Spectral Voices

Joanne Alain Cook

JACbooks
Published, 2022
ISBN 9781737589266

Dedication

To the middle child who glues everything together, just like
book two of a trilogy.

Prologue

Randy

An excess of stars, and an engorged yellow moon, shimmered behind a veil of wispy clouds, making a spectacular night sky for the city. It was the perfect night for possibilities. It took Randy twenty-five minutes to drive from the university to the edge of Thatcher Woods. That included his quick stop into CVS for a six pack of Icehouse Ale. He parked his Chevy Malibu under the soft glow of a streetlamp along the road edging the south side of the meadow. He fingered the written instructions Melissa had scratched on the back of a torn envelope.

If you really want to see me on Friday the thirteenth, Melissa had eyed him coyly, *meet me here at midnight.* Soft giggles escaped her lips, then, she gathered her books and walked away in a protected clump of girlfriends.

He totally wanted to see her. He'd dropped hundreds of hints during Ancient Native American History study group about getting together after midterms. He thought she never noticed. Then, she slipped that note atop his book and fluttered her mascara thick eyelashes at him. His heart pounded as he wondered if she could be the one. He read the note again.

Go down the Blue Prim trail and cut straight north toward the pond. There will be a dim light marking our spot. Come with an open mind.

Thatcher Glen Pond was really a bog. This early in the season the ground felt soft and mushy from deep layers of waterlogged soil. Luckily, the cool air kept the insects away. The entire River Forest area probably flooded due to a meandering river, hence the name River Forest, Randy guessed.

Randy climbed out of his vintage Chevy with the package of cheap beer under an arm. He guessed the girls planned an after-party to celebrate their first milestone in Ancient Native American History. Everyone warned them that the midterm would consist of a kazillion questions about absolutely nothing mentioned in class, and the warnings had mostly been right. He fished a blanket and flashlight from the trunk, they might come in handy, then turned toward the woods, picked out a landmark directly north and started walking.

Large oak trees peppered the area and the air suddenly became very cold away from the street. He could smell the acrid earth wafting through the weeds. He kept a towering tree front and center, and marched on. The elevation dipped to the right, and he surmised that it led to the pond. Soon enough, he spotted a twinkling light through the brush, a beacon guiding him in. As he drew closer, a soft rumble of voices carried through the cold air. That husky voice definitely belonged to Melissa. He smiled.

"You found us!" Melissa sprang to a stand, her eyes dropped to his blanket and bag.

"I brought beer," he said.

Her friend laughed while Melissa's eyes remained fixed on his. She smiled at him.

"Hush, Trish." Melissa gave her friend a little push with her foot. "I wasn't sure you'd really come."

Randy tossed the blanket to the ground and reached into his bag to pull out bottles of Icehouse Ale to offer. Melissa accepted a beer and stepped back, waving a hand at the third chair.

"I brought an extra chair for you," she said, "And Trish made brownies."

Randy crossed into their circle and offered a beer to Trish before dropping into the extra-fold out camp chair. *She brought him a chair!* He noticed the open bottle of wine between their seats and the brown grocery bag with a baguette sticking out. He helped Trish unscrew the tight top of her beer bottle before taking a sip of his own cool ale. They sat quietly for a moment and Randy glanced between the girls. He noticed Melissa giving him a shy survey as her plump lips bowed sweetly. He returned the smile feeling more and more confident. Trish leaned back, head tilted up, perusing the sky.

"That was a brutal test," Randy said to break the silence.

"Uh, no. No test out here," Trish blurted, "No school talk out here, not tonight."

"What are we doing out here?" Randy asked.

"There's a ghost—" Melissa started, but Trish quickly interrupted.

All term, Trish had interrupted consistently during their study group, one of the reasons Randy always sat far, far, away and never remembered her name. She never said anything about Native American History, but what she did say was always more important than what anyone else had to say, or so Trish seemed to think. Very different than considerate, careful Melissa. He wondered how such opposite girls became so connected in friendship.

"We heard it from one of the girls on our floor," Trish prattled on. "A ghost that only comes out on the full moon. An angry woman searching for something near Thatcher Pond wearing a U of C sweatshirt, that's why we wore the colors." Both girls wore school spirit shirts and threw their arms up in a cheer. "Everyone insisted we'd see a ghost out here on the full moon, and it's Friday the thirteenth, the perfect night for a ghost. She's is supposed to be so scary nobody dared come back."

"You two are roomies?" Randy asked.

Melissa and Trish both nodded. That explained it.

Sometime after they killed three bottles of cheap ale and one bottle of wine, Randy found himself stretched out on the blanket between Trish and Melissa gazing at the stars. Insects, frogs, and Trish eked out a steady stream of quiet noise. Randy now smiled openly at Melissa and she seemed to get over her shyness to return his undivided attention. With Trish chatting softly in the background, Randy sent Melissa silent messages. He stretched out his fingers until they touched hers and she didn't move her hand away. After a short pause, his fingers enclosed hers and he felt her gently return his clutch. They were definitely speaking the same language.

"What is that?" Trish abruptly sat up and her hand flew to her head. "Ooh. Blood rush."

Randy attempted to ignore Trish and concentrate on the silent messages between him and Melissa.

"I see something out there, look! What is that?" Trish's voice became high and sharp.

That sharp voice broke the spell and killed the mood. Melissa shifted to a sitting position, taking her hand far away. Randy moved quickly, also wriggling to a sitting position. He glanced in the direction Trish indicated.

"Oh yes, I can see her," Melissa said. "It's a person."

A very long way off, toward the pond, a person stood still as a statue. Or, perhaps, it was a tree. No, it was a person standing about a football field away. She stood bent at the waist, hand on a hip, hair hanging limp. Randy stretched his neck up to get a better look.

"She isn't moving," Melissa whispered.

The moment the words left her mouth, the person moved so startlingly fast that Randy felt his heart lurch, then plummet. Dread filled the place his heart had been. She had moved way too fast to be real, first one hundred yards away and then in the blink of an eye only fifty yards between them. Every muscle in his body tensed as he rose to his feet with the girls.

"Shit!" Trish snapped. "Did I miss something? Did she move?"

Melissa's breathing slowly warped into panting gasps. Her fear was contagious. He felt her inch closer to him, full of tense energy, while the person, a woman who now stood fifty yards away, slowly turned to face them. Had she really moved superfast a moment ago? He must have consumed more alcohol than he thought, or more likely, Trish spiked those brownies with something.

"She's trying to say something. I think she sees us," Trish's slurred voice broke the silence. "Hello there!" Trish waved. "Are you here to see the ghost?" Trish turned toward Randy and Melissa, "I think it's that one girl from our floor, the one down the hall. I didn't think she wanted to come. Do you recognize her?" Her voice had a pleading quality in the question.

They turned back toward the girl. She stood absolutely still, but startlingly closer again, maybe twenty-five yards away. Melissa took a small step backward, poised to spring away. The mystery woman wore a college sweatshirt with an old University of Chicago logo across the chest. Her long dark hair hung in perfect straight strands on either side of her narrow face, and her large eyes gazed at them, expressionless and dark.

Was she the ghost? Ridiculous!

At that moment, the woman seemed to register him and her eyes bore right into Randy's.

He turned his head slightly toward Trish, but snapped it back in the next moment. In the blink of an eye, the woman stood directly in front of him, and Melissa was gone. The pitter patter of her footsteps quickly dimmed as she receded into the brush behind him. Trish became unusually quiet and Randy felt frozen. He could not move. Petrified with fear, he stared into two dark pools of emotionless abyss. He barely felt capable of drawing in air and heard himself gasping. White skin stretched the surface of the woman's face and her thin lips moved ever so slightly. She leaned toward him, like she hoped to kiss him.

"Find it," she hissed.

Randy regained control of his muscles and ran. He stumbled into the same brush Melissa disappeared into and heard Trish screaming behind him, but he didn't care. He only cared about getting away. He ran haphazardly through the oak trees in a sprint, stopped when he realized he left the key to his car back on the blanket and he wanted to cry. It was on a simple little ring with only the one key. If anyone moved that blanket it would be lost in the grass for sure.

He cursed and kept running until he reached the road. He could see light in the far distance and moved toward it.

His mind flashed briefly on Melissa and Trish, but he dismissed them quickly because he could only think of one thing: keep moving away from that woman.

Chapter 1

Season Three Begins

Kiki

Spectral Analysis completed season two of their television program near the top of the ratings list. After an academy award for their feature length documentary on ghosts in a rural town, their popularity skyrocketed. The small group of paranormal investigators became tabloid favorites and household names. Hundreds of fan letters flooded their inboxes. People urged them to investigate ghosts in different corners of the country, but tired of traveling, and reeling from the effects of their success, they chose a ghost story near their own back yard to kick off the third season. Now, the night before cameras rolled for the season three opener, the *Spectral Analysis* crew found themselves in the city center of San Antonio along the famous river walk.

The new producer, Max Colliers, insisted on a new tradition; start each shoot with a casual dinner party on location, with the entire staff, for bonding purposes. *A good idea*, Kiki agreed, due to the changing aspects of the show, and the extra crew. They hired a replacement cameraman and master control panel operator, along with their replacement executive producer. Plus, behind the scenes helpers, gofers, hair dressers, and production assistants were all part of the team now. Everyone met briefly in Austin, but they hadn't gotten a chance to bond as a group until the dinner.

Kiki Mellow, the spiritual medium and a star of the show, wore a floral head scarf and overlarge vintage black sunglasses like a 1950s movie star. The dark lenses allowed her to covertly glance around. Carlos Fuentes, one of the tech specialists, brought his wife Maria. Apparently, his family hailed from San Antonio and their kids were tucked away with grandparents in town. Kiki met Maria several times and was always startled by her dark beauty and intense aura. Carlos doted on his wife, and Kiki couldn't help being amused at how the wise-cracking Carlos kept seeking spousal approval any time Maria turned her head.

She worried about her cousin, Paranormal Physics Professor Doctor Ian McNally. He shifted uncomfortably in his chair and hunched down with a Longhorns baseball cap pulled snuggly over his head. A thick, curly, three month old beard covered his lower face. After the last season, he grew the dark beard in an attempt to hide from a very public image. He assured them the beard would disappear before the taping at the Alamo. His attempts at hiding seemed fairly successful, as, no one recognized him outside of their small group. Ian had begun the evening quite chipper, but grew progressively low spirited as it became clear that Janine Stinger, the missing link, was not going to show up and "bond" with them.

The new executive producer called most of the preseason shots, and that came with pros and cons. For instance, they were booked into a very nice hotel and had a very swanky new office set up in Austin. He hired lots of extra help, but demanded the final word on film sites, story development, and their on screen images. Max focused on the money making aspect of the show more than the old producer. He pushed his fancy glasses up and plopped into the chair next to Ian. He arrived fashionably late and hadn't eaten dinner with them. He immediately sent several of the extra staff back to the hotel to prepare the newly reserved boardroom for the next day. The extra helpers were very excited to get started and went away happily. Only the primary investigative players, and Maria, lingered in the restaurant.

"Did everybody mingle well?" Max asked, and they all nodded happily.

Max hired the replacement cameraman and control board operator by outbidding other programs. The new cameraman, Don, came with years of experience behind a studio camera and Max "stole" him out from under one of the big stations in Austin. Don was a little older than the rest of the crew, perhaps in his mid-thirties by the look of him. By contrast, the control board operator, Ben, appeared to be a kid. He wore a Star Wars T-shirt with jeans and sneakers and was bright-eyed and bushy-tailed. He kept glancing toward Kiki from the corner of his eye and she pretended not to notice. He seemed curious and harmless. She remembered someone mention that Ben had just turned nineteen years old and already had a degree in computer science. He received numerous job offers out of college, but his big dream was to hunt ghosts with *Spectral Analysis*.

"I can't believe Ted ditched us," Carlos griped, then glanced at Don. "Of course, we're happy to have you Donny, it's just so unexpected to lose Ted too."

Max laughed, "Oh, come on, Ted wasn't going to leave Steve. They've been a team for a long time." Max grinned at him.

"I'm a little concerned," Carlos continued. "Has Janine contacted anyone? It's getting very close to show time and I wonder if she's checked in with anyone? I'm pretty excited to see her and hoped she would be here tonight."

Janine Stinger had been the missing piece of their puzzle for months. Toward the end of the last season, after the award winning documentary, she took an emergency leave of absence. A family tragedy hit. She touched base a couple times but had been impossible to reach since the night they won the academy award. Kiki glanced at Ian and watched him lapse into a deeper grey as he recharged his glass with the margarita from the pitcher. Janine skipping out of this get-together would surely rile all his sensitive spots. He'd take her absence as a personal avoidance of him due to her continuing hard feelings. He obviously felt the sting of rejection all over again.

"We've been in constant contact with her," Max assured them. "It's no secret that she wants out of her contract, but she will definitely show on time for the taping tomorrow night. She owes us several episodes before she can walk, and I made sure she can't walk early. To alleviate your immediate concerns, I did get confirmation that she checked into the hotel yesterday." His sparkling brown eyes fell on Kiki, and he paused. He loosened his tie a bit. "Have you spoken with Janine, Kiki? Do you know why she skipped this get-together? Maybe we should have stressed that it was mandatory."

"No." Kiki didn't move her head, but watched Ian to see his reaction. The idiot perked up. He appeared very drunk and not slowing down a bit on the booze. Kiki noticed several shot glasses between Carlos and Ian, most belonged to Ian. Maria seemed to have a modifying effect on Carlos and his consumption of alcohol. Hearing that Janine actually made it into town perked everyone up. For the past week, each of them harbored real concern that they'd be short one person for the season premiere taping, and no one wanted to start the season short one player.

"We finally get to meet Janine Stinger!" Ben grinned.

"Got a little crush on her?" Carlos laughed. "Get in line. After the feature, her fan mail skyrocketed."

"Did she drop out of last season because she got scared of the ghosts?" Ben asked.

Carlos shook his head. That was a common question. Carlos recapped the tale of the Biltmore Hotel, their first successful spectral connection, and Maria took the opportunity to move closer to Kiki. Both women noticed the waiter deliver more shots of tequila to the table. *Poison*, Kiki thought. Unbelievable that Ian continued drinking that vile liquid. As a nice Scottish lad, he usually stuck to single malt whisky or dark ale beer. Maria rolled her eyes at the shots.

"Kiki." Maria took her hands. Maria was a very tactile woman and beautifully dramatic. She projected a bright, bluish, happy aura. Not unusual for a woman with beautiful babies to love. "My niece Isabella is planning to visit soon. She is coming to stay with us in Austin for a visit. She is young, but not so young. My sister's husband says that she is different."

Kiki could guess where this was going, many young girls wanted to meet Kiki Mellow. As a famous spiritual medium and self-proclaimed witch, Kiki's considerable following of fans included people interested in the pagan arts. Most of her fan mail came from girls wanting to know more about the occult and ancient teachings. Most were bored, imaginative youths, but mixed into the letters were some gifted vessels, girls floating through life without a proper spiritual teacher. *Wasted talent*, Kiki thought. She already pondered her own transition from the ghost chasing TV show. *When I finally birth a baby girl*, she mused, *I'll focus on mentoring*. Kiki knew her time for reproduction was on the horizon and it excited her to imagine mothering her own daughter, her *Next* as the women in the coven called a first born.

"She's gifted," Maria hesitated, "and has asked if it would be an imposition to meet you sometime."

"Of course," Kiki said, "I would love to meet her."

The growing volume of the men interrupted their conversation. Rowdy laugher drew their attention. Apparently, the new cameraman had said something lewd. Young Ben appeared bright pink in the face and Ian wore a smirk, but Carlos appeared a tad upset. Kiki felt that something may have been said about their missing colleague, Janine, and Ian relished the snide remark as a patch on his damaged ego.

"Oh, come on, Carlos," Max Colliers shifted to the edge of his chair, closer to Ian. He seemed very interested in what Ian would say.

Since when did those two get on, Kiki wondered. Ian could barely stand Max Colliers and knew very well about Max and his inappropriate bad boy behavior. Max had quite the reputation.

"I'm sure you noticed the intriguing marks on her body," Max said. "On her chest even. She has an X carved over her heart, I've seen it. What does it mean? Does anyone know why it's there? I'm told it's body art. A symbol that means her heart is off limits. Like she's only interested in other things. I couldn't take my eyes off the…"

"Hey now." Carlos stood a little wobbly out of his chair. He glanced over at Kiki and Maria and seemed a bit startled that the women were actually listening in. He got his footing straightened out and turned to the other men. "Let's be respectful now, my wife is sitting right over there, and Kiki too. They don't want to hear this type of talk."

Max waved his hand as if to say they were all grown-ups.

Don grinned at Max. "Are you saying she's a wildcat then?"

"Guys." Carlos implored.

Max ignored Carlos and pointed to Ian. "He's the one to ask. Snatched her right out from under my nose, didn't you, McNally?" He chuckled. "Come on, what's the verdict? Don't hold back now, at that party, she was very hot and ready for something, I could smell it on her. I have a feeling her quiet exterior is camouflaging a dangerous, adventurous woman, if you know what I mean."

Kiki watched Ian open his mouth and knew he was about to say something incredibly stupid in his drunken, upset state. No one else could possibly guess what was going on in his head, and he would never admit it, but he fell for Janine Stinger like a ton of bricks and jumped in way too fast at her slightest encouragement. Janine proved to be a complicated girl for an idiot like Ian. She was dark, broken, and confused. Too many skeletons stumbled out of her closet, and thick headed Ian wasn't prepared to handle them. Kiki had warned him, but he didn't listen.

"Aye indeed, she's very sexy, and hiding quite a passionate side," Ian slurred to Don and Max, "She can seem very unassuming and uninterested, but, *wildcat* is an accurate description when you get her behind a closed door and…"

Smack! With a closed fist, Carlos flat out punched Ian in the eye and Ian nearly fell over in his chair. Of the scant people left in the restaurant, everyone turned to watch. She witnessed Ian get socked more than once and was afraid of what would happen. Those times were long gone, but he seemed to be in state of regression lately. Kiki watched Ian tense up and fought the urge to run over and placate him.

"Respect!" Carlos said sternly and pounded the table with his punching fist. He glowered at Max, who flinched with a respectable fear behind his glasses. Don scooted back and Ben appeared terrified of Carlos. Carlos shook out the hand he used to punch Ian, stretching his fingers. His voice became very calm and his typical joking tone came back. "Respect to the ladies please. I don't want my wife thinking this is common talk. She'll never let me go on site again. Ian, my brother, your stiff eye has made mush of my poor hand."

Ian managed to stand up and Kiki could see by his posture that he was not going to punch Carlos back. She let out a sigh of relief. Ian slumped over to hug Carlos quite heavily.

"I'm so, so sorry Carlos," Ian slurred. "Can you forgive me about your hand?" He pulled back from the hug, holding his own hand over his right eye. His good eye searched out Kiki and Maria. "I'm an arse. A bloody, idiot arse. Please forgive my mouth." Ian pointed at Max with his free hand. "And you're an arse too, a true bloody arse. And you too."

He pointed at Don, then Ian looked at Ben. "And you, don't be an bloody arse. Don't be like us."

At that point, Ian and Carlos began laughing at each other and Max joined a little hesitantly, adjusting his glasses, but Don and Ben sat stiffly, unsure of what to do. Clearly, Ian and Carlos were still a little shell shocked from how things ended the past season. Only the three of them knew how tough it was to film the final episodes of season two after what happened in California.

"I'm going to get those fools some ice." Maria slipped around her. Kiki could see the boyish grin Carlos shot at his wife in response to her very stern eye. Soon, Maria returned with bags of ice for each of them and then fussed over Carlos and his hand. When Ian's good eye found Kiki, all she could do was shake her head at him, the poor bugger.

Max Colliers reserved the hotel boardroom as the *Spectral Analysis* prep area. He was throwing a pot of money on their little television enterprise, so they'd no longer be squeezed into a small rooms in affordable roadside inns. Only a very fancy and elegant hotel along the San Antonio river walk proved suitable for the new executive producer. Not only did Max hire an award winning cameraman and a brainy control board operator, he added two image coordinators, a make-up artist and a hair stylist to prep them for the camera, just like a real TV show. Kiki looked forward to that positive change.

Kiki snuck into the board room well before the scheduled shoot and felt the buzz of excitement. Along with makeup and hair chairs in the corner, a short garment rack of zipped up items was propped in the opposite corner. Max Colliers must have hired a costume designer without consulting any of them. Kiki knew Max pretty well and expected the garments in those bags were likely on the suggestive side. Racy items that Kiki wouldn't mind, but the conservative crew might. Out from behind the rack, a tall athletic woman with long auburn hair stepped back as she unzipped one of the bags. She glowed with a nice tan, which made her light brown eyes appear golden. Janine noticed Kiki right away and instantly brightened as Kiki strolled over.

One glance told Kiki everything she needed to know. Janine had made it through the doldrums, not smooth sailing yet, but gliding slowly forward at least. She seemed heathy and strong, and her dark aura was not so thick it was frightening. When Kiki hugged Janine, she held on long enough to allowed Janine's residual grief to touch her. Kiki let out a sigh of relief that Janine had actually showed up.

Carlos jumped in on their reunion and the three of them huddled with their energies mixing for several minutes, then they turned to the garment rack and the bag Janine had unzipped. Her name was written on a card in the name placard. It appeared to be a full body suit in deep purple with flashes of bright colors as useless pockets on the sleeves, legs, and chest. It was made of a very thin stretchy material and cut with a low V-neckline. *Certainly not something Janine would choose*, Kiki thought.

"What is that?" Carlos asked. "Are you filming an episode of Star Trek, or are you ghost hunting with us?"

They all laughed as Janine zipped the bag back up. Carlos flipped through the rack.

"Whoa, look. There's a *Star Trek* suit for me too." Carlos opened the bag wide. The male version zipped all the way up to a crew neck but appeared just as form fitting. Carlos could barely contain his amusement. "I'm not shy about showing off my guns, but I'm afraid this material will reveal too much of the family jewels. I don't want to offend anyone with my overabundant gems, Maria would kill me." They laughed again, and it felt like they were right back where they left off many months ago.

"At least the new producer doesn't sexually discriminate in his exploitation," Janine said. "Is he's requesting we wear these suits or demanding it?"

Carlos pointed out three bags with Kiki's name on them. "Hey look, Kiki. Colliers has three outfits for you. Should we take a look at them? Should be interesting."

Kiki shook her head, the nerve of Max Colliers. Did he really imagine he could dress her up without discussion? More and more she felt like strangling the old producer for leaving them in a compromised position with Max. He proved over bearing and over controlling, sticking his foot into every aspect of the production without even considering the original vision of the show. Kiki and Ian McNally dreamt up *Spectral Analysis* for the sole purpose of investigating and revealing authentic paranormal activity. Max seemed to think the show was just spoofy fluff entertainment.

A mood change overcame the group and Kiki turned to see Ian standing near the main door staring at them. Clean shaven again, Ian managed to appeared chipper while chatting with the new guy, Ben. When he turned sideways, they got a good glimpse of his eye. *Ouch*, he would be bruised for weeks. A deep purple patch had developed over his right eye and a portion of his cheek. His eyelids began to flutter as he moved toward their small group. Ben followed closely behind him.

Kiki's cousin had once been a nervous kid. Extremely shy as a youth, Ian struggled through a stutter in his earlier years. Unlike the stutter, he was never able to completely get over his signature blinking, Ian's tell-tale sign of nervousness. Other than that little tic, he appeared calm and cool, ever the suave Doctor Ian McNally, paranormal investigative researcher and author.

"Look at this." He joined them and stiffly patted Janine's arm. "She's back. Ben, this is Janine Stinger. Janine, Ben is going to man the console. He's a wiz with computers."

A distinct dent lightened the dark aura surrounding Janine, but the tension in the air grew thick enough to cut with a knife. Ian and Janine avoided looking directly at one another. Ian was the easiest person in the world to read with those colorful expectant streams radiating from his head, so why did Janine have such a hard time seeing how happy he was to see her? What appeared quite clear to Kiki was obviously a cryptic puzzle to the two of them.

Janine noticed Ian's shiner and her expression turned tender. "Are you okay? That looks pretty painful. What happened?"

"Oh, you know, rugby and all." Ian glanced quickly at Carlos. "It's nothing, just a wee bruise, I hardly notice it. You look very well. Very nice. It's nice to see you looking so… so fit."

As always, Mr. Smooth. Kiki wondered how her bumbling cousin managed to attract so many girls. As if on cue, one of the beauticians, Lauren, crashed the group. Lauren bounced with excitement and everyone paused to consider her. She turned a tad red at the sudden undivided attention.

"Hello, Ian, I mean, Doctor McNally," she giggled. "Hello, Miss Mellow."

Oh dear God, Kiki thought, *he went and did it again*. Ian had a habit of befriending women and more times than she could remember, they always came off with the wrong idea. Many times, Ian became so guilt ridden for leading them on, he actually dated them. This little exchange would not help him close any divides with Janine.

"I'm Lauren." Her blonde head nodded all around and she beamed at Janine. "You're Janine Stinger, right? We're supposed to prep you and Miss Mellow for the show. I'm supposed to do your hair."

"I usually just pull it up into a ponytail," Janine told her. "It takes, like, two seconds."

"Oh no, Mr. Colliers asked for a set style on you. He instructed me to create a cascade of flowing ringlets. He hoped your hair was still long, it's very lovely. Miss Mellow, he said you would let us know what you wanted. I'm not supposed to let either of you out of here without some prepping."

There was an awkward silence.

Lauren's nervousness began to escalate and Kiki wondered if Janine could read the poor girl. Clearly, Lauren feared muffing up her first real workday on the show. Max had given her distinct instructions and Lauren definitely wanted to please the boss. Pushy Max, first the new outfit and now the girly hair. What would Janine do? Would she walk off and leave Lauren standing there, or would she play nice? Would she follow Max Collier's clear instructions or thumb her nose at him? Kiki wasn't sure what to expect. Janine's reactions had never been easy to predict.

"Sure, no problem," Janine said softly to Lauren. "But, please, call me Janine."

Lauren became visibly relieved as Janine followed her to the hair chair where Guy, the makeup artist, stood smiling at Kiki. He waited patiently for her to come to him. Kiki wondered if Janine might wear that new outfit. *Not a chance,* she thought as she followed Janine toward Guy and Lauren. Carlos called after them as they walked away,

"What about my hair? Doesn't anyone think my hair needs a curl?"

As they rotated through the makeup and hair chairs, Kiki briefed Carlos and Janine on the plan. During the past week, she interviewed several people who claimed to have spectral encounters in the Alamo complex. While she tracked down the stories, Ian scouted the entire five acres of Alamo grounds for hot spots with his EMF box. He found unusual energy inside the chapel, along the soldier's barracks, and near the wall between the Alamo and the Menger Hotel. Those locations were also cited by Kiki's witnesses.

Max managed to have the large planters blocking the plaza relocated, so they could park the van along the walkway in front of the chapel. He also reserved the entire Alamo for a single night of exclusive filming. Nobody would be in the complex except the *Spectral Analysis* crew.

Ben and Ian had gone ahead to meet Max and Don with the van. Kiki, Janine, and Carlos were delayed by the prep crew and followed half an hour behind in a hired car.

"The Alamo was originally known as the Mission San Antonio de Valero," Kiki informed Carlos and Janine. "It was built it in the early 1700s as part of a religious outreach program to indigenous people, to convert them. I felt a distinct presence in the chapel, the original structure. That presence may be residual energy from the Spanish Franciscan friars who built the church, it had a holy feel. Those friars may also be the six diablos that saved the building from destruction after the battle of the Alamo. It's a famous folk story that one of my interviewees tells very nicely. Then, out near the barracks, I experienced a strong melancholy energy, perhaps from one, or maybe from several spirits, it was hard to determine. I believe it came from someone who fought in that Alamo battle over 100 years ago."

"You think the spirit of James Bowie or Davy Crockett or even Santa Ana himself is wandering around in there?" Carlos asked excitedly, eyes wide open.

"Why would Santa Ana be a ghost at the Alamo, Carlos? He lived through that battle and had a long and successful career." Janine smirked, and Carlos creased his brow and frowned.

"People report three types of spectral energy," Kiki added. "A youthful energy that befriends children, fully formed spectral masses that resemble men dressed in old time clothes near the barracks wall, and ghostly whispers that emanate along the outer wall. I'm told the fully formed spectral masses are often mistaken for real people, and three separate witnesses have sworn to have seen one of them."

It was a short drive from their hotel to the old mission. As the car pulled onto East Crockett bend, Kiki spotted the newly painted *Spectral Analysis* Van on the wide stone-paved walkway. Instead of a simple decal, the entire van was airbrushed with a colorful rainbow. The rear doors were splayed open and they could see young Ben sitting in Steve's old captain's chair. Max stood outside the back door speaking to Ian.

Kiki, Janine, and Carlos jumped out of the car and made their way to the van. Kiki adjusted her overlarge Aztec poncho as they traipsed down the street. Something just snapped when she saw the ridiculous outfits set out for Janine and Carlos and she decided to go fully drab at first sight to freak Max out. She knew he expected her to be in a sexy outfit, but instead, she came covered from head to toe in bulky woven layers. Even Carlos couldn't think of a wisecrack for her oversized poncho. As they drew closer, Kiki delighted in Max's surprised, upset face.

Carlos started laughing when the new cameraman emerged from behind the van. He wore one of the *Star Trek* outfits and, unlike Carlos, Don's physique was not quite cut out for such a tight ensemble. His middle aged pouch was very well pronounced. Ian grinned at their approach, pleased with their costume decisions. The doctor wore a new version of his signature multicolored *Spectral Analysis* tie paired with a very nice form fitting shirt under his standard white lab coat.

"You look so sexy, Don," Carlos teased. "Ready to be beamed up, are you?"

Don visibly fidgeted.

"Didn't you guys find the suits I left for you?" Max stomped over and surveyed them. "Kiki, I left you three choices. What are you supposed to be dressed as?"

"I'm sure I have no idea what you mean." Kiki fluttered her eyes at him.

Max put his phone up to his ear and immediately began talking. He ordered someone, somewhere, to bring the garment bags from the hotel. He stared at Janine and Carlos. They both had donned their traditional gear, purple coveralls with red fishing vests and black work boots. Carlos pulled a pack of gum from an arm pocket and offered Max a stick. Max didn't take it. Their new executive producer did not appear amused at having his plan ignored.

"You're telling me you didn't see those designer new outfits?" he growled at Carlos.

"Oh, we saw them." Carlos chewed his gum. "They were very interesting. Were we supposed to wear them? I thought it was optional."

"Do you get that I am the executive producer here? I'm not sure you get it." Max inhaled slowly, then continued in a calmer voice. "The plan is to start the season with a new look. It's not unusual to tweak costumes for a new season, even the doctor has new ties and better tailored shirts."

"We get it," Janine stepped up. "We know you're in charge, it's my fault. I just didn't think I could get the zipper all the way up. It seemed to stop right about here." She pointed to a spot about mid-chest and stared straight at him. "It's an extremely revealing outfit and I'm not going to be able to wear it, ever. And Carlos and I always match, so he couldn't wear it, either."

Kiki relished the expression on Max Collier's face. Finally, he was at a loss for words. Over the past month he had hinted about his many plans regarding Janine Stinger. He wanted to take her under his executive producer wing and convince her to sign the contract by elevating her from the second fiddle chair. The fan mail pouring in proved the public wanted more of her, and Max planned to highlight her activity on the show. He wanted to polish her screen image and create a more alluring "character" for her. Obviously, being cast as the dowdy girl alongside Kiki's sexy image must be the reason she wanted to ditch the show. He felt certain she'd be thrilled with the changes and be appropriately thankful. Moving up in the hierarchy must be what Janine desired.

Max paused and studied them. Smart fellow, Kiki could see him backing away from this particular battle. He set his jaw and nodded. He put on a pleasant face.

"Okay, we'll figure out a fix for the next time," he smiled at Janine, but gave Carlos a critical gaze. "You hair looks wonderful, beautiful. That's a good update at least. I take it you girls are happy with the new stylist and makeup artist? Our plan is to up the ante a few notches this season and get the band out of the garage, so to speak."

"Lauren is terrific," Janine said sweetly, then she reached into her arm pocket to retrieve one of the many hair bands she always had stashed. She casually drew her lovely amber ringlets up and banded them into her standard ponytail. Max appeared both mesmerized and flabbergasted.

Janine barely noticed his reaction as she moved toward the air cases to gather her gadgets.

Max turned his attention to Kiki and she winked at him. "Thank you, Max. The extra attention and effort you put into the show is amazing. Those outfits were such a nice surprise, but I have a plan for tonight. Right now, I need to step away for a moment and get centered. I usually center my core as the crew gathers their trinkets, so no chit chatting for a few minutes, okay?"

Just as Max opened his mouth to exert his authority, Kiki whipped the large Aztec shawl up over her head and handed it to him. His eyes bulged at her cleavage and his mouth dropped open. Kiki knew her outfit was another over the top success story. She wore a very tight, skin toned, swede leather dress over her generous curves. It was extremely small and short enough that someone else might wear it as a long shirt. Her arms were adorned with intricate beaded bands. Then, she shed the overlarge sweatpants to reveal leather moccasins with straps crisscrossing all the way up her legs to finally tie together at her lower thigh. A small ornate knife was strapped to the outside of her right thigh in a dark leather sheath. She stuffed the sweat pants on top of the shawl in Max Collier's arms and leaned toward him.

"Be a dear and put those in the van for me." She purred, then sashayed away, consciously soaking up his undivided attention.

"Oh my God," Carlos's chuckle echoed over the pavement. "It's the real Poca-haunt-us."

Chapter 2

Inside the Alamo

Janine

The *Spectral Analysis* team stood in a semi-circle outside the main entrance to the world famous Alamo Chapel. At a nod from the doctor, Don activated the main camera and began panning from left to right.

Carlos pulled open the doors of the centuries old façade as Kiki recapped the history of the chapel. They entered the building one after another. Inside, Carlos quickly crossed to a far corner of the room to set up a low-spectrum infrared camera on a tripod. That camera had an wide angle lens designed to capture the entire room. Janine retrieved the spare thermal-panger from her side pocket and snapped it on. The thermal-panger was an elongated metal gage that recorded micro changes in air temperature. Over her arm, she carried the heavy coil of copper wire for the ultrasensitive large EMF box.

Janine remembered the last time she helped set up the magnetic antenna for that box, something went wrong and she took on quite an electric shock.

"We're setting the EMF box in the chapel to take readings while we wander the grounds," Ian spoke toward Janine, but he was really talking to the big camera. Don pointed the lens in their direction. "We'll try to tap into low frequency electromagnetic waves and see what happens. That large coil is a magnetic antenna. It's not feasible to capture electric pulses at ultralow frequencies, so we'll tap into the magnetic part of the wave instead. I'll place a monitor just outside that door and our backup recorder is in the *Spectral Analysis* van."

"Kiki says we might sense the six diablos in here, known to carry fire swords or something like that. Shall I leave my nice new thermal-panger right here, set to record?" Janine continued screwing the ends of the copper antennae to the box.

"Good thinking," Ian gave Don a signal to follow Kiki with the camera.

Kiki currently walked the perimeter of the room feeling out the energy. Don meandered away in his tight outfit and Janine almost giggled at the sight of his backside stretching the material. She noticed Ian rub the side of his face and wondered if the bruised eye bothered him. She watched him play rugby before and wondered why he loved such a brutal contact sport.

"Is the swelling giving you problems?" she asked softly.

He turned to meet her gaze. It was the first time, in long while, that they properly met each other's eyes. She felt a sudden shift in her chest at the full impact of it. She stayed stuck there for a moment, before dragging her attention back down to wrap the leads completely.

"Oh, no. I had a bit of a beard before this morning and it's a little getting used to. Itchy." His Scottish accent came thicker than normal. "I was a right, rough bloke there for a little while. You wouldn't have recognized me."

"I saw the beard," she told him, keeping her eyes down on her work. "I thought it looked nice."

Truth be told, when Janine spotted him at the hotel bar in his thick curly beard, all she could think about was running her fingers through it while kissing him. Her heart had been pounding and she felt very happy to see him. She almost ran to him, but hesitated, wondering how he felt. Was he still upset with her? Sad, or maybe angry? Or even worse, did he no longer care? Almost a year had passed since their very short fling. He was probably well past it, and maybe that was for the best, as she didn't plan on hanging around. Right when that thought crossed her mind, she realized he wasn't alone. He sat cozily with a very pretty woman, flirting, and so, Janine consciously hid from his view.

"You saw my beard? When, where?"

"I'll admit it, I spied on you for a little while right after I arrived. The beard looked very nice on you." She took a step back from the antenna. "Nothing's turned on yet, right? I want to stand clear before you flip the switch."

"Of course." He stood when she stood. His eyes intently watched her and she began to feel like she should have just kept quiet. Ian kept his voice low. "Why didn't you come say hello? I was hoping to see you sooner, and talk before we got busy here."

"I didn't want to interrupt your lunch." Janine avoided his gaze by looking across the room at Don and Kiki in the far corner. Ian kept staring at her and she lowered her voice even more. "You were with Lauren. I wasn't sure who she was until today, but you appeared a little busy."

Oh, the blinking eyes on Doctor Ian McNally. He stiffened and straightened and pressed his lips together.

"I know she shaved your beard this morning, because she told us all about it. Said she was nervous about hurting your black eye, but was glad you were ditching the beard, it got in the way with…well, she had a lot of nice things to say about you."

Lauren had chit chatted her way through styling Janine's hair and hadn't been the least concerned about throwing gossip around about herself, or Ian. She insinuated things without outright saying them, implying intimacy, confirming that she "socialized" with the doctor outside of work. Kiki grimaced through it all and got quite short speaking with Lauren, but that was Kiki's way. Janine just listened quietly and admonished herself, what did she expect after slamming the door so solidly in his face?

Ian was close to blinking his way into a coma and she became angry at herself for making him feel guilty. She was out of bounds here, being very unfair. Why did she say anything at all? Perhaps, she didn't expect her feelings to flare up so dramatically, not after her entire world had felt so completely dead just a few short weeks ago. It surprised her, the intense jealousy zinging through her veins. She could barely look him in the eye without wanting to either slap him or kiss him.

"Don't worry about it, Ian," she insisted. "It's all right, really. I'm not, I'm not upset at you about that, not at all. I'm okay with it, she seems like a very nice person."

He looked at his hands, "Crikes."

Kiki's loud voice urged them to the door, the haunted barracks awaited. Janine set the new updated thermal-panger next to the EMF box and set it to record. Unlike the original version, the new gadget was the size of a fat marker and able to record temperature readings for hours instead of one thirty minutes clump.

They trailed one by one out the rear door onto a nice paved path. The sweet fragrance of jasmine welcomed them into the night and Carlos, Janine, and the doctor finally inserted their ear pieces. Janine instantly heard Max Colliers giving instructions over the airways. He insisted everyone switch to hot-mic because he wanted to hear everything. He wondered out loud why they weren't already tuned in. His voice sounded impatient.

Throughout the first season, the *Spectral Analysis* crew wore bulky headsets to communicate with the control van. Over time, their communication equipment upgraded into better and better audio transmitters. Now, they each wore a minimal ear piece with an attached microphone. Both Janine and Carlos rarely selected hot mic. They always opted for the press to talk function, to ensure they didn't muddy the airways or accidently speak on top of the doctor or Kiki.

"Colliers, you may want to use the press to talk function," Doctor McNally's voice transmitted clearly through her receiver. "We can hear all the ambient noise in that van and it's quite distracting. We need to be able to hear each other out here. Don, you should turn your hot-mic off. Not sure why yours needs to be up."

"I want to hear him acknowledge my instructions, and I know his hands are tied to the camera. We're going to tighten things up this season. I'm committed to participating as your full producer/director here," Max came back. "I'm turning my transmitter down two notches so it should be a bit better for you. There, are the ambient noises gone?"

"Aye," the doctor answered him. "Are you insisting on constantly transmitting on hot-mic? Steve rarely transmitted during an active shoot."

"Get used to it," Max's voice came across the wire. "I'm running this thing now, McNally. Steve was a laissez-faire kind of guy, but that's not me. I've got a brain and know how to run a dynamic battle plan. Don't worry, I'll only give instructions as needed. You'll get used to me. Your first focus is near the long barracks, to your left."

"All right then," Ian responded. He glanced at Don. "Are you on com three or four?"

"Three," Don told him. "That's correct, right? Janine, Carlos, and I are supposed to be on com three. Kiki on one, you on two, and Mr. Colliers on four."

"Yes, that's perfect," the doctor told him. "Head over that way and stand just outside the courtyard entry, the one that leads to the mission well, next to that history wall. We are going to walk toward you and you can film us heading that way. Kiki and I will review the nature of the ghosts reported near the long barracks as we walk. Then, we'll…"

"Yes, yes. That's a nice idea," Max's voice interrupted through Janine's headset. "And don't forget to point out the history wall when you approach it. You'll want to mention James Bowie or Crockett, perhaps, and hint that their ghosts may be lingering about…" Max continued with his suggestions and Janine pulled the earpiece from her ear. Carlos laughed silently, holding his sounds in with a hand over his amused mouth.

The doctor shooed Don around the corner and then turned to Kiki, Carlos, and Janine. He held up two fingers and pointed to his earpiece, then to his microphone. Janine reset her transmitter and receiver for communications restricted to channel two.

The doctor covered the microphone with his hand.

"We're going to send and receive on com two, all of us." He whispered. "They will hear our chatter, but we won't hear them. I'll give a signal if we need to switch around. We'll do it as often as needed until he gets the message."

They each adjusted their settings and reinserted their earpieces. Carlos grinned, pleasantly amused by the power struggled playing out. Janine found it funny as well, but Kiki rolled her eyes.

"The long barracks proved very interesting from an electromagnetic standpoint," the doctor started walking ahead with Kiki. Carlos and Janine followed. Carlos had his low IR camera out and Janine monitored the air with an ion detector. Back to familiar ground, they grinned at each other.

She had to admit, it was a little fun to be looking for ghosts again. *Come out, come out, wherever you are,* Janine silently called to the ghosts. They could see Don in the distance filming their approach.

"There are several spectral masses haunting the long barracks," Kiki said to the doctor. "From my interviews this week, several witnesses spoke of general feelings of sadness flooding the area. Could those feelings belong to the ghosts of weary soldiers, Mexicans and Texans alike, wandering the area of their untimely death?"

"I measured distinct pulsing energy bands surrounding…" the doctor stopped talking when Kiki suddenly stopped walking. "What is it, Kiki?"

Kiki turned in a different direction, to face a small building, one made of light colored stones similar to the chapel. From the map she surveyed earlier, Janine knew it was the gift shop.

"Do we have access to that building?" Kiki asked. "Is somebody in there?"

"All the buildings are unlocked," the doctor told her, "and empty. Security is outside the walls, so we should be the only people on the premises. We have exclusive access until four in the morning. A contact man is at the Menger Hotel, if we need him, Reed something, remember? What is it?"

"There's somebody in there, or something," Kiki said. "It's calling to us. Urging us over."

Kiki stepped gingerly toward the gift shop building.

"Carlos?" the doctor pointed him toward Kiki.

"I'm rolling. Want me to go regular or keep it IR?"

"Keep it IR. Don, join us here, quickly," the doctor spoke calmly over the wire. "We are changing direction and heading into the gift shop. I can see you standing there, not moving. If you don't bring that camera this way, you are going to miss everything. We're following Kiki."

Don hurriedly toward them, balancing the camera on his shoulder, scowling. He must be listening to alternate chatter from Max on channel four. Janine turned back to follow Kiki into the gift shop and a cascade of pings went off on her ion detector. Ian and Carlos paused near the door to watch it pop off wildly. The doctor traded his portable blinking EMF box for her ion wand.

Kiki forged a path through the merchandise toward a back hallway. As she passed a table display, Janine noticed a book titled *Haunted Alamo* right in the middle of the souvenirs. Kiki always led them into unexplainable encounters when she ran off like this. Janine kept an eye on the portable EMF box for more blinking lights. Carlos skirted around the tables to catch up with Kiki.

"Tell me someone else feels this," Kiki tiptoed up a staircase to the second floor. "He's urging us to hurry. *We're coming.*"

Don finally caught up, huffing and puffing, balancing his camera on his shoulder. His angry eyes searched out the doctor.

"I heard loud knocking out there by the barracks," Don announced loudly. "Are we going to go back out there? Who do I listen to?"

"Hey, there, Max." The doctor calmly raised a hand up for Don to be quiet. "Max, just relax a minute. We're going to follow this up first, then we'll head to the barracks. When Kiki senses something, it is usually wise for us to follow her."

Kiki's voice came over the wire, "He's young. I think it's the boy. The boy ghost a couple of witnesses reported. I can't quite place him, but I sense him up here, in this general area."

The doctor smiled and made a motion for Don to remove his ear piece, which he did. His shoulders instantly relaxed. The doctor pointed up the stairs for Don to follow Kiki and Carlos. Janine followed next.

"*Where are you? Who are you?* Carlos, do you feel anything at all, I sense that he's right here, standing right here."

"I don't feel anything," Carlos said softly.

Janine did. She felt a temperature drop near the stairs and her stomach automatically clenched in response.

Temperature drops often came with unsettling encounters. Janine slipped the portable EMF box into her front pocket and retrieved her silver thermal-panger, the original temperature sensing device they used in the first two seasons. Very large compared to the updated version in the chapel, this gadget was embarrassingly shaped like a phallic device. She flipped the on switch and the silver panger confirmed a temperature drop with every upward step on the stairs. Kiki's voice continued rambling over the airwaves.

"*Are you in this room? No? Over here?*" Kiki's voice lowered in tone, a sign that she now addressed the crew. "He's very young. He prefers to watch people from afar, from out this window. I think, somebody here is making him nervous, one of us." Kiki's voice switched back to a higher tone. "*It's alright, dear, we just want to say hello.*"

"Kiki," Carlos said softly. "I'm picking up a nice blip of heat near your left hand."

"I can feel him there," Kiki said. "Don, be sure you've got an angle. I'm going to pull out a little mirror here, to look for a reflection."

The doctor crowded Janine in the close quarters of the dark stairwell and spied the readout on her thermal device. Did he notice her hesitation to continue up the stairs? She stopped one step ahead of him and her eyes fell right in line with his.

"Are you okay?" he whispered. He sounded concerned.

"Of course," Janine said sharply, then she shook it off, because what did it matter if she was a little spooked? Or, more honestly, off keel at being there again and acting like everything was normal. She probably should have met them earlier, at the get-together the previous night. They could have gotten this awkward reunion out of the way in a less busy situation, without worrying about ghosts. *Don't let procrastination and avoidance become your middle name in uncomfortable emotional situations*, her old shrink's voice echoed in her ear.

Suddenly, the ion detector popped off like a fireworks finale, startling them, followed by total silence. Shuffling sounds occurred upstairs and Kiki appeared on the top step with Don and Carlos right behind her. Kiki started down, cutting in between the doctor and Janine.

"He's gone. Just like that, he left," Kiki said. "He was a very strong presence, a very strong energy. He felt very young, only a kid, and he wasn't very sure what was going on."

Doctor McNally nodded and glanced at Don. He pointed to the earpiece dangling from his lobe.

"Don, your receiver is hanging. Let's head out to the long barracks now," Ian said.

Steady noise streamed from the long barracks. Shuffling footsteps and eerie voice-like sounds floated out the door. The crew stood just under the stone overhang, listening. The doctor glanced at Kiki and she shrugged, rolling her eyes in the opposite direction. Carlos peered downward, adjusting his camera controls. Don huffed, agitated, but his lens stayed on Kiki and the doctor. He openly glared at the doctor. Max must be trying to get their attention, Janine imagined.

"Doctor McNally, why don't you answer him?" Don appeared stressed about the whole situation and Janine felt sorry for him in that ridiculous outfit, shifting his weight from foot to foot. Don still didn't realize he was the only one listening to Max Colliers. This was his first night filming a live investigation and he was caught in the middle of a silly power struggle, and unlike Janine, he probably didn't want to lose his job.

"Oh, hey, Max," Ian stepped toward the overhang and glanced down the dark corridor. "We're tied up with our equipment here. Why don't you use Don as your go between so we don't all step on each other?" It was not typical for Ian to let a joke go this far, and Janine wondered what was really going on.

Don shook his head. He could see that Doctor McNally was not fiddling with any equipment. He opened his mouth, but Ian held his hand up.

"I'm just thinking here," the doctor told him.

"That was a pretty ominous moan," Carlos inspected the top of the stone overhang. "Could some of those noises be the wind rushing through the rafters? It almost sounds like a recording, doesn't it?" He angled the infrared camera to the top of the wall even though he knew full well it couldn't pick up anything through the stones. Perhaps he was looking for cracks.

Kiki's attention was not on the long barracks, "Where does that opening lead, that one over there? That the another little courtyard, isn't it?" Kiki didn't seem interested in the long barracks at all.

"It goes to the Calvary Courtyard," Janine told her.

"I admit that there are fabulous noises in there," Kiki said. "But I am very drawn to that little opening over there, to the Calvary Courtyard, and I have zero feelings about that place in there. Maybe we should split up. There's a very sad energy coming from the courtyard, much stronger than it was during the day. I don't want to ignore it."

"Okay," the doctor agreed. "Kiki will follow her nose with maybe, Don. Yes, Don, you should trail Kiki and get everything on the big camera. Janine, Carlos, and I will check out the noises in here, and then meander around to meet you at the tail end of the yard. I believe there's an opening at the far end of this hall, one that empties into your courtyard."

Don shook his head and glared anxiously. He pushed his microphone away from his mouth and leaned toward the doctor.

"No one is going to answer that question?" Don asked. "I'm not sure whose instructions to follow, who's the boss? Aren't you going to take that order into account?"

"Have you watched the show, Don?" Ian didn't cover his microphone. "I'm the boss here. During any investigative shoot, I'm the boss. I am the main scientist conducting an investigation of paranormal activity. That's what *Spectral Analysis* is, a paranormal investigation. Kiki is my spiritual medium, Carlos and Janine are my tech assistants, and you are my cameraman, for documentation. Do you hear that, Max? We are conducting a scientific investigation here, this is not a sitcom. Sit tight and see what happens. We are going to cover everything."

The doctor watched as Don flinched at whatever was coming through his earpiece.

The doctor continued, "I'm insisting, Max, that Don follow Kiki with the camera. The rest of us are going to walk down this hall and meet them at the other end. Carlos is going to record us on his camcorder, but right now, there is no script. Kiki always follows her nose and the big camera always follows Kiki."

They watched Don nod hesitantly, then nod to Kiki as they broke off. Janine trailed Carlos and the doctor into the dark museum while listening to Kiki prattle on to Don about the soldier spirits of the Alamo. She kept asking him if he could feel the sadness.

"*Oh yes,*" they heard Don say, "*I'm definitely feeling the sadness.*"

Faint, whispery, echolike sounds engulfed them inside the door of the long barracks. *Air flowing through a small opening would not sound like that,* Janine thought. Janine dug into a pocket to retrieve her audio recorder and set it for sounds in the lower sonic to subsonic range, then reinserted it with the microphone sticking out.

They watched their many gadgets silently. Carlos noted a very tiny hot spot down the hall and they slowly made their way toward it. Before the shoot, the doctor insisted that all the electricity on the premises be shut down. That small hot spot should not be an outlet or an electronic of any kind.

Kiki's voice suddenly turned to a higher pitch, a pitch she used when directly addressing a spirit. Janine focused on Kiki's voice for a moment.

"Sadness. *I feel you.* Overwhelming grief." Her voice changed a bit. "What are you filming? He's going over there." Her voice stopped for several seconds. "*Just calm down. I can feel you standing there.* Don, point your camera over there. Point it at… at him. *Oh my. Hello there.*"

The doctor turned toward Janine and Carlos with wide eyes.

"Kiki, what do you see? Is there somebody out there?" the doctor asked softly.

"I thought it was just a shadow," Kiki whispered. "But it's a man. He's moving in slow circles. Get up here and film this." She must be speaking to Don again. Her voice dropped lower. "Ian, get out here. There's man out here, and he's strange. He's looking all around, confused and so, so sad. He's becoming quite clear."

Ian muffled his microphone and pointed to the corner with the heat blip. "Carlos, check that out and then come over to the Cavalry Courtyard immediately. See if you can pinpoint that whispering sound. I'm going out there. There's something fishy going on." The doctor grabbed Janine's hand and pulled her along. They exited the museum and sprinted to the path Kiki and Don had disappeared into.

"Can you hear me?" Kiki used her higher pitch again. *"I can feel your sorrow. My goodness, you're energy is like a flood. You're in pain, I can feel that. Will you speak to me?"*

Don stood at the western end of the courtyard with the camera on his shoulder. Kiki stood just beyond him, facing the trees near an old cannon that was cemented to the ground. The foliage lay just beyond the cannon. Janine peered into that extremely dark corner, and, as they drew near, the figure of a man emerge from the shadows.

He meandered in a slow circle staring fondly into the sky. He wore an old military uniform which appeared weathered and torn. The edges of his sleeves were frayed at the wrists and the lower button on his breast was missing. That man was not a ghost at all, he appeared completely solid. His slicked back hair framed a dirty face and a pencil thin mustache lay crooked above his lip. The doctor's ion detector began to pop off and both Janine and the doctor stared down at it, startled.

"Can you tell us your name?" Kiki asked the fellow. He seemed completely unaware of Kiki, searching around in a spaced out manner. As they drew nearer, Kiki held out her arm to stop them. She waved at them to stay behind her.

There is something very strange about that man, Janine thought. A chill ran down her spine. If he was an actor, he was doing a terrific job. Janine glanced toward Don. His face wore an expression of absolute terror. His terror sent another chill down her spine. Don's eyes shot to the doctor, seeking him out. He waved the doctor over with an agitated hand.

"There is a very strong energy coming from this fellow, and he seems completely unaware of us," Kiki whispered. "I swear to you, earlier, he was not as solid as he is right now, granted, he was in the shadows, but look at him. I know what you're thinking, but this is not just some bloke standing in the trees, I don't think he's really there."

"Hey, buddy," Janine called out to the man, upset that he was trying to scare them. "Who are you? What are you doing out here? You can stop pretending now."

The man suddenly turned and his eyes went directly toward Janine, yet he behaved as if he couldn't quite see her. Kiki also glanced at Janine, surprised that the man responded to her.

"Do you need help?" the doctor asked, but the man didn't move.

"Do you need help?" Janine demanded firmly.

The man began to nod at her. He opened his mouth but no sounds emerged. He changed direction and moved slowly toward the wall of the barracks. The doctor moved closer to Don.

"What happened? Did he do something? Why are you shaking?" Ian asked softly, as he kept an eye on the strange man.

"He's not in the camera," Don said. "The camera's not picking him up."

They always shut down the digital display during investigative shoots, too much ambient light could spoil their night vision, so it wasn't easy to see what Don was talking about. The doctor bent to look through the eye piece and his body visibly tensed. Ian snapped his head back up to stare at the man. Ignoring Kiki's outstretched hand, Ian walked directly toward the soldier and just when he reached him, the soldier turned into the long barracks wall and disappeared into thin air. Janine inched forward to see better. *Did he go through an opening?* The wall was solid stone. While their mouths hung open, Carlos emerged from an escape door to the left of where the man disappeared. Carlos almost bumped into the doctor. He noted their shocked expressions.

"Yeah, yeah." Carlos nodded at them. "You guys figure it out too?"

"Did a man just pass you in there?" the doctor asked him.

Carlos glanced over his shoulder, confused. "A man, like a person? No." He hesitated, then turned his back on Don's camera and opened his hand. A small cube, the size of a die, lay in his palm. He handed it to the doctor.

The doctor inspected it closely, while at the same time keeping an eye on the long barracks wall. The doctor took his audio headset off and completely switched off his transmitter. Everyone else did the same thing. The doctor motioned for Don to keep the camera pointed at the bushes, then Ian tossed the cube back to Carlos.

"Is it a micro speaker?"

Carlos nodded. "The heat sig lead to it. The minute I handled it the whispering noises cut out. It's a pretty awesome sound system, wouldn't you say?"

"Son of a bitch!" Don muttered, he let out a huge sigh of relief. "I about had an accident over here. Who do you think did this?"

"Max." The doctor shook his head. "It has to be Colliers. He's planted some ghosts for us to find."

"Maybe the Alamo people did it," Don suggested.

Kiki took a few steps toward the foliage. "I don't understand. I got a very strong feeling out here, intense spectral energy, and in that gift shop too. I don't see how Max, or anybody, could do that. That can't be faked. How do you explain the man? His energy?"

"I don't know, a hologram?" Ian searched around the trees. "A projection device could be anywhere."

"A really incredible hologram that moved all over and seemed to respond?" Janine said. No one had any answers. "What's the plan?" They still had two other destinations to investigate, the battle cannon walk and the main chapel.

"Shall we go out there and confront Max?" the doctor raised his eyebrows at Kiki.

"Maybe we should play along with his little charade and toy with him before unmasking him." Kiki narrowed her emerald eyes. "See what he has in store for us in that chapel, he seemed insistent that we have our finale in there. Let's see how far he's willing to go."

They all agreed. The doctor put his audio back in his ear.

"Audio all now. We'll want to hear everything Colliers has to say, where he urges us, and such," the doctor said.

Janine tuned in to hear Max rambling about their failure to follow direction and wasting the camera. He informed them sternly that he was not just the executive producer, but he was also the director. He reminded them that a director directs and they needed to listen to him.

"Yes, Doctor, I get that this is an investigation, but to film it and present the story nicely, you need the direct input from your director. I am the eyes of Oz, so to speak, and can see things you don't. More direction would have helped you at the end of last season. Let's not let our egos keep us from getting the good stuff."

"Kiki talking to a ghost wasn't good stuff?" the doctor interjected.

"Oh good. You're no longer ignoring me," Max snapped back. "From my angle, Kiki appeared to be talking to a bush. Now we lost what happened in the long barracks with the ghostly noises. Those were super spooky sounds. I don't want to lose anything else. Do not give Don any more conflicting orders. I want Don pointing that camera in the right directions, especially in the chapel. Can we agree on that, McNally?"

"Aye, absolutely," Ian grinned. "Perhaps we should head straight away to the chapel. Carlos is a little shaken up about the long barracks."

"Oh yes," Carlos said. "Very unexplainable voices and footsteps echoing in there. I had to get out of there fast. I almost freaked out."

Kiki shot Carlos a look and he just gave her his dimpled grin. Max's voice filtered through the airwaves again.

"Let's put that behind us. I will say, I was hoping to get the Doctor-Kiki moment, the catch, in the long barracks. Maybe we can get something dramatic in the chapel. Don, get that camera up. I want everyone to head over to the chapel now. Don, this time film the group walking away from you. I'd like Kiki at the tail end, center shot. I love that outfit Kiki, very, very… well, very Kiki. Don, you know the angle I'm looking for."

They entered the chapel through the same door they exited earlier. Carlos disappeared into the chapel first, followed by Kiki, and then Don. Janine hung back with the doctor to look over the display for the EMF box. Nothing of note showed on the readouts. As soon as she entered the chapel, they noticed the interior felt extremely cold, as if someone ran the air conditioner on full blast. *Tricky to do without electricity*, she thought, *and an obvious stunt*. A room of cool air was not the pocket of coldness that preceded an interesting encounter.

"It's very cold in here," Kiki announced. "Do you guys feel it? Very cold."

"Let's check the thermal-panger you left and see what it tells us." The doctor nodded at Janine.

Max came over the wire. "Excellent idea. Don, you'll want a close up on those read outs."

Don rushed over to Janine and pointed the camera over her shoulder as she checked the panger. She skipped back over the past couple of hours to when she placed it on the ground, then set it to play back in quick-time.

"It recorded a steady drop in temperature that began soon after we left. It's roughly twelve degrees cooler than when we started the night."

"Must be a ghost on the horizon," Carlos said, "And do you hear that sound? Is that a clicking noise?"

"It is. It seems to be coming from the roof," the doctor looked up.

All eyes turned to the rafters. Then, the shuttered windows suddenly burst open, startling them, and the flutter of wings roared deafeningly. Hundreds of bats zig zagged manically overhead. The crew calmly gathered in the center of the main shrine room, crouching in a huddle. They watched as bats swooped up and down searching for a way out, but the shutters had closed, trapping them in. Several of the winged rats came to rest in the rafters.

"My word," Kiki gazed at the hanging bats. "There is definitely something afoot in this building." Her green eyes flashed irritably.

Max came over the wire, "Wow, you guys handled that pretty calmly. It looked scary as shit on the camera."

"We're professionals here," Carlos said. "Bats don't scare us. I'm getting warm bands coming from that room over there." He hit the playback on his infrared camera and showed the doctor his digital display where a definite human heat signature had moved.

Kiki added, "I also sense a strong feeling seeping from that room, like some sort of menace might be there. What is that room again? The monks' burial chamber if I remember correctly. The diablos were thought to be the men who built this chapel. Do you think we'll find six ghostly holy men lounging in there?"

"I detect a flame," the doctor said. Janine noticed a faint glow of light coming from the next room, pulsing, and the faint scent of vanilla finally reached her nose. Kiki narrowed her green eyes and shook her head.

Carlos tapped Janine on the shoulder. "It just hit me. Doesn't this feel like we're on an episode of *Scooby Doo*? Would you say I'm more like Shaggy or Scooby?"

"With your mop head, definitely Shaggy," Janine said.

Max Collier's voice cut in.

"What is going on in there? What is Carlos rambling about? Is anyone going to investigate that glowing light or are you just going to sit around? We only have the grounds exclusively for a couple more hours, and we need to get some good footage, spectacular footage. It was a big price tag, so don't fool around in there. If you guys don't start getting serious—"

"Oh, I'll go investigate it!" Kiki huffed as she stood up.

She reached dramatically down to draw the small dagger from the sheath on her thigh, giving the camera a nice shot of one near naked leg. She displayed the ornate grip for Don's camera lens. She held it by the silver blade and grinned wickedly. The wood handle was carved with an intricate Celtic knot.

"This is my witch's knife," she told the camera. "If the spirit of a holy man is trapped on Earth, I can release him with this dagger. I only need to be sure it passes cleanly through his heart essence. Come along with me and we'll try to release the holy devil from his earthly prison."

Everyone exchanged amused grins. Kiki strolled purposely toward the entrance of the monks' burial room and Don followed her with the camera. Janine, Carlos, and Ian all hung back, watching her swagger away. Was Kiki really planning to do something with that dagger?

Ian bent toward Carlos and Janine, "She's an expert at throwing the Sgian-dubh, she hardly ever misses her mark."

Kiki suddenly moved fast. She shifted her weight and planted her feet firmly on the ground. In one swift, graceful motion, she threw the knife into the next room, yelling, "Be free, ye devil!"

"Fuck!" an angry male voice echoed from the room. "That was a real knife!"

Kiki strolled backward, laughing. She smirked at Don's camera with her emerald eyes flashing impishly. "Well, kids, it's time to go out to the mystery machine and reveal the true identity behind the spectral madness we've witnessed here tonight. Hey, in there," she called into the chamber, turning her voice silky sweet. "Be a dear and bring my dagger with you."

Chapter 3
Debrief

Kiki

ax Colliers admitted ordering the miniature sized speaker for the long barracks and the bats in the chapel. The chapel was super-cooled per his instructions and he directed somebody to place another small speaker in the amphitheater. Max also admitted to hiring three actors to hide on the grounds, the guy in the chapel dressed like a monk, and two guys dressed as soldiers poised to shadow them in the garden near the arcade. Max would not own up to a hologram or other projection, or any other types of disturbances. He swore that nothing was placed in the gift store and never expected them to go into that building.

"Think about what made this show popular, the strange noises, the glimpses of a possible phantom, sexy costumes on a sexy woman," Max crossed his arms over his chest, defending his decisions. "Speaking truthfully, the last two episodes of the second season were duds without one spooky encounter of note. A terrible way to follow up your fantastic feature documentary and the very entertaining Old Town Sacramento episode. We need to jump start the enthusiasm right out the gate, or this show may die a slow and painful death. Those bats were very expensive and hard to do. You lost a golden opportunity tonight."

Ian, Kiki, and Max huddled in a corner of the hotel conference room, debriefing quietly. Everyone else in the room kept shooting them worried looks from afar. The extras stood near Lauren and the makeup guy. Before they changed clothes, Kiki noted that their costumes were very convincing, but new, clean, and pristine. Where was the guy from the courtyard in the tattered uniform? Her anger flared up just thinking about that fellow. Had it been a spoof or a spook? Kiki wondered how Ian managed to keep so calm.

Carlos sipped single malt whisky near the tech equipment watching Ben download different footage into the main computer. Every now, and again, he laughed loudly at things on the monitor. Janine was long gone. She ignored everybody to disappear straight to her room without a word about any of it. The man who played the monk glared across the room at Kiki. So what if her knife poked him in the shoulder a wee bit. It was his own fault for moving. Plus, his wound wasn't so large that a couple of Band-aids didn't cover it. She reached down to touch the returned dagger and smiled sweetly at him, then turned back to Max.

"That was over the top nonsense with the bats, Max. Messy, dangerous, and inhumane to the poor creatures,"

Kiki admonished. "And those guys over there, were we supposed to mistake them for ghosts just because you dressed them in old fashioned uniforms? Ridiculous."

"I don't see the man from the courtyard," Ian surveyed the room, "Are you still insisting you didn't have some sort of optical illusion out there?"

Max smirked at them. "It's not going to work McNally. You are not pulling my chain like that. I realize you caught onto my plan somewhere between the gift shop and the chapel, and decided to play a joke on me. You could have at least squeezed in the romantic Kiki catch at some point. In the middle of those bats would have been a nice place. Why you two are so riled up, just admit it, I threw some good stuff at you, stuff that could have been top notch entertainment. It's not any different than that catch you like to do, audiences love it. People want to be entertained. And those baggy outfits on Janine and Carlos, those two have assets we can use, they could be more appealing."

Kiki and Ian exchanged glances. They silently admitted that Max made a small point. When Kiki fainted into the doctor's arms on an early episode of *Spectral Analysis,* the audience loved it, because nobody knew Kiki and Ian were cousins. They often questioned their decision to allow that romantic tease to continue from episode to episode. It certainly proved valuable at making the show more successful. They realized the audience needed more than just the hunt for paranormal activity to keep them interested. Max was only guilty of exaggerating what they had already introduced into the show. It burned Kiki to have Max point it out to her. She watched Ian blow a deep sign out of his pressed lips.

"Okay, I get your point," Ian admitted. "But tonight was way over staged. We need to have a serious discussion about which direction we want things to go. We clearly have a difference of opinion here."

Max pushed his glasses into place and patted Ian's shoulder, "I agree. We'll tackle it in the Austin meeting this week. Right now, why don't we have a nice whisky and see if there's anything to salvage in those tapes? Let's mingle a with the troops, they seem a bit nervous. We need to calm our people down and project a united front."

Kiki didn't like to admit they almost sold out on being taken seriously back in season one, when they were desperate for success. That little bit of play acting just about cost them their reputations. Their feature documentary undoubtedly saved them, but they were right back on the fence again. How they dealt with the next few adventures would either mark them as real paranormal investigators, or just plain entertainers.

Chapter 4

The Office

Janine

The Austin office and studio relocated and expanded to include a dedicated sound stage with green screen, a conference room, a full workshop, and several offices in a suite of rooms. They occupied a lower floor of the First Bank Tower, to make it convenient for Max Colliers. The main Colliers business offices were fifteen floors above the less fancy *Spectral Analysis* space. It meant Janine and Carlos was expected to work between shoot sites and take on an expanded role before filming. Max asked them to keep regular hours at the new facilities, especially on Tuesdays and Thursdays, to attend meetings. Janine ignored that request, as she never signed the new contract and didn't intend to.

The *Spectral Analysis* reception area appeared larger than the entire old office had been. Cheryl, their original receptionist, squealed with delight when Janine strolled into the foyer. She hurried around her island desk to envelop Janine in long arms.

"It's so nice to see you," Cheryl gushed. "Let me show you to your office. You're sharing with Carlos, of course, but it's very spacious and has a nice view of river. I'm so glad you came a little early, you can get acclimated to your space before the big meeting. Everybody has been dying to meet you!"

Cheryl led her down a wide hall to a spacious room with two desks and a bookshelf. Carlos hadn't done a single thing to make the place homey. Clearly, he claimed the area in front of the shelves. Packages of his favorite gum littered the desk and random electronic gadgets were thrown haphazardly into the bookshelf. The desk closer to the window appeared to be a junk area with two cardboard boxes of papers on the desktop with another box in the chair. *J. Stinger* was scrawled across each of the boxes. Cheryl smiled at from the open door.

"Reminds me, there are a more up front. I'll have someone run them down, pronto."

"What is it?" Janine asked.

"Fan mail," Cheryl told her. "You've gotten a steady stream of letters since the movie. Well, since the electric shock." Her nodded and smiled. "I've had the reader sorting them. They're the usual; adoring fans, concerned mothers, kids. Your fan mail actually rivals the doctor's now. I'm not sure how you want to handle it, but the reader, Kristine, drew up a few form letters you can approve. The doctor does things that way, except, I'm told he writes a personal note on the rare occasion."

"What does Kiki do?" Janine asked.

"She does the same thing, only, she pulls a few out to answer *personally*. It's a little spooky how she chooses them. Her hand hovers over the pile, then she reaches in and clutches an envelope for a few seconds, then she either throws it back for Kristine or runs off with it. I think she's does it to spook us." Cheryl laughed.

"Wow, three boxes of fan mail." Janine stared at them. "Crazy, I think I only received about ten total letters the first season, and one was from my niece."

"Well, you came across very nice in the movie," Cheryl nodded. "People trust you. And you and Carlos have gotten much more air time than in that first season."

Carlos popped into the shared office a few minutes shy of the big meeting, or, more accurately, he had been in the studio with Ben and Ian watching Alamo footage while Janine sat reading letters from fans. If she had known those guys were in the building, she would have looked for them. She arrived early with the intention of seeing Ian. She finally felt like she might be able to chat with him, and she wanted to completely bury the hatchet so they could part ways as friends. Instead, a chattering Carlos guided her to the spacious board room. They plopped into seats at the large wooden table. Janine could hear Ben and Ian in the back room setting up the audio visual equipment. She debated running back to say hello, but the room began to fill in with people who stopped to greet her. In between the introductions, Carlos occupied her with photos on his cell phone, all of his wife, his toddler twins, and his long list of athletic brothers. Carlos shared photos of the house he purchased for his parents.

"We closed escrow on it last week," Carlos declared proudly. "It's down the street from mine, so Mama and Pop can live here instead of San Antonio. They need a big yard, cause they're gonna have so many grandkids. I'm telling you, Janine, you should consider staying on this season. Max is very generous in the new contract. Yes, we have office hours, but really, I just hang out in the green room, or in the doc's workshop, just joking around and smiling at people."

Lauren glided into the room like a ray of sunshine, followed by Guy, the makeup guy. Lauren flashed an over large smile at everyone and ferried two cups of coffee. She placed one cup on the table across from Janine. She gazed sweetly and said hello in a bright happy voice. She touched hands with several people before finally settling next to Guy in a chair against the wall. Another young woman joined them. Carlos identified her as the costume person, Sally, and the three, Lauren, Guy, and Sally chatted together in an fun way. Lauren seemed very popular.

Mike Dunn, the old lawyer, carried a briefcase in his hand and hurried to the far side of the table. He gave Janine a little nod before shuffling through papers. She wondered if any of that paperwork involved her contract. She doubted it. Management had been very flexible about her emergency leave of absence, but they were not so flexible about letting her out of the contract. Mike was probably tired of her queries. Over the past six months, she had called to insistently review her legal obligations to the show, and he took on the task of disappointing her over and over again. Janine finally came to terms with it, she owed *Spectral Analysis* payback time or a ton of money.

More people filed in and took seats against the wall. Carlos whispered, *he's in production, he's the graphic designer, she does something with the mail.* Don sat against the wall before someone reminded him to sit at the table. He blinked at Carlos and Janine but didn't really say hello. *Just like their old camera man, Ted,* Janine thought. Cameramen must be a grumpy bunch. An older woman with white hair and thick glasses turned out to be the letter reader, Kristine, who had been sorting Janine's mail. She carried a pile of papers in her arms and seemed preoccupied with them. Carlos could not identify a few others that strolled in, including another lawyer type who sat next to Mike.

Ben and Ian finally emerged from the back room and slipped into the seats across from Janine and Carlos. Ben smiled brightly at her. He seemed to get along terrifically with the doctor. The doctor noticed her and nodded. His bruised eye was now rimmed with a tinge of yellow skin and his jaw appeared very scruffy. He must not have shaved the past couple of days and looked a little like a pirate, rough and dangerous, very cute. She couldn't help smiling at the sight of him. He noticed and smiled back. The cup of coffee got his attention and he spun quickly around toward Lauren.

Lauren winked at him with bright, happy eyes. *How very thoughtful of her,* Janine mused. Janine watched Ian mouth a *thank you* and then he spun back to the table. His eyes met hers, but quickly darted away again. Janine watched his eyes begin to blink. Obviously, Ian had a beautiful new girlfriend and was worried that fact might hurt her feelings.

Boy, did it, but she decided she was going to just eat it. Being supportive and happy for Ian was the least she could do. She would soon be away from *Spectral Analysis,* and she could put that past behind her, with all the other stuff. She could hear her shrink virtually tsking in the distance, *Running away from uncomfortable situations just exasperates a problem, Janine.*

Oh, shut up, she wanted to tell him.

Cheryl followed Max Colliers into the room and flopped into the seat behind him with her computer pad out. Max beamed and personally greeted several people. He gave Janine an approving smile as he introduced her to the group. The season started weeks ago for most of them, and Janine got the impression that they were pleasantly surprised that she actually showed up to the office building. Max proceeded to give a very nice speech recapping recent events, including the shoot in San Antonio. There wasn't a hint of the disagreement during that shoot. Max glanced at the empty chair next to him, and shrugged. *Where was Kiki,* Janine thought.

"More things to focus on, promotions: We need to update everything with the new logo, everything. Nothing old out there, that includes the old ties and work suits. We have a few critical fixes in wardrobe to consider," Max glanced briefly at Janine. "Sally, your period costumes were very nice, and although everyone raved about the crew uniforms, Don tells me the new suit is a tad uncomfortable. He says it hinders his range of motion in the lower extremities. Perhaps we need a slight redesign, the crew will give you input on what they'd like. We've got a couple of solid weeks before our next shoot to work it out."

Though she just met him, Janine could not imagine Don using the phrase *range of motion*. She wondered if Max said that to keep the designer from knowing that she refused to wear the costume.

Max continued, "Now that Miss Stinger is here, perhaps she can make herself available for measurements. All of you, Don, Carlos, Janine, please see Sally sometime today so she can get your updated numbers. We're throwing out the old jump suits and need to make appropriate replacements."

The young brunette next to Ian's girlfriend raised her hand and waved.

"I'm down the opposite hall on the left, the middle door. It's always open." Sally smiled.

Max gave her an approving nod, "Thanks Sally. Please run your design ideas by the crew as well, we want to get their input so there are no surprises on location." Max gave Janine a handsome smile, all teeth. "We're also developing a plan for hair styles, and grooming. Carlos, how do you feel about growing some sideburns?"

Carlos laughed, "If you think sideburns are important for the ratings, why not."

"And what about you, Doctor? Lauren believes sideburns on the crew might be a nice touch this season, it'll jazz up your style in a subtle way."

Ian dragged his hand over his whiskery jaw. "I'm going to grow the beard back, I kind of miss it. Believe it or not, I've gotten a nice compliment or two about it, and it jazzes me up a bit, I think." He glanced fleetingly at Janine, then spun his chair to face Lauren. "I'll agree on a beard, and Carlos and Don can do the side burns. How about that?"

Max glanced at Lauren, "Beard on the doctor, chops on Carlos and Don, that sounds fun. Will that do, Lauren?" A little disappointment crossed her face, but she nodded and smiled. She must not prefer the pirate look for Ian. Then, Max rapped his knuckles on the table.

"I'm told, we have a little preview before breaking off into just the crew meeting." Max nodded at Ian.

"Yes, right." Ian straightened up as Ben disappeared into the back room. "After reviewing the material from our Alamo investigation, we were pleasantly surprised to discover startling evidence of a spectral entity haunting the mission grounds. What you're about to witness is film of Kiki speaking to a ghost. A ghost that everyone in the courtyard could see, but the camera could not." Ian pointed to Don. "Don here can attest to that, right Don?"

"Well, yes," Don wobbled as he adjusted his lounging position. "The man in the courtyard was not recorded on film. It was very scary."

People murmured around the room.

"But who's going to take our word for that?" Ian wondered out loud. "Nobody. At first glance, Kiki appears to be addressing the bushes, as Mr. Colliers first pointed out."

There were giggles and Max flashed his perfect smile again.

"But then, we put the video together with a subsonic audio recording." Ian waved an open hand at Janine, "Janine Stinger will often record encounters on her audio device. This time she set the device to record in a frequency band including the lowest range of human hearing down to an area in the subsonic zone. Ben noticed that the subsonic peaks matched patterns very similar to human speech. We decided to raise the pulses by a common multiplier so that they just reached the sonic zone. Sure enough, we heard an eerie voice."

The excited murmurs escalated. Janine recalled turning her audio device on in the long barracks, but had forgotten all about it.

"What you are about to see is footage of Kiki talking to the bushes. Superimposed on top of those images is the recorded subsonic voice, all time hacked together. So, you are going to hear the mystery voice in common time with our film clip."

Ben's head poked from the back room door and Ian gave him a thumbs up.

The conference room came with a supersized television and a surround sound system. In the next moment, the screen came alive with a still shot of Kiki standing next to the cannon.

Good lord, Janine observed, *Kiki's dress really was over the top.* It blended magically with her flesh and only the dagger sheath and bands of beads stood out against her skin. An excited murmur permeated the room.

Kiki always knew how to pose in a striking way on film. Her head swiveled from the background trees back toward the camera and her voice was very clear, "I swear, earlier, he wasn't as solid as he is now. Granted, he was in the shadows, but look at him. And I know what you're thinking, but this is not just some bloke standing in the trees. I don't think he's really there." Heavy breathing noises reverberated under her voice. With an outstretched hand, Kiki presented the bushes for the camera and the picture had just a hint of fuzziness in front of the foliage.

"Hey, buddy," Janine's sharp voice came from out of camera shot. "Who are you? What are you doing out here? You can stop pretending now."

A low-pitched, eerie response suddenly emerged from the breathing noises. "I am here on my watch. Women must congregate in the chapel, you shouldn't…"

"Do you need help?" the doctor spoke over the low-toned voice. The doctor's voice had been much louder, and it was hard to decipher what they just missed. Then, Janine's voice came in again, "Do you need help?" On the screen, Kiki's glowing eyes turned toward the camera, then her head swiveled toward the darkness again.

"Help is not coming." The low tone created an ominous voice that slowly began to fade. "There is no one to help us. Women must return to the chapel, and I must return to my wall."

Doctor McNally passed quickly in front of the camera and then the screen froze again. After a short silence, the room burst with excited chatter. Janine had to admit, that was a very spooky clip, wavering dark shadows behind an aesthetically pleasing Kiki, with a spooky low-toned voice answering her questions. It was spookier than when she actually saw the man standing in the bushes.

She glanced at Don and he appeared very unnerved. Ben reentered from the back room and Ian stood up to smack him on the back. The room continued to buzz with chatter.

"It was a brilliant, innovative idea from Ben here, and so simple really, pulling that pattern of energy into an audible range by increasing the frequency. Keep in mind, it was not a real voice, but energy transposed into a section in the human hearing range. Typically, we'd hear nothing but static, but in this case, the noise made words. Unexplainable, yes, but we believe we captured the energy of a spectral voice."

The room clapped for Ben.

"Fantastic work, Ben!" Max Colliers grinned at him. "Everybody, fantastic work! We are getting off to a fine start. Before I cut the support team loose, are there any questions? Anyone have something they'd like to add or ask?"

The reader, Kristine, raised a shaky hand and Max nodded to her.

"I think I'm asking for a lot of us here," Kristine grinned at Ian while peering over her square reading glasses, "but I'd like to know how Doctor McNally got that nice shiner. Was it during the investigation? Will it be in the upcoming Alamo episode?"

Good hearted chuckling permeated the room, from everyone except Carlos, Ian, and Max. That question appeared to stump Max for the first time. He glanced quickly at Ian, then at Carlos, then at Janine, then back to Ian. The room fell silent as everyone waited for an answer. Finally, Don spoke up to fill in the silence.

"It was Carlos," Don said. "He punched the doctor right in the eye during dinner."

As they began to review the season line up, Kiki finally waltzed into the meeting and sunk into the empty seat next to Max. She fluttered her eyes at him, then turned her attention to the lawyer, Mike Dunn. A few snags with local governing bodies had created last minute changes to the schedule. Janine realized that Mike's paper mess was about filming on location, not her personnel issues.

Kiki wore a pink sparkly track suit. She had rushed directly from her personal trainer and had to cut short her session with a metaphysical reflexology therapist. She advised Max that he needed to schedule meetings at least a day in advance if he required her presence. Lately, her life was a busy labyrinth of important obligations, and she couldn't just alter her appointments because he got a wild hair and wanted to meet at the last minute.

"You missed the meeting for a massage?" Max asked her. "This is hardly last minute, Kiki, we talked about this meeting days ago in San Antonio. It's a regularly scheduled event now. Between locations, we'll all be here."

"You didn't set an exact time," Kiki rebuffed, but she smiled sweetly at him. "And it wasn't just a massage. It happens to be very crucial recuperative therapy, vital for my well-being. Tuning in to spectral energy takes concentrated effort. It takes quite a toll physically, mentally and emotionally. You wouldn't want me to have an on the job injury, would you?"

Max couldn't help grinning as he readjusted his designer tie. "Okay, I get the picture. There's a diva around and I wouldn't choose anyone else to be that diva, Kiki. Mike, do you want to tell everyone the good news?"

Mike Dunn restacked his papers. "Seattle, Florida, Chicago, and Toronto quickly rubber stamped the show plans. We're still waiting for Santa Fe to decide, so you'll need to push that plan later in your lineup. Another little glitch, although Chicago approved everything, they won't guarantee exclusive access to Fort Dearborn Park and that other little park, not unless you guys go in the next month when the metro station is closed for reconstruction. They can do it then. Of course, they say you can access those parks anytime, but they won't close them off for you. You'll be part of the public parade."

"Okay, we push Santa Fe further back into the schedule and move something else up," Max said. "Kiki, Ian, where to next? Seattle? Janine, you're only obligated to film the next few shows, unless I can talk you into staying longer. Do any of those places strike your fancy? Personally, I like the idea of Chicago, I have some business that I can take care of out there, and we can take advantage of the exclusive access to that park. Why did we want that area again?"

"The Fort Dearborn massacre occurred on that spot," Ian said. "Lots of spectral activity in the area. Several years ago, I did a bit of research into the odd electromagnetic waves seeping from the Dearborn Massacre sites. I devoted a chapter in my book to the energy in that smaller park down the street. I'm excited to take Kiki there, for her take on it."

"We don't need exclusive access to any park." Kiki flipped through a thick planner, seemingly absentmindedly. "Chicago can wait, Seattle sounds nice."

"Exclusive access anywhere would be pretty nice, in Chicago. Chicago is a very busy, crowded city," Carlos said. "People are going to be stopping us, and talking, and butting in while we're filming. Have you been to Chicago? People are wandering around at all hours of the night. I don't think people know what dawn to dusk means in Chicago, it's crazy there."

"Carlos has a point," Max tapped his thick ballpoint pen on the table. "Think of the security problems we could avoid."

"We can hit Chicago later in the season." Ian rubbed his scruff.

Ian and Kiki hoped to avoid Chicago for her sake, because Chicago held traumatic memories for Janine. Back when she attended the University of Chicago, she was knifed in one of the wooded areas of the windy city and nearly killed. Recovering from that experience took several years of expensive therapy. Her therapist warned her that she might never completely recover, but she didn't want to be so fragile she couldn't go into the city again. If she went back to Chicago, she could prove to herself that she was finally past it. A *Spectral Analysis* shoot might give her the only excuse to ever go back.

"I vote for Chicago," Janine murmured softly. "Exclusive access to an open public area is surely a good reason to move it up in the schedule, rather than wait. Why would we wait? There's no reason to wait."

"Thank you," Carlos interjected.

"Are you sure about that?" Ian's soft blue eyes were focused on her. "It isn't a big deal for us to go later in the season. The small park I'm interested in is not a busy area."

Janine ignored those eyes and turned to Max. His eyes were equally soft, studying her. Did he sense the tension in the air?

"I vote for Chicago," she said firmly. "If you really want to make me happy, I think Chicago would be fun."

"I definitely want to make you happy." Max slowly removed his glasses. His attention flickered around the table. "We all want to make you happy, right, guys?" They all agreed. "I'm hoping you become so happy, you'll choose to sign on for the rest of the season, and more."

Max proved to be a savvy boss. Evidently, his goal was to make things so nice for Janine that she would change her mind about leaving the show. For months, Janine didn't understand why he wouldn't cut her loose, and then those boxes of fan mail provided a pile of enlightenment for her. People felt a direct connection to her experiences in the last season, and many of her fans confessed to having paranormal encounters of their own. Janine's obvious skepticism, followed by her very reluctant acceptance, liberated a number of viewers. They no longer felt the need to hide a ghostly encounter at the risk of being labeled a nut job. She unexpectedly developed a critical following that might be instrumental in the show's continued success.

Carlos distracted her by opening and closing the drawers on his desk. He appeared to be moving paper, pens, and other office supplies from drawer to drawer. He noticed her scrutiny.

"I'm organizing," he explained. "I never had a desk before, at a job, I mean. I'm going to figure out the perfect arrangement to streamline my access to things."

"You're streamlining office supplies, in case you need them in a hurry? Like in an office emergency? Like, maybe, important papers will need to be stapled quickly and you don't want to drop the ball on getting it done in a timely manner. Is that what you're thinking?"

Carlos flashed his dimpled grin and they both started laughing. They spun around in their very fancy, swivel and roll, bonded leather office chairs. Carlos grasped a three hole punch in his large hand.

"Why do I need this? Am I going to be punching holes in something soon?" He pointed to other supplies. "And this stapler with five thousand staples, five thousand! I don't think I've stapled fifty things in my life. And this set of highlighters, and look at this tape dispenser, and these paperclips. Why do I need all this stuff? I mean, how many paper clips does it take to do my job?" His eyes rolled to the ceiling, "Okay, I've summed it up, not one."

"This is definitely a different gig without Steve. Max is so much more…business. I admit, this place is tons nicer than that box of an office on Stone Oak Parkway, but it was fun. Remember how hot it got in the summer? Remember that time Cheryl's makeup melted, poor girl, she must be in heaven here. Was that a cappuccino machine by her desk? Even that hotel in San Antonio was nice with the private suites and fresh fruit, and real coffee after the shoot. People running around carrying the air cases for us, and that guy, Guy, powdering my nose and such."

Carlos nodded. "All the extra help is nice. Did you know, Max hired two tech guys from one of his other ventures to help in the doctor's workshop? They're down there perfecting and developing all kinds of meters and stuff. The big box is shrinking and the doctor's workshop is not lacking for tools. You should come down and see it, it's so cool. It's down two floors, next to the computers and green room. We call it the dungeon, but it's cool. The doctor is a happy man down there. He's having a hard time staying upset at Colliers for nosing-in during the Alamo shoot."

Should she ask? She wanted to know, so she asked, "Did you actually punch him in the eye at dinner? Is that how he got the black eye, or did Don make that up?"

Carlos widened his light brown eyes and blew the dimples out of his cheeks before tilting his head at her. "Yes, I punched him. There was a little too much tequila flying around that evening and it was sort of a reflex action, an accident. Don't worry about it. Everybody's good here." Carlos shrugged at her, "Guys punch each other sometimes. That's the way we are."

She wasn't buying that, something happened that they didn't want her know about. Carlos spun back toward his desk, and she decided to drop it. The older woman, the reader, popped her head in the door. Kristine wore her hair in a short beehive hair style, and thick glasses attached to a bright purple lanyard were propped in the hive. She exuded primary colors with a bright yellow shirt, navy blue pants, and a red scarf. She delivered three more letters for Janine. Carlos took the opportunity to slink out of the room as Kristine fully entered.

"Have you decided on putting a personal note in any of your fan letters?" Kristine asked. "If so, just take them out of the box and I'll have Keith pick up the rest so we can send out your responses, the generic responses. I wrote three samples for you to sign, one signature on each will do, and we'll keep a copy on file for the future. If you tell me the type of letters you'd like to personally read, I can set them aside for you. The doctor enjoys letters with science questions from kids, for example."

"Thank you," Janine touched one of the boxes. "I can't believe the pile of mail you've already sorted through."

"I've gone through them little by little since you've been gone. The first few months, I hope you don't mind, but we sent responses without asking. Back when Steve called the shots, he said you'd be happy we sent out those responses."

"Yes, yes," Janine agreed, "I'm happy you did it. I'm sure the generic response is fine, and recycling is fine. I don't need to see anything."

"We'd like to get an updated photo, a head shot and others. They can take them in the green room downstairs. Also, there are a few with no return addresses, or sender names. I rubber banded them together and stuck them in the miscellaneous box. I meant to point out a couple of them.

That long one in your hand might be from the same sender, I daresay. No name, unit, or whatever, but stamped from the Stateville Correctional facility." Kristine paused and glanced out the open door. She turned back and spoke in a hushed, excited voice. "Do you know somebody in the clink? Sorry, but I was tasked to read your fan mail and a couple of them made me curious. I assure you, I'll keep those letters strictly confidential, I'm like a priest in that regard. But is there an old boyfriend in prison perhaps?"

Janine plopped down in her swivel and roll, soft leather chair. Did *he* send her a fan letter? She shuffled through the five envelopes in her hand and found the one stamped in red, *Stateville Corrections*. She stared at it. He loved to write her notes, almost every day. He'd leave them on her pillow, or dorm door, or tapped to the soccer post on the practice field. They always made her feel special, loved, *adored*. She felt a bit of panic bubbling and tamped it down with a slow breath.

"Lots of inmates write to Kiki, from all over, nothing to get nervous about. She gets very raunchy letters from the inside. I've saved a few that I like to read on a cold night." Kristine giggled and adjusted the glasses in her beehive. "I banded your more amorous letters together and placed them in that box over there, good reading, you might want to save a few, but there were two others like that one. They're in the anonymous pile, and the wording led me to believe that you might know him, so I saved them for you to look at. Perhaps that one finally has a name on it."

"Hello ladies," Kiki suddenly stood in the doorway. "Hey, Janine, they're screaming for you over there in design. Sally wants your measurements." Kiki turned to Kristine. "Kristine, I need your help. I've got some new things for fan response that I'd like to run by you. Are you done here?"

"Yes," Janine said quickly. She smiled at Kristine but wasn't sure if it was convincing. "You know, I don't need to read anything, you seem to have it handled." Then, she threw the five envelopes onto the top of the pile as if none of them meant anything to her.

"Janine," Kiki stepped into the room and touched her arm. "Right after Sally measures you, can we meet? We haven't had a chance to catch up and I've got some stuff on the horizon that I'm planning. We can get out of this hell hole and go for a nice girl's cocktail or something. There's an important topic we need to discuss."

Janine nodded. "Sure."

As soon as Kiki pulled Kristine away, Janine fished out the Stateville letter from the box. She then rummaged in the miscellaneous pile and found the banded pile with no return addresses. She shuffled through to find the other two Stateville letters. They were each opened at the top with a single slit along the seam and she noticed a single folded piece of bonded white paper in each. She opened the lower drawer of her new desk and tossed the letters in for safe keeping.

Not because she wanted to read anything *he* had to say, but because she needed to confirm for certain that he really did send them. Janine closed her eyes. It would be very nice if they turned out to be written from someone else, but she doubted it.

Then, she went off to get measured by Sally.

Chapter 5

Rosemount Room

Kiki

Kiki could kick herself for not handling Janine's fan mail in her absence. She would have discovered those letters from the Illinois state penitentiary and kept Kristine from reading them, but things got busy and it never occurred to her. Kristine wasn't just a fast and thorough reader, she was quick to grasp the difference between a regular fan letter and a message from an actual acquaintance. Kristine might easily figure out Janine's carefully kept secret. What a media frenzy there would be if people found out the identity of *Jane Doe from Chicago*!

Kiki and Janine chose the Rosemount Room to take advantage of the plush private lounge and the fancy drinks. Kiki avoided the Twelve Grand because most of the *Spectral Analysis* staff found themselves in that whisky establishment after hours. Someone from the office always dropped in and Kiki wanted a private chat with Janine.

They found a spot behind two large potted plants and Kiki ordered a couple of old fashions right off the bat. She didn't ask because Janine normally said no to a stiff drink. She also knew Janine would love the Rosemount Room's version of the old fashion. They claimed the furthest leather sofa in the balcony area, in a spot secluded from most of the room.

"I'm guessing you want to talk to me about Ian," Janine said after the drinks arrived.

"Yes, a little about Ian," Kiki said. "But there's other stuff too. I want a good solid chat and to catch up." Kiki gave the waiter a signal for two more, best to have one waiting in the bull pen to keep the conversation pleasantly flowing. "You probably know that Gram and I keep in touch. She's kept me up to date with the goings on in California, and with your family, and with you."

Janine drained a healthy amount from her glass and nodded. Sure enough, their reinforcements arrived promptly. The waiter, Jeff, recognized them and Kiki laughed at a joke he made about ghosts. Kiki decided to go ahead and order ahead again. Even though she only took two sips of her first drink, she could see Janine was surprisingly ready to let loose.

"Let's try the fish house punch next," Kiki eyed the waiter. He was very bright eyed at her attention. "As long as you keep us a secret out here, we'll stay as long as you like." Kiki winked at him. "When you see these old fashions getting low, we'd like that punch? And how about a nice cheese board to nibble." Off he went.

"Kiki," Janine started, "I'm a little ashamed about the way I behaved. I put everyone on the spot and I need to apologize. Asking you to take sides…" She sipped her drink carefully. Her large doe eyes made her appear like a princess in a fairy tale, the kind that always needed saving. "Now that I've gone over things rationally, it was out of line to expect the show to accuse Caroline and Henry Webber of—"

Kiki reached out and grasped her hand. "That's behind you Janine. No one here blames you, and frankly, Henry Webber was not hurt. Caroline Govant was not hurt. Believing they were behind Sammy's loss was your need to solve things in a way that made sense to you. I don't blame you for pressing it so hard. You were grieved, anyone could see that, and everyone could certainly see the logic in your theory. It wasn't farfetched with the history in that town. I wish Ian could have been more understanding when you proposed it and handled it better. But he has his own issues."

Janine nodded, "What I'm trying to say is, I realize why Ian flat out refused to consider my theory for the movie, the legal ramifications, and, I'm sorry that I put you and Carlos in the middle of it when I reacted so harshly to him."

Janine blinked her emotions away and Kiki hugged her. Sammy had been Janine's very young niece, a bright eyed, beautiful little girl. Really, Janine's older sister adopted Sammy right after Janine had given birth to her. Sammy had been part of the aftermath of that life threatening relationship she survived in Chicago, and she disappeared mysteriously during one of their spectral investigations.

People believed a ghost took her, the one from the award winning documentary. They believed the ghost lured Sammy into the river, like all the other victims in the river ghost story. That's what Kiki believed.

The official verdict stated that Sammy accidently drowned and her body was washed away, lost to the river, forever.

Janine argued against an accident or a ghost. She accused two old people in the town of directly participating in Sammy's disappearance. Janine proposed that the kids weren't lured by a ghost, but by a living group of crazy people who believed they needed to sacrifice children to the river, a cult that possibly existed for years, generations. The authorities disagreed. Janine pushed to include her conspiracy theory in the documentary, but Ian wouldn't have it. He put his foot down hard at her suggestions, and said it was irresponsible to accuse people with absolutely no proof. Ian told Janine that she was not being rational. *She was being hysterical.*

Janine had been accused of hysteria before, back in the courtroom, after she had been stabbed. Her attacker nearly got away with everything by insisting she was irrational, hysterical, delusional. So, Janine stopped speaking to Ian completely. She wouldn't even acknowledge him. Then, she took that extended leave of absence.

"I know you felt helpless," Kiki held her hand. "Everybody felt helpless. We weren't careful, and it was just an awful, shit situation, Janine. A terrible loss."

They quieted down as Jeff brought out the cheese plate.

"Your Gram says you've been taking classes, at a university."

Janine laughed softly, "You think I'm crazy? I don't know what got into me, but I had to fill up my waking hours with something. I took an overloaded semester on top of a winter session. I actually have two more exams, one coming next week, so not quite completely done. It feels good to get caught up on the education I put off."

"It sounds like pure torture," Kiki said.

"It helps me. I feel like I'm doing something right. I stopped thinking about everything and just pressed right through. I guess it's my new therapy, no medication needed. I'd like to get back as soon as possible, but Mike Dunn tells me I'm bound by my contract to *Spectral Analysis*. Max could let me go, if he wanted, don't you think? I offered to buy out my contract, but he put a million dollar price tag on it. Can you believe that?"

Kiki nodded. "Oh yes, adorable Mr. Max, he is quite a little dobber. He certainly could let you out of the contract, very easily. I wouldn't like to see you go, but you have some compelling personal reasons for wanting to leave. I don't blame you one bit for wanting out of your contract."

Oh my, Kiki thought, *what was the look Janine gave her?*

"Is that why we're here? Are you worried about Ian? You said, you wanted to talk about him," Janine gulped her drink nervously. "Before you say anything, I want to repeat that I've accepted that Ian was right about what shouldn't go into the documentary, and I'm sorry for the way I reacted, for how harsh I was to him. To put your mind at ease, I'm not going to mess with Ian while I'm here. I realize I broke his heart back there and can see that he's moved on, so you don't have to worry. You can tell him…"

She stopped talking because Jeff came around with their new drinks. He could see that he interrupted and quickly left. Kiki touched Janine's hand to keep her from continuing.

"No, this talk has nothing to do with any of that," Kiki said. "Ian and you, and, well, it's none of my business. Anything you want Ian to know, you'll have to tell him yourself. That's not what I wanted to talk about."

"Then, what did you want to talk to me about? In regards to Ian?"

"His birthday," Kiki told her. "I'm planning his thirtieth and I think he would be very pleased if you were there. Steve and Ted and those two guys that used to fix the van. Current cast, crew and office staff will be there, also some of our past interviewees, the Savannah caretaker, Paul, and that crazy chicken girl, Foxy, from New Orleans, the one that scared the shit out of Carlos. Plus, Gram, maybe. I wanted to make sure it was alright with you. I'm setting a date and I don't want you to miss it." Kiki drained her drink.

"Go ahead and invite Gram. I'll come to the party. I want to end things as friends with Ian," Janine assured her. "I won't ditch it. Gram and I are good now. I'm not sure what she's said to you, but I can't very well drive to her house every weekend, not with the load of classes I took. Gram and I are talking again."

Kiki nodded. "Good. There is one more thing," she hesitated.

Janine was a terrible skeptic to almost everything Kiki believed. She and Carlos often laughed at Kiki and her witchy practices, and although Janine had come around to accepting some of Kiki's extrasensory perceptions, Janine would dismiss her own similar gifts. Kiki had itched to broach the subject for quite some time. Now that they were both a little tipsy, perhaps the subject would not be too brazen for Janine.

"Janine, I believe you're a *dragoma*," Kiki said bluntly. "In the spiritual sense, that's a person who can easily get their point across to spirits. Spirits listen and often obey a *dragoma*, and a strong *dragoma* can actually converse with a spirit."

Janine's eyes opened just a little wider. Amusement hovered in her expression and her shoulders finally relaxed with the change of subject. She downed the rest of her drink.

Kiki smiled back, "Laugh all you want, but I'm pretty certain of it."

Janine chuckled. "I'm taking this as a compliment, coming from you, Kiki, but I'm not into the psychic or medium thing. There's no longer a doubt in my mind that you have an uncanny ability to tap into that world, but I think I'm probably like most people, clueless. I don't even know what that is, a *dragoma*."

"Ian's mother, my Auntie Celeste, was a very talented *dragoma*," Kiki told her. "She was a true mystic seer, her callings were legend, and she taught many of us. She was the most gifted witch I have ever known. She spoke to many restless spirits, helping them find peace. Only a mystic who communicates easily with the spirits can do that, a natural speaker. I believe speaking to spirits might come easily for you too."

Kiki didn't mention that Celeste often spoke to ghosts as a child. It seemed to be the mark of a *dragoma*. Children could see and hear spirits easier than adults, perhaps due to unspoiled sensory receptors and an unbiased mind. Partnered with early learning, a child could carry certain talents into adulthood, like learning new sounds and training the ear, or training the tongue. If they're not practiced in youth, they could be lost to a person for life.

Janine laughed, "Only, I don't speak to spirits."

"That's not true," Kiki said. "You've communicated very successfully to spirits, and they've listened to you. They've obeyed you. Think back, Janine."

Janine stopped laughing because she could see Kiki was serious.

"You watched the playback of the soldier at the meeting, with the audio? He heard you, Janine, and apparently answered you. It didn't take any effort from you at all. Back in Rio Linda, you asked the river ghost to pull me under water, and she did, I felt her. She listened to you. When I slipped in the Biltmore Hotel and you made that wisecrack to Carlos about taking me to a party, directly after you said that, the ghost invited me to a party in room 1404. I know you think I made that bit up, but I didn't. You may have been doing it all along. I assumed it was me, getting better at projecting into the spirit world, but now, I realize, it was you. You were helping me. You whispered to them during our little excursions, haven't you? Calling them out."

Janine listened silently, her brow creasing. Kiki could see Janine trying to be open minded and that gave Kiki some hope.

Janine asked. "What if I have? What would it mean?"

"Not a whole lot," Kiki said. "Unless you want to develop your talent and explore it. I could help you there, or…" she hesitated.

"Or what?"

"Gwen. One of my coven sisters. She's the real teacher." Kiki watched Janine's smile grow. That was why she needed the drinks. Kiki was proud of her background, but knew Janine would not understand and make light of it. "You're laughing at me, but the sisters in my coven are also very nice girls of the Kirk. Gwen's father is actually our pastor, so, we're all very normal. Anyway, Gwen is coming for Ian's birthday and wants to meet you. An actual *dragoma* is rare to find. I shared my suspicions, and now she insists on seeing for herself. Gwen can be a bit much, and intends to bend your ear extensively about speaking to spirits."

"I don't care," Janine smirked. "She can ask me about anything she wants. I'm very curious to meet any of your friends. She's coming for Ian's party? Does she know Ian too?"

"Well, that's another thing," Kiki sighed. "There is a little history between Gwen and Ian. History long past, but history none-the-less. That's the most I'm going to say about it because I don't like to poke my nose in there, but it's only fair to let you know. So, Gwen might gossip with you about Ian too."

Kiki had a difficult time reading Janine. It was both unsettling and refreshing. There were rare people that Kiki could not read well and Janine was one of them. Janine's aura was just too dark to penetrate much.

"I'll be okay with your friend," Janine said.

"Are you also going to be okay with Chicago?" Kiki asked. "I don't understand why you did that, told Max Colliers you wanted to go to Chicago. Unless, you're ready to face the city again,"

Janine nodded. "Only, I'm beginning to wonder if I made a mistake, if I'm really ready to go back there. I've been scared of Chicago for years."

Kiki hugged her. "This is something you can do. And I'll be there with you, Ian too. You know you'll have our support."

Janine reached for her purse. With a shaky hand, she extracted three envelopes, the fan letters. She passed them to Kiki. Interesting sensations seeped through the paper, dark and intense energy.

"They're from the Illinois state pen," Janine told her. "I believe Rick sent them. Kristine said they weren't signed, but she guessed they were from…a friend."

Kiki ran her hand over the envelopes. "Do you want me to read them?"

"I need to know if Rick sent them, but I'm afraid find out."

Kiki would bet money that Richard Wilkens sent those letters. Who else would stamp dark energy onto a piece of paper addressed to Janine Stinger? But Janine the skeptic would not be satisfied with a psychic assessment. Janine needed to read the actual words for definitive proof.

"Let's read them together," Kiki suggested.

She pulled each letter from their covers and laid them in chronological order.

"We'll read them silently, one, two, three, and deal with it at the end," Kiki suggested.

Janine nodded and they both bent over the typed letters. None had a salutation, no dates, and no named writer. Only one short paragraph on each page, centered, giving them a similar appearance and indicating they came from the same source.

Letter one.

Your image popped up in the movie tonight. You look well, beautiful, not ruined at all. You did this so that I could see you again. Maybe you wonder if a second chance is possible. Forgiveness? I want it too. We're soul mates, after all. I miss you, and now know that you miss me too.

Letter two.

I found your first season. You appeared fragile, but getting stronger. Were you sorry? Why didn't you trust me? And, why am I still incarcerated? You realize, you're the one who broke your promise and caused everything to fall apart. You could fix it all with a word. Come see me. Speak for me. We can start again.

Letter Three.

Sometimes I wonder about our baby. I am not allowed to ask about it, but that doesn't seem right. No one will tell me, boy or girl. When we meet again, you can tell me what you did. I won't be angry. I know what went wrong now. You were haunted, and it mixed you up. You weren't ready to believe in us. I forgive you. Come speak for me.

Good Lord Kiki thought. Richard Wilkens still enjoyed scaring the shit out of Janine. Did he really think she would recant her testimony and get him out of jail, *just because he asked her to?* Kiki drained the rest of her fish house punch in one gulp. She moved the letters to the sofa between them. She did not want them in her hands any longer. Janine folded them over and stuffed them back into her purse. Instead of fear on her face, Kiki detected a flash of anger in her eyes.

"He's clever, don't you think," Janine said. "Didn't use my name or his name, and he typed them. There's no way to prove he violated his order to leave me alone. He's still covering his bases to keep from getting caught. Not admitting anything and still trying to play with my mind."

"Are you okay?" Kiki asked.

Janine fidgeted. "I'll be fine. I think, I need to go, if we're done here. I want to sleep and then start studying. I'd like to get back to UC Davis before the end of the week. Thanks for reading these with me, Kiki, you are a good friend."

Janine stood up and appeared unusually sober for a girl who never drinks. They hugged briefly and Janine left. Kiki plopped back down to finish the cocktails and cheese. *Good Lord*, she thought again. Then, she picked up her cell phone to ring Gwen.

Chapter 6
Chicago

Kiki

They booked everyone into the Lincoln House hotel near Millennium Park. As usual, Kiki and Ian arrived a week early to scout out the area. Aside from a plan to investigate the site of the Fort Dearborn Massacre, Chicago was a city teaming with reported paranormal activity. Criminals, disaster victims, and civil war prisons were all part of the city ghost stories. Kiki and Ian spent the week visiting possible haunted sites and conducting preliminary interviews to get a sense for where they could find authentic spectral activity.

They sat in a lounge finishing their notes while waiting for the *Spectral Analysis* team to show. They reserved the roof top restaurant for a pre-shoot dinner party, but planned on greeting people with drinks as they arrived. They also procured the Whistler Ballroom as their command center. Ben and another techie had arrived with the van the previous night and set up equipment in the ballroom. Kiki and the doctor conducted three camera interviews earlier that day. They interviewed the caretaker of the Graceland Cemetery, a maid from the Congress Hotel, and a gentleman who claimed to have photographic evidence of specters near the Dearborn Massacre site. Kiki and Ian found a comfortable spot in the lobby bar to enjoy a cocktail and wait for the others.

"I know it's popular with the ghost tours," Kiki tapped her pen on the paper, "but this Krill House devil child, I want to skip it. It's so clearly a farce and didn't you find that curator a bit over the top?"

Ian nodded, "I agree. We have equipment for four sites. We need to weed out one or two places."

"The post office," Kiki said. "You know, the Holmes Murder Castle. The building isn't really there anymore, except that one wall. I admit, it was an interesting wall in that basement, but I couldn't get a definite feeling about it. It came across like static energy more than anything focused. And the Valentine Day Massacre site, there's nothing there."

Ian agreed. "But let's definitely hit the water tower. It's one of the oldest structures in the city and quite garish in style, it'll look good on film. Who knows, maybe there really is a ghost in there. And I liked that wall too, the post office wall. I just wish there was more of the original structure. I wonder what the wall's composition is."

"You still gathering evidence for your theory on elements that take on a ghostly stamp?" Kiki watched Ian. He began developing his theory years ago.

"Magnesium and phosphorous," Ian said. "Those are prime energy elements. Gram hasn't detected a trace of that river ghost, has she? The boulders in the river not only contained rare earth elements, but the magnetite in the rock was jam packed full of magnesium and phosphorus in a slightly higher ratio than usual. I truly believe those elements absorbed the spirit of the girl who became the river ghost."

Doctor Ian McNally's theory about ghostly energy developed over years of research. He first noticed that spectral energy was connected to solid objects, like bone, wood, or stone. The doctor analyzed those objects for mineral content and found that tombstones associated with ghosts contained more traces of the elements magnesium and phosphorus. The foundations of haunted houses and old castles were rich in those elements, as well as the hydroxyapatite in bone found near paranormal activity.

Doctor McNally also noticed that when the material was destroyed, the ghostly encounters waned and disappeared. Ian and Kiki always accepted that spirits weakened over time, eventually faded from existence, Ian now theorized that it was due to the natural weathering and erosion of his trace elements.

Ian once attempted to entice the essence of a spirit to move from one tombstone to another. He used a concentrated mix of phosphorus and magnesium in the haunted Savannah graveyard. Kiki remembered that night well. Kiki told him he was being a nut and didn't want to participate. If a spirit "stamped" itself into things, as Ian suggested, Kiki believed it would take a very traumatic, emotional event to do it, not just some bloke with a few flammable chemicals.

"I've checked with Gram, and she says there's still nothing," Kiki told him. "She's happy to help with your theory development, and always asks after you."

When the boulders from her river were removed, Janine's grandmother no longer sensed the river ghost. Gram never realized that she always sensed the ghost, until the ghost was no longer there. When Kiki returned to Rio Linda for a short visit in November, she no longer felt the ghost, either."

Ian rubbed his new beard. "I'm going to go out on a limb and put the theory in my new book."

"You need to be careful of your reputation," Kiki told him. "You're the serious one."

Ian made a face. "I know. Okay, on day one, the crew sets up remote monitors at the Dearborn sites, the water tower, and the theater alley. After dusk, we film in those areas until midnight or so, then we head over to film your séance at the Congress Plaza. You want a two AM séance?"

"Two sounds good. Your mother always said two at two bells will fast the two heads," Kiki said. "It's midway between the change of day and the witching hour."

"I never knew what she meant by that," Ian said.

"A reference to the thinning of the veil," Kiki told him. "It's why two in the morning was her favorite hour for a séance."

"Day two," Ian continued, "We sleep during day, and then at nightfall, we run out to the Graceland Cemetery and Lincoln Park. We need to flesh out the area for the historic society. I owe them. If there's a need for any follow up interviews, we can stay for a day three."

Kiki added, "At that graveyard, we should both gaze directly into the face of that statue, the *Statue of Death*, to see if there's anything to see. It'll make for nice drama. That caretaker was pretty convincing and we can highlight his interview with the footage."

Ian agreed. He glanced into the lobby expectantly. Lots of activity occurred as folks arrived. "Looks like our people are here. Why don't you order some drinks and I'll wave them over?"

The lobby bar soon housed most of the *Spectral Analysis* staff. Everyone enjoyed a welcome cocktail and socialized nicely. They were no longer just six people in a van traipsing from place to place checking into affordable hotels. The money making machine behind the Colliers business empire treated them very well. Fancy hotels and a long list of extra helpers were nice improvements to their working conditions.

Kiki noticed the image people, Lauren and Guy. At first glance they seemed like peas in a pod, but Guy's aura was a tad murky. He must be working through something difficult in his life. Sally also came on location, in case someone needed to modify their new wardrobe. She carried a sewing machine into the lounge. She must not trust anybody with that valuable thing. Ben and his tech crew grabbed drinks and left for the ballroom. A few of the gofers sat together, laughing with the new van driver.

Kiki hoped Max and Ian got their control differences worked out. She detested how males loved to clash with each other. Everyone knew Max Colliers did not believe in ghosts and he probably thought they faked the subsonic voice, but he was happy to hear it and use it in the show. Luckily, the Alamo provided plenty of fun film to pull off a nice premier episode. The bats and knife throwing were funny, and Carlos's humor added a nice touch. Still, Kiki didn't completely trust Max. His aura broadcasted all ego and she imagined he'd try to exert himself somewhere during the course of the shoot. She hoped it wouldn't be in the guise of fake paranormal activity again.

Kiki lounged between Carlos and Don at the bar, admiring photos Carlos shared on his phone. Apparently, Milo Fuente, no more than four years, already showed signs of soccer superstardom and would soon be on the Olympic team playing alongside his Uncle Lonzo. At least, that's how Milo's father saw things. Kiki found Milo completely adorable. Same light brown eyes and dimpled grin as his father and uncles.

"He looks very sweet," Kiki sighed.

"Sweet? He's a world class, bruising, toe tipping second Cristiano. He's a monster!" Carlos shouted.

"And very sweet," Kiki insisted. *Carlos had the right focus in life*, Kiki thought; love your wife and adore your children.

Perhaps she should take another look at that eligible brother of his.

The doctor came around to say hello and Carlos showed the pee wee soccer photos all over again. Kiki noticed Lauren and Sally eyeing their little group. Just how involved had Ian gotten with Lauren? Lauren certainly wasn't shy about chasing after the doctor. Business trips in hotels were the worst for creating sticky situations and Kiki hoped Ian chose to be careful about getting involved. An entanglement with a coworker was a sure fire way to create a whole mess of trouble, did he need to learn that lesson all over again?

"Anyone seen Janine or Max?" Ian asked. "Our dinner reservation is in fifteen minutes."

"Max didn't fly in with us," Carlos told him. "He had some other stuff, upstairs work, to take care of. He has to manage the profitable business first, right? Said he'd try to make it out tonight, but not to expect him until tomorrow."

"As for Janine, well, she is flying out of Sacramento, isn't she? Maybe her flight gets in later, who knows," Kiki reminded him.

"Crikes, she's going to come at the last minute and ignore everybody again." Ian's eyes flashed around the bar but nobody had an answer. Kiki could hear it in his tone, he was certain Janine Stinger was avoiding him. "She's bloody planning to do the bare minimum, isn't she? Show up at the last second and fly the coop as soon as the camera's off, brilliant."

"Isn't that what she's always done? Maybe she doesn't know this season is being run differently, with welcome dinners and mandatory socializing." Carlos smiled at him. "Just relax, she'll be here."

Don patted Ian on the back. "Yes, relax. In the meantime, how about you get me in good with your friend's friend over there?" Don waved at Sally sitting next to Lauren. As soon as Ian looked their way, Lauren gave him a one thousand megawatt smile.

Kiki watched Ian consider Lauren a moment, then nod and motion Don over to the two women on the sofa. The girls made room for them, and when Ian hesitated, Lauren reached up and pulled him down. The grouped all had a laugh about the way he plopped into the sofa. It drew the attention of the entire room. Ian just smiled and stayed put. Kiki, along with everyone else, watched Lauren feed Ian one of the fresh strawberries from the coffee table platter. *The idiot*, Kiki thought, *he could at least be discreet*. She walked over and leaned down to whisper in his ear.

"Do I need to say it again? You need to be careful of your reputation." Then, she skipped out the back door to go find Ben and his crew. She wanted to remind them about the dinner upstairs.

Chapter 7

The Negotiation

Janine

Janine's big mistake was calling a Lyft to transfer from the airport to the hotel. Actually, she called two Lyfts. The first car's engine cut out at a stop sign and she called for another driver. The first driver begged the second driver for a jump start and Janine found herself teaching two Lyft drivers the proper sequence for safely jumping a car, *unbelievable*. The driver who had the jumper cables in his dead car also had a flat spare tire, a forward thinker. Long story short, she was more than an hour late getting to the hotel. She noticed everyone already mingling in the lobby floor bar and she hesitated.

Janine found herself spying on Ian McNally again. He seemed much more at ease when she wasn't in the room. She enjoyed watching him interact with the other people. The way he moved and flashed his smile fascinated her. His new beard was growing in nicely, not yet long enough to grab, but a thick dark mess never-the-less, and his hurt eye appeared practically back to normal. She watched him stroll to the sofa and grin down at the stylist, Lauren. Lauren playfully pulled him down next to her. He soaked up her flirty attention, appraising her with his soft blue eyes. *Ouch.* Then, Lauren feed Ian something in a very sensual interchange. They made a very nice looking, *sexy*, couple.

Janine flashed back to a time Ian had fed her food by hand. He did that on more than one occasion, in bed, after very starling nights of love making. A sudden heat flooded her body at the memory.

She watched Lauren run her hand along Ian's arm and remembered exactly how that arm felt, solid and corded with muscle, warm. Ian loved to wear silky, stretchable button down shirts and Janine imagined unbuttoning the dark green shirt he wore and seeing his broad, powerful chest emerge slowly under her fingertips as she climbed into his lap. She felt her heart rev up and sensations below moved in like a flash flood. Her eyes were drawn to the thick muscles of his neck as he chatted and laughed. Then, she watched his large hand rub the hair on his jaw and she imagined rubbing parts of her body in that curly mess.

She was suddenly startled out of her illicit musings by someone standing next to her, spying on the *Spectral Analysis* staff with her.

"Are you debating whether to go in there?" Max Colliers appeared amused. He wore a suit and tie and had a brief case in his hand. He watched the staff mingle a moment more before looking back at her. He must have noticed her flushed cheeks because he was taken aback slightly.

"You scared me." She let out the breath she had been holding.

"The fearless Janine Stinger? No way." He said softly. Max glanced into the room again. "I'm not going in. I've had a very long day and I'm not ready to be jolly right now. I hear they reserved the roof top restaurant for dinner. You are going to love it, enjoy."

"Wait a minute. You're not joining us for dinner?" Janine stopped him with a hand on his sleeve. Her heart was still racing and she took a deep breath to calm herself down. "We were supposed to talk at dinner tonight. Your secretary assured me."

He clearly did not want to have that conversation with her, he looked away and set his jaw. His eyes seemed weary. He had a bad day, she could see it.

"I'm beat, and I just had them send my dinner to my room. I'm not up for a crowd. I'm supposed to be backing off on location and allowing Doctor McNally to run the show. I'm afraid if I go in there, I'll start making speeches and…" He shrugged at her. "Unless you'd consider having a private dinner in my room. I have a suite. Very spacious."

"Okay, sure." Mostly because she didn't want to enter the scene in the bar, either.

"Yes?" Max perked up and his eyes lock on hers. "Wow, that would be very nice. I'll have them send something for you, what would you like? This will be a nice treat. A quiet, private dinner with a beautiful woman. Lately, all my dinners are either quick bites alone or big parties. This will be a very pleasant change. I like this idea. What shall I have them send for you? Got any preferences?"

"Just, whatever you're having, I don't need much. Just, anything, a salad, bread and butter." She found his giddiness amusing.

Max skipped over to the front desk and spoke to the desk manager, then he beckoned her to the elevators pulling his suitcase behind him. Janine picked up her backpack and got into the elevator wondering if a private dinner with Max Colliers was a good idea. He smiled like she just agreed to go on a date with him. Did he realize she wanted to talk about getting out of her contract? Of course he did, that's all she ever mentioned.

Max stayed at the Lincoln House in Chicago many times before. He raved about the spa on the fourth floor and wondered who might be up for getting a spa treatment. Kiki for sure, but did Janine think Carlos, Don, or Ian would go for a massage? He highly recommended the hot stone treatment. Then, he complained about the meeting back in Texas that made him late. Max had a brother that loved to foul things up and create messes for Max to clean up. Then, his uncle started questioning whether the company should be involved in show business.

"*Spectral Analysis* is my fun project," Max said. "I'm the one who actually got Steve Hanks interested in making movies when we were kids, we used super eight film for the fun of it. Steve studied whatever he wanted in college and he never grew out of it. My parents insisted on business and, here I am. Steve has all the fun, while I'm stuck funding the fun for everyone else. Work, work, work. I deserve to have a little fun too, right?" He noticed her silence. "Sorry, am I venting?"

"It's fine," Janine said.

Max's room was on the twenty-first floor. They stepped out of the elevator to see a flurry of hotel staff in the hall. The door was open and people were moving in and out of the room. They created a cozy romantic dining area in the suite, with candles, crystal glassware, and fancy folded napkins. Max let one of the workers take charge of his luggage while he slipped out of his jacket and tie. He handed those over and then hurried to the table and filled two glasses with the open bottle of wine. He ferried one to Janine.

"To a quiet dinner," he said.

"To a quiet dinner." Janine clinked her glass with his and took a sip of the wine. It was an incredible buttery smooth chardonnay and she took another sip, very easy to drink, very tasty. Max noticed her approval and was pleased that she liked the wine he chose. He slipped the waiter a tip.

"Shall I serve dinner, sir?" the waiter asked.

"I'll take care of serving," Max told him. "Maybe, send down another bottle of that wine, but don't knock, just set it right outside the door. I'll get it when I need it. On ice."

Janine set her backpack down and looked at the table.

"How in the world did they beat us with the dinner?"

Max laughed. "It's the same dinner they catered upstairs for the party, I had them bring down two plates. They only had one floor to go down, while we had twenty floors with four stops to go up. It's lobster and steak. The alternate was French chicken. Shall I have them send a sample of the chicken?" She shook her head.

Max positioned himself directly in front of her. He moved so close that a whiff of his cologne infiltrated her nose. His trimmed brown hair framed a manly face, and his brown eyes glittered behind his designer eyewear. He stared intently at her eyes. He was just as broad in the shoulders as Ian, slightly taller, and quite physically fit. She felt the heat radiating off his chest and it succeeded in keeping her blood stirred up. She didn't move away. His nice white teeth lined up perfectly in his grin.

"I want to get this out on the table before anything else is said." He kept his eyes on hers, and moved a tab bit closer. "I am very attracted to you. I don't mean to put you on the spot, or anything, but you should know; I consider you a very beautiful woman." Max sipped his wine, watching for her reaction.

Janine didn't know how to respond. Standing so close to Max after just spying on Ian, was confusing. Her nerves were all revved up and his aftershave kept invading her nostrils, egging things on. The first time she met Max she found him handsome. She excused his pushy attitude as a symptom of his success. She had been distracted with Ian back then too, but this time things were different, Janine was determined to let Ian be, and Ian had definitely moved on. Janine stared back at Max, considering him. She hadn't thought much about him in the past year, not until he became their acting producer. She took a deep sip of her wine, fully aware that her nerves were tingling from her clandestine musings downstairs.

"I'm here to discuss my contract."

Max nodded, "I know, and we'll discuss it, I promise. But first, let's get this out of the way, because I can see we're both thinking about it." He took her wine glass and set it on the table next to his. Then, he moved even closer. His hand brushed the hair away from her shoulder, surprising her. She didn't know what she wanted. Did she want Max Colliers to kiss her? Well, she wanted somebody to kiss her, she knew that. So, she didn't move when Max bent down to brush his lips lightly on hers.

Max grew bolder, and Janine closed her eyes. Not mind blowing, or earth shattering, but pleasant. It was very nice, she decided, and kissed him back a bit. Her hand touched his jaw and it suddenly felt terribly wrong. She pushed him away and Max grinned happily at her. He reached down and took her hand.

"Shall we eat?"

Like a perfect gentleman, he pulled out her chair and helped her get settled. He removed the silver domed cloches from their dinners and recharged the glasses with the buttery wine. *Crap*, Janine thought, *why did she kiss Max Colliers?* She was there to talk about her contract.

"I know you could let me out of my contract right now, if you wanted." She decided to be direct and get right to the point. "I can buy the contract out, if you put a reasonable sum on it."

"You don't want me to let you out of the contract just yet," Max softly said.

"Of course I do, why would you say that?"

Max chewed quietly, "Carlos. I don't feel right about letting him go."

"What do you mean? What does that mean?"

"You and Carlos are two parts of a duo," Max said. "When you were absent last season, Carlos didn't fit anymore. It was an awkward dynamic. There was no one for him to joke with. If I let you go, I'll have to drop Carlos as well. We haven't found anyone to fill your shoes and play off Carlos the way you do. We would need to create a whole new backup team for the doctor and Kiki."

"You're saying, when I leave the show, you plan on firing Carlos?"

Max shook his head. "You're taking this the wrong way. Look at it from the business point of view. Did you catch the final episodes of last season, after you went off on your emergency break? Did you see what happened? Boring flops. We can't have Carlos by himself as a support team."

"You're telling me, that unless I stay with the show, you are going to get rid of Carlos too?" Janine stood up, sizzling with anger.

"I'm saying that you being on the show is the easiest way to keep Carlos." Max didn't raise his voice, but his brow tightened. "It's going to be very easy for you to cast me as the bad guy right now, and that upsets me, because I have nothing but positive, glowing, thoughts about you, and of Carlos too. I think you two are fantastic. An original dynamic that's hard to match. I don't want to see either of you go. Believe me, we've tried to find a Janine Stinger replacement but you are one of a kind. Have you seen your fan letters? This won't make me popular, but that's one of the evils of running a business and being the boss, making the hard, unpopular decisions."

"I see your mind is already made up," Janine accused. "You're going to fire Carlos the day I leave. You're not even going to give him a chance to find a-a dynamic with another partner."

Max leaned back wearily. He looked just as tired as he had in the lobby. He rubbed his brow with a hand.

"It's hard to imagine him in a light other than the one you guys have painted," Max said softly. "Our attempts at changing his image have been flat out rejected. He's keeping loyal to you and won't bend from the image you two have created. I've got zero evidence Carlos can be flexible enough to fit with a new partner. Both of you were pretty hard headed about some of the simple changes I tried at that last shoot."

"Are you talking about those costumes?" Janine shook her head and searched for her backpack. She grabbed it up. "To me, that looked like you wanting to exploit us."

Max shot up and stepped around the table to block her exit. He pressed his lips together. She wondered if he would physically try to stop her. He was tall and appeared quite strong, the muscles on his forearms flexed as he stuck his hands in his pockets. He had a determined personality, and might be hard to fight. His eyes said that she was being unreasonable and unfair, causing trouble, when all he wanted was a pleasant dinner with her. *Would he stop her, or grab her, if she tried to leave, like Rick had?* She took a measured breath to tamp down the deep seated fear rising to the surface. *Was she reacting to him, or was she reacting to Chicago?*

"Work with me here," he said gently. "Wait a moment and listen to what I have to say." He took a small step back and relaxed his shoulders. *Did he register her fear?* "I made a mistake. Both you and Carlos have very nice physiques and I was trying for a different image. Truly, if we see Carlos in a different way, then maybe we'll have an easier time fitting him with a new partner. There is a distinct direction I envision taking this show."

Janine stared toward him, focusing on the air between them, trying to stop the panic attack simmering. *Was this always going to be a problem for her, reading men this way?*

"I realize the new outfit is revealing. You have a valid grievance with me about that, and I'm sorry. Believe me when I say that I never imagined you would be insulted.

After all, I've seen you dressed very sexy and looking quite comfortable. I can't unsee what I've seen. You have very nice curves, and the marks on your body are intriguing. I thought we could enhance your screen image and give you a sexy, dangerous look. With the way Kiki dresses, your reaction completely surprised me. You never came around for us to run it by you, nor did you respond to the queries. I took your silence, your disinterest, to mean that anything was okay with you."

There was some truth in there. The show sent her plenty of invites to participate in meetings before San Antonio. She deleted them all.

"Please, let's sit back down." Max stepped further away. He put on his perfect smile again. He peered at her from under his lashes. His voice was calm, nice. "Let's negotiate a plan we can both be happy with. I'm not kidding," he put a hand over his heart, "I want you happy with me. I don't like being the bad guy, especially with an lovely woman. We can negotiate and eat this nice dinner and become friends. Let's be friends."

Janine sat down grumpily. She couldn't just run off without knowing what would happen. How many chances would she get to speak directly with Max Colliers about her contract? And now she had Carlos to worry about. Didn't he recently buy a gigantic house for his parents? He couldn't lose his job now.

"If you want me so happy with you," her voice was low, "Why are you playing hardball? Forcing me to return and now threatening Carlos. You want to know what would make me happy? Let me out of my contract, right now, and give Carlos time to mesh with a new partner before writing him off."

Max nodded, sipping his wine.

"Your wishes are noted," he matched her low tone. "But, speaking from the executive producer's seat, the CEO trying to keep a business afloat, I forced you back to save the show. The audience needs to see you. If all we get are a few episodes, then I need to take them. Hopefully, the ratings and popularity get back on track, and losing you will not hurt us as much as I think it will." Max took a deep breath. "Right now, the best replacement option for you appears to be a replacement of the entire back up team, which doesn't thrill me, I don't enjoy letting people go. If I can talk you into staying the rest of the season, those worries will disappear, but I can see that's not going to happen."

Janine shook her head, "It's not going to happen."

"We vetted potential partners for Carlos. We screen tested and personality checked many candidates. He rubs people the wrong way. Look at how he grates on Don. Don is an award winning cameraman with an incredible reputation, we're lucky to have him. So, a new partner for Carlos, we haven't found the right chemistry yet. He tears everyone apart, and it's not always funny. But we do have an alternate backup plan. We found one potential replacement team that might work."

"Does Carlos know about this?"

Max's brown eyes shifted down. "Nobody knows. I hoped to change your mind; charm you into staying."

"What will it take to give Carlos a fighting chance?" Janine asked.

Max leaned forward. Carlos needed to show Max that he could be flexible and mold into a new image. Max planned on pushing a sexier back up team, but didn't think Carlos would follow through with that angle. If Janine wanted to help Carlos, she might take the wardrobe and image team seriously, and encourage Carlos to do the same thing. If Janine jumped on board with a few of his modifications, then Carlos might too, and if Carlos could pull it off, Max might be able to find a fit for him when she left. If he found that fit sooner, he could cut her loose from her contract early.

"You mean, let me out of my contract now? Like, right after this shoot?"

Max nodded.

"Why would you do that?" She didn't trust his complete change of heart. It was too easy.

Max poured out the rest of the wine.

"I now see how important it is to you. I misread you. I truly believed that you were tired of being the girl in the background," he said. "But, I want something in return." By the way his eyes flickered over her, Janine could guess exactly what he wanted in return. She picked up her crystal of expensive buttery wine. If he propositioned her, she was going to throw it in his face.

"And what would that be?" she asked.

He reached to the dining trolley and ferried two smaller plates to the table.

"That you allow me dibs on the carrot parsnip cake and let me believe the chocolate mouse is exactly what you would have gone for." He set the deserts in front of them. "I'm sorry, but I love the carrot cake."

That completely disarmed her. Janine drained the tasty wine and regarded him silently. She kept expecting Max to be more nefarious but he was actually quite nice, and though she didn't like to admit it, his explanation made a little sense to her. He chatted about his disaster of a brother who always took more of the cake than the standard lot when they were kids, always trying to steal things right from under his nose. Then, he insisted she have a bite of his carrot cake to see why he preferred it.

"I also, humbly, request a do-over," he added softly.

"A do-over?"

"Dinner. Promise to have dinner with me again, maybe, back in Austin, on a real date." He stared at her with his steady brown eyes and she could see that he wasn't joking. "Just dinner. To give me a chance to win you over, not for the show, but for me. I'd like to get to know you. That's not too much to ask, is it?"

Just dinner? Max was a handsome, wealthy, confident man, and she was very single. Why not? She even felt somewhat attracted to him. What woman wouldn't be a little attracted to him? And he seemed to be trying very hard to be nice to her.

"Okay," she agreed.

Max smiled. Then, he jumped up to retrieve the wine outside the door. He insisted she stay to toast their upcoming date and put the seal of approval on their agreement. He felt certain everything would turn out terrific for everybody; win, win, win. In the middle of opening the bottle of chardonnay, his cell phone began buzzing. He glanced at it and his eyes widened slightly.

"It's Doctor McNally," he picked up the phone, "Hello, Ian, how are you?"

Janine could hear the cadence of Ian's voice, but not the words. Why did she feel like she just got caught doing something wrong? Max poured the wine as he listened to Ian on the phone. Janine was limited to hearing a one sided conversation.

"No worries, I got room service."

"Is that right?" Max glanced at her.

"Let me put your mind at ease, she's here, she made it, no need to worry."

"Because…because, we're having dinner together. Don't worry, I'm sure she'll be on time tomorrow."

"Yes, okay. See you then."

He chuckled when he ended the call. He raised his glass to her.

"To our upcoming dinner date," he said, and she returned the salute. Max chuckled again. "He's keeping tabs on you. The doctor wanted to put out a search party for you. I'm not sure where he planned to look, but he was worried something may have happened to you between the airport and the hotel." Max zoned in on her small backpack. "He said you haven't check in yet."

She shook her head. "I haven't, not yet."

"Where's your luggage?"

She pointed to her backpack and watched his eyebrows shoot up.

"That's it? Wow, you travel light. I feel like a prima donna with my bags. Want me to call the front desk and have them change your room to one up here? I can have them send up a key."

Janine stood slowly, shaking her head. She needed to get out there, the wine was making her feel too comfortable, warm, and careless. She grabbed her backpack. Max followed her to the door and, like the perfect gentleman, he kissed her hand and said he had a wonderful time. He looked forward to seeing her again, the next day, and in Austin for their date.

When Janine finally checked in, she retrieved a note informing her to meet in the Whistler ballroom no later than nine in the morning. She recognized Ian's blocky letters. *Did they look angry?* Ian expected her to help set up remote cameras, audio, and other equipment in the morning.

Janine found Carlos in the small ballroom joking with compact blond Ben and another young man. They were loading audio and visual equipment into different air cases for protection. Carlos introduced the other guy as Mike, the van driver. Janine wore her standard *Spectral Analysis* T-shirt and saw that Carlos wore his too. From across the room, the image team, Lauren, Guy, and Sally, eyed them warily. After San Antonio, Janine didn't blame them for being hesitant of approaching her.

Janine waved and the trio instantly perked up, surprised at her spontaneous greeting. Janine nudged Carlos.

"Let's go over there and see what they have in store for us," Janine said.

"Did you give input to Sally when you got measured?" Carlos asked.

Janine gave no input. She hadn't planned on wearing anything new and assumed Carlos had a similar mind. Janine studied the thick and messy sideburns on his face. Those giant pork chops could not be what Lauren had imagined, they completely covered his adorable dimples. Janine suspected they were his way of following orders while rebelling at the same time.

"Are you going to let her trim those?" Janine asked him.

Carlos chuckled. "I found the design sketch they planned for me. They're going to transform me into an anime character."

"What if we cooperate with their design plans and see what happens?" Janine said.

"You mean, go Hollywood? Seriously? Or in your case, playmate of the month. I happened to see the design sketch for you, and they're going to outdo Kiki with the outfits, Janine. Are you sure about this?"

"I don't think it's going to be that bad," she hoped. "I had a conversation with Max and he gave some convincing reasons for the design ideas. Why don't we give one or two of them a try? We can ham things up to make it fun."

Carlos studied her. "The doctor said you were with Colliers last night instead of at the dinner party. I'm not going to say I totally object, because Maria says that he is an awesome catch for some girl, and he's filthy rich, insanely rich, and they might buy the Spurs. I just want to make sure you're being careful. Don't squander the milk, Janine, girls often squander the milk with guys like him. My mama always said, why buy the cow if you can get the milk for free. That's sound wisdom, from my mom!" Carlos raised his finger to drive the point home. "Even more important, don't give your heart away too fast, okay."

"No chance of that," Janine giggled at Carlos and his clumsy big brother advice. "I don't think my heart is very keen on him." A thought just struck her, "I guess, that might make Max Colliers the perfect man for me."

"Hi!" Lauren and her gigantic smile had snuck up behind them. She glanced between them expectantly. "Are you two ready to get prepped for the morning segment?"

Janine nudged Carlos. She could see him hesitate.

"We're really going to do this?" He stared at her.

"I am," Janine told him. "I'm going to go all in with this." She turned to Lauren. "I'm all yours."

They crammed into the van with a plan to hit four sites. Don would film the crew setting up the remote sensors, and the footage would be used as backdrop and filler. They packed regular and low IR cameras, audio recorders, and a mini weather station that could record data on temperature, pressure, and humidity. Most of the information would be sent via wireless communication to their control center in the ballroom. Ian instructed Ben to have someone remotely monitor each site over a twenty-four hour period. The doctor settled next to the driver and Janine rode in the rear with Carlos and Don. Ian hardly said two words to her before jumping into the van. He barely glanced her way. *Well, hello to you too*, she thought.

Their new *Spectral Analysis* shirts were athletic, form-fitting, moisture-wicking, long sleeved shirts. They were brightly colored in the visible bands of the electromagnetic spectrum, starting with a red left sleeve and ending with a deep violet right sleeve. A small logo was stitched into the fabric along with their first names over the left breast. The female version of the shirt had a generous scoop neck to show off her cleavage. They paired their colorful shirts with dark stone-washed jeans and heavy duty work boots. They looked a bit like comic book characters. Everyone wore the outfit, except the doctor, he wore another nice shirt with his updated tie.

"The plan for this morning," the doctor read from his clip board. "We are going to set up remotes at the old water tower, the alley behind the theatre, Fort Dearborn Park, and also that little park near 16ᵗʰ street and Indiana Avenue. All, hopefully, before taking an afternoon lunch at the hotel where we will touch base with Kiki and Colliers before getting in a good sleep. After sunset, we'll head back to those sites and film segments with Kiki and mix in a little ghost theory. We'll conduct an onsite investigation in the smaller park before our séance at the Congress Plaza, so it'll be an all-nighter. The more we do tonight, the less we worry about tomorrow."

The old tower in Chicago was a historic water landmark on Michigan Avenue in the shopping district. It happened to be the second oldest water tower in the United States, built in 1869, and was originally constructed from limestone blocks. As one of the only surviving structures of the Chicago Fire, it represented an important event in the city's history. Periodically, the police received reports of a hanging man in the tower, only to investigate and find nothing at all. The hanging man ghost was rumored to be a victim of the Great Chicago Fire. A lone man who refused to abandon his post during the blaze, and later hung himself in the 154 foot tower rather than succumb to the flames.

Doctor McNally stood just inside the entrance with their point of contact, a short man with a thick neck and round, bulging eyes. His bulging eyes kept returning to scan over Janine and she felt self-conscious in the skin tight shirt and push up bra Sally dressed her in. She silently repeated "you are a badass" to herself over and over again, the mantra Kiki once suggested to pull off a racy outfit. Janine found it worked well at boosting her confidence. Don filmed the doctor's conversation with their bug-eyed contact man while Carlos and Janine posed stiffly, like bad asses, next to the equipment cases. Carlos's biceps bulged quite nicely in his form fitting shirt and she doubted she looked even remotely as tough.

"Can you point out which of these blocks in the building are of the original limestone pillars?" the doctor asked.

Their contact pointed out the different columns and talked about the past renovations with the doctor. After the short interview, the crew filed into the main stairwell of the tower and climbed the spiral steps into the top dome. The doctor and their contact man led the way.

"You go ahead," Don said to Carlos. "I'll film from the rear following after Stinger."

"Oh, come on, Don," Carlos chided him. "My ass is going to look ten times better on film than hers." Carlos pushed Janine up ahead of him. "No offense, Janine, but I doubt you do any squats in your spare time? I really doubt it. Let me tell you, Don, I do squats from all around the world. Bulgarian squats, DMZ landmine squats, Japanese sumo squats, Donny dumbbell squats. You probably do those. Believe me, this is the ass you want in the shot. I've been working for this opportunity, I deserve it."

Max was right, Janine noted, *Carlos didn't try to get along with anyone.*

At the top of the tower, they rigged a remote infrared camera, a regular camera, a small weather box, and an ion detector. The doctor seemed uncertain about the audio recorder and then decided it wasn't needed. A hanging man wasn't going to say anything.

"We'll save it for the alley." He gave Don the signal to start moving down the stairs. Janine and Carlos snapped the gear boxes closed and gathered them up. The doctor moved closer to them, keeping an eye on the bug-eyed contact man.

"Carlos, do you think we can swipe a sample of that wall on the way down? Just a wee chip? Maybe at a corner, low. I'll tell you where," the doctor whispered.

"Yeah, sure. I've got a little tool." Carlos glanced at the bug-eyed man.

The doctor softly added. "He's not going to give us much of a chance, unless…" the doctor didn't quite look at her, "Janine could distract him a wee bit."

"How do you suggest I do that?"

"You're distracting him already without even trying." Ian's eyes avoided hers, then they aimed downward and scanned her skin-tight, low-cut, moisture-wicking shirt. "You could easily get him to start walking down the stairs with you, right now. If he resists, stand up nice and straight and look him in the eye. He'll easily follow you. You know, lure him ahead and be flirty."

"Fine," she snapped, knowing she sounded very pissed off.

Their next stop was a pathetic little patch of grass near the 18th Street metro station named the Battle of Dearborn Park. The entire park was corded off and reserved for them. They quickly set up a camera on a lamppost before driving a couple of blocks away to a smaller patch of grass on the corner of Mark Twain Parkway. Again, the police marked the area as reserved for the *Spectral Analysis* TV show. Those signs were sure to attract a late night audience, so Ian removed them and threw them into the back of the van.

The patch of the park the doctor directed them toward was separated from the main play area by a set of railroad tracks and fencing. Several mature trees stretched across the grass, shading the area nicely. A few of the trees had low, thick branches and looked very easy to climb. When Janine had been in Chicago for college, her soccer teammates often had climbing contests to see who could get up a tree first, or go the highest, or brave the thinnest branch. The trees reminded her of that nice memory.

"That park back there," Ian told them. "That's where the massacre occurred. But this place right here, this is where they buried the dead, on this little triangle of land, especially in this patch of trees here. In the past, I recorded some eerie low frequency electromagnetic pulses on this spot. We're going to bring the magnetic antennae and the big box tonight. Right now let's get the remote audio and cameras in the trees. Maybe higher up, then angle them down at that spot. Kiki wants us to suspend small mirrors from the branches as well."

"Why did you want a piece of the wall from the water tower?" Carlos asked him.

"It's part of the original stone," Ian said. "No worries, the historic society said it was okay to take a wee sample, but that guy wanted to give us a problem and I wanted to avoid a long discussion about it. I'm going to have it analyzed. The tower was constructed from limestone, you know. Some limestones are more dolomite than calcite. Calcium magnesium carbonate. I'm interested to see the amount of magnesium in the minerals."

Janine listened in. Why was the doctor concerned about levels of magnesium in limestone? That seemed random. Janine stared up at the trees and really wanted to climb one. Maybe this was one of those places they could ham things up and have a little fun.

"Hey, Carlos, think you can climb that tree before I can get up this one?" Janine called over. "I'll put the audio in mine and you can put the camera in yours."

Mike brought out a ladder but Janine and Carlos waved him away. They started climbing and Don started filming. Janine grabbed a low branch, then swung her legs up to curl around a higher limb. She pulled herself easily up to a standing position. She was about seven feet off the ground looking down at the doctor.

"How high would you like the audio recorder, Doctor?" she asked.

He unexpectedly turned his soft blue eyes on her. "About that high." Ian smiled at her and she melted a bit. "You make a very lovely monkey."

"Thank you, Doctor." Then thought, *That's the first time he's looked directly at me today.* She turned to start strapping the audio device to the tree, feeling suddenly sad. A whisper of a breeze blew through the trees that sent a chill down her spine. It felt familiar, like a ghost from the past. She glanced at Carlos and noticed that he had climbed much higher than her.

"My camera is just a little harder to attach," Carlos said. "I've got this swivel attachment to hook up."

"You win." She told him, gripping the tree because she felt slightly dizzy. "Just be careful going down."

Janine moved to a lower branch then jumped dramatically to the ground. She gave Don a little gymnastics end salute as Ben delivered the small mirrors.

The alley behind the Nederlander Theater was their final destination before lunch. Back in 1903, a fire broke out in the theater killing more than six hundred people. Most of the victims fell to their death on the back alley ground. That event was still considered the deadliest single building fire in United States history. The doctor said that many people claimed the *Alley of Death* was haunted and reported hearing whispered voices when walking that stretch of pavement.

Doctor McNally directed them to set up remote cameras on both sides of the alley with audio recorders tuned to cover the sonic range. They finished rather quickly and were happy to know they were a couple of blocks away from their lunch. Although, the doctor suggested they might swing around to the river to set up the extra camera. Apparently, that intersection was the actual site of Fort Dearborn. He checked his watch and saw the time.

"Tell you what," he surveyed the crew. "You lot pack up and go back to the hotel. Have lunch, then take a nap so you'll be fresh tonight. I'll set this one up on my own. Just tell Kiki and Colliers that I'll be straight away, and that we're on schedule." The doctor ran down the street with the camera and soon disappeared around the corner.

As they began loading the gear into the van, Janine noticed one of the small wire connectors used for attaching antennae to cameras or audio devices. It could be one of the many extras, but it also might have fallen off the camera the doctor took. It lay on the ground, right outside the van door. Janine picked it up and looked at Carlos and Don.

"Did the doctor drop this?"

Nobody knew. They debated calling him, but Janine volunteered to run after him. If he didn't drop it, then no problem, but if he needed it, he'd have it right away. Mike suggested they drive around as soon as they got the van packed, but Janine insisted that she could get there sooner if she started running immediately. The doctor obviously wanted everyone to go eat and then sleep all afternoon.

In the corner of her mind, she knew there was a different reason she wanted to run out alone to Doctor

McNally. A reason she refused to formulate in her head just yet. She imagined that little connector as some sort of cosmic sign urging her along.

Janine ran in her clumpy new boots as her lovely curls flew all around. It didn't take long to catch up to Ian. She'd been running the track regularly and had gotten into top shape. She closed in on him, just as he reached the corner of Michigan Avenue and East Wacker Street. His was surprised to see her right behind him, and she held up the little connector. The doctor paused, examined his camera, flipped it around, then shook his head.

"Not mine," he said.

They stood quietly, catching their breath. He watched her with eyes that blinked a little quicker than normal, probably wondering why she ran after him like that. *Why did she run after him like that? Damn you*, she cursed herself. *What are you doing here? You told Kiki you were going to leave him alone.* Janine reminded herself that she wasn't planning to hang around Texas or *Spectral Analysis*. Her plans were separate from his plans and she needed to let him move on in peace, with someone who didn't have the issues she had. She straightened up and brushed the tangled hair out of her face. He waited patiently for her to speak.

"Ian, I want us to be friends," she said softly. "I know it may take some time to completely forgive each other, but maybe we can try to forget some of what happened and be friends again."

After an excruciating long moment the doctor nodded. He gave her a weak smile. Of course, he wanted to be friends too. He stepped over and hugged her briefly. Then, Ian took a step back and eyed the tall lamp post.

"Since you're here, we could attach it up higher. That would be the optimum placement. Come on, I'll give you a boost."

She unlaced her boots and took them off. The doctor readied the camera and flexible clamp for easy attachment. Then, using the post for balance, she stepped into his hand and he easily propelled her up.

"Stand on my shoulders?" he said.

She stepped up and was soon on his shoulders using the lamppost to steady herself. She reached down and took the camera from him. She quickly wrapped the clamp around the post and began tightening all the loose ends. Ian started talking.

"People report seeing spirits out here and along the river walk down there. I doubt it, but since we're investigating the massacre site, we may as well monitor out here as well. We've got the extra camera and all. Don't forget to adjust the panoramic lens horizontally." His warm hand patted her foot. "You really do make a brilliant monkey."

When she finished attaching the camera, Ian tried to squat to make her descent less dangerous, because she couldn't jump to the pavement without her shoes. She grabbed the lamppost.

"Don't do that. You're going to break your back. I'm going to slide down this pole fireman style, no problem," she said.

"Too bad Don's not here to get this on camera. It would go nicely with your new sex kitten image."

They started laughing, shaking with the giggles. She slid down safely and let go of the post, but she wasn't paying attention to the ground. The lamppost was on a little pedestal and her first step was a misstep that set her balance off and she stumbled. The pavement was going to be a very hard landing.

But she needn't have worried, because Ian happened to be a world class catcher of falling women. The show definitely capitalized on that skill during the first season. The doctor saved Kiki from one nasty fall after another. He even caught Janine once on the show. The Doctor-Kiki catch provided a little side event the audience always looked forward to. The human drama of a possible romantic interaction was the first thing the audience latched onto. True to form, the doctor did not let her hit the pavement.

It was a perfect catch. Janine felt his strong, solid arms embrace her as he spun a bit. She remembered him once explain, in his doctor voice, that he spun in order to slow the fall, which lessened the force of impact between them. More collision time, less force, same impulse, basic physics, he had explained to the camera. *Yep*, Carlos had chuckled, *he's a real nerd.* Janine felt Ian's hand move slightly along her back and the base of her neck. She got her balance back quickly but her arms moved up automatically to hold him in a loose embrace. One hand reached over to steal a feel of his curly beard. *It was so soft!*

Ian released her and they quickly separated, but he still faced her. He stared into her eyes. Her pulse raced. There was no way to hide what was in her heart as she looked at him. She desperately wanted to move closer.

A car honked. And honked again. Janine realized that someone called out her name and a man stood a few feet away snapping photos with a cell phone. Then, a deep voice, that Janine instantly recognized, called her name again. She turned her attention quickly toward that voice.

"All right, that's enough. Run along," the deep voice ordered the photographer.

An extremely thin man in an oversized crumpled suit shooed away a man with a cell phone. The cell phone guy raised his hand and said, "Nice catch Doctor," before moving away. The thin man walked toward Janine and Ian. He had wiry brown hair and thick, light-sensitive glasses. Janine wondered if that man would know she had returned to the city. She wondered if he would visit her. She was very happy to see him.

"Detective Anderson," she said.

"Janine Stinger," he responded.

Detective Anderson smiled his toothy smile and nodded with a very pleased expression on his face. He glanced at Ian.

"Do you mind?" He held his hands out like he wanted to hug Janine.

"What?" Ian appeared confused. He saw that she was happy and turned back to the detective. "No. Aye, go ahead."

Detective Robert Anderson stepped in to give her a giant hug. Even though she was a tad taller than him, she felt very safe in the presence of his quiet, solid strength. Once upon a time, Janine and the detective spent the better part of a year getting to know each other. After Janine survived a brutal knife attack in a section of Chicago woods, Robert Anderson was the lead detective tasked to investigate, solve, and see the case to conviction. There had been an extended period of time when she only felt safe in the vicinity of Bob Anderson and his crumbled suits.

"I dropped in at your hotel," Detective Anderson said, "looking for you."

"We were setting stuff up," she smiled at him. Janine glanced at Ian. "Ian, this is Detective Robert Anderson. Detective, this is Doctor Ian McNally."

The two men shook hands and exchanges pleasantries. Detective Anderson informed Ian that he read his book on paranormal electromagnetic energy. He was curious after watching the show, but hardly understood any of it.

"Do you mind catching up?" Detective Anderson asked Janine. "Maybe over lunch?"

"Why don't you join us at the hotel," Ian suggested. "We have a generous spread and you can meet the rest of our team. If you need a private spot, there's plenty of room."

"Thank you. I think I'll take you up on that offer." The detective waved away the car parked on the side of the road. Was it his partner? After Janine got her boots back on, the three of them started the short walk around the corner to the Lincoln House Hotel.

Chapter 8

The Detective

Kiki

A local catering service provided a large spread of various salads and sandwiches. The hotel often sponsored groups in the ballrooms and pulled out nice dining tables for one corner of the conference room, creating a lunch area. Apparently, Max Colliers often booked the Lincoln House for his business trips. In fact, Kiki discovered that he reserved a smaller boardroom to meet with folks the next day, for business unrelated to *Spectral Analysis*. Kiki watched Max stroll toward her table with his lunch plate.

"Well, hello, Kiki Mellow. You look very fetching. May I have lunch you? I promise to behave."

"Please, sit down."

"I saw Carlos and Don, but what happened to the doctor and Stinger?"

"They're setting up one last camera around the corner," Kiki told him.

Most of the team ate, socialized, and left before Janine and Ian returned. Just a few stragglers hung out in different corners, chatting. When the doctor and Janine entered the ballroom, Kiki noticed an unfamiliar man following along. That man joined them at the buffet table. He projected a very strong and interesting energy. Kiki was delighted to see such a fascinating array.

The man's aura blended pink and radiated out of his trunk, hands, and head, which was an incredibly rare thing. There was further light around his crown, and Kiki concentrated to pick it up. Yellow and orange and a bit of emerald green intermingled. Definitely a peaceful shade of green, not the darker shade of envy more often seen in a halo. The yellows resonated confidence, while the orange tint hinted at perception. Kiki knew the man must be analytical. Ian vibrated some of those same patterns. But mostly, the mystery man exuded a gentle pink energy with open and loving vibrations in all directions. His aura fascinated her. Masculine, but certainly not a typical man's aura at all.

Kiki suddenly felt nervous as the trio turned toward her table. She felt as if this would be momentous meeting. She wore a very snug, low-cut shirt, no bra, and a flashy gaudy belt, like a rock groupie. She knew it was a very tantalizing ensemble, a Kiki Mellow ensemble, and now she wished she had change clothes after setting up for the séance. Ben had filmed the setup, which included a little banter with the manager of the Congress Plaza. The buzz of sexual tension always made an interview more fun, and helped Kiki tune into the energy around her. Now she just felt silly, and she certainly didn't want the man with the pink aura to presume she was frivolous.

"Who's that man?" Max asked.

"I haven't the faintest," Kiki said. "But he's absolutely gorgeous."

Max laughed softly. "Yes, that's a gorgeous wrinkled suit he's wearing. And look at that curly wiry hair, and those safety glasses. He winked at her. "I never knew you to be so sarcastic, Kiki."

"I wasn't being sarcastic."

Max rose to greet the trio as they reached the table. Janine introduced the man as Detective Robert Anderson, an old friend. *Her detective!* Max insisted that Janine and her old friend join them to eat. Kiki could see that Max's curiosity was as piqued as hers. Of course, he had no idea about Janine's past in Chicago. Max arranged things so that Janine took the chair next to him, and he make a big point of helping Janine get comfortably seated. Max seemed obvious about what he was after. Kiki wondered how Janine was handling the Max Colliers seduction experience. Kiki admitted that she enjoyed watching Max in action, he tended to be quite successful and always ended up on good terms with each of his conquests.

"Are you part of the park security the city is providing tonight?" Max asked.

Detective Anderson shook his head slightly. "That's a special job, not really my area of expertise as a detective." He smiled at Janine, "If I get a chance, I might drop in on one of your shoots to see you in action. We've plenty of interesting ghosts here in Chicago."

They all agreed that he should come out, anytime. Ian recited their rough timeline and gave him his cell number in case he wanted to call ahead. The detective whipped out his little book to jot it all down. Kiki gave him her personal number.

"In case Ian doesn't answer," she said.

He glanced at her and she could see that he understood her completely. In regards to Janine and Chicago, Kiki was the confidant. Kiki asked if he had any paranormal experiences.

"I might not have been paying attention properly," the detective admitted to her, "but I've been to a few places that give me the feeling someone hasn't quite left. That back alley you're visiting is one of them. It's a very cold stretch of pavement, I would say."

"How did you and Janine become old friends?" Max asked. "It's kind of unusual, isn't it? A young Texas gal and an old city detective. How do you know each other?"

Janine answered quickly. "I went to the University of Chicago my first two years of college. I met the detective back then."

Kiki noticed that Janine's aura had altered into softer hues under the influence of Detective Anderson's pink pulse. *Wow, his energy proved powerful enough to brighten Janine's dark cloud.*

"That's right," Max said. "I remember seeing U of C in your personnel file. That's a pretty impressive school. Did the detective break up a frat party or something? Is Janine hiding a party girl past from us, Detective? Or did she get into some other type of mischief?" His attempts at light hearted teasing were falling flat.

"Well," the detective smiled calmly. "It's nothing like that at all. I just happened to be in a position to help Miss Stinger one day and we became fast friends. If it was a story worth telling, I'm sure she would have told you by now."

The detective pegged Max pretty quickly, Kiki thought. The detective gave Max an even look. His big brown eyes were firm, but not mean in the least. *He's likely a terrific detective*, she thought. He'd probably make a terrific father as well, and Kiki wondered if he already was a father. He looked to be in his late thirties, or older. The thought of him being married with children caused a little flutter of panic to rise in her chest.

"Are you married, Detective? Do you have children?" Kiki blurted. After a stunned moment, everyone chuckled.

"Why, no, Miss Mellow. I've never had that pleasure." He gave her a generous smile. "Of course, I love the idea of marriage and raising children. How do you feel about it?"

"I love the idea of having children. With the right man." Kiki smiled at him. She absolutely enjoyed gazing into his eyes. "Very much so."

Max Colliers let out a big laugh. "Be careful." Max patted the detective on the shoulder. "Kiki's a bit of a man-eater. A real ball-buster, some would say. You can't be too keen on marriage, Kiki. I know two guys, who very recently came calling with outlandish diamond rings, only to be sent away with their tail between their legs."

"Feel free to air all my dirty laundry whenever it strikes your fancy, Max," Kiki said sweetly to him. "Not that any of it is your business."

Kiki didn't think there was anything wrong with dating men she found interesting. She loved being in the company of attentive male energy and often channeled that attention into honing her mystic senses, and she never, ever, promised anybody anything she wasn't willing to give. That last fellow wasn't interested in a real marriage anyway. He only wanted to prolong the illusion of their flashy romance for the sake of his reputation and growing fan base. It had been a mutually beneficial arrangement for them. Date and have fun in front of the media without the pressure of a real relationship. Her vow of chastity and his homosexuality would cleverly stay hidden. But then he wanted to up the ante in their game. He believed the extra payout for Kiki would be in obtaining citizenship. He imagined she would jump at that offer. She didn't and broke it off immediately. Fake or no, she did not plan on marrying anyone, ever.

"Perhaps you misinterpret Miss Mellow," the detective said. "I believe she is what one might call a coquette. A lovely woman only having a little fun, but means no harm."

"Who was the other bloke?" Ian raised an eyebrow at her. He only knew about the basketball player who wanted to improve his second string reputation by dating a TV personality. Kiki waved the question away, miffed, because Ian likely agreed with Max regarding what he once called her "callous" treatment of men.

The detective stood and excused himself from the table. He begged their pardon but desired to privately catch up with Janine. They moved across the room to sit in the plush chairs near the coffee dispenser. Kiki wondered if the detective could see auras. He must be able to see something, because he seemed to understand her perfectly.

Kiki, Ian, and Max quickly reconfirmed the plan for the evening and Max requested a spot in the séance. Kiki anticipated his request and agreed rather quickly. Max could provide some vital male energy to the table. They were going to attempt to contact several famous spirits at the Congress Plaza, but Kiki believed the room 441 ghost might be the only real specter they'd encounter. That ghost was notorious for waking guests with noises and moving objects. Many people even reported the manifestation of a dark shadow in the shape of a woman in that room.

Lauren suddenly plopped into the chair beside the doctor. She gave him a bright smile and casually placed her hand on his arm. They each said hello, then turned back to their personal notes. Max turned his attention across the room to Janine and the detective. In truth, all of them covertly watched Janine and the detective, Max was just very obvious about it.

Lauren already knew the man was a police officer, she spoke to him earlier in the day. Guy, Sally, and Lauren were very curious when he popped into the ball room looking for Janine Stinger. They wondered if she witnessed a crime, guessing it was the reason she missed the welcome dinner the night before.

"She's quite the mystery lady, isn't she? I wonder how they know each other, a windy city detective, no less. She's hiding a notorious, dangerous past. That's my guess. Maybe she ran with the wrong crowd once upon a time," Max grinned. "I wish she'd let on more. We had dinner last night and she doesn't give away much. Think I can crack her shell and discover all her dark secrets?"

"I think so," Lauren nodded brightly. "I probably shouldn't say this, but I overheard her and Carlos. Guess what she said?" She beamed at Max, "She thinks *you* might be the perfect man for her."

"Really?" Max grinned back at Lauren. "Finally, someone on my side. The perfect man for her, how about that, Doctor, Kiki, I might be the perfect man for Janine Stinger."

Max enjoyed pushing Ian's buttons. Kiki glanced at Ian and his blinking eyes.

"Max, obviously, that was sarcasm," Kiki purred. Lauren gasped, shocked.

"Come on, Kiki," Max smiled at her. "Why can't you be nice to me? Are you jealous?"

"Of course I'm jealous. You know how I like being the one to bust your balls." She winked at him, reminded Lauren about their hair plan, then excused herself to go start her beauty rest.

Kiki couldn't sleep. She was waiting for Janine to respond to her text. She insisted Janine message when she finished with the detective to confirm that everything was all right, or if she needed to talk. Kiki texted that she would not go to sleep until she heard back. Then, a soft knock came at her door.

Janine stood in the bright hall and Kiki ushered her in. Janine carried a bottle of wine.

"What's that for?" Kiki asked.

"It was sent to my room, from Max Colliers," Janine said. "We had dinner together last night and he noticed I liked this wine. Kind of a sweet of him, don't you think? Do you have an opener?"

"Careful with Max, he's quite a player." Kiki found a cork screw and handed it over. Then, she checked the cabinets in the suite and found a couple of very nice wine glasses. She held them while Janine poured.

"Are we celebrating or medicating?" Kiki asked.

"Just drinking," Janine said.

Kiki took a taste of the wine. Oh yes, a very elegant, creamy, full-bodied papaya taste. It slipped down very easily. Kiki could see why Janine preferred it. They sat silently enjoying the wine. That was one of the nice things about Janine Stinger, she was a quiet girl. Many of the women Kiki knew needed to chatter. Not Janine. They could sit and enjoy a quiet room and soak up some calm vibes.

"Detective Anderson wanted to tell me in person that Rick has his first parole board soon, in a couple of weeks," Janine said softly. "He's been the perfect prisoner and has a better chance of being released than most. Prisons are overcrowded and all, and it's not like he successfully killed anyone. The local politicians love him, I hear, especially the new governor."

Kiki sat up. Janine did not seem very upset.

"I've been anticipating it," Janine said softly. "He's very good at acting normal. He can be very convincing, likable, appealing. He even made me doubt my own memory at first."

"I remember that," Kiki said. "It was part of his main defense; That you didn't accuse him right away. That you must have been coerced into blaming him, by some detective."

Kiki knew the story from news features that referred to Janine as Jane Doe from Chicago to protect her identity. While Janine was a student at the university, she fell head over heels for a charming psychopath. Sometime during that relationship, she tried to leave him, but he didn't let her and held her prisoner in his house. When she finally escaped, he caught up to her and stabbed her multiple times. Janine had garish knife wounds on her back, stomach, and chest. She almost died. Later, in the hospital, it took more than a week for her to tell people that the man holding vigil at her bedside happened to be her attacker. A notorious trial followed, one in which the defense harshly questioned Janine's state of mind and memory. The defense claimed that she was irrational, hysterical, and in a hormone-induced emotional state. She was an unreliable witness. Her reckless defamatory allegations slandered their client, and she was accused of spreading false testimony. Different media outlets took opposing sides in the scandalous case, mostly because her identity was kept locked tight.

"Did you tell the detective about the letters?" Kiki asked. "They may be enough to keep him locked away."

Janine nodded. "He has them."

They polished off more than half the bottle of wine and Janine poured herself a little more.

"I really like your Detective Anderson," Kiki said out loud. "I mean, I *really* like him."

Janine smiled at her. "I think he really likes you too."

They started giggling about the detective. Janine told Kiki that the detective always came off very gentle and sweet, but once, she watched him take down a large burly drunk, completely immobilizing him in a matter of minutes. Then, he talked the man into being calm and quiet without further need of force.

Kiki described his aura and Janine had a hard time believing that it was pink. 'Crusty Detective Anderson with a pink aura, no way,' Janine said. Kiki also described the hues of yellow she found so attractive in his halo, and the little touch of tan that was similar to Ian's aura.

"Kiki, I know we need to get some sleep, to be fresh for tonight, but I have a favor." Janine stared into her glass of wine. "There were flowers with the bottle from Max, and a note. And then there's Ian. I'm sorry to say, I may have looked at Ian in a suggestive way on the street today."

Kiki shook her head. "You're afraid someone might come knocking on your door?"

"Does that sound arrogant?"

"You can just say no, Janine. Or you leave the door unanswered," Kiki told her.

"If a certain doctor shows up, I don't think I can just say no," Janine confessed. "I don't know what's wrong with me that I don't think I can say no to him. But I won't do that again. Would you let me nap in here with you?"

"It's part of that dark aura of yours. There is a streak of pure red underneath, the passion speaking. You thrive on the physical plane. Some of it is the trauma you're holding onto, but mostly, it's just your sensuality. Yes, you can nap in here. I've got plenty of room on that king size bed."

It was Ian that Janine was wary of, but Kiki would be worried about Max. After what Lauren said in the ball-room, she doubted Ian would be knocking on Janine's door. Especially after those conclusions he jumped to the night before, and the fact that he hadn't broken it off with Lauren yet. But that fantastic bottle of wine was a different story. It shouted that Max certainly would come knocking and expected to share that sweet chardonnay. Kiki knew very well Max's modus operandi, his notorious reputation, and the pride he took in it.

They were on a strict schedule for the evening shoots. They would walk down the alley at nine, visit the water tower at ten, and be in the parks by eleven. Then, they would meet Sally, Guy, and Lauren at the Congress Plaza for a touchup before her séance. Kiki planned a wardrobe change between the street investigations and the séance. If everything flowed smoothly, they'd be back in bed before dawn.

The guys already left for the alley and a fancy car waited to ferry Kiki, Janine, and Max after the girls were prepped. Max lounged in a chair completing paperwork and sipping an evening cocktail. True to his word, he planned to watch the filming from afar, from his limousine. Janine rushed into the conference room and did a double take of Kiki's hair.

"Wow, that's quite a red," Janine said. "I didn't know they could dye hair down here."

"Lauren colored it in my room. There's no plumbing down here," Kiki shook it around. "You were pretty conked out and slept through the whole thing." Then, Kiki leaned in and lowered her voice. "I want to try something tonight, in regards to you being a *dragoma*. Will you try a little experiment with me?"

"What kind of experiment?"

"Just one in which you mimic what I say on purpose, with concentrated intent, when I call out with my summons,"

Kiki said. "Speak to the spirits with me. Come on, I'll give you some insights while Lauren curls your hair."

"More than a century ago, hundreds of people lost their lives right here on this spot. The Nederlander Theater replaced an earlier theater called the Iroquois, which burned down, tragically," Kiki spoke to Ian in front of the camera. "It occurred during the opening night of a show called Mr. Bluebeard in 1901, a show for children, so, many of the dead were very young. Today, people claim to hear whispered voices echoing down this alley, youthful voices. Perhaps they hear the ghostly cries of victims who tried to escape through a door on the upper level, a door that opened into nothing; no fire escape, no balcony, just open air. It wasn't the fire, but the fall, a plummet of over three stories, that led to their untimely demise," Kiki pointed to the top of the building. "An unknowing crowd pushed victims out the door as the flames closed in behind them."

Ian fiddled with his subsonic audio detector and monitored the needle swings. They sent Carlos and Janine down the alley with a small EMF box and a thermal-panger, but being in a paved back alley between two active buildings was not an optimum site for many of his gadgets. They gradually moved toward Carlos and Janine while Don filmed their conversation.

"We've been monitoring this alley for close to six hours, remotely," the doctor continued. "So far, we've detected nothing out of the ordinary. It doesn't help being in such an active area of the city."

"I do feel a deep hum back here," Kiki said. "A buzz of excitement that could be the energy from the people surrounding the area. Perhaps we should come back to the *Alley of Death* in the dead of night, when we know all the actors in this building have dispersed."

"Let's attempt something before we move on," the doctor said. "In our last investigation, we discovered one specter speaking on a subsonic level, in a range inaudible to the human ear."

"We've been told that people hear their own names being whispered in this alley," Kiki added.

"Yes. Let's see if we can mark a discernable pattern with our names, and then see if any matching patterns pop up in the subsonic range."

They finally reached Janine and Carlos. Their new *Spectral Analysis* investigative suits were very similar to the ones Max proposed at the Alamo. The main difference was in the trouser area. Sally added more leg room and added large cargo pockets to give them a military flavor. She also topped them with a thick web belt of clips and carabiners for attaching gear. Janine's outfit was cut low enough to expose most of the dark knife marks on her left breast. Those marks were in an X pattern and Kiki knew that Janine preferred to hide them. Many people mistook that scar as body art and tended to stare when it was exposed.

Carlos raised his eyebrows at Kiki's ensemble. He often teased her about her outrageous show costumes, but this time he didn't say a word. Her skin-tight, zipper up the front suit happened to be a knock off of the crew's new uniform. Only, she did not have the cargo pockets or the web belt.

The doctor tasked everyone with saying their names into the audio recorder. He then saved the pattern and set his device to beep for any slower, similar wave fluctuations in the subsonic zone.

They huddled in a circle watching the meter. After a few moments, the doctor let out his breath.

"It was worth a try. Wait a minute, maybe I should reset it before we give up." The doctor studied the bottom of the meter. "I need something small, like a pin or something." His hands were searching his pockets.

"I've got it." Carlos frantically patted around his own pockets. "I've got what you need!" He handed his camcorder to Janine and dug in deep on his arm pocket. Then, he pulled out a paper clip, which got Janine and Carlos to laugh hysterically as he unbent the small metal loop.

"Let's try something else as well," Kiki turned to Janine. "Let's have Janine summon the ghosts this time. Speak as if you're calling through a tunnel. Your voice needs to echo to the end of that tunnel. It can be a whisper, or just thoughts in your head, but you need to project it. Ask any spirits to speak to us, and really feel the words while you ask."

Janine took a few slow breaths. "Speak to us," she whispered.

A series of pings went off on the doctor's meter startling them. They all stared at the meter. Did Janine or the paperclip set it off? Then, it went silent. Kiki wasn't surprised at all. Now, she knew the secret to their success. *Her poor ego*! Kiki had been convinced she was becoming better at sending messages to the other side. She had been pumped up with her own importance and even bragged about it to a couple of the sisters back home, *there's a new* dragoma *in town*. Now she knew, all along it had been Janine whispering to the spirits.

"What was that?" Carlos said. "What just happened?"

"A lot of subsonic noise," the doctor said. "It was a burst of energy. Mixed, so it's hard to see a pattern. The machine believes there were some matches, but we'll get this back to Ben and see what he comes up with." He glanced around. "To the water tower?"

"To the water tower," Kiki agreed.

Don and Ben rode in the van with the driver, while the rest of the crew piled into Max Collier's hired car, a very roomy and comfortable short Limousine. Carlos and Ian took the rear facing seats, while Janine and Kiki sat on either side of Max on the forward facing seat. Max seemed very pleased with his spot in the car. He made no attempt to be discrete in gaping at both Janine and Kiki in their near matching *Spectral Analysis* suits.

"You girls look fantastic," Max gushed. "Do you guys see what I'm trying to do here? Now, this is top rated stuff.

We are going to have the audience going bonkers over this episode, I can't keep my eyes off of these girls!" He glanced at Carlos. "And you look like a god, Carlos, aren't you glad you let the image people do their stuff?"

"My kids say I look like Astro Boy," Carlos laughed lightly. "I admit, I like this batman utility belt. I will give wardrobe an A plus on the bat belt."

"Can we focus on this shoot?" Ian sounded very irritated and they all went silent for a moment.

Poor bloke, he was blinking again. Kiki noticed Max casually resting his hand on Janine's thigh. He was doing the same to her, so it was nothing for Ian to get overexcited about. He must be upset because Janine and Carlos fell in line with Max's design ideas. Kiki knew Ian had been pleased when they refused to comply back at the Alamo. She could see the tension rising from Ian's corner of the car, green and orange sparks streamed from his halo. Max tossed his cell phone at Carlos.

"I want a picture with these sexy women." He put his arms around Kiki and Janine and pulled them in close.

Carlos feigned having trouble working the camera, he kept muffing things up, like he wasn't sure what to do, or maybe, there was something wrong with the phone. Whoops, another failed attempt. He asked the doctor to assist, but the doctor snapped at him and didn't look up from this computer pad. Carlos's attempts at creating a lighter atmosphere were not working.

"Just take the picture, Carlos," Janine said irritably. "It's fine."

And then they were at the water tower.

The tower consisted of a gothic building made of rough faced rock that the doctor told them was carved limestone blocks. It no longer pumped water because the main sand pipe had been removed years ago. When Kiki spotted the winding staircase that led to the top of the tower, she wondered if they actually needed to climb those stairs. Had the remote sensors picked anything up? She definitely did not get any sense of paranormal energy in that direction. They only included the tower because it was such a historic landmark.

They made the decision to skip the climb and gathered on the steps where Kiki briefly spoke with the bug-eyed point-man regarding the hanging man ghost. Don filmed with a single camera and boom microphone set up. The doctor planned an experiment on those front steps with a substance he called sodium thiosulfate. Ben delivered a tray of materials. Everyone gather on the steps to watch the doctor with the looming tower providing a nice backdrop behind them.

"I want you to remember this," the doctor said to the camera. "A wee lesson on the absorption of energy, the storing of energy, and the release of energy. Understanding energy exchanges like this can help us understand what may be happening with spectral or ghostly energy. Perhaps we can begin to understand why ghosts are attached to certain locations, and how they migrate from life energy into something else."

He added a few drops of water to a small vessel of the crystal pellets and then proceeded to warm the mixture with a small blow torch.

"Are you melting it?" Carlos said.

"Aye, but I will quick-cool the crystals below the melting point, so they shouldn't remain a liquid. I'm only heating them now to allow them to better dissolve in that wee bit of water. The absorbed heat will allow them to remain dissolved in what is known as a supersaturated solution. This is the energy absorption phase."

"That's not enough water to dissolve that much stuff," Carlos observed.

"Not unless the crystals absorb and retain this heat," the doctor told him.

The crystals and water soon appeared to be a clear fluid. The doctor transferred his mixture into a small bucket of ice. It was dry ice, so the solution cooled very quickly. The doctor carefully retrieved the container of clear liquid and set it on the steps, propped up in a test tube holder.

"Go ahead and feel the outside of the test tube," the doctor invited them.

"Cold," Kiki said. "Very cold."

Janine used a thermal-panger to get a reading of the cold temperature, well below zero Celsius.

"Aye," the doctor said. "Much colder than when we first began. If those pellets were not dissolved in those few drops of water, they would have solidified, froze to a solid as soon as the temperature reached their normal freezing point of forty-eight degrees. They can only stay dissolved in those drops if they retain the heat used to melt them. This is an example of a substance storing enormous amounts of heat energy. It's hard to tell, because it's so cold, but believe me, the heat that melted those crystals is trapped inside that cold, clear solution waiting to be released."

"How do you get the solution to release the energy?" Kiki asked.

"A simple disturbance. Like adding a seed crystal," the doctor said. "Keep this in mind for later, when we talk about paranormal energy. The science behind this energy exchange may mirror a similar process that happens in ghostly events. Most substances will absorb energy, store it, and then release it, but supersaturation is a little different. Not every substance can hide this much energy, nor do they require a trigger to release the energy."

Then, the doctor added one small seed crystal to the supersaturated solution and the sodium thiosulfate instantly began to crystallize. The entire container appeared to turn from a clear liquid into a solid block of ice in a matter of seconds.

"Go ahead and touch the outside of the container," the doctor invited. "You will feel the heat those crystals had been storing."

"That's crazy!" Carlos touched the container. Janine used her thermal-panger to get a readout of the temperature again, forty-eight degrees and rising.

Kiki also felt the container and it was indeed very hot. A moment ago, as a liquid, it was freezing cold, now frozen solid, it radiated ample amounts of heat. Clever Ian, he was setting things up nicely to reveal a bit of this theory. Janine volunteered to help Ben clean up. She gave the doctor a very nice compliment on his presentation and Kiki watched him nod stiffly before walking away.

This time Janine jumped in the van with Ben and Don. She surprised them with her last minute decision. Kiki imagined she wanted a break from Max and Ian.

"I don't understand why you're not using the earphone microphones. It's a state of the art audio system," Max said. "I could listen in while I make my phone calls. And why does eight o'clock in Moscow have to be so late at night here?" Max chuckled. He was enjoying a large drink and offered one to Kiki.

"We don't drink until the night is over," Kiki told him. "We don't want to impair our perceptions or put them into question."

Max quickly set the drink down. "Sorry, I didn't know." He grinned mischievously, then glanced at the doctor. "Why don't you guys go on audio for this next stop? I'd like to hear everything. I promise to only use push to talk. I'm on the phone anyway."

The doctor agreed that was a good idea. He planned on separating the crew in the second park, so being hooked up made sense. He had fetched the crazy coil of copper wire that he used as a magnetic antennae and was checking to make sure the wires weren't crossed. Kiki could see the animosity emanating back and forth between Ian and Max, their clashing auras. Carlos flipped through the messages on his cell phone, trying not to look up. Clearly, he felt it too.

Then, Kiki felt Max's hand. His warm fingers caressed the small of her back. Max pulled that maneuver before. She caught him scanning over her scanty outfit, so she leaned forward to give him a better view, then pulled his hand away to let him know that looking was about all he'd be doing. He grinned and had a little more of his drink. He must be compensating for being brushed aside by Janine. Max gambled that Kiki would flirt back, because she often did. He was very good at focusing his energy, and at that moment, he focused directly on her.

A group of people were gathered outside the police tape at the Battle of Dearborn Park. A squad car and two uniformed police officers stood near the crowd and people carried signs with *Welcome, Spectral Analysis* drawn on them.

"Terrific," Ian grimaced at the crowd of about twenty spectators.

"Don't be a grouch," Kiki purred. "We'll go out and mingle before we get to work. Good thing we skipped a climb up that tower."

Janine and Ben were already chatting with people on the sidewalk. Carlos filed out first, then the doctor, but Max held her back with a firm grip on her wrist. He pulled the door closed and the dome light dimmed.

"Wait a moment and make an entrance. They're eagerly waiting for you, Kiki." He was staring at her cleavage again. "You're about to burst out of that thing, are you sure you won't give me a quick peek? I love that you asked Sally make you one, and just the way I designed it." He moved his hand down her thigh. "We think alike, Kiki. We know what it takes to make things happen. We could be a good team."

"How much were you drinking?" Kiki asked.

"Don't be coy with me. We understand each other, and I believe you were jealous earlier today. Do you miss being the object of my attention?" He ran his hand up and got a nice feel of her buttocks. "She may be athletic, but you are all woman. Are you going to change your mind about us?"

"Let's not revisit that old conversation." Kiki slowly removed his hand from her body. "I love flirting with you, Max, but we need to work together, so let's not mix things up."

Kiki popped out of the car. She actually relished the flirty sparring match with Max because it came at a very opportune time. Having him shower her with that stream of desire energized her. She could turn that verve to her advantage. Male erotic energy was a powerful stimulus for mystic receptors. It was an age old practice, well known to the sisters of her coven, and people didn't realized that her show outfits weren't just for show. It wasn't anything that hadn't happened before, with Max. She'd bet money that he propositioned almost every woman on his staff at one time or another. Feeding off his desire was harmless to a player like him.

The small crowd immediately encircled her, snapping photos and asking for autographs. Kiki noticed the doctor and Carlos speaking to three young women, while Janine spoke with an older couple, Kiki attracted everyone else, including the burly policeman hovering behind her. Her core energy well would not be waning anytime soon.

After the fan meet and greet, the doctor rallied the crew toward a single tree in a round area of grass. It was surrounded by a cement walkway and three benches in an arc gave them a place to gather. Kiki and the doctor took one bench, while Janine and Carlos settled on another. Don filmed their conversation from a standing position. The doctor handed a computer pad of digital controls to Carlos. On the small screen, Carlos could zoom in on their group through the camera they planted earlier that day. The doctor encouraged them to hunt for ghostly images on the screen. Spectral reports regarding the Dearborn massacre always involved ghostly images on camera.

"The Potawatomi may have been acting in retribution for broken promises from the US government on that August day in 1815. It's pretty safe to say that the natives were caught between the British, the Americans, and other native nations, and choosing sides was likely very chancy and incurred dangers from multiple angles. The possibility of being double crossed, high," the doctor told them. "Whatever the reason for the attack, whatever caused them to target the people in the fort, it resulted in a terrible loss of life for the United States troops and their families. It was mainly the young men of the tribe that attacked, so no one can blame the entire Potawatomi nation."

"This must have been a quiet spot, beautiful, very close to the lake like this," Kiki said. "It's hard to imagine such a savage event occurring in this serene location."

"Savage it was. The records state that native warriors bludgeoned twelve children on this very spot in a brutal and senseless act. The history of the entire tragedy is commemorated as a star in the city flag. The Chicago flag has four red stars. The first represents Fort Dearborn, marking it as an intensely emotional event." He held up his hand. "But, was it intense enough for a part of their life energy to be absorbed into something? I think, yes."

"That's fascinating," Kiki said. "Usually in areas of traumatic loss, especially involving children, I feel an abundance of psychic energy. But I don't feel anything here. Do you think there's a possibility that this isn't the massacre site? That perhaps the historians got it wrong?"

"Not a chance, Kiki," the doctor said. "I believe you don't feel anything here because this place is missing the elements needed for a ghostly stamp. Remember, not every chemical can trap heat and become a supersaturated solution. Perhaps it takes a key substance to absorb and retain that intense psychic energy you often feel. Something in bones and wood, or in certain minerals found in some types of stone, such as—"

"Such as boulders in the river?" Janine's voice interrupted sharply. "Like the mineral deposits in those boulders in the river? Is that the theory you've been hoping to push? It is, isn't it? Why you so adamantly refused to even consider…" Janine closed her eyes and stopped herself. She stood abruptly and everyone stood with her. Janine pressed her lips together and shook her head. "I need to take a little break," she moved quickly down the path, away from them.

"I'll go." Carlos set the computer pad on the metal bench and took off after her.

Don raised an eyebrow at the doctor. The doctor gave him a ten minute break and he meandered toward the van as Max emerge from his car. Max hurried down the path to where Carlos and Janine stood under a lamp. Kiki couldn't hear what was being said but watched them talk. The group of spectators also watched. Both Max and Carlos stood very close to Janine and she wiped her eyes, but held herself pretty solidly. She was not accepting any hugs. A slow moving train rumbled behind the park, shaking up the atmosphere. Ian dropped a fisted hand on the bench.

"Crikes. Maybe I should go over and apologize or something." Ian's voice sounded perturbed. "What would I be apologizing for? We've already been through this one. Even if I didn't have a theory, she knows—"

Kiki stopped him with a hand on his arm. "Hush, Ian. You don't need to go over there, just give her a minute. She'll be fine."

"She's fallen for Max Collier's game," he spat under his breath. "I'm certain of it, and it's burning me up. I thought she was smarter than that," he shook his head. "I'm such an idiot. This morning, I almost thought…I went to check on her, you know, after the detective, I was worried about her. It turns out, she wasn't even in her room, and she was definitely with Max, because he wasn't answering his phone either. Both of them indisposed, and look how giddy he's behaving and how he keeps touching her. She doesn't seem to mind it at all. Can you believe it? Do you think she's trying to rub my nose in it?"

"I knew you were jealous, but that's why you've been so hostile?" Kiki patted his hand. "No worries, Ian, she was not with Max Colliers. She's not rubbing anyone's nose in anything."

"How can you be so sure? Look at her over there. She's totally playing into his hands, letting him dress her like that." He glanced at Kiki's outfit and pressed his lips together. "Sorry," he said.

"Ian, Janine slept in my room this afternoon," she nodded at him. Kiki watched his aggravation begin to break down into pieces. "I'm not going to go into detail, but she wanted to hide in my room to take an undisturbed nap. She was actually avoiding both of you blokes." She noticed

Carlos and Janine heading back and stood up. "Here they come."

Kiki gave Janine a quick hug and the doctor nodded at them.

"I'm sorry about that," Janine said. "It just hit me unexpectedly. The mention of innocent children must have set off my emotions, I guess. Obviously, I still harbor reservations about things, but I'm fine, everything is good. I'm sorry. Let's continue."

They went back to the benches. This time the doctor switched with Carlos. He hovered over Janine, full of concern, but she glared at him until he backed off. Don trotted up with the camera.

"We don't need to talk about my theory, we can change the plan. I can talk about it in the green room later," the doctor said softly. "We can wrap things here and go to the small park. That's where we have the best likelihood of getting some odd stuff."

"Nonsense," Janine snapped. "Keep going with your theory." She eyeballed Don. "You're rolling, right? So, energy absorbed, stored, and released. Different substances absorb differently, like having a different specific heat capacity, or something? But it's not just heat energy, even light can be stored, right, Doctor? Like a fluorescent mineral or glow in the dark stickers. You're thinking some kind of special psychic energy is being stored. In what? You mentioned magnesium earlier today. Magnesium in those limestone pillars at the water station."

"Aye," the doctor said softly. "There may be something I've missed, but magnesium seems to be one of the elements that absorb spiritual energy, phosphorus as well, maybe others. Those elements are found in bone, wood, and rock forming minerals."

"Then why don't we see ghosts everywhere? Those are pretty common elements," Janine asked him.

"I'm still working on that answer. Perhaps there's a specific ratio, or an isotope, or a key arrangement involving other substances. Sodium thiosulfate needs to be in a solution to store energy, mixed in a small quantity of water."

"You would need a traumatic event to stamp in that kind of energy, don't you think?" Kiki added. "Like when the doctor added heat to get the sodium thiosulfate to dissolve in the first place. Spirits are associated with tragic events. Murder, sorrow, disasters."

"What kind of energy are we talking about here?" Carlos asked. "What type of energy is being stamped into these elements?"

"Aether, life energy," Kiki said. "Psychic, spiritual, the energy that's part of what we call our feelings, our souls, I would imagine. Think of this, who hasn't felt the presence of another person standing behind you? Maybe that energy. Or the intensity of being observed from afar? Everyone projects an aura. It's part of the energy of life, but it isn't really alive."

"A mystery energy we haven't yet discovered," the doctor nodded, "Or found a way to measure. Quintessence, maybe? Or something else. Aether might be the right word for now. Those low frequency EM waves I always get excited about, that's not it. Those low frequency pulses result when our mystery energy is transformed from one medium to another. Like a friction of sorts, it's not a completely efficient transformation when the energy is released and we get leaks resulting in low frequency electromagnetic waves. The mystery energy is not going to be electric or magnetic. We are not going to measure that mystery energy on the EM spectrum. It's on some other plane, some other dimension. Right now, all we can do is measure the whispers of when that energy seeps into parts of the world we understand."

"Okay," Janine asked, "then wouldn't the energy, the aether, be released sometimes… spontaneously, similar to radioactivity for instance? We've been monitoring this place for hours now, with very little to look at, according to Ben. Why would we expect to see a ghost right now, just because we decided to go looking for one?"

"There needs to be a trigger to release some of the energy," the doctor explained. "Perhaps something inside a living person, living energy is the trigger. But, not all people can see or hear ghosts, perhaps it takes a certain type of person, projecting the right type of vibe, to be a trigger. The correct type of disturbance on the surface of the solution, so to speak. Like a seed crystal or a catalyst. A person like Kiki probably provides a bigger disturbance than most."

"I would agree that Kiki provides a pretty big disturbance everywhere she goes." Carlos nodded thoughtfully.

Kiki flashed her cats eyes at Carlos as they chuckled.

"Very interesting," Kiki said. "Now earlier, you mentioned that this place is missing the elements for the ghostly stamp of aether. Where do you suggest we find that stamp of energy?"

"In the small park a few blocks from here," the doctor said. "That's where they buried the massacre victims, and some of those bones are still trapped in that plot of land. Bones don't just store calcium, you know. Traces of magnesium and phosphorus are mixed in as well. I believe, if we show up with our lovely trigger here, we may see some interesting things." He glanced around. "Shall we head out to the small park?"

They all nodded and said in unison, "To the small park."

This time Carlos snagged the extra seat in the van. Kiki, the doctor, Max and Janine all piled into the back of the hired car, with Kiki and Max on one side, the doctor and Janine on the other. The doctor picked up his large copper coil to inspect it again. Max had another drink in his hand and his brief case in his lap.

"If you don't stop drinking, I'm not going to let you sit in on the séance," Kiki chided him. Max just smiled pleasantly at her.

It was a short drive to the next park, just down South Prairie Street and then a turn onto 16th Street. They hopped out of the car pretty quickly and had to wait for the van.

There wasn't a crowd at their little triangle of the park, but Kiki noticed a squad car with a small gathering on the other side of the railroad tracks near the playground.

"Someone should run over and greet that crowd," Ian said. "Pass out stickers or something, placate them so they don't head this way. This is our critical location, where we want a little privacy."

Max volunteered to run over in the limousine. Would the doctor object if he took a little speaker and hooked up the audio? He could divert the folks with a little preview and give them a listen in on the investigation, a reward for being dedicated fans, and the way he said it, he'd already made up his mind. To Kiki's surprise, the doctor agreed with him. Ian shrugged at her.

The van rolled up and Ben jumped out. He rigged an audio set up pretty quickly. Max grabbed Kiki's hand and pulled her toward the car, then he grabbed Janine's hand as well.

"I'll take the girls with me," Max said. "Just for a few minutes, to greet your fans and take a pictures while you set up." Max grinned at the doctor. "You don't need Kiki or Janine for anything, do you? I'll send them right back."

Kiki could see a confrontation on the horizon, so she moved closer to Max and slid her arm into his. Max smiled at her. Kiki glanced at Janine and winked, then looked into the doctor's stern face.

"We should go," Kiki said. "Those fellows won't stay over there unless we give them some attention. Don't worry,

Ian, it's going to take time for you to connect that big box of yours, and we'll be back in fifteen minutes. Twenty, tops."

Max was positively delighted with her, and a little drunk. He must have completed his long distance phone calls and was winding down. His tie was gone and his smile constant. He lounged across from them for the short drive around the corner. His eyes gleamed in a devilish way.

"I'm sorry I've been drinking so much, Kiki," Max said. "I don't want to worry you about my behavior in the séance later, so I've lined up my replacement."

"No kidding?" Kiki asked. "And who will be replacing you?"

"Lauren." He grinned wickedly. "She's quite pretty, don't you think? That's natural blonde hair on her, you know, gorgeous lips, and smile. Gets along well with Doctor McNally. She's been hinting at the possibility of being on camera for quite some time. Did you know, she did a screen test with Carlos a couple of weeks ago and looks good on film, natural? We're vetting her to possibly replace Janine if she leaves. When she leaves." He shot a look at Janine. "This could be a continuation of that screen test. So, is it alright with you, that Lauren takes my seat in the séance tonight?"

Well, that was a lot of information, unusual for Max to share so much. Kiki imagined it was spurred on by whatever he'd been drinking and to get a reaction out of Janine. *Which button was he trying to push*, Kiki wondered. Janine didn't budge and inch. Good for her.

"She'll make a terrific replacement in the séance, Max," Kiki told him. Janine agreed with a nod.

Then, they pulled up to the curb to greet their fans.

Chapter 9

Ghosts In the Park

Janine

A flurry of flashes blinded her, setting her nerves off and irritating her. Kiki, on the other hand, relished the rowdy attention. She strutted in her racy costume and flashed her glowing eyes at everyone. Janine couldn't fathom how she managed to feel comfortable in that crowd of boisterous young men. Then, Kiki suddenly rushed away. She beelined toward a woman with a baby carriage leaving Janine abandoned in a laughing group of frat boys. They were university students and Max lost no time in telling them that Janine once attended the University of Chicago as a student. They became over excited and squeezed in to take photos while shouting "U of C, U of C!"

Max carried a bottle from the limousine bar to share, definitely in a party mood. A few of the men told her that a guy named Randy knew where to find *Spectral Analysis* that night, a ghost had whispered the location in his ear. Kiki, still speaking to the woman with the baby, must have heard that talk, because she perked up and faced them at that very moment. Kiki finally started moving back toward Janine when a young man decided to grab Janine's hand. Max instantly jumped to the rescue and shot the guy a scrutinizing look.

"Here there," Max admonished, "hands to yourself now," which Janine found very ironic. Max had barely keep his own hands to himself in the car, with her and with Kiki. He appeared quite drunk and was acting extremely strange. Perhaps he really had knocked on her door expecting to share that bottle of wine with her. Janine had no idea what type of women Max was used to. Either way, she felt a touch of agoraphobia in that crowd of university students and couldn't wait to escape into the car.

Max instructed the driver to set up the speaker system at a table in the playground. That drew most of the attention away and she breathed a sigh of relief. Kiki ran up gushing about the baby. They drifted closer to the car, but a small group blocked their path. It included the same grabby young man from earlier. His wild hair half hid his eyes, and his mouth was pressed into a tight line.

"Randy saw a ghost," one of the fellows announced. "A real ghost. He's totally possessed. The ghost talks to him in his sleep." He indicated the man who had grabbed Janine's hand.

"How interesting," Kiki's glowing green eyes narrowed on the young man. "In his sleep?"

"Go on, Randy," the friend pushed the nervous one forward. "Did you bring it? Give it to her. He has something for you, for Janine Stinger."

"Come here, handsome." Kiki pulled him closer, and he relaxed a bit. "You say a ghost is haunting you? How do you know it's a ghost?"

"I saw her by the pond." His bloodshot eyes briefly landed on Janine, but darted away quickly. "She comes back in my dreams."

"You poor dear." Kiki reached up and stroked his hair. His friends got a kick out of that and snickered, but Kiki ignored them. Her voice was soft, soothing. "You say you have something for Janine?"

"I don't need anything," Janine continued moving away. She avoided contact with the mystery guy and nodded toward the car. "Come on, Kiki, we need to get back to the other side." Janine waved to the other college guys. "Sorry, but we need to go."

Kiki nodded reassuringly at her, then turned back to Randy. He seemed transfixed by her attention. "I certainly believe you, Randy. Come around to the Lincoln House to see me, if you like. Day after tomorrow would be best, in the afternoon. I want to hear all about your ghost." Kiki smiled flirtatiously at the other guys and Janine was never more irritated at her unending quest for male attention.

Randy gave a jerky nod before glancing at Janine. Finally, Kiki climbed into the limousine. After the door closed, Janine turned an angry face to Kiki, perturbed that she needed to flirt with every male that crossed her path, and now, she was trying to drag Janine into it. Janine regretted wearing that ridiculous, stupid jumpsuit.

"Why did you invite that guy to the hotel? He was beyond creepy and I don't want to talk to him."

"He's haunted, Janine." Kiki ignored her upset attitude. "I could feel it all around him. You could feel it too, it was that creepy feeling you noticed. Haunted people have a very distinct aura." Then, Kiki took Janine's hands. "Let's talk about what we're going to do in the park. We have different talents, you know. While you may be a natural *dragoma*, a sender, I'm a natural receiver. I can focus my energy on receiving if you can do the summoning. Ian thinks I'm the only trigger out here, but I believe it's really you."

"I'm still not certain what you mean by talking from my core," Janine snapped, still irritated.

"Just repeat what I say out loud, or silently if you prefer, but not passively like you do, but with determination. When you hear me speaking to the spirits, recite it and try to *feel* the words, Janine, *in your core,* your heart. Direct your intent and project it to where you feel a soul might receive it. I'll vocalize as much as possible out there, but you will need to open your heart and really feel like you're talking to them."

The doctor placed the copper antennae on a branch and the large EMF box along the edge of the tree line. He planned to man the box and communicate over the wire on channel two. Anything they wanted people in the park to hear, they'd transmit on channel one. Carlos would trail them into the trees and record low spectrum IR images with his camera, and Don would film the normal stuff with the big camera. Janine clipped a thermal-panger, ion detector, and portable audio recorder onto her web belt.

Kiki wanted to meander toward the mirrors hanging from the trees. The doctor aimed his magnetic antennae in that direction. As Kiki stepped away to center herself, Janine turned to the doctor and found him quietly regarding her. Whatever had been bugging him earlier had passed. *Out of sympathy regarding her little outburst?* She didn't want to know and turned back toward Kiki. She simmered thinking about it. Her conspiracy theory was no more lunatic than a ghost, did he need to be so harsh about it, calling her hysterical and irrational? *No, no, don't get upset again*, she told herself. *He had been right to shut her accusation down quickly*. Luckily, Kiki became "centered," and they began a slow stroll into the trees.

The atmosphere transformed the moment they crossed under the canopy and the trees obscured the sky. Kiki reached for Janine's hand and pulled her close. She insisted on walking hand in hand. She whispered something about sharing their gifts. *When witches hold hands, their gifts are shared*, Kiki conveyed. Kiki spoke in a soft voice, a whisper.

"We seek yon souls of near to there, we call on you to us appear, reveal yourself for us to see, so I command, so mote it be. Project that, repeat it, open your heart," Kiki instructed Janine, then turned to the spirits, "*Hello, hello. We wish to speak with you. You can trust us. We want to help*." Janine concentrated on repeating

all of Kiki's words, but she felt very silly hearing her voice muttering that witch talk.

The doctor's voice came softly over the audio, "We're getting definite ultralow frequency pulses. I've seen those here before."

"*We seek yon souls of near to there, we call on you to us appear,*" Kiki continued softly. "*We come to help you.*"

Janine grabbed her thermal-panger and clicked the button to record. She felt the temperature begin to drop. The ion detector on her web belt popped off a couple of times.

"*I can hear you,*" Kiki said. "*I hear you. You're fine now, please calm down, it's all right. Don't be afraid.*" Then, the tone of her voice changed, "Janine, are you focusing? We need to talk to these spirits. Are you repeating this?"

"Yes, sorry, I'll focus. Go on."

"*Please calm down. You are fine now, it's over.* They're afraid, Janine. I sense that they are afraid. We need to let them know that they no longer need to be afraid," Kiki whispered, but changed her voice for the spirits again. "*Your ordeal is over, and we want to help you.*" Janine very softy whispered a repeat of most of that, feeling completely idiotic.

"My camera is picking up a cold spot," Carlos's whispered voice came over the audio. He stood six feet behind them. "To your right, beside that tree. The one you climbed today."

"Tell me about it, the panger is picking it up too," Janine told Carlos.

Kiki gripped Janine's hand firmly and pulled her toward the tree.

"*Don't cry*. They're crying." Kiki said. "I feel scared children, several children, Janine, they're frightened, can you feel them? We need to help them calm down. Maybe we can sing them a song. Do you sense them at all?"

The doctor's voice came over the line. "Do you think you sense kids from Fort Dearborn? Maybe try to ask. Ben says the audio receiver is getting flashes with speech patterns across the sonic zone, but just faintly. Do you hear anything?"

Kiki squeezed her hand. It was too dark to clearly see under the trees. "Really feel the words now. Open your heart and communicate this." Kiki took a deep breath, and Janine did too. "*We are here to help you. You're no longer in danger. We come to help. Sing with us now, sing a little nursery rhyme to calm down.* What's something old?" Then, Kiki recited, "*Pat-a-cake, pat-a-cake, bakers man, bake me a cake as fast as you can. Pat it, prick it, mark it with a 'B,' and put it in the oven for baby and me.*"

Janine joined her. An eerie feeling cascaded all around and Janine could feel movement in the air, gentle swirls of molecules. It felt as if someone moved passed and the pressure fluttered on her skin. Someone kept moving past. It couldn't be a breeze. The feeling barely stirred in every direction, circling them.

"Do you hear them?" Kiki asked, chuckling softly.

Janine concentrated. *Was it her imagination? The power of suggestion?* She heard a faint, almost imperceptible giggle.

Childish giggles and then the rhyme. More giggles from a little girl. *Could it only be in her mind?* The pounding of her own pulse made it hard to determine. The air took on a heavier feel. Then came a burst of giggles, sudden and strong, and her heart pounded loudly in her temple. *She did not just hear that!* A warm pocket of air pressed into her ear and Janine barely heard the whisper of a voice say, *I love you, girl.* Her heart bottomed out. She broke away from Kiki and her eyes flew wide open. Janine searched frantically around.

She called, "Sammy? Sammy?"

Faces were everywhere, flickering in the trees. Young faces, smiling, frowning, confused. Janine spun around, scouring those faces as every eye bore down on her, waiting. They wanted her to say something to them, imploring, earnest, attentive young faces, watching her. She hunted for a familiar face, but couldn't find it. Her chest felt very heavy, and she couldn't breathe. Her pulse flooded her head and she no longer heard the giggling. She turned to Kiki, seeking direction. *What should she say? What should she say to them?* Kiki's mouth moved, but Janine could no longer hear anything. And then, the world turned black.

Kiki also saw the faces. She always insisted that spirits were more easily seen as reflections than directly. Kiki also detected faint ghostly forms moving under the shelter of trees. Ben planned to zoom into the footage later, to see if any camera picked up the impressions she described. Janines' blackout only lasted a few moments, but she felt very sluggish. Kiki was usually the sluggish one, but she seemed just fine. She wished Janine had not let go of her hand.

"Just drink this tea and rehydrate," Kiki advised. They relaxed in the back of the limousine while the guys stood outside talking to the fans that drifted over. Janine could hear Ian's voice as he explained his electromagnetic box to someone.

"I don't get it," Janine said. "I'm not a fainter. Is this how you usually feel?"

Kiki smiled at her. "Don't worry, it'll pass."

"I feel like total crap. Are you going to do the séance without me? I heard some talk out there about rescheduling it or sending me back to the hotel. I can't believe I feel this sluggish, like I just ran ten miles or something." *Why did Kiki appear unfazed?* Usually, she was all droopy after an extreme encounter.

Kiki shook her head. "I don't want to do it without you, so we'll try the séance another time, if needed. Maybe, it's not needed."

Janine became the weak link, the runt of the team. She didn't want to be the reason the entire schedule got wrecked. Didn't they invite guests to participate in the séance? Would a delay add another day to the schedule? She needed to fulfill all of her obligations for it to count for the contract. If she bailed on part of her duties, Mike Dunn warned that she could be strung along to make up for it later. Janine sat up and drank the tea.

"I'm going to be okay," Janine insisted. "I just need a few more minutes, then you can tell the guys we can proceed. There's going to be food at the plaza, right? Carlos said there would be a late night snack while we mingle with your séance guests. It'll give me more time to rest and get some sugar into my system. I don't want to be sent back to the hotel, Kiki, I'm okay. You always recover just fine, so I'll be fine too. You're back to normal already."

"You did the sending out there," Kiki told her. "I kept my focus to receiving those spirits. Janine, I don't believe this energy drain is from sending. I believe you were trying too hard to see and hear them, and it taxed you. I should not have asked if you could hear them, because it encouraged you to focus on receiving." Kiki watched her curiously, then reached to the limousine bar and poured a very short touch of whisky into a nice crystal tumbler. She handed it to Janine. "Just drink that."

They never drank alcohol unless they were done for the night. Kiki must not think Janine would be much help at the plaza and Janine had to agree with her. She could barely sit up without feeling achy in the head.

"Want to know how I can bounce back so easily?" Kiki pushed her blood red hair behind her ears. "How I can manage to go from one encounter to another some nights? Why I have so much energy right now, tonight? You'll need to keep an open mind. You could try it, if you want to feel better."

"Of course I want to try it," Janine pushed herself to a better sitting position. "I'll try anything, what do I need to do?" She was willing to try whatever ritual Kiki was about to come up with. She had plenty of positive results using Kiki's methods. Where she once used to laugh at Kiki's antics, she now believed Kiki possessed effective mystical knowledge. Crazy things always happened around Kiki Mellow.

"Male sexual energy is a powerful thing, Janine. It's one of the quickest, most powerful resources for a witch," Kiki said. "If you want to recover quickly, you could tap into some of the testosterone driven energy out there."

Did Kiki just flip her lid? "Are you suggesting I have sex with someone right now?"

"No, absolutely not." Kiki burst out laughing. "Now keep an open mind, every witch in my coven knows this trick. When male sexual energy is directed at you, you can soak it in and use it to feed your core. The momentum can open and fuel your psychic receptors. You have to be careful, though. You can't think about where it usually leads for you, physically, I mean. Try not to slip down that slope or the energy won't make it to your core. It'll seep in your Base Well, and then you'll be up a creek. Just welcome the energy in, accept it openly, and send it to your core. Then, use it for psychic purposes. It can be very restorative."

Janine was at a loss for words.

"I do it all the time. When you think I'm flirting with a fellow, it's not real flirting. And I can use any male. Old, young, all that matters is the energy. Don is a terrific cameraman in this regard, and Carlos is another nice source in a pinch, but that might be a bit awkward for you."

"You want me to flirt with one of them? The guys?"

"You don't need to actually flirt," Kiki said. "Just be open and receptive to any passion energy that's directed your way. Let the fellows admire your womanly form without reproof. Flirting accelerates the process and focuses the energy on you, which is a must. You'll need the energy aimed directly at you. This suggestive outfit can do the flirting for you. That crowd of fraternity boys was a powerhouse of energy. If you had opened up to their attention, instead of blocking them out, you wouldn't be in the position you're in right now. Those men provided a ton of sexual energy and you completely shunned it. Some would have naturally seeped into your core and kept you from feeling this way. Next time, absorb it, like I did, and use it. Many women do it without even realizing what they're doing."

Janine agreed to give it a try, as long as the plan didn't include Ian or Carlos. Kiki insisted she needn't to do anything beyond openly receive the energy directed toward her, and that didn't require anything physical on her part. In fact, Kiki instructed her to avoid any sexual thoughts at all. If she did, the energy might get trapped in the wrong well.

Kiki opened the limo door and waved to Ian. She informed the doctor that they were feeling better and wanted to start moving toward the plaza. Kiki insisted that the doctor and Carlos give Don a break from the van and let him ride in the limousine with Max, Janine, and Kiki. Then, Kiki slipped into the rear facing seat and pulled Janine with her.

"Just relax," Kiki said. "I'll get things ramped up. Be open and receptive, none of your normal deflecting, okay? I'll get them focused directly on you as quickly as possible. This isn't a long drive, so we'll have to get straight to the point." Kiki urged Janine to lay across the seat with her head in Kiki's lap.

Don scooted in first. His eyes darted around the interior of the fancy car and noted the small bar and the stereo controls. He fiddled with the overhead lights, then nodded at Kiki and Janine.

"I hope she's okay," Don said to Kiki. "That was quite a tumble. Mr. Colliers said it was a missed opportunity. He wants me to film the doctor catching one of you."

Kiki broke into a sly smile. "No worries, Don, we'll get that catch in the graveyard tomorrow night."

Max jumped in, still chuckling at something said outside the car. His eyes skirted over Kiki and Janine, then he set his empty tumbler on the bar. He gave Janine a concerned closed lipped grin. Janine could tell he was still quite intoxicated.

"How are you doing over there, Janine? Are you up for the séance? I'm told you're only needed to monitor stuff in the background. Carlos can do it all if you want to sit this one out," He said gently. "I think it would be fine if you'd like to sit out and the doctor agrees."

"Janine doesn't like to sit out, she's always all in." Kiki used her super silky voice, almost purring like a cat. She often used that voice during interviews when she wanted to woo information out of someone. *She certainly could change the mood with that voice*, Janine thought.

Kiki stroked Janine's long auburn hair with a slow hand. Her fingers paused to play with the curls at the end, and though Kiki was hamming it up for the men in the car, her caress delivered a nice healing touch to Janine's pounding head and a soft sigh escaped Janine's lips. She noticed that both Don and Max were trying not to stare at her, and failing. A buzz of intense energy streamed off them.

"Just relax, sweet girl," Kiki murmured in that silky voice. "Don, you were right about these outfits, they are very constricting. I better loosen her up a tad, don't you agree?" Kiki's hand dropped to the zipper on her outfit. *What was she doing?* "Let me help you, my sweet girl. Give you more room to breathe." Kiki gently tugged at the zipper and gave Janine strikingly more cleavage, so much more that she felt almost completely exposed. Certainly, that lacy red push-up bra was no longer hidden. Kiki leaned down and whispered in her ear. "Accept it, and soak it in. Stop deflecting. Breathe deep and open your core."

There was indeed an energy spike directed at her from the men. Dons mouth gaped and Max eased back into the leather seat. His arms crossed over his chest as his eyes fixed on her exposed lace. Janine had his undivided attention, but he also appeared a little confused. *Kiki was right*, Janine thought, the buzz of desire got her blood flowing, and she no longer felt as sluggish. Kiki removed her hand and helped

Janine sit up. Kiki whispered into her ear so that the men couldn't quite hear.

"Channel it to your core, Janine." Then, she turned to Max, "Switch with me, Max."

"What?" he asked sharply.

"Switch seats with me, she might get faint again and need to lean against you, or something." Kiki reached over and took his hand. "I want to make a short drink for Don, I've seen some of the playbacks and Don is making me look very nice on film. He has a good eye for accentuation. I haven't gotten the chance to tell him how happy I am at having such a talented cameraman on staff." Don actually appeared scared of Kiki.

Kiki pretty much forced Max to switch seats with her. Don dribbled off a stream of words to Kiki that Janine couldn't quite analyze because Max had moved very close to her. He stared down at the X knife scar and she watched the bulge in his pants grow. His proximity made her very uncomfortable, hot. She could hear him take in air and she wanted to zip back up, but that zipper would take a little fight to get started and she was afraid the fight would draw even more attention. Max opened up his arm and offered his chest as a pillow. She wasn't sure what she should do, so she leaned in and lay against him. She could feel the hard muscles underneath his shirt and the warmth radiating from him. Her body responded to his proximity, and she was afraid to move. She glanced at Kiki and those green eyes held a warning. Kiki sharply shook her head.

"Direct it to your core," Kiki said evenly, her brow creased with worried.

"Direct what to her core?" Max asked.

"The tea," Kiki said. "She needs a little more tea." She passed Max the tea cup and clearly meant for him to feed it to Janine. "It looks like we're here. Can you manage her, Max, help her out of the car, and make sure she drinks that tea. I'm going to run to the ladies' room."

Max stretched out his legs after Kiki and Don departed. Janine shakily turned away from him and zipped up her front. She felt a whole lot better physically, but was very embarrassed at the same time. She couldn't quite meet Max's eye. He held the tea cup for her, then set it aside when she didn't take it.

"I'm not sure what Kiki's up to; teaching me a lesson, maybe? That short drive sobered me up quick," Max said. "Before you run off to do the séance, I want to apologize for my behavior earlier. I haven't been acting exactly a gentleman. Is that why you participated in this? Is it because I was being a sore sport about it?"

"A sore sport about what?"

Max pulled out his cell phone. He called up a GIF of the doctor catching her by the lamppost. Somebody, that man, posted it, and it apparently caused quite a stir. People were very excited about the *Spectral Analysis* team being in Chicago. It certainly painted a romantic scene as Janine gazed so fondly at the doctor. The clip gave the impression that a very differently ending had occurred.

"It started popping up right after lunch. Our lawyer contacted the fellow to have him take it down." He glanced at her from under his eyelashes. "Look, I admit, I was a juvenile tonight. I was excited to make a little headway with you at our dinner, and then very disappointed when I saw that clip. You got the flowers, right? I actually imagined us sharing that bottle over a romantic conversation." Max raised his eyebrows, "And then that showed up and I can guess why you were unavailable. He outplayed me again, I assume." He studied her. "I completely understand, he did mention that you two can be very hot at times, very physical, so he must be hard for you to pass up. I get it."

"What are you talking about?"

Max glanced at her body again, focusing on her marked chest. *What was his obsession with the scars about?* "I'll be honest with you. I imagine that's a message that means your heart is off limits, and I can respect that, if that's what you want. But maybe you can give me a chance next time. I'm getting the message that you might be open to it. I know you two aren't exclusive. I mean, there's Lauren, and…"

"Ian talked about me? To you? What exactly did he say?"

"Not much. He was very complimentary, of course, and it was entirely my fault. I've always been curious about you, since that thing in Sacramento, and I probably pumped him for the information. You know how men talk when they've had a few." Max indicated himself as an example. "Maybe I filled in the blanks, after his wildcat comment. Don't worry,

Carlos stopped him from going too far with that punch in the eye, but, the conversation did reboot my curiosity. I'm very interested in getting to know you better."

Wow, so those guys had some type of sordid discussion about her. No wonder Max Colliers presumed she'd be open to his advances. At least now he was being up front about his motive. He gave her a nice smile and a little more room.

"I'm headed back to the hotel. I've got a board meeting at ten in the morning, so you probably won't see me again, until Texas. I'm jetting home tomorrow evening. I want you to know that I'm looking forward to our date in Austin. We still have a deal, right? You give me fair shot at impressing you, and I'll take a good look at the contract. I'll take it any way you want to play it."

Chapter 10
The Séance

Kiki

They secured room 441 in the Congress Plaza hotel for an early morning séance. The haunting in that room included a mystery woman who assaulted sleeping guests. Kiki invited five participants, because six was an optimum number for a séance table: Agatha, a maid who cleaned 441 regularly, an elderly couple named Walter and Emily Croager who once stayed in room 441, Lauren, and Doctor McNally. Kiki touched base with Lauren to see if she'd ever participated in a séance before, and other than teenaged fooling around, she hadn't. Lauren's aura burst with bright, happy energy. All that life force would surely attract curious spirits.

"I'm happy Max asked you to sit in for him," Kiki told her.

It wasn't the best set up for a séance. Kiki usually included a virile male for the energy they provided, and the doctor didn't count for her. She had actually been banking on Max Colliers to provide that small service. Kiki might need to tap the spectators for supplemental energy, or, she could only pretend to call on the spirits and bank on Janine to send the messages. Kiki needed to discuss it with Ian, why calling to spirits completely drained her of energy, but tuning into them did not.

Lauren, the old couple, and Agatha mingled near the refreshment table and Kiki glided toward them. She had changed into a flowing outfit with beautiful silk scarves and accented her outfit with jewelry laden with precious stones. Sally had made a stretch lace tie-up top with dangling coins that she wore under a sheer shirt. Compared to the *Spectral Analysis* suit, her gypsy attire came off more modest. Still sexy, but not blatantly so. Kiki preferred the more sensual profile the translucent material created. She always enjoyed a subtle feminine mystique when conducting a séance. At the moment, they waited for the second hour to draw nearer and the doctor meandered over. She retied the silk strip in her red hair.

"I sent Ben to the hotel to start processing the earlier tapes," he whispered to her. "We're going to be wiped out at the end of tonight and will want to see things fast. I'm not sure anyone got any shuteye earlier."

"We've tried the mirror trick before," Kiki said. "All we can do is cross our fingers. I'm interested to see what the audio picks up."

"You and me both." The doctor spotted Janine and a smile creased his lips, his eyes tracked her movement across the room.

How did Janine manage to capture Ian so completely with all that dark energy? Was it because her physical shape was copy of what Gwen's had been? Or, perhaps, it was because her aura mirrored the streams his mother often projected? Janine had an underlying array of pink below the murk, and Ian's mother had similar layers. Could he detect it? He always claimed he couldn't see an aura, but maybe he didn't realize that he could.

Ian interrupted her thoughts, "She seems quite recovered. Max didn't take her back to the Lincoln House after all."

Kiki patted his hand, she didn't dare tell him what they attempted in the limousine earlier. Ian knew her coven tricks and always frowned upon her using them. He chided her more than once about the sexist teaching in her pagan education. She walked toward Janine, who was standing by the snack table eating fruit. Janine looked up at her.

"I feel a tons better. I guess your method actually works. Although, I'm not sure I can do that on a regular basis, and it may have backfired on me. I can't believe you left me alone in the car with him after that." Janine banded her long hair into a loose pony tail as they stepped away from the group.

"I genuinely needed to pee, sorry," Kiki said, then scolded softly, "You know, you would feel ten times better if you would have channeled that energy properly. You should be buzzing, receptors on fire, tuning into everything on heightened alert. Max sends some extremely good vibes." Kiki mused. "You may need help on finding your core. You feel better because sexual energy accidentally leaks into the core. It always happens that way for women, mixing love and sex energy, but most of Max's efforts went straight into all the wrong places, Janine. Oh well, no worries, we'll work on it."

Janine appeared miffed, but Kiki didn't have time to worry about her hurt feelings. At the moment, she needed Janine to focus and pay attention. She was a smart girl with natural talents. If she could get past her passion energy, and over active analytical mind, she could be quite powerful in the spiritual realm.

"I need you to go around and rally the spirits in this building. Tempt them into coming to the séance. This is a very old hotel and may be haunted by more than just that woman in room 441. Remember, they will obey you if you direct your intentions properly. Open your heart and feel the words."

"I'm not sure I understand," Janine's face erupted into a smirky grin. "You want me to wander around the hotel and whole heartedly invite ghosts to come to the séance?"

After everything that happened that night, Kiki expected a more tempered response. She waited for the chuckling to end.

"Sorry, it just sounds a little comical, crazy to me. I guess I'm not as convinced that I'm speaking to ghosts."

"You speak to them. And it's no more crazy than glimpsing those faces in the mirrors, and you saw them," Kiki felt a little angry. "Why do you refuse to accept your own perceptions? You need to get out of your head for a little minute and get out of your skin too. Try to sense with your core, your heart, pretend if you have to. Pretend until you believe it."

"Can I just whisper to the ghosts, softly? Maybe even, not say anything out loud. It makes me feel a little conspicuous, speaking out loud to ghosts."

"Whatever you need to do, just do it, and then get to 441 right after," Kiki snapped. "And don't try to see anything, Janine, just transmit. I've got a theory that your energy drain is on the receiving end. And remember, whatever you say, or think, you should end it with: *as I command, so mote it be.* For instance, *you will come to the séance in 441, as I command, so mote it be.*"

Janine trudged off and took Mike the van driver with her. Janine didn't want to do it alone. Kiki turned to her séance guest and guided them to room 441.

They had rearranged the room earlier that day. A round table had been placed in the center of things, and salt lamps glowed in the corners. Kiki arranged a crystal grid on the table with a quartz ball dead center and six trails of colored minerals radiating out of it. Each radiating line led to a heavily cushioned chair. Most pieces in the grid were smooth, tumbled gemstones, but she included purple amethyst pyramids for protection.

Kiki placed Agatha, the maid, in the chair on her left and invited Walter Croager to sit in the one on her right. Lauren came next, on the left, and Walter's wife Emily sat next to him, on the right. The doctor took the spot directly across the table from her. A small white candle, a silver tray, a small square pad of paper, and an old fashioned fountain pen flanked each of the six mineral lines. After settling into their seats, Kiki dictated a series of breathing exercises to calm their nerves.

"At times during the ritual," Kiki touched each item in front of her, "I'm going to ask that you use the pen to write a word, just one word, on a little square of paper. It's called automatic writing. It's critical that you don't dwell on what you write, just do it, no matter what the word is. No matter how crude, grotesque, embarrassing, or if the word makes no sense at all. Those words won't be coming from you. Write them down immediately, when you hear the command *write*." Kiki reached for a long taper. "We're going to light our candles now. Mindfully, take three cleansing breaths before igniting your flame, then pass the taper to your left."

Kiki illuminated her candle and passed the taper to Agatha. As Agatha lit her candle, Janine slunk into the room and settled herself against the far wall directly behind the doctor. The taper soon made its way around the table and Kiki blew it out, then, she reached for the hands of both

Agatha and Mr. Croager. Everyone joined hands at that signal.

"*Hear us now.*" She used a voice to cross the veil. "*Speak to us, bring us light, in this dark night, and we will listen and heed your voice, your choice.*" Kiki stared at Janine, willing her to repeat the words. Janine dipped her head slightly in acknowledgement, but rolled her eyes.

"Hear us now, speak to us now, bring us light, in this dark night and we will listen, and heed your voice, make your choice." Kiki repeated those words over and over until the air had become heavy and thick.

A faint flutter descended on the room and a faint hint of lavender wafted in the air. Kiki hadn't detected that scent before. She felt a buzz of energy skirt the edge of the table.

"I feel a woman in this room," Kiki said aloud. "Are you the woman who haunts this place?" She paused to give Janine time repeat her questions. A faint haze descended on the table and Kiki felt a momentary pressure against her shoulder. Lauren visually fidgeted and she locked eyes with Kiki. Kiki tilted her head and focused on the crystal in the center of the table. "What do you desire to tell us?" A buzz hummed in her ear. The crystal began to shimmer. Kiki commanded, "Write."

She put the pen atop the stack of paper and allowed her hand to move freely, unaware of what she scribbled, ignoring her hand until the pen dropped. Kiki noticed the others writing. Janine's brown doe eyes bore directly into hers and Kiki shook her head slightly. She hoped Janine understood that she should not *tune in to the ghost, just transmit.* Kiki felt certain Janine's energy drain occurred when she tuned in. They were like opposite sides of a coin.

"We will each read aloud our words," Kiki told her séance participants. "And, after you've read your message, you shall burn it. Obliterate it in your candle flame and place the burning paper on the small silver tray. If you're feeling taxed, breathe deeply, to calm yourself. I'll read first. We'll go around the table in the same direction that we lit the candles. That will be how the message was given."

"Why do we need to burn them?" Lauren asked softly.

"To cleanse us of this communication," Kiki told her. "Burning the words will release us of this message and sever our link with this spirit. Automatic writing can cause an essence to feel powerful, like they can control you, because, for a brief moment, they controlled one little part of you. Don't be surprised if you don't recognize the handwriting."

Mrs. Croager glanced at her paper and gasped. Kiki locked eyes on the woman, and sent her a friendly smile.

"No worries, the crystal grid will contain her ambient energy. Only your hand is in that realm."

"Are you sure?" the old woman asked. Kiki nodded at her.

"Let's read our messages. *Intrusion.*" Kiki touched the corner of the paper to her candle flame before placing it on her silver tray to burn away.

"Privacy," Agatha mumbled and lit her note and placed it into her own tray.

"Silence," Lauren added softly, and burned her note.

"Annoying," the doctor said, and burned his note.

"Quiet," Emily Croager's shaky hand lit her post-it, then moved it to the tray.

"Uncomfortable," Walter Croager huffed before burning his note.

Their words hung in the air as they quietly waited. Kiki closed her eyes and used each word to create a mental picture, a picture that *somebody* wanted her to have. Random colors spun behind her eyes as the jigsaw snapped together. Kiki could feel her, an introverted woman, upset and unnerved.

"She feels annoyed with the guests here. This is her domain and people keep invading her peace. Living energy is too loud for her." Kiki stared at Janine. "We should assure this spirit that we'll be out of her space soon. We apologize for the intrusion."

Kiki retrieved the hands of Agatha and Walter, and instructed the circle to take three deep breaths to clear their cores. The density of air had gotten very thick and she focused on the movement of energy that circled the table. She could detect sparks of spectral energy along the crystal grid. Kiki wondered if anyone else could see it, but no one else seemed to notice. Several souls competed for their attention and she studied the central orb closely for signs of life.

"I feel others here, many others. I feel a young man lingering near. Please, tell us why you have come," Kiki said. The orb in the center of the table changed faintly. "Write."

Each person gripped their pens and scribbled. Starting with Kiki, they read their words out loud again.

"Music."

"Booze."

"Party."

"Smokes."

"Party."

"Crazy."

They each went through the ritual of burning their written words. This spirit felt confused and eager. Kiki felt spirits like this before, a whiff of life energy completely unaware that their life was gone. They always attempted to mingle with the living.

"He's looking for entertainment," Kiki said. "He came searching for a group of people having fun, but he's leaving. I feel another woman, a different woman. Look!" The orb in the center of the table glowed dimly. Someone in the circle let out a startled sound. "Quick, write." Kiki ordered. They wrote swiftly, then read them out.

"Forsaken."

"Terrified."

"Sorrow."

"Empty."

"Regret."

"Helpless."

This spirit had commanded the table easily, and felt powerful. It had purpose and a very dark center. But the spirit did not show Kiki any images, just confusing feelings. This particular spectral voice was eager to tell them something, while at the same time, it desired to stay hidden.

"She is very sad and may have done something regrettable. She's afraid of what she has done. Her actions came from a place of deep sorrow and feelings of… abandonment," Kiki whispered.

"What has she done?" Emily Croager's scratchy whisper hung in the air.

"She may have killed herself," Kiki said softly. "And someone else. A child, yes, her child. That's it, I think that's exactly it. She wants to take it back. She's desperate to take it back." Kiki stared at Janine and locked onto those glittering brown eyes. "A *dragoma* might counsel a spirit like this one, find words to ease her guilt. She yearns to find peace and needs solace. Sometimes, people act from terrible grief and regret rash actions that cannot be undone. This poor soul carries a burden past her own death and feels that she can never right it."

Maybe Janine would know what to say to that spirit. Commiserate on regrets. Janine once abandoned a newborn. Kiki knew that she had awful regrets about it, but she would never be able to make amends, because Sammy was gone. Janine shut her eyes on Kiki. Kiki glanced around the table.

"I think I feel her sorrow," Lauren whispered. Agatha and Emily nodded.

"You probably do," Kiki said.

"I also feel weary," Lauren said. "Exhausted."

"Me too," Agatha chimed in. Emily Croager nodded.

Kiki felt the quiver of energy intensify. There were several conflicting vibes bouncing inside the room, most were weak, but there was one focused point of energy hovering near the table edge and running along the lines of the crystal grid. It was an insistent voice demanding to speak through the void, a very impatient presence bearing down.

"We'll try one more," Kiki said. "But first, rearrange the stones in front of you. Take the nearest stone and trade it with the pyramid in your line. Place that pyramid at the end, closest to your seat."

She watched as they rearranged the stones. Kiki approved, and they all joined hands. She searched out Janine but did not think anyone needed to help this spirit. This spirit wanted to talk without encouragement, and that scared her a little.

"Okay, three cleansing breaths," Kiki began, but the orb was already glowing. "Write!" This was definitely an aggressive spirit, but their distraction had a moderating effect on its vitality, and the orb pulsed. The group seemed a little unnerved and Kiki saw why. Her hand had written in a distinctive spidery thin cursive.

"Ignored."

"Misunderstood."

"Disregard."

"Entitled."

"Respect."

"Bad."

Kiki nodded. "He's angry. He isn't held in the esteem he believes he's due and feels overlooked. He wishes violence on those who would dismiss him. Perhaps, he is a violent criminal."

"Al Capone?" Walter Croager asked timidly.

The table vibrated suddenly and Agatha almost jumped out of her chair. Both Lauren and Emily Croager pushed their seats away from the table. The tension in the room skyrocketed.

"No, no," Kiki slowly stood. "Not him, this spirit is someone else," *or something else?* "Someone who feels very important." *Someone who feels important to Kiki? Or to one of the others in the room?* The spirit felt animosity and it still had a message. The orb began to glow again. Kiki stared at it.

"Write," she said softly. Her pen began to move on that square paper, deliberately and forcefully guiding her hand.

"Curse."

"Souls."

"Irene."

"Vengeance."

"Control."

"Nothing."

"I feel an overwhelming dread," Emily Croager squeaked suddenly. The age lines around her eyes were etched deeper. "My hand is weak."

Kiki locked eyes with Janine. "We ask this spirit to leave at once. To be gone! Make sure you mean it. Tell it to be gone! We ask all the spirits to leave. Please go." Kiki reached out to grip Agatha's hand to calm her. "We are going to block ourselves from any lingering souls. Snuff out your candle, then touch the tip of the small pyramid with your index finger. Breathe, and try to connect within yourself. Close your eyes if needed and stay quiet. Stay connected to that pyramid. Keep your connection until you've completely calmed your heart."

Kiki shut her eyes and retreated inside herself. She listened to the spectral sounds echoing as they faded away. So many voices wanted to speak. On her earlier survey, she had no clue the old building contained so many restless souls. After a moment, she asked Carlos to activate the lights.

"Oh my goodness, I can't believe that happened, ghosts were in here." Emily Croager clutched her husband's arm. "They touched me."

All the participants buzzed as they recovered. The doctor held Lauren's hand, and he had moved closer to reassure her. Janine walked around the table to Kiki. She appeared in fairly good shape.

"Good job, Janine," Kiki told her. "This room was jam packed with energy. I couldn't tell how many life forces were here, but more than I could count. Whatever you communicated in the halls worked." Kiki shook her hand, "What exactly did you say? It might be worth writing it down for future use. You can begin your own grimoire. We need to get you a diary, soon, so you can chronicle your charms."

Janine rolled her eyes. "I had a hard time thinking séance, so I projected party. I projected that there was a party in room 441 and everyone should come. It just seemed easier, and I felt less silly."

Kiki stared at her, then laughed. Okay, probably not a spell for a true grimoire. *That explained the party ghost.* Who would have guessed, even spirits have a hard time resisting a good shindig. Yet, that last spirit confused her. It was a strong, angry energy that felt slightly familiar. It easily controlled her hand, and those extra words didn't spark anything but dark shadows in her mind.

Chapter 11
Debrief

Janine

There was an hour left till dawn when they returned to the Lincoln House ballroom. Janine and Carlos helped unload the van, then changed into their normal clothes. Carlos vigorously combed his hair down, no longer an anime knock-off. He had been a good sport about it, so Max couldn't say Carlos was inflexible after all that. Four nice varieties of alcohol waited on the refreshment table and Janine wasn't shy about pouring a generous helping of the Macallan bottle. Kiki came around and handed her a slip of paper.

"Max left you a note," she whispered. Janine opened it, skimmed it quickly, then crumbled the paper and tossed it into the small garbage bin next to the refreshment table. Kiki gave her a questioning look.

"He can't stop thinking about the limousine ride and hopes to meet for an early breakfast before he's in meetings and I'm asleep all day. He suggests breakfast in my room in about," Janine glanced at her watch, "an hour. I think that energy boost you suggested is coming back to haunt me."

Kiki chuckled, "You weren't ready to try that yet, sorry."

"I'll just hide in your room again," Janine said irritably.

"Fine," Kiki said. "I'm going to check if there's anything worth waiting for."

Janine didn't know how long Kiki wanted to stay, but hoped she would be quick. Between the long day and the chattering Lauren, Janine itched to disappear as soon as possible. It wasn't like the old days. They weren't actually putting anything together in the debrief. That would happen back in Texas now. Janine caught up with Carlos in the back of the room. They lounged in the nice leather chairs clinking their glasses of whisky. Janine ferried the expensive bottle over, so they were set for a nice draw down to their long night. Up near Ben and his console of electronics, Kiki and Ian kept nodding at a very animated Lauren.

Stop judging her, Janine admonished herself. She just participated in an exciting paranormal event that will soon be on television. And, who wouldn't flirt with handsome doctor McNally given the chance? *Plus, they were a thing, right?* Yet, the way Lauren kept touching Ian's arm and flashing her mega-smile irked her. She just wished Lauren would stop lighting up the room in her upbeat, peppy way and act like a normal person. *Jealous much?*

"Lauren worked out well in the séance, don't you think?" Carlos noticed who she was staring at. "Don says she's very photogenic. Comes off nice on camera. Doesn't have a bad angle."

"Do you think she could be my replacement?" Janine asked.

"Oh no, she could never replace you." Carlos smirked. "You are the least photogenic person I know. We would have to mess up her hair and wipe off that perfect lipstick, and maybe teach her a little sarcasm and slouchy posture."

"Jerk." Janine kicked at Carlos. "At least I'm not a cartoon."

Carlos chuckled and poured them more whisky.

"I don't have slouchy posture. So, was Lauren there when you punched Ian in the eye, in San Antonio?" Janine asked.

"Oh, no. Most everyone took off by then," Carlos shook his head. "It was just the guys, and Kiki. It was nothing important, just guy stuff."

"You mean like— just you and Ian and Max? Or, was Don there too?"

"Well, Don and Ben. I think that was it. It was nothing," Carlos said. "What put that in your head?"

So then, Ian McNally boasted to all the men she worked with that she was a wildcat, or something, in bed. No wonder Don leered at her and Ben acted so shy, and Max believed she would be interested in getting together in hotel rooms.

"Just something Max said earlier," Janine told him.

Kiki and Lauen appeared next to them. Ben did not have anything for them to see on film, but did confirm that the pattern on the alley's subsonic recordings matched the sound signature of their names. It felt like years since they were in that alley. Kiki grabbed her hand and pulled her up.

"Come on, lets walk up together. Lauren is going to get my color back before bed," Kiki told her. "We can have a girls only debrief in my room."

Wow, Lauren offered to correct Kiki's hair before going to sleep. Not just totally adorable, but over the top nice too. Nice, pretty, positive, shiny and bright as a new penny. Definitely an upgraded replacement for quiet, morose, messy, marked up Janine. Lauren likely lacked all the complicated relationship issues too.

"Sure thing," Janine snatched the bottle of whisky to bring along.

Kiki prattled on about the séance while Lauren used a special cleanser to wash the temporary red from her hair. Kiki complimented Lauren on her ability to open up during the séance. She showed a natural ability to use her *core* to channel psychic energy. Kiki flashed her emerald eyes toward Janine when she said that. Janine lounged on the bed, glaring, not adding much to the conversation. Kiki winked at her, then grew serious and asked Lauren about the last word she had written.

"What was it," Kiki's brow creased. "Was it a name or a word?"

"I think it was a name, Irene." Lauren said.

"Odd," Kiki said. "A name."

After Kiki's rinse out was complete, the three of them had a celebratory shot to conclude the night's success. As Lauren made her way to the door, she glanced back at Janine.

"Are you sleeping in here again?" she asked Janine.

"We still have a few things to go over," Kiki told her. After Lauren left, Kiki refilled their tumblers. "We probably shouldn't, but why not. I can see you're pretty far gone already, so what will one more hurt? Self-medicating again, I see." Then, she turned and peered deeply into Janine's eyes. "Shall we talk about the park? Do you need to talk?"

"No, I'm too tired and intoxicated." Janine shied away from Kiki's penetrating gaze. She definitely did not want to talk about the park. She pointed to the door instead. "You realize that girl is putting two and two together and coming up with five."

"She probably is," Kiki chuckled, then purred. "It'll just add to our mystique. Let's not worry about it and get some sleep. By the way, your detective messaged me when we were out tonight. I have an early dinner date with him tomorrow. What do you think about that?" Kiki beamed at her.

Very hot. Physical. Wildcat. Carlos had to punch him before he said more. So, what did he say before that punch? What exactly did Ian McNally say about her? Never in her wildest imagination would she believe that Ian McNally would speak ignominiously about her to Carlos, or Max, or to two guys she hadn't even met yet. Janine lay in bed, still very drunk, and growing angry that Ian would betray her so casually. She was terribly tired, but she couldn't sleep. Kiki had no problems and snored softly beside her.

Janine thought about that voice in the park. Did she really hear a little girl's voice say, *I love you, girl?* She was half afraid Ben would have visual playback of the park, that Don's camera had picked up the faces in the mirrors and that one of those faces would be Sammy's, calling from the other side. *Crap!* She could not let those thoughts spin out of control. She should go back to the anger instead. *Grab onto the anger!* Just what did Ian say to those fellows? Did he get super explicit? Is that why Carlos hit him?

A thin layer of whisky lined the bottom of the bottle and Janine eased out of the bed to reach it. It always helped on a sleepless night and it stopped the dreams when she did sleep. She was afraid of those dreams. Why were so many restless ghosts children? It was heartbreaking. Was Sammy's ghost out there somewhere, restless and lost, abandoned? *No, no, no, focus!* Janine told herself. *Don't think about that.* Focus on that dammed asshole, Ian McNally, running off his mouth and getting Don, and Max, and probably even Ben, to objectify her before she even showed up to meet them. They were all probably passing around the stories and *imagining things.* She was not going to wear that *Spectral Analysis* outfit again. Perhaps she should go across the hall and tell Ian off. She should pound on his door and just do it, get it off her chest, and then she'd be able to sleep. But what if Lauren was in there with him? *Even better.* Maybe he needed a dose of his own medicine. She could gossip about him for a change. She could out him good with some uncensored talk. She would tell Lauren that Ian was so… so incredibly tender, sweet, and unbelievably satisfying? So irresistible? *Crap!* No, she would think of something else. Like, he was a blinking idiot. *Ha ha, that's it.* That's exactly what she'd say, that was funny. She drained the last of the Macallan whisky.

Janine searched around, then remembered her clothes were sent to the laundry, all except the thin T-shirt Kiki lent her and the panties she wore. Her jeans and shirt would be cleaned and delivered back by noon, before she planned to wake up. She needed it done, because she only brought the one small backpack, with one change of pants, two shirts, and extra undergarments. She barely packed anything because she didn't really want to be there. The extras must be down the hall in her own room, cleaned the previous night and returned. *Crap again!* Wait! There were perfectly luxurious hotel robes in the closet. Janine snagged a plush robe and wrapped it around herself, then, she quietly snuck out the door and went directly across the hall.

She stumbled over and knocked hard. She immediately regretted it. The bright hallway was unforgiving, and she suddenly didn't want to see Ian, or especially Lauren, on the other side of that door. She turned back and realized that she didn't bring the key, any key. Not to her room, or to Kiki's. She would have to wake Kiki up. *Crap,* Janine thought. She'd rather sleep in the hall than wake Kiki up.

Then, Ian McNally's door opened and he stood there staring at her, bleary eyed. He wore pajama bottoms, but his top was bare. Janine's eyes drank in the muscles of his chest and stomach. The sight of his muscular hairy torso felt more intoxicating than the whisky. Her eyes drifted to the base of his throat and over his broad shoulders. Clearly, he'd been working out in the past year. *No, he had always looked that good. Good lord, was she actually salivating?* She swallowed.

"What are you doing out here?" He searched up and down the hall. He reached out, grabbed her wrist, and pulled her into the room. "Come in here."

They stood just inside his room, but he didn't close the door all the way. He took a step away and stared at her in a confused manner.

"Why are you wandering around in a bathrobe? Are you drunk?" he asked. "You are. Are you alright? Shall I walk you to your door? Or, are you staying in Kiki's room again?"

"I'm locked out," she muttered. "I didn't bring a key. Kiki's sound asleep."

"Where were you going?"

"Here," she confessed. Then, she reminded herself of why she was there. She tried to call up the anger, but it wasn't quite catching. She peered deeper into his room to see if anyone was in there. She lowered her voice, "So, is she in here? Do you have someone back there?"

"No, no one is here." He shut the door completely. "Do you need to talk about something? Something bothering you?" His voice became very soft and his eyes were so tender, she felt like she was melting in them. Was he doing that on purpose? "I heard who you called out to, in the trees," he whispered.

"Oh, no, I don't want to talk about that." Now that she knew no one was there, she went all the way in. Right to the bottle she knew would be on his night table. She needed a touch more to help fire up her nerves and squash that voice from the trees. "I want to talk about you, and why Carlos had to punch you in the eye." *Yes. Yes, think about how he called you a wildcat, providing him with hot sex that he must have described to tons of random guys, probably hundreds.* "I heard that you were talking about me. That you were having a nice time giving out explicit details of—of our past. Putting ideas into people's heads. To all the fellows, Max, Ben, Don, anyone I left out?"

"Crikes, you're completely drunk." His eyes were blinking up a storm. "Maybe we should talk about this another time."

Janine laughed. "Fancy that. Did I disturb your sleep? I'm so sorry. Why isn't your girlfriend here disturbing your sleep? Is she not wild enough for you? Do you talk about her with the guys as well, or is it only me you discussed? Are you going to deny it?"

"Crikes, Janine. I, I'm sorry. You, you have every right to be angry. Did somebody s-say something to you?"

My goodness, was he stuttering, Janine thought. It was not right of him, to look so sorry and sad when she wanted to be angry at him. He was in the wrong here! She stared at him, fully aware that she was very, very drunk and wobbly. She saw that he was getting his blinking back under control, but he still wore a flush of shame. *My goodness*, the thought struck her, *his eyes were absolutely beautiful.* Blue and surrounded by thick lashes and his curly black beard was so dark and crying out to be touched. And his hair was all mushed up from sleeping. He crossed his arms in front of his chest like he was protecting himself from her. *From her!*

He shook his head. "I, I was a complete arse that night, I won't deny it. Totally drunk, and an idiot, waiting to see you. I was disappointed. I, I felt like you were personally ignoring me by avoiding that dinner. Snubbing me. I just wanted to hurt you back, lass. I'm sorry."

She wanted him to look at her. Not with those eyes he wore at moment, all sad and sorry, but with the eyes he wore on the street, full of desire. Like he couldn't wait to draw her in and make love to her. If he could talk about her like that, then he should look at her like that, shouldn't he? Maybe a little flesh would change his attitude. Let the outfit do the flirting, as Kiki advised. Janine untied the Lincoln House hotel robe and let it fall to the ground. She knew she was practically naked in front of him. *Crap*! She was pretty far drunk and in the back of her head some part of her did not agree with her actions here. Well, fuck that part of her! She needed to feel Ian's male sexual energy and channel it into her core properly. As his eyes changed to the smoky ones she desired, she stepped toward him.

Then, she had him like she had fantasized, running her fingers through his dark beard as she kissed him. It was overwhelming and so, so satisfying. That electric charge was still very much alive everywhere they touched. His taunt muscles felt so nice. They sunk onto the bed as his large hands left a hot trail all over her. He was just as eager, until… he suddenly stopped. Ian pushed her away. He was moving further away from her and holding her at arms' length. She couldn't believe he had stopped kissing her. She was infuriated. What was this? Her entire body burned for him and he was pushing her away.

"We can't do this," he gasped. He stood up from the bed, and stepped away. "You're totally drunk. You're upset. We can't do this. I know what you're upset about and I don't want you this way."

"What do you mean?" *Was he kidding?* He could talk about having sex with her to everyone she worked with, but he couldn't do it when she needed it? "What are you talking about? You don't want me?" Janine stood up and she slapped him, hard. Ian just took it, and she was instantly ashamed of herself. She reached over to grab his bottle of whisky.

"Why are you drinking so much?" He took the bottle away from her.

"Give that back! It helps me sleep," she added softly. "It helps me forget." And then she burst into tears. Cold, dark, desolate tears.

Ian instantly engulfed her in a tight embrace. He held her close, taking in her grief. He didn't let her push him away. He radiated a comforting sphere all around her. He was whispering things she couldn't understand in his thick Scottish accent and it sounded so sweet.

She'd never forget, she knew, but at night, it was always worse. Her dreams gave her hope that things could be changed, that events could be undone.

If she wished hard enough, then Sammy would return. She'd emerge from a hiding place, giggling that everyone thought she washed away in the river, how silly- *and that oppressive weight would blissfully be gone.*

Sometimes, Rick was still the man she first met and she had been mistaken about things. His kisses were filled with love, *love, love,* and he, and her, and that little girl were a happy family- *relief would flood her chest.*

Or, she made a silly blunder believing such a horrible thing happened. There were no knife wounds to hide, no scars, and her body was nice again, smooth, normal. She had never been a victim, or stupid, or powerless. She was whole- *the pressure in her head would ease.*

In some dreams, Sammy turned out to be Ian's daughter, how lucky was that? *A sliver of hope would dribble in.*

Happy images invaded her sleep, giving her peace, such peace…but then, she'd wake, and fully realize her folly, and gravity would yank her back down, *down, down*…and she'd have to face her harsh reality all over again.

Ian put her in his bed and covered her with his sheets and blanket. He brought back something and made her drink it, all of it. It was some sort of sports drink. He sat on the edge of the bed and stroked her head like she was a baby. It was already very cold being out of his embrace. Did he notice that she had slapped him really hard a moment ago?

"Go to sleep, lass." He didn't look upset at her. "You'll be better after you sleep it off."

Janine sat up. She was past the sobbing wreck phase of her tantrum. It had cleared her head a little.

"No. I'm not going to kick you out of your bed," she said. "Hand me my robe. I'll go back to Kiki's, or to my own room, you need to sleep too."

He pushed her gently back down and tucked the sheets in firmly, all around her, like a mummy.

"You're going to stay right here, where I can keep an eye on you," he ordered. "No arguments about that." He climbed over her, onto the bed, and lay on top of the covers next to her. "You see, I'll sleep right here." He lay very close to her and draped his arm across her body. He whispered into her ear, "I do want you, lass. I want you right here." And that's how she was finally able to fall asleep.

Thick blackout curtains kept the room dark and everything seemed turned around. Then, she remembered. She had been totally drunk and went into Ian's room. She sat up and looked around. The room was quiet and deserted. The hotel clock blinked the time, four forty-three in the afternoon. She had slept soundly for eight hours, a world's record. She actually felt very good. She spotted a note at the foot of the bed next to a small folded pile of her clothes, a room key, and an extra toothbrush. She picked up the note. It was written in Ian's blocky square letters, which happened to match the blocky L and H on the hotel stationary paper.

The hotel sent up an extra key, so I fetched some things from your room. There's water by the bed. Crew dinner at six upstairs. We get started at seven thirty. Hope you feel better. Ian.

Janine slipped her jeans and shirt on to make the short trip down the hall to her own room. She needed to shower and get ready. She was embarrassed. She wanted to skip the dinner, but somehow, she felt like Ian would be insulted if she skipped it. She made it to her room without bumping into anyone, but then she saw what Ian must have seen when he came to get her things.

Now there were two vases of flowers, violets and roses, *very lovely*, another bottle of wine, and a small bowl of strawberries. She spotted another handwritten written note and picked it up.

Thinking of our kiss and that ride in the limo. Sorry I missed you this morning, Max.

Ugh! Fine. Good. There were worse things in life than having a handsome, wealthy man shower her with flowers and attention, but she couldn't think of one just then. She decided to get cleaned up fast and run upstairs for the dinner. She didn't want anyone to think she was ignoring them.

Most of the *Spectral Analysis* staff sat outside on the terrace overlooking the Chicago River. Janine glanced around and spotted everyone except Kiki. Ian lounged at a table with Ben, Carlos, and Lauren. *Why did that woman have to be so pretty and perfect?* Max was there and brightened up when he saw her. He wore a very nice designer suit and tie. Janine wore a faded old *Spectral Analysis* T-shirt and jeans.

"Hello there, we meet again," he said.

"Are you coming from one of your board meetings?" she asked.

"No, I'm about to catch my flight," he said. "Sorry to say, I've got a few fires to put out back home and you guys will be on your own for the rest of this outing. I think the doctor prefers it that way. If last night is any indication of what goes on during the shoots, then I think we're going to have a successful episode."

"And, you got a good look at Carlos in a different light, right? It's easier to imagine him teaming up with someone new. A more glamourous girl, maybe, like Lauren, even."

A tiny flicker of caution passed through Max's eye as he smiled at her.

"Why don't we save that conversation for our date in Austin? I've got a few things to nail down first, but I think you'll be happy with the outcome. I have a feeling you'll find it a celebratory date." He lowered his voice. "I missed you this morning, for our early breakfast," he smiled at her.

Janine glanced away, embarrassed.

"You're just more alluring than ever. I enjoy that, believe it or not, a challenge," he smiled. "Part of the fun is in the chase."

She didn't answer him. Other people came around, and the conversation turned to other things. Max Colliers was in high demand. Most everyone wanted to curry his favor.

Janine grabbed salad and bread from the buffet, then settled at an empty table. It didn't stay empty for long. Soon, Ben and Carlos and the doctor plopped down next to her. The doctor gave her an amused smile that she definitely deserved.

"Guess what," Carlos said. "We found images in the mirrors. On the IR clips anyway, not on the regular camera."

"There appear to be thermal images on Carlos's camera," Ben chimed in. His big bright eyes beamed at her.

"Ben fine-tuned the infrared clips and found patterns captured in the mirrors. They appear very face like," the doctor patted Ben on the back. "But there was nothing on the audio, just crackling noises under the voice tape of you and Kiki."

"Are they recognizable faces?" Janine asked. "Do they look like anyone?"

Ben and Carlos shook their heads.

"Did you do your subsonic trick?" Janine asked Ben. "For the audio in the park?"

"Not yet," Ben said. "The camera doesn't pick it up well. I'll have to analyze the audio recorder you attached to that tree when we recover it." Ben saluted and said he needed to run downstairs to make sure everything was loaded into the van correctly. Carlos took another trip to the buffet.

"You look remarkably recovered," Ian said when they were alone.

"I'm sorry about… " Janine briefly met his eye, then glanced to where Lauren sat spying on them from a corner table. She wondered if Lauren knew what Janine had done that morning, if Ian told her. "Did I make a total fool out of myself?"

Ian shook his head slowly. "You were very charming, no worries. I'm just glad to see you looking yourself again. Before I head downstairs, I want to apologize for the jackass things I said behind your back in San Antonio, and for any problems it's caused you. I'm very sorry," he said. "See you downstairs."

Kiki perched in the makeup chair chatting to Guy. Apparently, Kiki was going goth for the graveyard shoot. Her eyes were outlined with thick, dark, smoky liner which always made the green pop, and she paired it with jet black lipstick, and Lauren had succeeded in getting her dark brown hair back. Janine sat on a stool to watch. Carlos came around and sat next to them. He gave Janine an interesting look. His brow was furrowed and, for once, he was not smiling.

"Don't worry, we're not going goth," Carlos said. "I got a look at tonight's outfits and we're basically going to be dressed as Kiki's biker back-up squad. Why isn't the doctor being dressed up like this? I never thought I'd say it, but, I want to wear a rainbow tie and button down shirt like the doc."

Guy smiled at his remarks, "I'm still supposed to blacken your eyes. Doctor McNally doesn't like anything that isn't casual conservative and he won't wear makeup. Sally's been buying him nice shirts, though. His rainbow ties match everything, and I love the statement they make."

Very nice shirts, Janine silently agreed. Kiki gave her a small manila envelope. A silver chain snaked out of it followed by a pendant of a *patron saint?* She didn't recognize the saint. *Saint Comba* appeared to be a naked woman, *very Lady Godiva-ish*, with an animal at her side. There was something odd about that darkened silver metal, it repulsed her. Very ornate and old, it felt cold and heavy, an unwelcome weight in her hand. Was it lead? No, it wasn't soft. Janine poured it back into the envelope and returned it to Kiki.

"That guy," Kiki told her, "from last night, the haunted one. When I was running out to dinner, he was standing out on the steps. Poor dear, he looked confused, like he didn't know what he wanted to do. He begged me to give that to you."

Janine remembered the haunted one. He had been very creepy. "I don't want it."

"Are you sure?" Kiki took the envelope and flipped it over. "That's his name and number. I'm going to meet him tomorrow and ask about his ghost. He's eager to get things off his chest. That woman is Saint Comba, on the pendant, you know. My auntie had a similar charm, maybe even, exactly like it, and she wore it on a special occasion. I often wonder where it went. Saint Comba was a witch and a Christian saint, Janine. Some insist that she's the patron saint of witches. She's important to my coven. Isn't it strange that he said a ghost wanted you to have it? Do you mind if I wear it tonight? I feel streams of interesting energy seeping out of it."

"Go ahead," Janine told her. "It's all yours."

"I'm not going keep it," Kiki said. "I'm going to hold onto it for you."

Janine decided to check out the garment rack and see why Carlos was so upset. Carlos followed on her heels. His garment bag already lay open and his outfit spilled across the table; black leather chaps and a silky see-through netted shirt. Over the top, he'd wear the bat belt. *Good grief, that was quite a getup*, she thought.

"And look, silver metal wrist bands like I'm some sort of slave, or something, and is this a metal collar?" Carlos laughed without humor. "The doctor doesn't care what we wear, but said there was an agreement that Colliers called the shots for design changes, like our onscreen images, which includes costumes and such."

They unzipped the garment bag for Janine as Sally wandered in. Sally smiled, excited to see them examining her creations.

"Want me to help you get suited up?" Sally asked. She pulled out the female version of the sexy biker gang outfit and it was quite a sight. Leather chaps again, but where were the pants for underneath? All Janine could see was a very small leather bikini bottom. Then, the top, leather again, with a lace up back. Or was it the front? They couldn't be serious about that outfit.

"It's the front," Sally said. "Very tricky to hide everything, but I'll show you how to lace it up so nothing important gets exposed. Mr. Colliers designed this costume for the graveyard scene, he's actually a very good artist. He said you guys might go for it after last night." She smiled proudly. "Of course, there's a toned down version I can pull out, but this is the ensemble he hoped you'd choose tonight. So, how about it, feeling brave?"

"I'm not going to ask what type of film you made costumes for before this show," Carlos said.

Sally didn't seem to understand his comment, then Kiki appeared. Her eyes popped open at the leather outfits and she let out a startled laugh. She gave Janine an amused eye. Was Kiki daring her to wear it? Janine spun to Sally.

"Can we have the room to ourselves for a minute? I'll call you, if I need help."

Sally shrugged and walked off with a frown. Kiki raise her eyebrow and caressed the skimpy leather top.

"If you're not going to wear this," Kiki said, "I think I'll give it a try. It looks like one size fits all. It's much better than the top I had planned. My goodness, this is absolutely wicked. I'll want those chaps in the future as well." Kiki laughed, apparently happy there was someone dreaming up crazier outfits than her. "Max is going to get us a more risky rating, and maybe a later time slot as well."

"Tell me we're not going to wear this stuff, am I right?" Carlos appeared relieved. "I gotta say, last night was incredibly awkward, I only did it for you, Janine, but this leather stuff is not okay. Maria would not understand this. Maybe we should just wear those stretch shirts from yesterday, they weren't too bad, just a little form fitting."

"Look, Carlos," Janine started, "Max Colliers is having trouble finding a replacement, for when I leave. The only reason I wanted to dress up was, well, because he wanted to see you in a new light, to better match you with a new partner. Otherwise, he's thinking of replacing both of us at the same time."

"You mean, like firing me?" His eyes widened.

Janine nodded, "But he said something just now, upstairs, that made me think he's seen what he needs to see, and you'll be okay. But, for tonight, I'll be frank with you, I can't wear this either. I don't want to wear any of it anymore. I'm thinking, this T-shirt and jeans for tonight, it's the type of uniform I signed up to wear. I never agreed to wear this type of stuff." Janine pointed to the leather chaps.

Kiki shook her head. "That arse! I was wondering what got into you. You should have come to us with this right away."

"What good would that have done?" Janine said. "He was pretty convincing."

"We've got a package contract, Janine," Kiki nodded her head. "Ian insisted on it. None of us are officially signed, until you sign. We've been waiting for you, you're the final signature on the block. If you don't sign the contract, then they have to draft a whole new document with whoever the new person is going to be." Kiki patted Carlos on the shoulder, "We could all jump ship on Max if he tried to pull something like that. He would shite his pants."

"You would do that for me?" Carlos asked.

"Of course, sweetie," Kiki said.

"Are you sure about that, Kiki?" Janine asked.

"Absolutely."

If she wanted, she could check with the doctor, or better yet, give Mike Dunn, the original show's lawyer, a call. But Kiki knew, beyond a doubt, that if Janine did not sign the contract soon, and they wanted to include someone new, then everyone would have to sign again.

"He cannot spontaneously drop Carlos," Kiki said. "Seriously, Janine, Max threatened all those things to either convince you to dress in his outrageous outfits, or to get you into bed. That's how he operates, and he's clever at getting his way. Carlos is a big part of this show and we could not do without him. Max knows that."

"Thank you, Kiki," Carlos hugged her. Kiki pushed him away and took the scandalous black leather lace-up body shirt off Janine's rack. "Very soft lamb's leather, very witchy. So, I guess you won't be needing this sultry thing." She winked at them before running off to change.

"She's in a fantastic mood," Carlos watched Kiki skip away. "Someone at dinner said she had a hot date. Only Kiki Mellow can reel in a fish on such short notice in Chicago. Who do you think it was? Another athlete? Maybe she had a connection through the last guy. I wonder, how she juggles her suiters so smoothly without them killing each other? My brother Lonzo has a terrible crush on Kiki, he begged me to set them up, but I am not going to let that happen. She would eat him alive."

"If we're going to go grunge tonight," Janine interrupted, "we should probably bring an extra shirt for Don. They already took off and I bet he's dressed in something like this. You have an extra *Spectral Analysis* tee, right?"

Carlos laughed, "But Don loves dressing sexy. Sometimes, I wonder if Sally and Don came off the same show before this one."

They were scheduled to hit the Graceland Cemetery first, then head over to Lincoln Park during the wee hours of the morning. If things flowed smoothly, they'd rap up filming on location before dawn. Then, they'd gather the remote equipment the next day and fly back to Texas the next evening, just in time for the birthday bash Kiki planned.

The doctor, Ben, and Don drove ahead in the van, while Janine and Carlos would follow after Kiki was ready. Max left the limousine for them. Sally was visibly upset that they did not wear any of her designs. She sat on the other side of the room, next to Lauren, pressing her lips together and feigned reading a magazine. She snapped the pages audibly. Janine turned away from them and pulled her hair into her standard pony tail. The only new items they allowed was the dark eye makeup and the bat belts over their jeans.

"Well," Carlos lounged in the limousine, "this is more like it. So, Kiki, are you going to tell us who your date was with? Was he perhaps a Bull, or a Bear?"

Kiki smiled demurely at him. Her hooded cape draped all the way down to the bottom of her black boots. The boots stretched all the way up to her knees and she wore a dagger strapped on her thigh. Janine wondered if Kiki also wore that silver ornament with the witches' saint. As if in answer, Kiki opened her cloak a fraction and fingered the silver accessory. It dangled between plump breasts which were scarcely contained under that laced up leather shirt. *Oh my goodness*, Janine thought, is *she's trying to recharge her receptive batteries using Carlos?*

"You are so astute, Carlos, how did you know?" Kiki gazed at him in wonder, shifting suggestively so that most of one leg escaped from the cloak. She used her sultry voice on him. "He's a definite bull, very strong, very powerful, and very virile. In Celtic beliefs, the bull is the symbol of fertility. Don't laugh at me, but I think it's a sign, the heavens throwing a powerful bull at me, less than a year before my twenty-eighth birthday, when I need to start making good use of my eggs. I need a virile male, don't you agree, for that activity? Next spring, as the delicate blooms bud, I'll be free to enjoy all the fruits of the Beltane festival for once in my life. That's a fertility festival, you know. Yes, that date of mine was a definite bull."

Carlos glanced at Janine, and she could tell he was a little flustered. "What are we talking about here? When I said bull, I was asking if he was one of the Chicago Bulls?"

"He's definitely a Chicago *bull*," Kiki purred. Then, her entire demeanor changed and she smirked at Janine. "But even better than that, he's got the prettiest aura, head aura mind you, that I have ever seen. I have never been in the presence of a man so, so in touch with his entire triquetra, his body, soul, and spirit in perfect harmony. You know, we often use the word spirit incorrectly on our show. We use it referring to a ghost. What we should really say is soul, because that's the essence of a person." Kiki's green gems glowed out of the dark black eye powder. "I have never met such a soul, Janine. If you believe in soulmates, then you could probably bet that I met mine. Detective Robert Anderson is my idea male. Our cores connect, and I'm convinced he can see my aura."

Carlos and Janine exchanged glances. They both tried not to laugh, because Kiki came off very seriously. This was something new, Kiki never gushed about anyone she dated before, and Kiki had gone on dates with very attractive, eligible men.

"Is Kiki telling us she's in love?" Carlos asked. "With a detective? Have I seen him? Was it the big guy at the park last night? He was very interested in speaking with you, Kiki, but I didn't think he had the guts to do it. I have to tell you, he did not, exactly, come off as a brain. But he did look a little like a bull. Did you see him, Janine? He was a giant, I'll give you that."

"No, no, not that bloke," Kiki giggled. "Janine already knows the detective. He is much more powerful than that fellow in the park. Imagine a cosmic burst of solar energy. Like, an extreme coronal mass ejection that creates an aurora so spectacular it lights up the entire northern hemisphere."

Now they were all laughing and Kiki held up her hand.

"Okay, okay, that may be a wee bit of exaggeration," she grinned playfully. "Let's just say, I adore Bob Anderson."

On the corner of Clark and Irving Park was Graceland, a classic example of a decorative garden cemetery. Their main goal in the graveyard was to film clips in front of varied tombstones and monuments. They wanted to use the footage as a backdrop for Kiki's voice overs. Many of the *Alley of Death* victims happened to be buried in that patch of land. Markers from Lincoln Park had also been transplanted to Graceland, though, it was rumored that many of the remains had been left behind.

"If you're so gaga about Detective Anderson, why didn't you recharge your receptors off him instead?" Janine whispered as they walked toward the *Spectral Analysis* van. The van sat in front of the Getty Tomb, an ugly box-like mausoleum with an ornate iron door. "You shouldn't use Carlos like that."

"It's because you misdirect the energy, Janine. Man is of the sun and woman of the earth, even Plato knew that.

We'd wither without the constant radiant energy men shower on us, and, admit it or not, Carlos is a very red blooded, masculine man. He directs his energy at every girl he sees, and does it in a very nice way, all of the time. What do you imagine his humor is covering up? He tries to disguise it, so he doesn't offend, but believe me, his wiseass comments are a projection of admiration. I use his energy often, but I never do anything naughty with it. His energy never touches my passion zone." Kiki rolled her eyes. "And, if I ever did return some of that energy, Carlos would never, ever, stray from Maria, not for me or anyone else. He isn't molded that way."

"I feel like you just threw feminism right into the trash can somewhere in that speech," Janine huffed. "I'm just saying, couldn't you have reset your batteries on your date, instead of on our friend?"

"Well, Janine, I was like you were last night. I had problems redirecting Bob's energy to my core. It took me by surprise, and frankly, I didn't want to redirect it, he is so genuine. Gosh, if that's what happens to you all the time, no wonder you need to hide in my room." Kiki patted her hand, then went over to meet the doctor at the van to discuss the shoot.

Don emerged from the van as they approached. He took one look at Janine and Carlos, stamped his foot and cursed. Carlos shook as a slow rumble of laughter rolled from his chest. Don wore the chaps. He wore the sheer, tight, muscle shirt. He wore the metal collar and clumpy wrist bands. His eyes were dark colored cavities of blackness.

"This is not happening," Don spat out. "Why aren't you two in costume?"

Carlos pressed his lips together. "I didn't think I could pull off that outfit the way you do." Carlos grabbed Janine and pulled her aside. "Don, I have to hold this girl back, you're so sexy! Maybe you should cut her a break and change into something more toned down." Carlos laughed at his own antics. He let go of Janine and pulled out a first generation *Spectral Analysis* T-shirt from his backpack. It was a basic black cotton shirt with the electromagnetic spectrum stamped across the chest.

"Sorry we didn't get to you sooner," Janine said to him. "We decided to go grunge for tonight's shoot, back to basics. You would rather wear a regular T-shirt than that outfit, right?"

"Isn't that going to get us into some kind of trouble with management, the producer, Mr. Colliers?" Don still wore a scowl. Carlos held the T-shirt out and, after a pause, Don grabbed it and stomped behind the van to change. The doctor noticed the commotion and joined them.

"You two look very nice, very retro, I like it." His eyes smiled at her, and Janine felt herself blush.

Kiki and the doctor posed in front of different grave markers discussing his theory regarding elements that store ghostly energy. They began the conversation at the Getty Tomb, then changed locations as they continued the discussion.

They next moved toward the Shoenhofen marker, which was basically a small pyramid and sphinx. The doctor theorized that the stone composition of the pyramids were perfect for absorbing paranormal energy, because they were composed of limestones and granites, with a generous helping of micas. No doubt many workers were killed during the construction, under harsh conditions, Kiki added. She said that the shape of the pyramids lent to the focusing of cosmic energy. She often used stone pyramids to focus energy during a séance.

The Greek temple of Potter Palmer was another extravagant burial chamber. Kiki elaborated on the mystic oracles and lamented the loss of that ancient knowledge.

They filmed short clips at smaller tombstones, all victims of the fire who died in the *Alley of Death*, and discussed the unusual whispery recordings they gathered from the sensors planted behind the theater. Finally, they congregated at the Dexter Graves site where an ominous life-sized figure loomed before a black granite backdrop, the "Eternal Silence" statue. The figure appeared to be oxidized bronze, or copper, and wore a metallic cloak very similar to Kiki's velvet one.

"Dexter Graves was originally buried in the old City Cemetery," the doctor told the camera. "Which is now Lincoln Park. People from all walks of life were laid to rest in that old cemetery. For political or financial reasons, the city closed that burial ground to accommodate a surging population. Many bodies were exhumed and sent to other places, like this one, Graceland. That movement didn't happen overnight, it took years. The final graves scheduled for relocation had markers made of wood, and when the Great Chicago Fire hit, those markers were reduced to ash, which made it near impossible to locate graves to be moved. Basically, unaccounted for remains are rumored to still be in Lincoln Park, our next destination.

"The curator shared something interesting with us," Kiki reminded him. "This monument is also known as the *statue of death*. Many people have stared into the face of this monument and received a vision of their own death. Shall we try it?"

Don filmed the doctor and Kiki stroll up to the statue from different angles, from the front, from the rear, and in slow motion. Kiki allowed her cloak to drift open, just enough to show off her racy suggestive outfit, and she pulled her hood up for the start of each clip. As she lifted her face to the statue, the hood always drifted dramatically back, exposing her startled, glowing eyes. Carlos filmed one take in infrared for a spooky effect. After a few clips, the doctor nodded at Kiki, apparently done.

"I guess that's a rap here. To Lincoln Park?"

"Oh, no," Kiki pulled him back. "Now, we must peer into the face of that statue, seriously, and seek a vision of our deaths. I'll use a prophesy charm, and we'll give it at least three minutes." Three again, her witching number, Janine recalled, all things divisible by three.

Carlos and Janine strolled toward the van to stow their equipment, one small EMF box, a thermal-panger, and an infrared camera. Behind them, Don shouted. Janine turned just in time to see the famous Doctor-Kiki catch.

The doctor spun round and caught Kiki in one fluid motion. *Was it a staged fainting?* Kiki mentioned a *graveyard catch* in the limousine the night before. Yet, Kiki appeared very limp and drooped dramatically. Her cloak hung open, scandalously exposing the lace up shirt. Max Colliers was going to love that shot. Ian lowered Kiki to the grass and knelt beside her. Janine and Carlos double-timed back to the Dexter Graves monument.

"Kiki, Kiki?" The doctor rubbed her hand as Don hovered over them with the camera.

The statue of death loomed in the background. Janine didn't dare move her eyes to that figure. *Did Kiki see something in that stone face?* Kiki's lashes fluttered as the doctor helped her to a sitting position. Kiki's trembling hand reached up to grasp the pendant hanging from her neck. Her bosom heaved against the laces of her shirt, and her legs peeked haphazardly from her cloak, creating another great shot for Max. Kiki's brilliant green eyes glowed like cat eyes in the dark.

"Someone killed me with their bare hands," Kiki breathlessly declared. "I was choked to death. That's how I die."

Janine, Kiki, and Don rode in the limousine. Janine managed that combination by insisting Kiki needed to stretch out across one of the seats. She insisted that Kiki might need Don to recount exactly what he saw when she fainted. It sounded ridiculous, but if Kiki needed to soak up some male sexual energy, Janine did not want young Ben or her friend Carlos to be the sacrificial lambs providing it. The doctor raise his eyebrow when she proposed that seating arrangement, but didn't say a word and went along with her suggestion. *Did Ian know about the witches' trick?* She would be incredibly embarrassed if he found out she tried it on Max the night before. They made a plan to meet at Clark Street, near the old Couch Tomb in Lincoln Park.

Kiki stretched across the rear facing seat with Janine and Don across from her. Janine assured Don that Kiki fainted regularly and snapped back quickly. Kiki smiled at him.

"Don't worry, Don, sometimes the mystic world takes a toll on a girl."

"Did you actually see your death in that statue? By strangulation?" Don asked.

"Yes, I did. My killer felt familiar, like someone I knew, but he isn't someone I've met yet. He strangled me with his bare hands," Kiki whispered. "Could you be a dear and pour me a bit of water? I'll tell you exactly what I saw. I'll need to recite it for the green screen later, but let's hear how it sounds out loud, right now."

Don poured the water. He added a cube of ice to it, and Kiki released a little sound of appreciation with her breath. She glanced through fluttering eyelashes as he handed the tumbler to her.

"Thank you." She sat up straighter and was quite a sight. Under the cloak, in that lace up shirt, she looked like a character from a racy vampire movie. Dark, dangerous, and unpredictable.

Kiki tilted her head back and closed her eyes. "The vision commenced with me hiding from someone. Someone who felt like my lover, but I couldn't quite decide. Was he, or wasn't he? That was in question. One thing was clear, I had no doubt that he wanted to kill me. The sky was dark, definitely night, and a full moon reflected on a body of water, or, perhaps the moon was low in the sky? The image seemed to waffle and the moon went from horizon to water. The grass beneath my feet felt cool, smooth, then scratchy. Again, I couldn't decide. The images were very tricky, because it felt like I was in two places at once. One place was cool and breezy, while the other was more stagnant. Heather bloomed everywhere, but then, the heather morphed into cattails, very confusing. A gentle breeze stirred my hair, and for a moment, it felt a wee bit like Scotland on a warmer winter's night, peaceful. For some reason, I wasn't afraid to die. I realized that being killed wouldn't matter at all and that it was somehow needed." Kiki fingered the silver charm with a faraway look in her eye. "But then, I turned around and he was there, and I was terrified, and his hand felt hot with passion and tight on my throat. It began as a caress but turned into anger as he squeezed." Kiki ran her hand along her own neck. "He smiled lovingly at me, squeezing tighter and tighter, and the world around me dimmed until there were only pinpricks of light before there was nothing at all."

"Jesus Christ," Don exclaimed. "Did you get a good look at him? Maybe you can avoid him. You can watch out for him. I don't believe the future is fixed, Kiki. You can change things. You don't have to date him if you know what he looks like."

"The darkness made him hard to see," Kiki glanced from the corner of her eyes at him. "But I noticed that he had strong arms."

"There you go," Don said. "You can avoid him. If you believe all this psychic stuff, maybe this prediction is a 'maybe,' right? Has anyone ever died after looking at that statue? It's got to be an old wives' tale."

Kiki shrugged, "The images point to a definite strangulation, but I think you're right, Don. I don't think the future is fixed. The environment kept changing, so nothing was fixed. You are a very observant man."

"Could you identify anything else, other than his arms?" Janine asked.

"He was a devil," Kiki stated. "Or a demon. A man with no soul, no aura radiating from his core. I just need to be sure that I don't cross paths with a demon." She inhaled deeply, and accidently spilled the water. Droplets dribbled into the crevice of her chest starling her. Kiki attempted to pat down the drops through the laces of her shirt in a very ineffective way. *Good, grief,* Janine couldn't believe she had participated in that behavior the previous night.

Of the tombstones left in Lincoln Park, the largest was the Couch Mausoleum next to the Lincoln memorial, near the final resting place of one David Kennison, their spectral focus for the night. Although a plaque annotating Kennison's life lay blocks away from where they stood, the doctor's research suggested his original burial site lay near the Couch tomb.

"It's believed that David Kennison's bones were never exhumed and moved with his marker," the doctor rambled as they drifted through the park. "He was a larger than life figure who live well past one hundred years old. One hundred and fifteen, people insist. He didn't want to leave this world, and many reports suggest that he never did. His ghost wanders this area regularly."

The doctor carried his ion detector and waved it around. Carlos carried the infrared recorder, and Janine clipped a thermal-panger and subsonic audio recorder to her bat belt. The doctor anticipated too much ambient electromagnetic noise for the big box, so they basically followed Kiki, hoping she'd pick up a hint of paranormal energy and lead them to David Kennison's ghost.

"Ghost sightings have waned in recent years, so there's a possibility that the spirit has faded away," Kiki said, still dressed in her gothic cloak. She struck quite a pose on that grassy mound. "Well, Doctor, care to elaborate on your theory regarding a fading spirit?"

"Of course," the doctor said. "When the substance a spirit has locked into is broken down, weathered and eroded, scattered, the energy is lost. Burn down a haunted house and the ghost leaves too. Pulverize and scatter the minerals of a rock or bone, and the energy becomes dispersed. Over years of erosion, a spirit can fade away as the tainted elements are reabsorbed into nature."

"You believe this ghost was stamped into the bones themselves?" Janine asked him.

"Yes," he answered. "Probably the best material for trapping the energy of a soul, as bones are likely stamped from the inside, very deep. It would take years to erode bone down to the particles that store ghostly energy, perhaps centuries. This particular soil is very moist, due to the proximity of the lake, and with the excavation of the cemetery, and the building of this lovely park, the remains were disturbed, bones possibly broken. Any fragments left behind would decompose at a much quicker rate than in a dryer, more neutral environment. I'd wager that this soil is also quite acidic, due to the fertilization of the gardens and grass."

"Who was David Kennison?" Carlos interjected. "Anyone of note?"

"Heard of the Boston Tea Party? Well, David was one of those guys," the doctor told him. "He fought in the revolutionary war and the War of 1812. He was a busy, active man, larger than life. One historian said that Kennison was too busy to learn how to sign his own name, until he was sixty. His exact resting place is unknown and the city office asked…" The doctor continued rambling to Carlos and the camera.

Kiki came close and slipped her arm through Janine's. The silver necklace reflected in the darkness, dangling back and forth under the laces of her shirt. *Why did that pendant bother her?* They walked together, like they were casually strolling through the park.

"Let's see if you can call him out," Kiki whispered. "I'm feeling a buzz of energy radiating from an area up ahead, but it could be a lot of things. It's very faint. Do you feel anything?"

"Not a thing," Janine confessed.

"Remember my favorite summons? *We seek yon souls of near to there, we call on you to us appear, reveal yourself for us to see, so I command, so mote it be.* Say that."

Janine whispered it, barely audible.

"Be direct, Janine. Be nice, but be direct. Say it again, and this time don't ask, order him to talk to us. Demand that he tell us why he's here. My Auntie Celeste always tried to release trapped spirits, instead of expecting some erosion process to occur. Maybe we can help him find peace sooner rather than later. We need to know what's keeping him in this realm to do that."

The doctor stopped talking, and all three of the men turned back. Don pointed his camera at them as Janine silently request that David Kennison reveal himself and speak out. Janine pulled her thermal-panger from her pocket and watched the temperature drop minutely, not unusual for a night near a large lake.

"What are you two up to?" The doctor straightened the lower portion of his tie. "Do you feel something?"

"I do," Kiki said. "Something over here."

Kiki's long cloak trailed in a wake as she directed them to a nice patch of grass and stopped. As they drew closer to her destination, the temperature took a severe nose dive.

"Whoa," Carlos said. "There is a major cold pocket of air right here. Just a bubble of cold air."

"It's him," Kiki said. "He's here, and he's upset."

"Tell us why you're upset." Janine spoke toward the air surrounding them. The doctor gave her a surprised look. It was usually Kiki saying such things. "What do you want us to know?"

They shifted and formed a small circle. The ion detector popped off, the thermal-panger temperature numbers still decreased.

"He's missing his head." Kiki touched her own head. She allowed one sleek leg to slip from her cloak. "And his left thigh, and a few fingers, but he's not worried about those. How large is this cold patch, Carlos?"

"I would estimate about ten feet in diameter," Carlos said. "Give or take, a little."

"Well, he's scattered all around." Kiki spread her hands out and spun slowly. "And he's very anxious about his head and thigh. He's upset that someone took his head away."

The doctor pulled a collection of small survey flags from the pocket of his lab coat, the type workmen use to mark underground water lines. They set about marking the edge of the cold patch using the IR camera as a guide. Kiki stood directly in their intended circle with her eyes closed, listening.

"He's very faint," Kiki said, as they positioned the flags. "Barely here."

The city was very interested in finding the remains of David Kennison. Kiki spent the next ten minutes trying to confirm who she was communicating with, but never got a definite answer. The spirit kept insisting he cared more than three straw for his head, she chuckled. After they marked the site for the Historical Survey, Don snapped off his camera, rapping the Chicago shoot.

I made it, Janine felt a mass lifted off her back. *I made it through Chicago without begging out anywhere.* It was so simple, really. A near fatal knife attack paled in comparison to losing a child. She was the only one scarred in Chicago, whereas, the loss of Sammy scarred everyone she loved.

Chapter 12
U of C

Kiki

Ben, Don, and Mike drove the van back to the hotel, while Janine, Kiki, Carlos, and the doctor cruised around in the small limousine. They hit up the small bar and took the scenic route to the Lincoln House. They discussed the contract and Max Colliers, and the doctor confirmed everything Kiki told them. They had a little leverage on Max, if he tried to release one of them, but he could levy some hefty fines if they jumped ship. At the moment, they were in a compromised position.

"Don't worry about me," Carlos suddenly said. "Pay wise and fun wise, this job is hard to beat, but I have other prospects, you know."

Kiki wanted to discuss the fainting spells, and why it drained her of energy to summon a spirit. If spectral energy, the aether, was stamped into an inanimate object, why would her personal energy be sapped at all? She requested the doctor's scientific explanation. He considered her question as he removed his multicolored *Spectral Analysis* tie and loosened the top buttons of his shirt.

"The doctor inferred that you were like a catalyst," Janine interjected gently. "Using that analogy, a catalyst implies that activation energy is required to initiate a reaction, the disturbance on his supersaturated solution, for instance. Perhaps your energy sap is the activation energy needed."

"That's an idea worth considering," the doctor poured the drinks. "Or, perhaps it's in the translation of the messages that take the energy."

Ian offered a dram of whisky to Carlos and Kiki, but he offered Janine an iced soda. Janine's light brown eyes flashed, but she took the cola without a word, glancing at him from under her lashes. *Those two seemed to be getting on much better than the previous evening, but not easy friends yet*, Kiki noted. Janine's dark aura waned considerably any time Ian fixed his eyes on her. Then, Kiki witnessed something she never thought she'd see: Ian poured himself an iced cola too. When had that man ever passed up a wee dram? Never. When they arrived at the hotel, Ian and Carlos ran off to the ballroom to see how the download was progressing, while Janine and Kiki escaped to their separate rooms to sleep. So, Kiki noticed, no more hiding.

The next day, while the gofers were busy packing up the ballroom, Janine and Carlos took the van to retrieve the static recorders left around the city. Kiki recorded a voice over for her vision of death clip and conducted a short interview with

Lauren regarding the séance, then she was off for a mid-afternoon rendezvous on the other side of the city. She agreed to meet Randy Ivy, the haunted college guy, at a coffee shop near the university. The limousine driver waited outside the main entrance, and Carlos and Janine happened to roll up as Kiki exited the hotel. Carlos stuck his head out of the van's driver's window.

"Where do you think you're going, young lady?" Carlos demanded, all dimples. "Not another date with the mystery man, is it?"

"Not the fellow you're thinking of." Kiki told him. "But mysterious he is."

"Not the bull?" Carlos asked.

"Not the bull," Kiki winked at him. Janine popped out the passenger door wearing a scowl. "Come with me, Janine, just a little coffee run, it'll be fun. I'm meeting your creepy, haunted college man for a latte."

She shook her head grumpily, "Count me out."

"I feel like you need to come," Kiki urged her. "This fellow needs to talk to you more than me. He's haunted. He's been hexed by a ghost to do their bidding and we might be able to help him. He claims that it's you he needs to talk to. You're the one he delivered the charm to."

"Fine," Janine's doe eyes softened as she reluctantly climbed into the limousine. "But I'm going to need a stiff shot of something to get through it."

Kiki poured them both two fingers of whisky as the car pulled away from the hotel. She passed the tumbler to Janine.

They clinked their cups but neither of them tasted the golden liquid. Kiki worried about that sullen attitude and itched ask.

"Anything interesting to tell? Last night, I noticed you weren't hiding anymore," Kiki said softly. Her Aunt Celeste always demanded the girls steer clear of matters of the heart, but Kiki worried about her thick skulled cousin. Until meeting Detective Anderson, she had no idea what was at stake.

"Well, after being denied the traditional whisky after our shoot, I had a whole bottle of Max's wine waiting in my room, and I didn't have to share it with anyone, if that's what you're asking." Janine sunk into the limo seat. "I guess, I'm pretty arrogant after all. It doesn't matter, everything is as it should be. I don't know what I expected."

Too bad, Kiki thought, *no wonder she's in such a foul mood.*

She's surely avoiding dreams with all that alcohol. Janine hadn't taken one sip of the whisky in her hand. She only drank near bedtime, and then she really poured it on, medicating herself into a stupor. It just prolonged the pain, avoiding dreams. Dreams play a crucial role in putting the pieces of a fragmented soul back together. People needed to endure their night visions, painful as they may be, so that the jigsaw could be worked out and the pieces replaced correctly. Nightmares included. But try suggesting that to a wounded soul and they might snap your head off.

"Are you going to advise me not to drink so much," Janine challenged. "To find my core, stay away from Max, and try to make things up with Ian? Advise me what is, or isn't, best for me?"

"No," Kiki said slowly. "You already know what's best for you." She set her whisky down. "If I'm going to tune into this fellow properly, I'd better save this for later."

Janine set hers down too and stared at Kiki. "So, how exactly do I find my core?"

Randy Ivy crouched in the back of Build Coffee, a little shop on the south side of campus, with hair falling over his eyes and a gloomy frown on his lips. The skinny barista was the only other soul in the place. His eyes grew wide when they entered, then darted to where Randy slunk in his corner.

Randy scrambled to his feet and stared through blood shot eyes.

Kiki nodded at Randy, then chatted with the barista as she ordered coffee drinks. He gaped at her from under his lopsided bangs, but quickly worked the espresso machine, steaming milk and mixing drinks, grinning nervously and trying not to stare at Kiki's bosom. When the drinks were done, he quickly returned to his counter and hid behind a book. He clearly meant to listen to their conversation. Kiki and Janine moved toward Randy and they all sat down simultaneously.

"Tell us about your ghost," Kiki got right to the point.

"She moved without moving," Randy mumbled, examining his own dry hands. "She moved fast."

"Are you describing things in a dreams?" Kiki asked.

"No. This happened in the park, at night, that night," he mumbled softly. "We were partying after our midterms. The girls heard a rumor of a ghost that only comes out on the full moon, so, we went to check it out. At around midnight, we saw the ghost. She appeared far away, and, at first, I thought she was a tree." An odd laugh sputtered out of him and he shook. "Then, she was right next to us. She didn't move at all, but she moved real fast."

"So, she appeared in the distance, then she moved closer?" Kiki said. "Was she transparent? Shimmery? Floating? An odd size? Anything you can add?"

Randy's eyes darted all around. "She was real. Like a real person, only intense, very intense. She commanded me to find the necklace, right up in my face. It was terrifying, only, I didn't know what she meant. But when I found it, I knew. The necklace… " His eyes rolled haphazardly, then stopped suddenly on Janine. "She wanted you to have that necklace. She demanded I find it and bring it to you."

Janine glowered, she scowled at the poor guy, but Kiki gently gathered Randy's hand into hers. She could see that he was shaken through to his core and guessed that the spirit had touched his heart. He must have been feeling love when the ghost appeared. Only a heart feeling love could open sufficiently for a spirit to enter. Randy visibly calmed with Kiki's hands covering his.

"Did she guide you to the necklace?" Kiki asked. "Did she lead you to it?"

Randy shook his head. "I found it with a metal detector. My key got lost in the meadow that night and I took the detector out to search for it. I found the necklace instead, buried beneath the soil. It was dirty and I cleaned it, polished it, I felt compelled to prepare it. The saint is chained to the wall on that pendant. I've never heard of that saint."

"Why do you believe the ghost wanted Janine to have the necklace? Did she mention Janine by name?" Kiki asked.

Randy shook his head again, then glanced at Janine.

"That part came in a dream." He lowered his voice. "She kept entering my dreams, over and over again, and hounding me to find you." He stared unblinkingly at Janine. "She screamed, find her, find her. FIND HER!" His fist slammed on the table, hard. Kiki took his hands again and asked him to calm down. He nodded, red eyes fixed on Janine, voice firm and harsh. "At first, I wasn't sure who she was talking about, and she kept insisting that I deliver the necklace, because you needed it. Or, you needed to do something with it, or, something."

"Janine needs to do something for the ghost?" Kiki asked.

"That's the feeling I got," Randy conveyed. "I got the feeling that she needs something done, that someone owes her. You owe her, and you would know what to do."

Kiki nodded. "Then, we probably will know what to do, if you got that distinct feeling. We just need to figure out what that is."

"You didn't tell us how you came up with my name, from the ghost." Janine clipped in sharply. "How did you determined that it's me the ghost is interested in."

"I knew it when I saw you," Randy said. "On the TV. When we were watching the ghost documentary. You were in the movie, talking, and I knew instantly, you were *HER*. The ghost meant you. You need to take that necklace and do what she wants."

"Well, what does she want?" Janine snapped.

"I don't know," Randy finally seemed calmer. "You're the ghost experts. You can figure it out, I just want out of it. I delivered the necklace, I delivered the message. I should be out of the loop now. I did my part. One of the girls, a girl who saw the ghost with me, who went out there that night, well, she dropped out of school at the break. She went home and doesn't contact anyone anymore. Nobody. The other girl won't talk to me and acts like I'm a leper. Most people say I'm cursed." He stared at Kiki. His eyes pleaded with her. "Am I cursed?"

"Do you still feel that way?" Kiki asked softly. "After passing on the necklace?"

"I feel better." He blinked. "I feel more better now that we've talked. Maybe, after you figure out what needs to be done, maybe, I can get back to normal again. You'll let me know, right?"

"Of course," Kiki assured him. "Perhaps you're on your way to being back to normal already. I don't believe you're cursed at all, Randy. You were tasked with a message to deliver, and you did it. You delivered. You can move on now."

Randy let out a long sigh and his shoulders relaxed.

"Could you give us a complete description of the ghost? It might help us figure out who she was," Kiki requested.

Randy described the vision in his dreams, and the one in the park. Tall and slender, but solid, with long dark hair. She appeared much prettier in the dreams, alluring, and alternately much scarier and sinister. In the park, her large oval eyes were bottomless and dark, while in his dreams they resembled kaleidoscopes of dark shadows. She wore a University of Chicago sweatshirt, but it changed styles in the dream. Her face was narrow and thin, and her voice sounded painful, scratchy, surreal. From a distance, at the very first, he mistook her for one of the girls in his dorm, but he was sadly mistaken. He couldn't describe her main feature, it wasn't something visual. It was a feeling, *like cold despair?* He had no words to do it justice.

"Would you be willing to accompany us to the park where you had your encounter?" Kiki asked. "Show us where you found the charm?"

Randy jerked his head side to side, no question about it. "I'm never going back there."

Kiki's eyes softened and she patted his hand. "Of course not, but would you draw us a map? A rough sketch of the park with marks where you found the necklace and where you met the ghost."

"Okay," Randy agreed.

Janine remained quiet, observant, frowning. The barista delivered complimentary scones with the pen and paper, and he joined them. While Randy took up the pen with a shaky hand, Kiki examined the barista's palmar flexion creases and allowed him to stare into her eyes. Kiki gushed over all the lines that indicated his good characteristics and ignored all the bad ones. Janine kept her own eyes on Randy's pen as he scribbled faint lines for streets and a squashed circle for a pond. He added small dots that he labeled with wobbly letters. Randy explained that the "G" was where he first saw the ghost. The "M" was where the ghost came upon him, and the "N" is where he found the necklace. He forgot the park's name, but one of the streets along the edge of the woods was very easy to remember. He wrote it in severely slanted script, and Janine's doe eyes narrowed more and more with each letter that emerged from the pen; *Edgewood Street.*

"Edgewood Street or Edgewood Place?" Janine asked in a soft, sad voice.

"I don't know," Randy answered just as softly. "I could show you on a real map, if you like. It's not around here, it's a little drive away."

Janine rose and Kiki realized she meant to leave quite abruptly.

"It was nice meeting the two of you." Janine gave the two men a brief smile before turning her head away. "I'm going to wait in the car."

"I'm coming with you," Kiki accepted the map drawing and thanked Randy for his bravery. She left the barista a huge tip and hurried after Janine. She slipped into the limousine just as Janine drained her tumbler of whisky. Janine pressed her palms into her eyes. Kiki told the driver to start rolling and unfolded the drawn map. "He didn't write the name of the park, but I guess he didn't have to, did he?" Kiki said. "You know exactly where this is." She held up the drawing.

"Yes," Janine told her. "And I'm not going to tell you where it is until we get back to Texas. Don't even think about driving past that park, it's not going to happen, not with me in the car. Just, let me get out of Chicago before we talk about it. Okay, Kiki, please? Let's wait until we're out of Chicago to talk about this."

Ian chose to drive back to Austin in the van with Ben and Mike. He wanted to meet the historic society in the park near his survey flags and chat with the director. He assured Kiki that they would get to Texas in no time, driving in shifts, if needed. Kiki wanted to kill him. He very possibly might miss his own thirtieth birthday bash if they got delayed. On the bright side, she could finalize the party plans without Ian butting his nose in. Their own flight was delayed a few hours due to thunderstorms, and they did not get into the air until just prior to midnight. Most of the crew fell asleep after liftoff, but not Janine. She sat doing the crossword puzzle in the inflight magazine.

"Okay, we're out of Chicago," Kiki said when the plane leveled off at altitude. "People will project, Janine. Just because that fellow tied you to his ghost doesn't mean you're really tied to it. People observe us on the show and they add us into their own stories, it's not uncommon. Even if that park is where I think it is, it could just be a coincidence."

"It's a map of my woods, Kiki, of Thatcher Woods, but his map is of the south side of Chicago Avenue and my side is the north. I know exactly where that pond is and all of his dots. I used to go on early morning jogs in that park." Janine stopped working on the puzzle and eyed the sleeping people in the dimly lit cabin. Back, two rows behind them, Sally and Lauren chatted quietly. "There's something else I want to talk to you about, something Randy mentioned, but not here, okay? Maybe tomorrow. I'm trying not to think about it right now. This isn't the place to talk about it."

Kiki nodded. "I'm supposed to fetch Gwen tomorrow afternoon, so maybe we can meet in the morning, or for an early lunch. I can run by your place before fetching her. Where are you in Austin these days?"

Janine stared at the crossword puzzle and shook her head.

"Janine, where are you staying in Austin?"

Janine sighed. "I haven't decided. Last time, I stayed at the Holiday Inn, and I'll probably stay at the Holiday Inn again. I don't really have it worked out yet. My home is in Davis and I'm not planning to stay in Austin very long. If things go according to plan, I'll probably be back home in Davis this weekend."

She planned to disappear that quickly, unfortunate, just when Kiki figured out why they were good at summoning ghosts. She'd miss having a sister witch around, even one that didn't consider herself a witch.

"Stay at my house. I have two extra rooms. That way I can sleep in and go to church before picking up Gwen. I should get it out of the way before seeing her. We can iron everything out and settle all our questions before you leave. We won't have to rush our way through any conversations if you stay at my house."

Chapter 13

Witchy Ways

Janine

Kiki lived in the luxurious Westgate community of Austin in a million dollar home on the banks of the Colorado River. She claimed to have two spare rooms, but didn't mention that the other three bedrooms belonged to her cousin Ian. They shared a large kitchen, dining room, den, pool, playroom, and living area. No worries, Kiki told her, sometimes days passed without her bumping into the bloke on the other side of the house. Besides, Ian was in the van, driving back from Chicago at the moment. It would be at least another day before he made it home. The girls would have the house all to themselves in the meantime.

The décor was surprisingly normal, conservative, urban. A display of large minerals in the living room was definitely the doctor's doing. It was a spectacular showcase of pure specimen, each crystalized in a different geometric pattern, each the size of a cobble, and each nested in their own lit up cubby of a wooden shelf system that spanned the entire wall. Very nice, Janine admired the collection of crystals. The only item in the common area that appeared remotely Wiccan was a round table with a carved Triquetra under the glass top. Even the guest room was void of mystic influence. Just a regular queen size canopy bed and a generic empty dresser. Janine didn't know what she had been expecting. Luckily, the room also had a private bathroom. Kiki confessed that there were more bathrooms than bedrooms in that house.

Janine slept until just after noon and woke after Kiki had already left for church and the airport. She was curious to learn what type of church Kiki attended. Was it Wiccan? She did mention that her coven were girls of the kirk, was that Catholic? Kiki left a note and an extremely small string bikini if she wanted to go for a swim. *Fat chance wearing that.* Instead, Janine lounged on the plush sofa admiring the mineral wall, reading, and enjoying coffee with a bagel. Kiki's house was much nicer than a hotel, and more serene. Janine noticed several messages on her phone, most came from California, but two were Texas numbers.

Ian McNally texted; *Just checking to see if you got in okay. I know you're planning to leave soon, but please stay for my birthday party. And let me know where you're staying.* Janine texted that they made it just fine and that she would be at his party. She wasn't sure about letting him know where she was staying, in case she wanted to clear out before he got back.

Max Colliers also texted; *Lets have that date tonight or tomorrow.* She texted that she would get back to him soon, she didn't have anything appropriate to wear for a fancy date. Then, her phone rang, Max.

"I'm glad you're back. You aren't still living out of that back-pack, are you? No roots in Austin?"

"Well, if it's good news for me, then I might only need what's in that back-pack," she said.

"Except for our date. I can have Sally leave something for you in the office, or she can deliver, she has your measurements." He paused. "Not like the show stuff, I promise. Sally told me you didn't go for the chaps." He chuckled, "Can't blame me for trying to up the ratings."

She told him that he didn't need to send anything. She would drop by the office and decide if she'd wear any of it, or find something on her own. Not to worry, she wouldn't be in jeans and a T-shirt and promised it'd be a real date. They could go out the next night, if he liked. She'd meet him somewhere, *the sooner, the better*, she thought. The day after that was Ian's party, then she could head back to California and get back to her real life.

She texted back and forth to her grandmother Gram, her next door neighbor in Davis, and her niece Ashley. Kiki had groceries delivered and Janine carried them to the kitchen. She noticed fruit, vegetables, pasta, chicken, and a box with a dessert inside. So then, Kiki planned on cooking. The large kitchen window had a nice view of the backyard pool and river. Janine watched the speed boats pass by as she put the groceries away.

Kiki soon returned with her friend from home, Gwen. Janine came out of the kitchen to greet them and was surprised to see that Gwen was just as tall as Janine, at least five foot nine. Flowing red hair framed the spectacular freckled face that greeted her. If Kiki's eyes were a glowing emerald, then Gwen's eyes were a sparkling sapphire, and Janine sensed an analytical mind behind those eyes. No generous womanly curves on Gwen, but a strong, muscular, athletic build, flat chested, yet still feminine. Gwen gave Janine a good dose of scrutiny before smiling.

"Gwen, this is Janine Stinger," Kiki formally introduced them. "Janine, this is my oldest friend, Gwendolyn Allina Murphy, Gwen."

"Oh, the tales I've heard about you." Gwen hugged her.

It turned out that Kiki was not doing the cooking, Gwen insisted on preparing the feast. She insisted they relax in the kitchen and get better acquainted while she prepared a chicken scaloppini for dinner. She poured three large glasses of wine as she made herself at home in Kiki's kitchen. Kiki and Janine sat at the breakfast bar to watch her chop everything up.

"Kiera knows well that I unwind by cooking," Gwen said as she delivered the wine glasses. "Nothing is as relaxing as creating a culinary masterpiece, and then enjoying it with a pair of common allies such as yerselves."

"Unwind by cooking!" Kiki giggled. "Can you believe she said it? It's a witch's ploy, Janine, feeding you. Gwen is using her kitchen magic to open your heart to her ministrations. She wants to hear what you have to say about that guy's ghost."

"Ho, ho," Gwen laughed back at her. "Listen to this wee yin, cryin' about how one needs to tread lightly and then go spillin' the beans." Gwen turned her amused freckled face to Janine. "I mean no harm here, lassie. Kiera tells me you have something important to talk about and a little wine and spice can only help. My cooking is a wee attempt at coaxing me into the conversation, and I really do love to cook. Of course, I understand if you girls need to take it off in private."

Wow, Kiki discussed the creepy college guy with Gwen. Did she mention the woods? Janine wasn't upset, it was very hard not to like Gwen, she exuded warmth. Janine wondered what else Gwen knew.

"How much do you know already?" Janine asked.

"Only that a haunted lad gave you a charm of Saint Comba. Tis a very rare charm to be had, indeed, and very similar to a dear charm we once admired. And that you're familiar with the area he found said charm," Gwen told her. "And you had something mysterious to add, something you wanted to save for private. So, maybe, I'll need to entertain myself for a wee bit later? Or maybe not?"

"She doesn't know anything else," Kiki told Janine. "Nothing."

"That's not true." Gwen was busy mixing things. "I know that you may be a *dragoma* and that you made good use of sweet Ian not too long ago." They all shared a little light hearted chatter about Ian. "It's likely none of my business, but I'm always curious, and Kiera, sorry Kiki, keeps a tight lip. Perhaps I can just listen in then?"

Janine really liked Gwen. She needed to tell Kiki about the ghost, because Kiki would understand, and if Gwen was like Kiki, wouldn't her insights be valuable too? There didn't seem to be any harm in Gwen knowing everything.

"The woods, where that college guy saw a ghost and found the charm, it's the same woods where I was brutally stabbed and left for dead some years ago," Janine told her. "Maybe you heard of the story. The news called it the Coed Captive case, and they referred to me as Jane Doe from Chicago."

Gwen glanced over, and Kiki nodded slightly to Gwen.

"I heard of it," Gwen said slowly. "One of the reasons I argued against Kiera moving to America. The guns and violence, and incredibly, that story in particular."

"Good, then you know what happened to me," Janine said. She sought out Kiki's green eyes. "That description the college guy, Randy, gave of the ghost. Long dark hair, slender, strong looking. I think, I saw her, the ghost." Janine drained her wine and Gwen refilled it. They waited patiently for her to continue. "When I was being attacked, she came. Only, I didn't notice a university sweatshirt."

In the past year, Janine no longer needed to suppress memories of that ordeal and she analyzed them all over again in her solitude. When her captor unlocked the tether that kept her restricted to the upstairs area of his house, she automatically bolted. It startled both of them, as evidently, they both assumed she had no fight left inside of her. She was the one who carried the hunting knife into the woods. She snatched it off a side table near the door as she ran by. She remembers wondering why it had been there. Janine ran, or hobbled more accurately, directly into Thatcher Woods in the dead of night. Terrified and weak, bruised from his abuse, she didn't really believe she could outrun him, or fight him off. It didn't take long for him to catch up and push her to the ground. Her weak arms were feeble, and her spirit was nearly broken. When he noticed the knife, he slapped it out of her hand and snatched it up. He stabbed her in the back more than once, to teach her a lesson. *Her fault*, he growled, *for bringing it. Did she mean to stab him with it? Consider it karma.* He flipped her over and she remembers begging for her life, apologizing, promising never to run away again. She'd stay as long as he wanted. Anything. But he kicked leaves and rocks over the top of her, saying he was going to bury her in the park. He wasn't angry, Janine recalled, but disappointed. She felt warm blood pooling underneath her and wondered if she was already dead. He leaned in close and demanded that she say it one more time, *that she really loved him*, and to promise they could start again and that she'd stay forever. And so, she promised, still hoping he would go get help. He glared at her and asked, *cross your heart and hope to die?* Then, he carved that X on her chest and called her a liar, finally looking angry. He continued placing rocks on top of her, saying it was too late, she was ruined. *Ruined.* And that's exactly what she believed, for a very long time.

"At the moment I realized he meant for me to die, I called for help, but it was only a whisper. No one would have heard me. Deep inside of me, I was screaming for help, but I could barely make a sound. And then I saw her, standing in the shadows, absolutely still, frozen in place, staring, with dark, indefinite eyes. I wondered if she was really there."

Janine certainly had their undivided attention. She pointed to the simmering chicken and Gwen moved it off the burner, then turned back to face her.

"The ghost heard you," Kiki softly said, "And listened, because you're a *dragoma*."

Janine nodded. "Maybe. She stopped Rick, because she startled him and he was instantly terrified of her, like he recognized her. She appeared exactly as that college guy described. She commanded him to stop, *she used his name*, that's why I thought she was real. I remember wondering how she could scare him so easily. Who was she? But I didn't care, because he ran away."

"Did she say anything to you?" Kiki asked.

Janine hugged her arms to her chest as the images materialized in her mind. "No. I passed out staring at her eyes, deep and dark. I wondered why she didn't go for help. I wanted her to find help, begged her silently, but she remained a statue. For years I believed I only imagined the woman in the woods."

Janine initially told the police about the woman, but no witness ever came forward. They concluded that she imagined someone, because there was no physical evidence that anyone stood at the spot she described; no footprints, no damaged vegetation, nothing. A dog found her in that tucked-in back cluster of trees. If that dog had been five minutes later, she would have bleed to death.

"Kiki, do you believe animals can hear ghosts? Animals, like dogs?" Janine wondered.

"Oh, absolutely," Kiki nodded.

Gwen agreed. "Some dogs have a talent for sensing spirits, like humans. Why do you ask?"

"The dog that found me. The owner said he acted strange the moment they got on the trail and became antsy. He only let the lab off the leash to have a dip in the river, but the dog ran straight to me instead, in the opposite direction, at least a quarter of a mile through the woods. He'd never done that before. He knew right where to find me. Would it be pure conjecture to say the ghost sent that dog and now she wants me to do something for her, in return? What would she want?"

"Finding out who she is and why she haunts those woods would help," Gwen said. "Let's eat while we talk about it. This is best hot off the stove, and I'm famished."

Gwen prepared their plates and Kiki quickly mixed up a salad. They all helped cart the meal and wine to the large dining table. Kiki fully opened the blinds to reveal an orange tinted sky of setting sunbeams over the river. Gwen asked

Janine about her family and her studies at UC Davis. Janine discovered that Gwen worked as a nurse specializing in pediatric oncology.

"It's all very crude medicine, chemotherapy," Gwen told them. "Gruesome, but miraculously gentler on the youngsters. Adults are barely able to endure the same treatment. It breaks the heart. The children are always so brave, and the parents sit helplessly watching as it's done to their child. The kids rarely get stirred up unless their parents are stirred up. I find myself praying for those parents as often as the kids. Dark energy can have a negative effect on healing, you know. It can eat away at a healthy person and jump from soul to soul. Those kids need their parents to be strong, and prayer works. Prayer brings positive energy to everyone involved. It nurtures the soul."

"Praying, like to God? How does that work with claiming to be a witch?" Janine asked. "Kiki ran off to church today. What kind of church? A Christian church?"

"It's a Presbyterian church, very like our kirk back in Scotland. You just don't understand what a witch is, Janine. It's someone who follows a type of practice. Our pagan beliefs are shared with most modern religions. In our coven, we each made a vow to attend regular services at least once a month. To stay connected to the male aspects," Kiki told her.

Gwen considered them both for a moment.

"Most modern religions are very similar at the deepest level," Gwen told Janine. "That symbol on the coffee table out there. The Triquetra or the Trinity knot. A nice Christian would say it represents the Father, the Son and the Holy Ghost, while the original meaning is the Mother, Maiden, and Crone from the roots of our pagan practice. Many Christian symbols come from pagan roots with the meaning altered to accommodate a masculine ego. Very simply put, most modern religions are just the old ways, rewritten from a male point of view."

"Women naturally follow a path of empathy and caring and community, generally speaking. Spirituality is a natural facet of a female aura and men have a much harder time. It's all ego with men and base instinct," Kiki interjected. She was startled to see Gwen giving her a stern look. Gwen turned back to Janine.

"The masculine end of the spectrum is not naturally tethered to the nurturing Earth like the feminine. Masculine energy, and a vivacity for the physical, make it very difficult for a male dominated personality to recognize and grasp a world outside of themselves. Modern religions strive to bring those with a masculine nature closer to the center, to embrace their spiritual side. Now dinna think we're just a bunch of sexist females, thinking we're all that. A feminine soul needs a good dose of physical pleasures to bring them closer to the center as well. It's impossible to grow spiritually without experiencing the physical world, and each needs a little of the other to become whole."

"Male energy is very animal, whereas female energy is very spiritual," Kiki interrupted again.

Gwen grew red as she gave Kiki another stern look.

"A theological discussion such as this conversation should take days," Gwen grimaced. "In a nutshell, male dominated religions were created to help men, or rather the masculine dominated personality, to stretch beyond their base tendencies and experience a spiritual side. Over the years, like any good plan, the details got muddled in the misinterpretation. People often tweak the rules to suit themselves and many male religious leaders did the same. Kiera's a terrible teacher of coven principles, tossing around generalities so loosely. And it's nae exactly men versus women, but masculine and feminine, or more like the concept of yin and yang."

Kiki threw a napkin at her, "I beg your pardon, but who is the more gifted witch here?"

"Ho, ho. You've heard the saying, *those who can, do, and those who can't, teach?*" Gwen said to Kiki. "It should be, *those who can do, because they can't teach.* Seriously, Kiera, you *do* because you are the more gifted witch, but those who *do* are sometimes the worst teachers of all. It all comes so naturally, and easily, for you, and you have no clue how to help someone over a hurdle, as you dinna recognize what a hurdle is yourself."

"She's taught me a little about speaking to spirits, being a *dragoma*," Janine said softly. "I think that's how I put things together, that I must have called that ghost in the woods when I needed her. And she's taught me a little about absorbing—" Janine felt herself flush as she recalled the experience, "Absorbing male energy to recover from… Kiki says it recharges the receptive batteries."

Gwen's eyes were round balls of shock. She soon dissolved into laugher, along with Kiki, and then Janine. Apparently, Gwen knew the exact practice Janine tried to describe. Kiki did say that every witch in the coven used the trick.

"So, lassie, tell us how that went," Gwen requested.

"I felt better right away," Janine confessed. "But it was very uncomfortable."

"She failed to divert the energy to her core," Kiki told Gwen. "Most of it went straight into to her Base Well."

"Did Kiki give you any direction on finding your core? Or how to divert passion into your core?" Gwen watched her confused expression and gave Kiki another stern look. "Seriously, Kiera, you really are the world's worst teacher. Not everyone knows the Triad of Wells, and even so, not everyone naturally absorbs passion into their core, like you. You think everybody has the skills of a Core Master? None of the rest of the sisters are even close. Most of us girls naturally allow sex energy to flow where it belongs, into the Base Well."

Gwen seemed truly miffed at Kiki, then turned to Janine and reached for her hand.

"Don't try it again," Gwen advised. "Not until you can solidly find your core. It'll be playing with fire, I know. Unlike our perfect little witch over there, it took me a very long time to learn how to divert passion energy into my core, because typically, it doesn't flow that way. Also, better to practice on a fellow you won't mind slipping up on, in case it leads to a nice coupling. Kiera never had a problem sending any type of energy into her core. She's a bit of a savant, she is. Lacking any understanding of the passions, but a gifted Core Master. That's why she's still a coven vestal," Gwen shrugged at Kiki. "What, she dinna know this? You try to have her brim the well, but leave out any foundational information?"

"Janine is a classic skeptic," Kiki defended herself. "She needs a concrete experience before hearing, or considering, what she thinks is silly nonsense."

Janine shook her head, "It's alright, I don't want to cause a stir."

"No stir," They both chimed in unison, then laughed.

Kiki confessed, "Gwen is quite right about a lot of things. I truly don't understand where the hurdles pop up for most people. For instance, when we're on an investigation in the presence of an extremely strong spirit with a very obvious buzzing of energy, and not one of you feel anything at all. Sometimes I think, *you're kidding me*! As if you're ignoring a glaring light in front of your faces."

Gwen came around to give Kiki a hug. Her bright blue eyes fell on Janine.

"This should be another long conversation," Gwen said. "Kiera should have begun by telling you of the three wells, or caldrons. What we call the head, base, and core. Those are the wells from which we create and take in the universe. The aether flows easiest between like wells, but energy can always leak in every direction. That's why we feel love when there's passion. It has mixed up more than one person in the world. If you're aware of your wells, you can divert or alter energy from one to the other. Each person has their distinct strengths. Kiera is definitely tuned into her core, that's the heart, or soul well. It's why she can hear ghosts easily and can see auras. Most ghostly aether is of the core. I'm nae kidding about her being a savant. Most folks are more focused in their heads and the passions. And it's true, one of the quickest most intense sources of energy is testosterone driven sexual passion, from the base. Most will go directly into your own passion center, unless you divert it. Energy doesn't divert or change without effort, you know. Learning to redirect passion is a tricky process that usually takes years to develop." Gwen gave Kiki a look.

"I thought she'd be a natural," Kiki said simply.

Gwen and Kiki both displayed the tattoos on the back of their necks, a small, simplistic Triquetra, or Trinity knot. Most witches in their coven had one in the same spot. The three wells, or cauldrons, that every witch hoped to fill equally. Janine had seen Kiki's tattoo before and always wondered about it. Now she knew.

"Three is a sacred number in the universe," Gwen told her. "You study science, right? Think about those building blocks of matter. The nucleons that make up atoms. What are they made of? It's a trio too, right?"

"You mean protons and neutrons?" Janine said.

"What are they made of?" Kiki asked.

"Quarks," Janine said. "Three quarks a piece."

"A Triquetra of quarks. And quarks have distinct orientations, right? Opposite orientations, just like the feminine-masculine dichotomy, but it's a trio that make up the whole. Two up and one down make a proton, if I remember correctly. And it's a trio of wells that make up a person, each with opposing aspects. Three is a very sacred number. The Triquetra happens to be one of the oldest symbols known to humankind."

Gwen offered to keep in contact with Janine and answer any questions she might have regarding their coven belief system. Gwen and Kiki were excited that Janine was interested in the ancient teachings. Janine admitted that she had many odd experiences around Kiki and was truly curious. Then, they cleared the dinner plates, and Gwen asked to see the charm. Janine disappeared to find it. Kiki had placed it in Janine's room earlier that morning, because Randy insisted the charm was meant for Janine.

Chapter 14

Detective work

Kiki

Kiki could see Gwen's emotions had gotten stirred up at her for encouraging Janine to practice coven secrets without any sort of education, but it wasn't like open heart surgery, was it? Either a girl had the talent, or she didn't. Janine definitely possessed some talent, and it was perfectly natural to assume a *dragoma* could find her own core. Spiritual communication emanated from the core, didn't it?

"Well, Kiera," Gwen craned her long neck to spy down the hall. "You said she had a dark aura, you didn't mention she had that dark past."

"She's working through it. She might be close to being over it."

"Maybe," Gwen gave the opposite hall a glance. "So, tis Ian's lair back there, is it?" Gwen took two steps toward Ian's side of the house. "Maybe I'll just pop over and do a little snooping. He knows I've come, doesn't he? He would be truly insulted if I didn't care to invade his privacy a wee bit."

Gwen disappeared down Ian's dark corridor. Kiki didn't put up a fuss because it would do no good, Gwen would sneak back there eventually and she had a valid point, Ian would expect it. Janine returned, and they moved into the den with the comfortable sofa. Kiki prepared a tea pot and cups, and Janine put the creased envelope containing the charm on the coffee table next to the pot. They lounged quietly, observing the early evening stars through the back windows. Kiki checked her messages.

"Gram isn't coming to the party." Kiki studied Janine, who gave a small nod. "Says she's too busy. We rented this house because of the windows. It's a little like your Gram's back patio. Ian loved her big sky."

"She texted me."

"The detective messaged me," Kiki showed her the text. "His words declare that he cares deeply for me. I believe he's feeling love. This is an *I love you text*, look at it."

Janine examined the text. Her eyebrows went up in amusement. "He asked you to let him know that your flight made it in okay."

"It's a very blatant *I love you* text," Kiki declared. "It must be. Clearly, Janine, you need to learn to read between the lines. Detective Anderson is thinking about me, and his concern about my whereabouts speak volumes. He reached over a great distance to stay connected after only just meeting. He's visualizing me in his mind, tracking my movements in the world. Those words are definitely a message of love."

Gwen emerge from Ian's hall sporting a little smirk.

"You're cousin is a neat freak," Gwen squeezed between them brushing her red curls behind her ears. She poured the tea. "He doesn't have a single photograph of me back there. The nerve of him, after all the effort I put into Ian McNally in my youth. The fun we had with me trying to divert his energy to my core and failing so miserably." Gwen winked at Janine. "Dinna worry yourself, that's all ancient history by now. He's all yours."

Kiki couldn't help laughing at the face Janine made; wrinkled nose and pouty lips. Janine shifted around to face Gwen. She shook her head.

"What do you mean by that?" Janine asked. "We're not— Ian and I are also ancient history. It ended a long time ago. In fact, it was barely anything at all, just a very short fling. So, if you've come to reconnect with him, go right ahead, it's perfectly fine with me. Although, he may have a new girl, right Kiki? He's with Lauren now."

"Nae danger of a reconnection for me. I've got a very nice pediatric oncologist back home, but let me divulge a little secret. Ian has several photos on display in his office and bedroom, only three with people in them. One of his dear mother, and two images of you." She nodded at Janine. "Anybody wonder what that means?" Gwen didn't wait for an answer, she pointed to the manila envelope instead. "Is this the necklace?"

Janine grinned after that secret and the beautiful undertones in her aura sparked dramatically. Would Auntie Celeste have considered that meddling? Gwen definitely approved of Janine Stinger for Ian, even with the dark past. Kiki noted the similarities between Janine and Gwen; both tall, same hips, similar manner of movement, and radiating the same red undertone in their auras. Janine tipped the envelope and they watched the charm and chain spill onto the coffee table. Gwen's hand hovered over it and Kiki knew that Gwen felt energy radiating off the charm.

"This is a very old medallion," Gwen said.

Kiki agreed. "I sense that as well."

"Is it haunted?" Janine asked. "Is that ghost in it? I wonder what type of metal this is?"

"No ghost or a spirit here," Gwen cupped the charm in her palm and studied the raised image. "This is more akin to an ambient emotion. Nae different than the way a musical instrument takes on the character of a musician and gets flooded with a taste of their soul. This trinket has had a number of musicians. Faithful owners who gave part of their heart to it. It must be centuries old."

"Does this image of Saint Comba seem familiar? It's an uncommon one," Kiki asked.

Gwen narrowed her bright blue eyes and raised her ginger brows. "It is exactly like hers, you're right about that, though it was years ago when I last saw one. Meg had one too."

Kiki nodded. Gwen confirmed it. Her Auntie Celeste often wore the same ornament. She would have to ask Ian's father if it still existed.

The image depicted a woman with long flowing hair, naked, and her left wrist was chained to a wall. An unidentifiable beast lay near her feet. The words "Saint Comba" was stamped across the bottom in clumpy letters. Kiki noticed Janine eyeing the image through narrowed lids. *What was she thinking?* Janine had been chained by the left wrist as well, and still bore a scar from the handcuffs. *Was she thinking about that?* Did Janine know any of Saint Comba's story? Imprisoned, raped, saved by an animal. Did she draw parallels between Saint Comba's story and her own?

"Was the woman, Randy's ghost, a witch?" Janine asked.

"Hard to tell," Kiki told her. "But I would wager more than one of the women who wore that charm practiced something of the arts. I sense four owners, maybe more. The freshest vibe reeks of anger, and the metal radiates… guilt?"

Gwen wrinkled her speckled nose, and nodded. "We have a few clues. She wore a university shirt, was tall, with long dark hair. Anger such as this might come from a young woman in the heat of her passion years, or an older woman, severely betrayed by life. One thing is certain, she was dead long before Janine ever went into that park."

"I'm going to go to bed," Janine rose suddenly, her dark aura thick again. "There was a girl before me, with Rick, a track star. Someone warned me about her. She's supposed to be living abroad, but someone didn't think so and flat out accused Rick of doing something to her. Could it be her? The ghost? Back in the woods, the ghost called him by name and he was startled. And, she may have attended the University of Chicago, at least that's what Randy implied."

Kiki nodded. "I can contact the detective and confirm if she's is still missing, he probably knows about her. It's a lead, at least."

They watched Janine retreat to her room, and Gwen slipped the charm back into the manila envelope.

"Here, finish your tea, Kiera… sorry, Kiki. How am I going to remember that? Everyone calls you by your baby name? Brilliant. It's absolutely comical, this TV personality you've invented. Now drink that up, I want to see if the person you were whispering about is in there."

Kiki did as she was told and handed the cup over. Gwen was a gifted psychic, a prophesier, able to detect how energy swirled around a person and to work out how the currents might spin. Kiki felt a little nervous at what her leaves might reveal. Would there be a death mixed into the sediments? A strangling? Gwen flipped the cup and peered into the dish. She glanced at Kiki with a small smile.

"Nice, I see him here," Gwen said. "And you're thinking about a baby. Please assure me, Kiera, that you haven't jumped the gun on that one. We intend to arrange a proper coming out for you, a true awakening. You've been focusing on babies, I can see it. It's also obvious your Base

Well has begun to shimmer and swell. You want this fellow to be the father?"

No hint of a strangulation, Kiki sighed. Perhaps the vision in the cemetery belonged to a soul connected to that charm. It had hung next to her heart when she saw those images, and her heart had been vulnerable, unlocked, *feeling love*. Gwen's blue eyes bore into her inquisitively, waiting, likely worried the prime vestal had fallen off the pedestal.

"I only just met him," Kiki told her. "He has a pink aura and he's the detective Janine mentioned."

Gwen chuckled. "A pink aura? This ghost and the mystery charm is a reason to call him. Maybe we'll see you finally get flustered over a nice lad. Of course, there's a few bets running round the girls that you've already done as much."

Kiki waved that comment away as she watched Gwen peek into Janine's cup. Gwen flipped the cup once, then gazed at the leaves with a creased brow.

"I'll be honest, there's a lot of darkness in there," Gwen set the cup down. "But, it might belong to that monster who chased her. Those shapes could be in the past, but indications imply that darkness still follows her. I'm going to add her to my prayer chain tonight, I can have a hundred of devoted mothers directing their positive energy to eradicating the darkness on her back. It'll fade before we know it. We need to help that lass, for Ian's sake."

Kiki researched Thatcher Woods after Gwen finally collapsed for the night. She matched up the marks on Randy's crude drawing to a real map. She googled the Coed Captive story. No photos of Janine, but there were several of Richard Wilkens. He was quite handsome, angelic. Kiki often had difficulty recognizing acquaintances in photographs, because she required their energy to really *see* them. She suffered from a condition called partial prosopagnosia, or face blindness, according to one doctor. Kiki recalled the day she realized most folks couldn't see an aura. It stunned her. Kiki assumed everyone identified people by analyzing their energy. She stared at the photos and wondered what type of colors he emitted, a man brutalized the woman he loved. How were his sacred wells intertwined? For Janine to misinterpret him so completely, his energy must be a twisted knot of contradictions. Either that, or he was a true devil without a core, perhaps the soulless demon from her vision.

Kiki studied contours of Thatcher Woods. It encompassed a very large area. Too large for a typical ghost to wander. Perhaps the woods contained more than one ghost, or perhaps, Janine's summons was so compelling the ghost couldn't resist. Several hiking trails snaked through the area and it would be near impossible to hide a body for any length of time. Kiki left a message for the detective because the midnight hour had already passed. Detective Anderson was a rare gem, very in touch with his feminine side. Kiki wondered how he became a police officer. She sent him a photo of the charm with a short message about the ghost.

Kiki and Gwen spent the day preparing for Ian's thirtieth birthday party. Gwen insisted they bake a birthday cake from scratch and hand-whip the icing. To ensure a cake filled with love, they needed to use raw ingredients, so they spent the better half of the morning baking and mixing up a delicious frosting. Luckily, Gwen didn't eliminate the caterer too. Kiki was not fond of kitchen magic.

The party would take place in the common kitchen, living room, game room, and pool area, and Kiki hired a service to clean and set up the premises. A caterer brought several small tables with nice cutlery, and a dance troupe set up a small square floor on the far lawn. There'd be Irish dance instruction and a drum heavy Scottish band. Lauren arrived partway through the day with decorations. She seemed very eager to put her stamp on Ian's birthday and flittered about adding nice touches to the party layout. After Gwen transferred the cake to the cooler, they all lounged on the pool deck watching the dance floor being snapped together.

"Thanks for finding that troupe," Kiki said to Lauren.

Gwen crinkled her nose when Lauren turned away. She seemed irritated with Lauren's dazzling smile and bright chatter, and Gwen's eyes kept drifting to Lauren's petite feet, ogling them in their strappy high heels. Lauren grew curious about Ian's side of the house, but Gwen put a stop to her snooping. Better let Ian show people around at his own pace, Gwen suggested firmly. Lauren then proposed ordering a professional cake, raving about some designer bakery and Gwen finally snapped at her. Lauren just giggled at the outburst, surprised and amused.

"It can be an extra cake," Lauren beamed. "Marino Brother's makes a *to die for* three layered Chocolate Decadence."

Kiki patted her arm. "We've got it covered with the caterer, but thanks."

"Sally delivered dresses to your office," Lauren gushed toward Janine. "They're there right now. I would have brought them if I knew you were staying here. I can drive you to the office to pick them up, if you'd like. I go right by that area on my way home."

Kiki gave Janine a questioning look. Sally made dresses for her? Janine appeared caught in a tight spot as she avoided eye contact. Did it have something to do with Max Colliers? Before she could ask the question, Kiki received a text from Chicago. She scanned it quickly.

"Her name is Miranda Daily and she lives in Turkey. Her family insists she's alive and well," Kiki read it out loud. "But when he mentioned the charm, they were very interested in seeing it. He's going to meet with them soon, to show them the picture. He wants to see their faces when they look at it."

"Maybe we can look her up, do an internet search," Gwen suggested.

Janine turned away from the conversation, frowning. The previous night, she had left the charm in the living room.

It lay abandoned on a side table. Why did she find that necklace so repulsive? Kiki felt positively attracted to it.

"I'll take that ride if you're ready to go," Janine said softy to Lauren, then turned to Kiki. "I'll be back late. I've got a dinner date, so don't wait for me. And don't worry about anything, I know what I'm doing."

"Be careful, Janine." Kiki noticed Lauren's curious gaze, but couldn't be bothered with what she might think. She pulled Janine into the house for more privacy. "You think Max plays fair, but not all the time, not when he feels dismissed. He can be quite a brat, I've seen it. He's going to make sure he wins something. I wish you could record exactly what he says about the contract so we can find the loopholes later. And Carlos isn't going to like it, if you try to save him by agreeing to something you wouldn't normally do. Like wearing the costumes."

"Okay. Don't worry about me, I won't be fooled again. Worse case, I miss the summer session at Davis and move in with you for a month or so," Janine said. "Or until you get tired of me. I think, I only owe two more shows."

Lauren caught up to them and Janine ran off with her. Gwen raised her ginger eyebrows as she watched them run away.

"We've got an hour before we can ice the cake," Gwen said. "Shall we have a go at finding Miranda Daily?"

They searched her name first. With a name like Miranda Daily, they could see that tactic wouldn't work. Mostly, they found photos of a celebrity named Miranda in her daily routines. Then, they tried Facebook. Several accounts for Miranda Daily popped up and they perused them carefully, but, none of the Mirandas lived in Turkey. They found a few old accounts that had been abandoned, none with a connection to Chicago. They did find one Miranda Daily from Boston.

"Look at this," Gwen pointed to a woman in her family photo. "This old lady is wearing a charm necklace. Too small to tell which saint is on it, but, it's the right size and color. Let's click through her friends and see what we find."

Although Miranda Daily halted all activity on her Facebook account several years ago, her friends were alive and well, and posting up a storm. Most of them limited their personal information, but a few of her old friends were not shy about listing their phone numbers for the world to see. Kiki and Gwen jotted down two promising numbers to call. Both women listed the University of Chicago as their alma mater. The first number went directly to voicemail. Kiki left her name and number.

They meandered into the kitchen to make the next call. Gwen needed to frost the cake and declared that it was late enough to open a bottle of wine.

"Hello," Kiki said when the phone picked up. "Hello, I'm trying to contact Lisa Welks, a University of Chicago Alumni."

"I'm not interested in donating," the woman on other end snapped. "Please don't call…"

"Don't hang up, I'm not looking for a donation," Kiki said quickly. "I'm calling about something personal, about someone you might know."

"This better not be a sales call," the woman said. "Who is this?"

"My name is Kiki Mellow. And I'm calling about —"

"Kiki Mellow? Like the TV ghost whisperer? From that show, *Spectral Analysis*? Is that who you think you are?"

"That's exactly who I am," Kiki said. "Can I ask you a few questions?"

Lisa Welks informed Kiki that Miranda Daily moved to Turkey, or somewhere close to Turkey, in the wilderness. She left unexpectedly during their final semester at college and never returned. They had been roommates for three years and Miranda always talked about living abroad. Lisa felt certain that Miranda was in Europe, because she still received cards from Miranda, always around Christmas and on her birthday. But, Miranda no longer engaged on social media, and it was against her beliefs to be photographed or to use a phone.

"This may sound funny," Kiki said. "But, what does she look like?"

"Right now? I have no idea, but in college, she was on the tall side, with dark hair, very long, tall and thin, and she was a runner. She was on the varsity track team, I don't think she would ever give that up. Smart too, she completed her requirements early, that's why she left early."

"Was she religious? Have a favorite patron Saint?" Kiki asked.

"I assume she's pretty religious now. She converted to some sort of cult out there, but back in school she never went to church or anything. I don't think she was very religious."

"Do you remember if she had a boyfriend?"

The woman laughed, "She had several boyfriends. She liked them handsome, blond, ripped, and tall. Other than that, I don't remember much about them."

"I see," Kiki said. "Well, thank you for talking to me."

Gwen gave a little smile. "Sorry you hit a dead end. It looks like this Miranda girl really is in Turkey. That ghost must be someone else."

They enjoyed another home cooked dinner by Gwen and discussed Kiki's future. There were several new sisters in the coven and Kiki had missed a few important pagan events. She felt like she was losing touch with her roots. Close to three years away was an awful long time, and things had not gone as she expected with *Spectral Analysis*. Regardless of how much film footage they shot, the world was not ready to believe in paranormal activity. All Kiki really accomplished was obtaining a mountain of money and a popular persona that some of the sisters teased her about. She may have gone overboard as Kiki Mellow, she admitted, but had a lot of fun doing it. Suddenly, a text pinged.

Kiki and Gwen read the text together. *Miranda Daily is dead. And your friend is lucky to be alive. I warned her. Don't contact me again, I'm going to block your number.*

"That was the number for who? The Lisa Welks number? Or the Mary Kline?"

"Mary Kline," Kiki said. "I wonder if Detective Anderson knows about Mary. Mary certainly knows about Janine Stinger."

Chapter 15

Men

Janine

Janine learned a few things on the drive to the office building. Sally believed that Janine and Carlos wanted to get her fired, Guy petitioned for the company medical plan to cover his transition, and Lauren hoped to compare notes on Ian McNally. *Sorry,* Lauren grinned impishly, *but it was common office gossip that there was history between Janine and Ian.* Don had confirmed that information for them. Janine learned that Lauren and Ian hadn't yet transitioned from a casual dating relationship into something more serious and exclusive. Lauren felt ready to jump all in, but like most men, Ian seemed hesitant. *Sorry,* Janine thought, *but I may be a little happy with that information.* Lauren also considered Max Colliers a fantastic boss. She never understood why Kiki Mellow always derided him. From her perspective, Max created opportunity after opportunity for everyone in his employment. So what if he came across a little flirty? He always behaved like a gentleman around Lauren.

Janine decided to wear one of Sally's dresses, a cute sundress. It was perfectly acceptable and it would save her shopping for something else. All she needed to do was sit through a nice dinner, make polite conversation, and get out of her contract. She would stay cool, reserved, and soon be home free. She would not ignore Max and be a nice date. She'd keep an open mind, or at least try to. Janine noticed that Carlos left a couple of small audio recorders on his desk and wondered if she should borrow one. She slipped it into the small pocket on the cute sundress Sally provided.

Max Colliers chose a fancy seafood place called Bobby D's for their date. A live piano played in a far corner and Max hovered near the entrance waiting for her. He broke out in a broad smile and delivered a glass of wine as she walked in the door. A tiny bit of his aftershave infiltrated her nose as he leaned in to pecked her on the cheek. He was acquainted with three or four people in the vicinity and introduced her to each of them, all while holding her hand in his. A steady stream of soft jazz floated out of the lounge. It felt nice to be on a date again. She didn't know why she had been so apprehensive.

"I can order a semiprivate table, or we can become part of the scene near the piano and people watch," he whispered. "What does the lady prefer?"

"Either way is fine."

He eyed her critically. "You are going to give me a fair chance here? Before we start our date, you should know that you're officially cut loose from the show, if that's what you want. Scot-free, no penalty fee, no more obligations to *Spectral Analysis*. We might ask for a few promo photos, and maybe an appearance at a future press function, but that would be the limit. And, don't worry about Carlos, we're going to make it work. He stays as long as he wants." His eyes softened and he squeezed her hand. "Admit it, I just put my pretty date in a very good mood. You're happy with me now."

A long envelope emerged from his inside breast pocket, which he handed over. "Here's the official copy, all you have to do is add your signature. We can do that right now, or wait till later. Hopefully, it'll put your mind at ease, and you can relax. We can focus on getting to know each other, something I've wanted to do since the first time we met. Do you remember?"

Janine read through the short document while they sat at a semiprivate table. They were shielded with a shimmery canopy and the table was set with crystal flutes, sparkling silver, and napkins bended into the shape of mini-swans. It was a very fancy, romantic setting. Max took her hand again, and caressed her palm. He suggested she sign the document later, then send it to Mike Dunn. Max already signed it, so it was official on his part, unless she ripped it up or delayed acting on it.

"I'm not asking you to rip it up," he said. "I actually prefer that you're not in my employ tonight. This way nobody has an upper hand or feels pressured in any way."

Max poured them both a little more wine. "Let's put this part of the conversation aside, shall we? I'd like to focus on finding out what makes Janine Stinger tick."

Max turned out to be an intelligent and entertaining date. He was quite funny and Janine found herself enjoying his conversation despite herself. He studied at Columbia University, then at Wharton for his upper degree in business. Steve Hanks, the last producer, was his cousin and they lived next door to each other growing up, although, next door for them meant a couple of miles between houses.

Did she know, Max had always been the main contributor to *Spectral Analysis,* since its conception? He admitted to chasing after Kiki quite ardently at the beginning, but soon realized he was no competition for the professional athletes she preferred. He told her about his family and a past fiancé that had been arranged, a thing he never wanted, and thank god, she didn't either.

He tried to tease information out of her. He charmingly tip toed his way around personal questions he could see she avoided, but he pressed her anyway, trying to be light-hearted about it. He pried for the sordid details regarding her knife scars. Her quiet, shy demeanor didn't fool him, he *knew* she was into *interesting* things. Max clearly believed her chest X was a self-inflected personal statement. Her marks seemed to excite him. She didn't know what to say, so she let him believe whatever he liked.

After dinner, they migrated to the lounge area to listen to the jazz pianist and bass. They slow danced. Several people stopped to say hello and Janine felt envy from a few of the women in the room. Max charmed every pretty woman that chatted with him, but that wasn't so strange for a bachelor like him. She questioned why Kiki was so wary of Max Colliers, he seemed pretty typical of his station. She tried to imagine how a romance with a wealthy sophisticated playboy might play out. Too many fancy dinners and uncomfortable situations, she imagined, and his fascination with her scars felt very odd, a major red flag. Although he talked nice, she sensed a sinister goal underneath his surface. She wondered why he put so much effort into a girl who was not interested in hanging around.

Janine originally planned to call a taxi, but Max appeared hurt that she didn't assume he would drop her off, especially as his car and driver were waiting in the parking lot. It seemed silly to say no to that very nice chauffeured Mercedes sitting in front of her. Max helped her into the back of his car and then climbed in beside her.

"Mind if we take a scenic route? Are you staying somewhere nearby?" he asked.

"I'm staying with Kiki," Janine said. "Do you know where that is?"

Max chuckled and nodded. "Yes, I've been there a few times, it's actually one of my rentals. Let me tell the driver." Max opened a little window to give their destination and then closed it. His driver was partitioned off from the rear by a thick tinted barrier. When that barrier shut him out, she noticed a distinct change in Max's demeanor. He shifted closer and cozied up to her. He reached over to touch the very top edge of her scar and Janine brushed his hand away.

"Don't do that."

"Why won't you tell me about this cut mark and why you did it?" He considered her angry eyes and narrowed his own. "Don't be like that, I know you're attracted to me, I can feel it. You've been having a good time and you've been sending me signals since we bumped into each other at the Lincoln House. I'm not sure what you and Kiki were cooking up in that limousine, but you led me to believe that getting physical is not out of bounds for you."

Janine shook her head slowly and Max stiffened slightly. His calm, cool, unpredictable behavior had a unsettling effect on her.

"Have you been toying with me?" he asked. "That isn't nice. I've been more than fair with you, out of my way accommodating some would say, and I know you're leaving as soon as you can, so…I'm not asking for a lengthy commitment," he touched her scar again, "Just a chance to play. I'm interested in why a nice girl gravitates to this type of harmful behavior. Is it something you still do? This dark, dangerous stuff? Would you do it with me? I want to understand it, I'm curious. We could go somewhere private and you could tell me all about it."

"I'm not going to sleep with you," Janine told him.

Max nodded. "You sound sure about that. That's okay, but I know you've considered it." His eyes made a pass over her body. "How about showing me everything, as a thank you, a parting gift? Would you be willing to show me all your scars? That entire blemish between your breasts and the one on your back, it went pretty far down. I'm just imagining how far. Are there many more? Someone told me there were lots more, all over. Did you let different guys make them, or was it the same man? Does it turn you on before it happens, or when it happens? I'm dying to know."

"You want to see a body riddled with knife scars, as a thank you?" Janine glanced at the driver to see if he could hear any of it. So, this was what Kiki sensed, some kind of odd, creepy fetish. It didn't cross his mind that her scars were the result of a life threatening, violent attack. He seemed convinced that she invited them on purpose, *for fun*.

"You let your beautiful body get marked up, more than once. That's fascinating? I want to know what type of play precedes them, and why you wanted it. Did anyone go too far and get carried away? What harm would it do, to show me and tell me about it? Not here, but somewhere private. We can get a dual massage, I can easily arrange it, it's the polite thing to do, return the nice favor from me, with a harmless favor from you. You're the only woman I know who's done anything like this, this Marquis de Sade stuff. I admit, it excites me."

"Are you making this a condition, for that document?"

"No," Max said. He shook his head. "No, I already signed those papers and I always keep my word, guaranteed. I'm only asking for a small favor, yours to give freely, just to be nice. What would it hurt? Haven't I been extremely nice?

Very fair? I'd settle for just seeing the scars and hearing the stories, but if you wanted to give more than a look, that would be very appreciated. You could tell me what to do."

"I don't think so," Janine said softly. She couldn't look at him.

"Or, you girls could let me watch. I know what you and Kiki were up to in Chicago. I got it all wrong, didn't I? Someone told me, but I should have guessed. Did Kiki make one of those marks with her special dagger? Did you let him watch? I wonder how that dynamic works for the three of you. Did you know that they're related? Cousins. Did they tell you that? Kiki's extremely sexy, isn't she? Did he worm his way in and burn a bridge somewhere? Is that what happened?"

Janine stared at Max in his tailored suit and expensive designer eye glasses. He was so polite and nice in public, always behaving like a perfect gentleman, keeping his distance and not overstepping social boundaries. What did he really want? Did he really expect a response from her? Did he expect her to seriously participate in this conversation? She glanced out the window. At least they were driving in the right direction, in another ten minutes she would be free of him.

"He's making quite a few messes, wouldn't you say?" Max settled back comfortably, studying her. "Has one girl fleeing due to his harassing behavior while he works on another. I'm told quite a few young women find him a little too friendly, and it might be prudent to start an investigation. It's the responsible thing to do."

What was he talking about? Where was he going with this? What was he up to?

"Sexual harassment in the workplace is a multimillion dollar problem these days." Max stared at her. "I could back him up, of course, because I don't believe he harassed you. Or, I could flush him out and question his reputation. Not a hard stretch to assume he forced you to flee a promising career. Did he? Is he the reason you're leaving?"

"I haven't accused anyone of sexual harassment," Janine said.

"You don't have to, there's already a fair amount of gossip about it. Everyone is wondering why you avoid him and are hell bent on leaving," His light brown eyes smiled at her. "I can always ignore it. Loose talk usually fades with time, but what do I get for going out on that limb?"

Max Colliers was a snake, who didn't think he was a snake. Kiki warned her, but she didn't see it coming. His charming and accommodating demeanor fooled her. She needed to learn from this and not play into his hands.

If Max investigated the doctor for sexual harassment, he could make it stick. A minefield of pretty women worked in that building and would say just about anything Max asked. After months of ignoring her requests to be released from the contract, she should have realized that he wouldn't just give in. Not without a triumph in the end, or some way of making it clear he controlled the outcome. She needed to *reveal his true nature with undeniable proof.* She reached into that small pocket on her dress.

"You don't think that this, what you're doing right now, is sexual harassment?"

"You no longer work for me," Max smiled. "You owe me nothing and I owe you nothing. This is just talk, and we're on a date. If I do you a favor, or you do me a favor, we're just friends, doing each other favors. You don't have any obligations here and there are no direct repercussions on you, no matter what you do. And I always keep my word."

"You're asking for a favor then, to keep a target off the doctor? Exactly what type of favor, so I can think about it?"

"Nothing harmful. My top choice: you come on a private weekend with me. It'll be very nice. We can take my jet to a warm, exotic location. We can keep it private, no one needs to know." He grinned and raised his eyebrows. "You and I could have a lot of fun. I'm not squeamish. Maybe, you'd let me add my mark, I would love to see what that's like."

He waited, but she didn't say anything.

"Okay, second choice, you can invite me over and allow me watch you and Kiki. Just three friends hanging out, I would be quietly respectful. That's fair, after the game you two played in the limo."

He waited to see her reaction to that.

He smiled, "Fine, that's just wishful thinking. Last choice, but one you might find easiest, you allow me to see everything and tell me the story behind each of your interesting scars. Why you allowed each of them, who did them, and how you felt when it happened. Fair choices, don't you think, harmless really?"

Harmless, wow, what a delusional fool. Why was he so upset at her? Janine noticed Kiki's driveway and was relieved when the car pulled in. Janine didn't know how to respond to Max Colliers other than saying, *get the fuck away from me.* How clever of him to invent this tough spot for her. Using her departure as evidence that Ian harassed her. Was this another trick, like the one he pulled with Carlos and the contract? Was he really expecting her to do one of those things, or was he only being mean because she wasn't interested in him? Was Janine that easily fooled?

"Let me know by the end of the week, or when you turn in that paperwork. We wouldn't want rumors surrounding your departure to spark an investigation." The driver came around to open the door for her. "I could be your date to the party tomorrow," Max offered.

"No thank you." She couldn't get away from him fast enough. She stood in the driveway and watched his car fly off, then Janine reached into her pocket to turn off the audio recorder.

She searched around the front porch for the spare key. Kiki said it was under a rock, but a garden full of rocks speckled the beds around the porch. She could ring the bell. She noticed it was half past midnight and the house appeared quiet. Maybe Kiki and Gwen were still out on the town.

Janine rolled over a few of the rocks and found the key by chance. She opened the door and slipped into the house. A tall shadow stood in the foyer and she jumped. Ian McNally.

"Kiki messaged that you were staying here," He grinned at her. "You're back early. Where is everybody? Kiki and Gwen with you?"

"No, I was with Max. He let me out of my contract." She waved the long envelope. "When did you get back?"

"Just a bit ago. We drove for twelve hours straight on that last stretch, taking turns." He rubbed his head. "I guess Kiki and Gwen are out tearing it up, just as well. I couldn't stay awake for the grilling Gwen has for me," His eyes perked up. "So, did you two get on?"

Janine nodded, "She's very nice."

"Did Gwen tell you that I proposed marriage when we were both eight years old?"

"No." Janine had a good laugh with him about that.

"It's not like Max, caving in. I guess, he had to accept you wanted out." He shrugged. "I'm glad things went your way."

Janine debated telling him about Max, but she still wasn't sure how she was going to respond. Then, she decided to let Ian relax and enjoy his birthday. He appeared exhausted in his T-shirt and sweats. He must have already been in bed when he heard the car in the driveway. His hair was mushed up and his beautiful eyes were rimmed.

"I guess, you're pretty tired." Janine inched toward Kiki's side of the house.

"I'm glad you decided to stay for the party," Ian said. "It means a lot to me."

"It's really no problem. I wanted to wish you a happy birthday, in person," she said. "Only, I didn't get you a gift. That's pretty lame of me."

"I don't need anything," he moved his arms casually across his chest as he watched her. What was he thinking? He was beginning to make her nervous. Could he read her mind? See right through her?

"Okay, that's a lie," she confessed. "I did get you something, a bottle of Glenmorangie Signet. It's supposed to be one of the best, and it is, very smooth. But I opened it last night to help me sleep. It's still pretty full, but... I should have come out here to get something from the bar, but Kiki and Gwen were still up, and I was," she closed her eyes a moment, "Embarrassed. So, I ruined your birthday gift. Would you like it anyway, the rest of it?"

"Do you know what I want for my birthday?" Ian spoke softly and his eyes started slowly blinking. "I want what we did in Chicago. You know, where I got to hold you and help you fall asleep. You didn't let me do any of it last year when I should have been there, helping you get through things. I wasn't allowed. That could be your birthday present to me, let me be there for you tonight. You're still having trouble sleeping, you just admitted it. I could be there tonight, and every night, until you leave."

She felt sudden hot tears behind her eyes that she had to blink back. He still wanted to comfort her, after she had shut him out so brutally and broke his heart. She had to admit, she slept very deeply under his arm in Chicago, and loved it. Just the thought of being cocooned in his protective sphere felt peaceful. She dreaded going off to bed with her wandering mind and wanted nothing more than to lay under Ian's arm and listen to him breathe. But wouldn't that open up an old wound?

"Ian, I'm leaving," her voice was very soft. "For good. I don't want to lead you on about anything."

"This is not about trying to win you back," his voice was also soft. "It's hard to describe how I feel, like I was robbed of something. A role that should have been mine. One that I really wanted. I really wanted to be there for you, even, just as a friend. You could give that back to me, like you did in Chicago. What do you say? It would mean a great deal to me. I really liked being there for you in Chicago. It would be the finest birthday gift you could give me. Just let me hold you and see you through the night, that's all I ask. No funny business, I promise."

Chapter 16
Birthday Party

Kiki

Kiki stumbled out of bed halfway through the day. That's what a visiting Gwendolyn Murphy will do to a girl. Gwen insisted on visiting some real Austin hotspots, and they spent a fair amount of time in the warehouse district taking in the up and coming music from local bands. Gwen begged to visit a real Texas honkytonk and twostep with real cowboys. So, they found themselves at the Patient Pony and danced around a track the rest of the night. One thing Kiki loved about Austin, she could run around an entire night and not be recognized. Her secret was to dress, and talk, as Austin Texas as possible, and use her real name. No one was ever the wiser. The funniest moments were when someone accused her of trying to look like Kiki Mellow but didn't the quite make the mark.

She stumbled into the kitchen and found Gwen and Janine at the table drinking coffee and eating fresh scones. Did Gwen wake early and do another kitchen magic trick?

Oh yes, one bite of the scone and Kiki could detect a certain witch behind them. Perhaps she should practice more in the kitchen. Kiki wondered if Detective Anderson enjoyed a domestic type of girl. Surely, all men admired a woman who could cook. To think she could have been practicing all these years.

Kiki searched for her purse. Good, on the counter. She pulled out her cell phone and saw that it was dead. One of the problems with coming home tired and tipsy, no one cared about charging a cell phone. She plugged it in.

"What are we talking about?" Kiki drank her coffee black.

"Just a little of this and that," Gwen told her. "You missed your handsome cousin by a wee bit. He ran off to work, got in late, I hear. You didn't tell me he grew a beard! He looks very tough. I forgot how cute his blinking eyes were," Gwen chuckled.

"Did you tell Janine what she missed last night? The two-stepping cowboy and his rodeo winning friend? Did I invite them to the party tonight?" Kiki and Gwen went into fits of laughter. "And did I see you trying to teach those girls an Irish jig?"

"Ho, ho, don't try to push that one on me," Gwen said. "Couldn't blame me anyway, they were very lovely."

"Well, you missed quite a girls' night," Kiki told Janine. "I'm sure your night came off well?"

"Max let me out of my contract," Janine told her. "I'm going to meet with Mike Dunn in an hour to have him look over the paperwork, in his downtown office. I want to run something by him."

Kiki spontaneously hugged her. Too bad seeing her go, but it was what she wanted. She wondered how Ian would take that news.

Janine said, "Summer session doesn't start for couple of weeks, so I might linger a few days, if that's okay?"

"Stay as long as you like," Kiki told her. "Gwen's here for two weeks and you could pick her brain about the Trio of Wells and get things straight." Kiki glanced at Gwen's freckled face. "Have you mentioned our little research project?"

Gwen shook her red head. "Oh no, we were too busy harassing Ian." Gwen retrieved the coffee pot and came around to refill everyone's cups. Kiki stretched her phone to the table and tuned it on. It should have enough of a charge to show Janine the texts.

"We did a little sleuthing on our own, and found a thing or two about Miranda Daily. She has a Facebook account that hasn't seen business for eight or nine years. We got a hold of two people from her friend list. One friend places her in Turkey, still gets letters and such, but no photos or phone calls. The other insists that she's dead and says she warned you. Wait, here it is." Kiki showed Janine the message from Mary Kline. "She knows who you are and that we work together."

Janine studied the message and number, then pulled her own phone out. She punched in the number for Mary Kline. Kiki and Gwen exchanged quick glances.

"Hello, Mary?" Janine said into the phone. "This is Janine Stinger, don't hang up. I want to thank you for trying to warn me. I should have taken your notes seriously." Then, Janine just listened, her brow took on a very worried crease. After a moment, she put the phone face down on the counter.

Wow, what did Mary have to say, Kiki wondered. Nothing good by the look of it.

Janine carefully sipped her coffee. "She doesn't want anything more to do with it and I think we should respect her wishes."

"She said something else," Kiki could see the caution coming off Janine. "What did she say?"

"She's terrified. Expects he'll come after her if he ever gets out." Janine covered her eyes with her hand. "He always suspected she sent those warnings and has harassed her for years over it. At least now he seems to have forgiven her, so she doesn't want to be involved. She has a family and she doesn't want anyone to call back. If she gets another call, she's going to change her number."

"Do we have any idea how she knows him, or Miranda," Gwen said. "I wonder if the other one, the roommate, Lisa, knows Mary Kline. Maybe Lisa knows all of them."

Kiki called Lisa Welks again. Lisa might recall a Mary Kline, but couldn't be sure. Lisa railed at Kiki for calling and pumping her for information. If the questions were for the ghost show, shouldn't she be compensated in some way? If they needed her input, why didn't Kiki interview her? She's seen the show and watched Kiki interview people all the time on TV. Lisa would be happy to help, but she didn't want to be used. Kiki thanked her for her time and said she'd call back soon for a more formal interview, then set the phone down.

Kiki lent Janine her car for the meeting with Mike Dunn. Kiki trusted Mike. He would ensure the paperwork was in order with no funny business from Max. Mike would certainly make sure Max worded things correctly in that document he gave Janine.

"Looks like my prayer chain is working wonders already." Gwen said after Janine left. "She's looking well."

Kiki did notice. Janine's dark aura had definitely lightened and her undertones were amazingly bright. Perhaps getting out of that contract was exactly what she needed.

Ian's birthday party turned out to be a spectacular bash. The entire *Spectral Analysis* staff, the old producer, cameraman, neighbors, a smattering of friends, and a few gate crashers crowded around the pool and party room. Several of Ian's rugby mates stumbled in, and Carlos brought his wife, Maria. Kiki noticed Max arrive with a familiar female executive from the upper floors. Kiki watched all the mingling with satisfaction, Texas horseshoes around the corner, Irish dance across the pool, food and drink under the awning. When Janine finally returned, they found a quiet corner to chat.

"You must have good news," Kiki said.

Janine slipped Kiki a copy of an audio on thumb drive and disclosed what she discussed with Mike Dunn. She floated suing Max for harassment, unless he completely backed off on anything to do with *Spectral Analysis*. She asked Kiki to be the one to talk to Ian about it. Janine wondered why she wasn't surprised, and Kiki said she's warned her plenty of times about Max Colliers. He did not play fair in love, and Kiki suspected it was mostly idle talk to get what he wanted.

"Why do women believed any of his nonsense. Max only wants to win the game. He must be bluffing about whatever he threatened to make you squirm and give in." Kiki told her.

Carlos quickly insinuated himself into their conversation. He left his wife in the company of Gwen and they appeared to be laughing hysterically. Was Gwen flirting again? She always became very flirty at parties.

"I'm officially jobless," Janine gushed to Carlos. "I mean, I'm going to miss you, but I'm pretty happy about it. We'll keep in touch, right? And I got confirmation that you'll stay on the show through the end of the season, if you want."

Carlos nodded and then shot them a funny grin. "I already know about it, and I may not stay on, either." He flashed guilty eyes at Kiki, he shrugged. "I confronted

Colliers when we got back from Chicago. He asked me to finish the season, but I've been offered the weather job at KVUE and decided to take it instead of signing again. This is something Maria and I have been discussing since last year. There's too much traveling with the ghost show. At KVUE, I can stay at home and coach peewee soccer year round. Meteorology was my original plan before I got sidetracked with you guys. Mimi and Milo already notice when I'm not at their games. I can't have that."

That news was not unexpected. Kiki hugged him.

"With those wee bairns, I don't blame you."

"You're sounding more and more Scottish with your friend around." Carlos laughed. "She's hilarious by the way, telling some funny stories about your friend Kiera Lovett, a gal who's gotten into a brawl over sports. She may be perfect for my brother, Lonzo. If she ever comes to visit, let me know, 'cause I want them to meet."

"I believe she's already met your sweet brother, a few times." Kiki winked at him and walked away. She heard Janine explain it to him as she wove through people toward Gwen and Maria. She smiled when she heard Carlos laugh out loud. If Gwen continued running off at the mouth, Kiki's mysterious image would be lost forever.

Kiki asked the Celtic Lads rock band to stop playing and help shoo people away at two in the morning. She did not plan to party till dawn. Unfortunately, the Celtic Lads were not big on leaving themselves. She should not have fetched her collection of daggers for a little target practice, but couldn't resist when she bumped into the guy who had dressed as a monk in San Antonio. He stared at her with a mix of hostility and lust, so Kiki coaxed him over to show him how to throw a knife properly. Most people probably imagined she was flirting with that group of hunky blokes, but she really just wanted that one fellow to realize she didn't have to miss in San Antonio. The band also took turns throwing knives at the target and Ian rushed over.

"Kiki, are you sure it's wise to encourage a bunch of drinking Scotsmen to throw knives back here?" Ian asked.

Lauren tagged along after him, holding his hand and staking her claim. Ian seemed a mite perturbed with Lauren, especially after the very spirited and public kiss she landed on him when he blew out the candles. Apparently, Lauren was tired of waiting for him to make a move and decided to go for it.

"Someone is going to get skewered," Ian said, but he grabbed a dagger and had a go at the target himself. "I'll get these lads under control if you can start clearing out the rest of the crowd."

It took an effort, but soon folks cleared out. The last of their guests gathered in the den for a final drink. Gwen engaged Max in an intimate discussion near the kitchen, and the others sat along the sofa, chatting. Apparently, Janine had hidden a nice single malt scotch in her room for Ian's birthday and shared it for the nightcap. They toasted Ian's thirty years one last time.

"I got a message from the parole board earlier," Janine quietly confessed to Kiki. "The letters are inadmissible without proof that they came from Rick."

The small group shift around when Carlos and Maria left. Then, Lauren succeeded in convincing Ian to give her a tour of his side of the house. Everyone watched them walk down his dark hall wondering if they were gone for the night. Ben shifted to chat with the woman Max brought to the party.

"I can make another statement to the parole board," Janine continued softly. "In writing, or in person. At first, I wasn't even considering being there."

"Are you considering it now?" Kiki asked.

"It's early next week," Janine said. "I've another favor to ask. I can bring someone with me, as support, Rick might be in the room. My sister, Juliana, and I are still in a rough place. I spoke to her, earlier, but I couldn't bring myself to ask her to come. I know you have Gwen in town, so it's okay to say no. I think, I can go by myself, but… "

Kiki took her hand and squeezed it, Janine never asked for Kiki's help with anything before. "I think Gwen would enjoy Chicago. She can come with us." Kiki hugged her. "It's no problem, I could introduce her to my detective and we could go to the Congress Plaza and have another little séance." Kiki also wanted to see Rick Wilkens in person, to get a good look at him.

"Your detective?" Janine smiled, very relieved. "You mean my detective."

"We'll see about that," Kiki pulled her in for another soft embrace. She whispered, "You're not alone, Janine."

Max noticed their interaction with a devilish gleam in his eye, so Kiki gave him a sly smile. Ian and Lauren retuned to break up the group again. Ian babbled idiotically and Lauren appeared a bit stung. Things must not have gone her way back there. People shifted again, and Gwen migrated to Janine and Kiki.

"She's even more beautiful when she's upset," Gwen whispered, glancing at Lauren. "Her smile tries way too hard, but her pout is positively captivating. It makes me want to cheer her up."

"How did you enjoy Max Colliers?" Kiki asked.

"He's a charmer," Gwen grinned. "I felt like he was wooing me. Did you know, a huge part of his parent company invests in the direct research and production of cancer therapies? His family hosts a local fundraiser for the Saint Jude Society every summer. He's a real philanthropist, that one, and he knows his stuff. Sorry, girls, I can't help it, I like him. Part of my rebellious nature, fancying the naughty ones. He even offered to show me some of the Austin sights, if you were too busy."

"Am I too busy?" Kiki asked, and Gwen laughed softly. She obviously found Max a harmless flirt.

After a while, their final guests began to depart and Ian stood at the door thanking everyone who came. Max offered rides to anyone who needed one, ever the gentleman. An uncomfortable moment occurred when Ian hugged Lauren in a stiff way, then they closed the door on the last guest. Kiki felt relieved, but happy. Throwing large parties always got on her nerves.

"I guess, I'm off to bed," Ian said. "That was a brilliant party, thank you all."

Kiki hugged him generously, then Gwen came around to embrace him and slipped in a nice peck on the lips. She laughed when he shooed her away.

"That's a fine thank you after the cake I slaved over." Then, she pushed Janine toward Ian and his side of the house. "Go along then, nae need to tip toe around us. Everyone here already knows everything anyway."

Ian and Janine exchanged guilty looks; caught red handed. Then, without a word, Janine followed Ian into his lair. Kiki gaped at Gwen's amused flush face.

"I didn't know about that," Kiki said.

"Why else would he send that gorgeous girl, Lauren, away?" Gwen smirked. "Shall we tidy up now or leave it for the morning?"

Kiki listened to the thumb drive recording after cleaning up a bit. Max Colliers had a very vivid imagination and quite an ambitious playlist. He was a complete and total brat. If Janine believed for a second that he was serious about investigating Ian for sexual harassment, then she didn't know Max. He would never destroy the primary character in his entertainment investment and have it all implode. Max was smarting because unassuming Janine didn't care for his advances, and no amount of wealth, charm, or romantic overtures worked. She shut him down cold without explanation or apology. He probably felt like a fool and wanted her to squirm a bit. He was smart and leaned in the right direction, Janine would definitely protect a friend. But his big mistake was not understanding Janine Stinger. She was not the kind of girl to call a bluff, or to cave in, or play his silly games. She was the type to quietly access the situation and then counterattack. That's probably how she survived that brutal episode in Chicago.

Kiki rang Mike Dunn and got the run down on everything. Janine planned to go full public on Max Colliers with that audio tape. It could spoil the future in politics he always talked about. Janine might even sue the greater company, if he continued to stick his nose into *Spectral Analysis*. Max was on his way to becoming a very silent producer once again. Kiki wasn't sure how things would play out, but if a senior Colliers, his uncle or father, caught whiff the tape, Max would be knee deep in shite. Poor Max, all he probably wanted was another notch on his bedpost.

Chapter 17

Parole Board

Janine

It was the second time Janine woke since falling asleep. The first time followed a semisweet dream that left her crying softly. Ian stirred beside her, then embraced her until she drifted off again. It was the third night she slept with Ian in his bed. Kiki and Gwen assumed more was going on, but Ian was very clear about what he wanted. He only wanted to cuddle and help her get through the night. He was right, as usual, she could bear the dreams better with him embracing her when she stirred. The past night had been the easiest, but, it was also the final night for them. She needed to fly to Chicago for the parole hearing and then return to Davis. The past two mornings, Ian woke first and was already up and about before she opened her eyes, but this last morning, she woke before him, so she got a chance to study him without him interfering with her scrutiny.

His brow furled and he murmured in his sleep. His eyes moved beneath his lids in a dream. His lips bent up in a momentary smile The previous evening, she watched him draw diagrams in his journal and type out a paragraph for his new book. Along with his ghostly theories, he studied basic energy exchanges in common minerals. He made mapping the difference between rocks with more or less feldspar versus quartz sound very exciting, and Gwen enjoyed his discourse regarding the large mineral collection as much as she did. Then, he spoke excitedly about elemental allotropes and the possibility of a fourth phosphorus or second magnesium. He wondered if there was an unknown crystalline shape that hadn't been discovered. *C60, the buckyball for carbon, wasn't discovered until the 1980s,* Janine had mentioned. Then, Ian pulled out his collection of rock slices, gathered from ghostly sites, and slid one under his binocular dissecting scope to show her. It was fun. She could definitely see why he had been a popular professor.

She was going to miss listening to him speak in his Doctor McNally voice about small details in objects that he found so fascinating, and then how his eyes began to blink when he couldn't find the right word. She'd also miss the way he grinned when those two witches teased him unmercifully over their morning coffee, trying to embarrass him, and his smooth crawl, as she spied him swimming laps in the pool through the kitchen window, and then those whispers in bed before he fell asleep about something amusing that happened earlier in the day. But mostly, she'd miss being cocooned under his arm as she slept. His nearness generated a peaceful feeling, and she was glad they had become friends again.

His hair was all mushed up and his beard needed a bush. He must be uncomfortable, because he slept on top of the covers in a sweatshirt and sweat pants. Not the most comfortable sleeping attire, but it was part of their unspoken agreement, padding to tamp down any simmering flames that might develop. She knew she wrecked things for him, with Lauren. That picture of herself on pier 39 in San Francisco was propped right on his dresser, and there was a second photo in his office, tacked haphazardly to the wall. Sure, it was part of a sea of photographs, but she was the only person in any of them. Mountains, valleys, shorelines, rocks, the aurora, and then Janine. He didn't seem to realize the message those pictures sent out. No way Lauren missed them on her tour the other night. Here she was, messing with his love life without even trying. *Maybe he wants it messed with*, she thought.

She reached over to touch his beard and found that she couldn't stop herself. Her fingers slipped right into the curls and she found his jaw. His whiskers were soft and silky. She felt a tad guilty for invading his space, but he did grow the beard because she liked it, didn't he? His eyes fluttered open and he stared right at her. They were beautifully blue and so clear and happy. She realized both her hands were in his beard and she quickly pulled them back.

"What are you doing?" He yawned.

She didn't know. She didn't know what she was doing. He watched her closely and she became embarrassed.

"I'm sorry about that. Your beard just looks so… so soft. It is soft. Very soft. I just wanted to, you know, it was a little out of sorts there." That sounded very stupid. "It was my last chance to see how it felt, sorry."

Ian shifted around to give her his full attention, but keep a space between them. He propped himself on one elbow, silently attentive.

"You should put that photo away." Janine couldn't maintain eye contact with him. His constant steady stare and his wall of space aroused her senses despite the padding. "You might not realize it, but if you bring a girl back here, the photo on the dresser is not going to help you. It's going to cramp your style. I'm afraid it may have already messed things up for you, in regards to Lauren."

Ian turned his head and spotted the photo she was referring to. "I like that picture. It's a very nice sunset over the San Francisco Bay, look at the colors in the sky." He squinted at it. It was not male sexual energy he directed at her. It was something else, but it had a similar effect, causing a blanket of warmth to flood her core. *Did she just realize her core?* Was that the sensation she'd been noticing each night? Ian feeding her core, but not with sex energy, with something else, something better. She should share this breakthrough with Kiki and Gwen. She moved to rise from the bed, but he took her hand and tugged on it a little, so she turned back to him.

"Were you going to kiss me? The way you did in Chicago when you were drunk?" He looked amused.

She let out a soft laugh and pulled her hand away. "I guess, I was considering it. You don't have to tease me about it."

His hand fell to her hip now, and he deliberately pulled her closer, bridging the gap. The heat from his fingers seemed to penetrate right through the heavy net cotton of her track pants. Janine watched his gaze change, and her heart started beating faster. *Was he shifting his energy, or was it only her?* He slowly guided her hand back up, toward his jaw, and his attention went to her lips. The sparks in his eyes lit fuses on her nerves as she vividly remembered that kiss. Her fingers sank back into his soft curly beard again. His eyes locked onto hers and he let down his guard. *He had guarded himself from this!* And now, his eyes had altered to a deeper shade of blue.

"So then, lass, what will it be?" he dared her.

What will it be indeed? Her heart pounded in her ears. *What would one little kiss hurt?* She leaned in to brush her lips to his and felt a thousand tingling points start right there and shoot all the way down to her toes and everywhere in between. It was a sweet kiss that turned into a passionate, urgent need very fast. They had slept in close quarters for three nights, just simmering, but this heat was searing. She flashed on fantasies she secretly had about him, thoughts of rubbing suntan lotion over his muscular shoulders after he rose dripping from the pool, or kissing his thick chorded neck when he bent over his dissecting scope, or climbing into his lap as he drank his morning coffee, or rubbing her breasts into the soft curls on his chin. Before she knew what she was doing, she tore off her sweatshirt and straddled him, practically attacking him. Ian removed his sweats too, all of them, and she saw that he was fully aroused. Then, he took over and pinned her down, kissing her neck and running his hands everywhere, speeding her up and slowing her down at the same time. He meant to take his time with her, she could tell. And, he was right again, as usual.

She lay spent in his arms, embarrassed for tearing up. His kisses were slow and sensual, and he held her close. His scent was intoxicating, musky and arousing. They both knew it was getting very late in the morning and her phone pinged with a message from Kiki. They were due to leave soon, to catch their flight to Illinois.

"I don't want you to go," Ian whispered. "Tell me that we'll see each other as often as possible, between your terms and whenever I can go out there. You'll finish up out there soon, right?"

"I'm never coming back to this TV world, Ian. And I'll want to go to graduate school too, maybe. I'm going to be in school for a very long time, who knows where." Her head lay against his chest, so she couldn't see his face. Janine worried if making love with Ian had been the wisest thing for them. Deep inside, it certainly felt like the most natural thing. She whispered softly, "I certainly will visit you, when I can. And I'll welcome your visits too, anytime. But, I don't want you to put your life on hold for me, okay? Promise me that you'll do what you need to be happy. I'll totally support whatever you do and whoever you end up with. I realize I have a lot of issues. But if, eventually, we find ourselves in the same place, and it works out in the end, then that would be very nice."

He didn't say a word. He just held her close until she absolutely needed to go.

Janine and Kiki rode the train to the parole meeting with Detective Anderson. He would submit her taped statement as Janine waited in the wings in case they invited her in. Janine's hands shook in her lap. She had not seen Richard Wilkens since the day he was found guilty of aggravated assault, battery, and unlawful imprisonment, the only three, from a slew of charges he had faced.

Kiki and the detective chatted quietly together for most of the train ride, then, the detective moved next to Janine and took up her shaking hands. The detective shared news regarding Miranda Daily. She resided in a mountain village in Turkey and posted letters home at regular intervals during the year. Her family recognized the Saint Comba charm and were surprised that Miranda never mentioned losing it. They sought its return, as it was an old family heirloom. They could prove the charm was theirs, and shared many photographs of their last matriarch wearing the pendant.

"Have they spoken with her lately? Can we get her phone number?" Kiki asked.

Detective Anderson shook his head. "She only corresponds through the mail with very little telecommunications. The family got the feeling that her cult frowns on modern technology. They implied that she's called in the past, but not very often."

"So, it's a strange situation." Kiki tapped her own chin. "Have you ever heard the name Mary Kline?"

"Kiki!" Janine interjected. "She doesn't want to be part of this."

Detective Anderson patted her hand again. "I won't bother her," he assured her. "I know about Mary. I know she wants nothing more to do with Richard Wilkens. I met her many years ago. You may not know this, but Mary is his sister."

His sister? "He claimed to be an only child," Janine said.

Richard Wilkens had both an older brother and an older sister. His brother went MIA years ago, likely killed, during a skirmish in the middle east. At the time, his sister lived near the university, as a student, and his parents resided in the house on Thatcher Road with a very young Richard Wilkens. Within a year, the father had an unexpected heart attack. Curiously, the mother was missing. No one knew where she went, or when, but the younger Richard Wilkens says it was soon after his brother was reported killed in action. Mary Kline became the guardian of her minor brother for the next few years. It was not an easy situation for the two siblings with the parents gone so unexpectedly and the sister recently out of college. Their relationship turned extremely sour, and a few odd accusations were made by the sister." The detective double checked the details when he investigated Janine's case.

"That's a lot of mystery," Kiki said.

Detective Anderson nodded. "An unusual amount of mystery, I would say."

The parole board did not have questions for Janine Stinger. They reviewed her filmed statement and sent out a thank you for her input. The detective disclosed that Richard Wilkens had not been in the room. The detective was scheduled to give his own statement after the lunch hour, and then they would leave. If they preferred, he could have someone drive them to the town center to wait, and they could hop on an earlier train back to Chicago. Then, an announcement for visitors blared over the loud speaker and Janine stared at Kiki. Kiki knew exactly what she was thinking.

"Are you sure about this?" Kiki asked. "It's the one thing you were dreading."

Exactly, and it was the reason Janine dragged Kiki to Chicago with her; to hold her hand in case she had to face him. For days, Janine psyched herself up for that meeting. She wanted to look Rick in the eye and show him that she was no longer afraid of him. *She wanted to see him.* Detective Anderson said he could pull some strings, it wouldn't be hard. Rick waited in a nearby room, very available, and it was not unusual for a prisoner to have visitors on a hearing day.

He sat chained to a table on a much shorter tether than the one he used on her. He appeared undamaged by prison and actually thriving. Two suits sat near, clearly part of his legal representation. When Janine entered the room, his eyes lit up as he tracked her motion. It used to put a flutter in her chest when he reacted that way. He looked the same. *It was going to be harder than she thought.* But, she didn't waver, or run from the room. She continued steadily to take the seat across from him. Kiki followed, along with a prison representative, and they sat somewhere behind her. Rick didn't even glance at them. He silently beamed at Janine, as a his handsome smile stretched across his face. Janine forced herself to breathe easy.

"You have no idea how happy I am to see you," he gushed. "I'm overwhelmed. You look absolutely beautiful, wonderful, Janine. Have you come to speak for me? You have, haven't you?"

"Are you still claiming innocence? That I misidentified you as my attacker?" Her voice was shaky. She forced herself to meet his eyes. Pale, grey, clear and pretty, just like Sammy's eyes, and she quickly glanced away. She forced her emotions down and turned back to face him. He used that same expression in so many different situations with her: after a tender kiss, when she a cooked meal for him, the night she lost her virginity. She swallowed down the lump in her throat, because those had once been happy memories.

His eyes filled with concern. "I forgive you, for saying that, for thinking it. Deep down, somewhere inside, you know that it wasn't me." His voice wavered with emotion. "That attack traumatized you, and I'll never forgive myself for not protecting you better, and for the stupid argument that sent you out of the house. I've studied in here, about how the brain changes images in the mind after a disturbing event. I understand how your mind transferred those actions to me, because you were angry with me. I made you angry the day you left. Someday, I hope, when you realize your mistake, you can forgive yourself. I already forgave you, long ago, and I don't blame you at all, Janine. I'm just happy to see you looking so well."

Janine realized that his lawyers believed whatever bullshit he'd been feeding them over the years. Their stern eyes bore into her. Even Janine felt herself wavering. He appeared so earnest, open, and full of concern, sweet. But, she wasn't fooled. She was prepared for this duplicity after experiencing a similar game with Max Colliers. *Thank you, Max, for that warm up round.*

"You're so full of crap," Janine hissed softly. "I came to tell you, and whoever will listen, that we both know there's no misunderstanding. Stop lying, Rick."

When the parole board questioned him, they very likely might believe every word out of his mouth. His handsome features and perfect smile were pleasant and disarming. He certainly came across as innocent. Did she really think she would find a chink in his façade after those letters? It infuriated her, this overconfident smugness that he could get away with anything. And they were going to let him get away with it too, she could feel it in the air. *Okay, okay, think! There must be some way to expose his true nature with undeniable proof, so he could never fool anyone again.*

"People realize a mistake was made," Rick told her softly. "It's not your fault, you were traumatized, but others are starting to listen and accept the *truth*. Actions speak louder than words, Janine, I could never harm anyone. Not many people continue to believe that I could do the things you accused me of. I wish you were not so clouded. I still love you, you know, and I always will. We made a vow to each other, do you remember? And, you're the mother of my child, I will never forget that."

He paired his soft voice with a tender smile and resembled the Rick she fell for in the very beginning. Janine felt herself fidget because the visit was not going the way she wanted. She needed an admission from him, no matter how small. She needed to eliminate the last little bit of self-doubt that she might be unreliable or irrational. *Prone to delusions, ghosts, and conspiracy theories.* But how could she get an admission when he wanted her confused? Needed her confused. *Don't fall for his nonsense. Don't fall for it!*

"What about Miranda Daily?" Janine asked softly. "What would Miranda say?"

His lips tweaked almost imperceptibly. "Miranda? I don't know. I assume, she would be concerned about you. She would definitely speak on my behalf."

"You think so?" Janine continued softly. "I'm planning to meet her later, and speak with her again. We'll see what she has to say."

His face relaxed a fraction. His mouth bend in a near imperceptible sneer. Did he allowed his real thoughts to peek through, *did he slip?* She spotted amusement behind his expression. He didn't believe there was any chance in hell that Miranda Daily would speak with her. *Because she was dead?*

"Again?" He shifted in his seat. "I didn't know that you two ever met."

"Again," Janine confirmed. "We're meeting *again*, in Thatcher Woods, where we first met. You remember? When you were burying me in those leaves, that was Miranda, wasn't it? Standing there, watching. The woman near that tree, the one who told you to stop."

Ah, now that smug expression melted off his face. A shadow of stark fear passed over his eyes. It was that recognition of the truth she wanted. *He remembered the ghost in the woods*! She felt something loosen from her chest. It was the last little thing she needed for closure, even if he didn't say it out loud, his eyes said it all, she wasn't delusional.

"She haunts the woods, Rick, because you left her there." Janine leaned forward, speaking softly. "And she knows everything."

One lawyer stood up and took a step toward him. He could see the fear in Rick's eyes, the rapid breathing. The lawyer meant to protect him, but didn't know what caused his fear. *Only someone who has seen the ghost would understand this fear, ask Randy.* Janine relished watching the confidence drain from his face. He glanced down and tried to rebuild his façade.

"I have her Saint Comba pendant, found in those woods." She watched his eyes flicker toward her at the mention of the pendant. *He knew the necklace she meant!* "And when I summon her tonight, I'm going to find out where you left her, and when I do, her remains will tell everyone here exactly what you're capable of." Janine glanced at the two lawyers, "All these people you've been working, they'll turn on you, and if they're smart, they'll make sure you never get out of here."

They ended the visit after that statement. Janine didn't care, seeing the smug confidence drain out of him was enough for her, and she was convinced, beyond a doubt, that Miranda Daily was buried in Thatcher Woods. They needed to find her, *for that undeniable proof,* before the Illinois parole board concluded anything. Kiki remained unusually quiet on the walk back to the waiting area.

"Kiki? Kiki, what did you think?"

"He's a true demon," Kiki told her. "That man, Richard Wilkens, has no core aura, no soul. It's scary to see a missing core, Janine. He's a demon," Kiki repeated. "A very charming and dangerous one. The other people in the room, they all had positive feelings for him."

On the train back to Chicago, Detective Anderson recapped his own statement in the parole hearing, then asked about their prisoner visit. He filled them in on what he remembered of the investigation regarding Miranda Daily. He didn't work the case, but read about it when Janine's case came up. Cadaver dogs canvased every inch of Thatcher Woods and found nothing. Before the family began receiving letters from Miranda, someone accused Richard Wilkens of duplicity. The investigators later discovered that it was his sister, Mary Kline, and found that bad blood had existed between the siblings, for years. When their father passed away, all the assets went directly to Richard and Mary felt her brother was not capable of managing the sizable estate. Mary developed a pattern of accusing her bother of different crimes in an attempt to make him ineligible to collect the family assets. Stealing the mother's jewelry, for instance, and hiding the heirlooms. She even accused him of killing their parents, both her father and her mother. Mary always claimed her mother either "escaped" or she was dead. Apparently, the father had been a very controlling individual and passed that characteristic on to his namesake son. Mary warned them not to listen to people on the block who found both the senior and junior Richard Wilkens personable and nice. Those people had no clue what occurred behind closed doors.

Bob Anderson's large brown eyes focused intently on Janine. "Miranda's family is satisfied with the letters from Europe. They claim that Miranda always threatened to run off to exactly where she went. They insist she is alive."

Kiki watched the detective offer assurance without making false promises. He felt the parole board leaned toward forgiving Rick Wilkens, especially as they approved of his conduct in prison. Even Kiki observed how easily Rick charmed people. The board believed a different inmate was responsible for the letters Janine received and that Rick had no knowledge of them. Although her identity had been protected, it wasn't top secret information. They advised her to be prepared, in case there was a media revelation. Perhaps, she shouldn't have taken such a highly visible job.

Chapter 18

The Woods Ghost

Kiki

Gwen had devoted her day to exploring The Art Institute of Chicago with an old friend who happened to be a nurse at one of the pediatric cancer hospitals in the city. She listed all the pros of being a tourist when they met for a late dinner. Gwen's bright chatter improved their mood.

Kiki soon tuned them out, in order to revisit her death vision again. Something about it tugged at her; did that vision seep out of the charm? The charm reeked with the auras of many powerful people, but those conflicting images of the strangulation unsettled her. Did cattails or heather litter the landscape? Wind or no wind? Kiki worried that perhaps more than one vision had been intermingled. The heather definitely reminded Kiki of Scotland, and though the image of the man was very dark, he definitely resembled the Rick Wilkens she'd seen in the flesh. *Could he have killed more than one person?* Gwen pulled her from those thoughts by asking a question.

"So then, Kiera, did you invite Detective Anderson to the summer solstice?"

"I didn't quite get the chance as of yet," she answered.

"Did you lose your nerve?" Gwen giggled.

That wicked witch, Kiki thought. "Of course not!" Kiki lied. "But he's likely very busy being a detective, isn't he? And though he's quite an understanding fellow, I worry the ways of our solstice festival, and especially the other ritual, is not something he has encountered before. I hesitate to broach it with him because, frankly, I'm not sure how to word such a thing. Will I will shock him with the invitation? I mean, to my awakening?"

"Nae doubt he will be shocked." Gwen chuckled. "Many fellows would be shocked at such an invitation. But, he may be delighted as well."

"If you're inviting Detective Anderson to a pagan festival, I'm sure he'd take it in stride," Janine told Kiki. "He's very open minded and I get the sense that he's a bit enamored with you. Good gracious, I never imagined you could be nervous about inviting a man anywhere, and it's only Detective Anderson. I'm positive he'd be beyond flattered that you're asking him to go anywhere."

Gwen continued laughing up a storm. The skin between her freckles became so red that her complexion appeared to smooth out, yet Janine remained completely clueless. Well, this subject proved a bit mortifying for Kiki. She assumed that Janine had caught on in earlier discussions, but perhaps she hadn't. Kiki planned to have coitus for the first time in her life during an awakening ritual after the solstice. Because the detective was a powerful man, in the cosmic energy sense, he'd make a special partner. He could possibly be the perfect man to sire Kiki's future child. A baby conceived during an awakening came with a special blessing.

Kiki waved Gwen away from the subject, feeling a dreadful conversation in the making. There was nowhere near enough time to go into all the nuances of the coven hierarchy, the traditions, or the importance of practicing celibacy to master the Core Well. Plus, Kiki didn't think she could survive explaining it to a skeptic like Janine.

"Let's focus on tonight," Kiki said. "Since Gwen is here, and is a *master teacher*, she can give you tips on finding your core. You'll need to beckon from your core when engaging this spirit. It'll be interesting to see what happens when you exert your full center into calling a ghost. If you can manage to reach from your core, that is."

"I may have found my core," Janine mumbled shyly. "With Ian. I felt light, weightless, and Ian was being so sweet and caring. The entire weekend, I felt him all around my heart, leaving his love. Not passion, better than that. This feeling was light and pure, and went to the center of my body. That's my core, right?"

Kiki and Gwen nodded at her.

"I'm sorry, Kiki, I told you that I would let him be, but I couldn't help it. I think, I love him. You two probably believe I should return to Texas. Think I'm making a huge mistake for going off on my own. But I need to do something first, to find my purpose, and it's not being on a TV show. And before I can accept what Ian was offering me, I need to get my issues settled."

Kiki nodded and patted her hand, happy she figured that out.

Gwen said, "I don't think you're making a mistake. People have it all wrong these days. Women following a man's ego and becoming lost spirits in the process, it's the downfall of humankind. You're right to go out and find your own purpose. Never forget, woman is of the earth, Janine, the fertile soil, the cradle of life, the home. If it's meant to be, Ian will find his way to you, he won't be able to resist. All you need to do is open up your world to him when he does, and bask in his sunlight."

They parked the rental car on Thatcher Avenue in front of the Wilkens house. Janine stood motionless as she stared at the structure, the front yard ran deep, at least 30 yards from the curb. Light streamed from two windows and it felt occupied. Did it still belong to Rick Wilkens? Perhaps a service rented it out while he was incarcerated. The neighborhood was well cared for and nice. Quiet. No one would guess that such a normal house owned that notorious past. Janine quietly turned away with a pensive expression on her face.

"I ran this way," Janine abruptly crossed the street and walked into the woods. They each carried an electric torch and Kiki snapped hers on.

The lack of lunar light created a very dark woods. The college guy, Randy, claimed that the ghost only emerged on a full moon, but Kiki knew that the moon affected spirits similarly to the tides, and the new moon pulled on the aether just as vigorously as a full moon. Just in case, Kiki carried a special candle to woo the spirit. She also brought the mystery charm. Three strong witches performing a traditional séance could surely summon Miranda Daily from the void, especially since the ghost specifically sent for one of them.

Janine kept a quick pace, so it was hard to keep up. She had long legs and she was a runner, while Kiki was mainly a yoga girl. Gwen glanced at Kiki. *Did Gwen sense the tension streaming off Janine?* The twigs and leafy debris crunched beneath their feet as they veered off the regular path. Janine turned to enter a small clearing, just a small open circle hidden between the oak trees. She stopped to glance around. Kiki met her eyes through the dark shadows.

"This is where he caught up to me." Janine aimed her torch at the ground to reveal fallen leaves, twigs, and stones. She moved the light around, searching. "I almost bled to death right here." She sounded winded and far away, as if she was talking to herself. "A stone, maybe like that one there, lodged into my back and slowed the bleeding, saving me." Her light hovered over a large stone. Then, Janine turned her light to the left and illuminated a tall tree, her expression was expectant, "She stood next to that tree."

They meandered around the clearing, but Kiki couldn't detect anything unusual, not even a hint of a presence.

"Have you tried calling to her?" Kiki asked.

"Not yet," Janine said. Her doe eyes shone in the dim light. "I didn't think I could ever come back here, but this place means nothing to me now. It's just the woods." But when Gwen came around to hug her, the tears came fast. *When would Janine realize that she didn't need to play brave with them?*

"Go on then, get it out," Gwen urged softly. "It'll empty the murk so you can think clearly. Never fight your tears, lassie, or be ashamed of them. Crying is a sign of strength. It's a fallacy to believe holding your emotions proves you valiant. It's the exact opposite."

They moved south, toward Chicago Avenue and the pond. They searched for the spot Randy first spotted the ghost. They followed his crude map. The pond emerged from behind several trees under a blanket of stars. They traced the water's edge to a less weed covered spot. The quiet was broken by croaking frogs. Kiki noticed the serene surface of the water and the many cattails poking through the liquid. Goosebumps trickle down her arms as they gravitated toward two fallen weathered tree trunks.

Kiki felt certain they entered the climatic location in her vision of death. The smell of the air, the soft grass, the call of the insects added to her memory, but it wasn't the right night. The glass surface of the pond reflected a moonless, cloudless sky, and unlike the vision, no gentle breeze stirred her hair. Kiki drew in a breath to calm herself. *Don't worry, the strangling devil is still in jail,* she told herself.

"Kiera, is something amiss?" Gwen noticed her distraction.

Kiki nodded. "What time is it?"

"Well after midnight, and the veil thins." Gwen turned to Janine. "Do you recall the hour you faced the ghost?"

Janine shook her head. "I was disoriented. All I know is that it was night."

"Randy's encounter occurred around midnight, but well before the witching hour," Kiki said. "Let's set up a candle." Kiki's inner meter sensed a scant energy brewing in the air.

"I thought the witching hour was at midnight," Janine said.

"Only in Hollywood, Janine," Kiki told her. "The actual witching hour is on the third bell, when the curtain thins and the spirits swirl, transcending the void as they seep into our world."

Janine found a rock. She insisted they not place a burning candle directly on the dry grass. She hunted for a good spot to place the stone and Gwen gave Kiki a raised eyebrow. Did she wonder if that was instinct on Janine's part, delivering the needed alter and placing it? Traditionally, the *dragoma* always placed the altar.

Kiki pulled out a thick candle of bay leaves and cinnamon, a perfect summoning aroma, and she handed out the small pouches Gwen put together. Each contained a sample of brittle black tourmaline, smoky quartz, and jet, a petrified wood, to help guard against dark spirits and negative energy. Mixed with the minerals, Gwen had added anise and cloves to complete the protective sachets.

"Petrified wood and tourmaline would have some of Ian's elements in them," Janine whispered. "And so would the anise."

Kiki smiled at her. "Your science grew out of alchemy, which first grew out of pagan practices. Trial and error, it's how the ancient sisters did things. What is that really? Experimentation without the male ego. What Ian doesn't understand about his theory is, that it already exists, just not in a man's scientific terms. He likes to narrow it down to a few elements, but I wonder if he's missed something in the combination of things."

Kiki could see Janine become a little miffed about that. Good for her, smarting on Ian's behalf. A woman needed a man in the world, and a powerful witch needed a powerful man, and very powerful men had attempted to attach themselves to this girl, that devil in the prison and then her cousin. Surely, Gwen would agree that a powerful witch lurked in this friend of theirs.

Kiki passed the candle and matches to Gwen, but Gwen relayed them to Janine to place on the rock. *Let the* dragoma *build the altar.* Kiki retrieved the charm and gave it to Janine. They each tucked one of the sachets into their shirts, next to their hearts. Kiki waited for Gwen's signal. As the senior sister, it was Gwen who should dictate the evening's events.

"We should leave a place in our circle." Gwen nodded at the space closest to the pond, and they shifted to make room. "If Miranda Daily is a witch, she'll want to join our ring."

"If she isn't a witch?" Janine asked.

"Then, she'll do whatever it is that she wants, I suppose," Gwen said.

They giggled nervously on that for a moment. Gwen turned to Janine.

"Ian's mother was one of our spiritual teachers," Gwen told her. "A powerful speaker, a *dragoma* like no other. She spoke special spells and charms that only a *dragoma* would use. There exists a book, back home, which contain many of her writings and it was placed into my care. It's meant for our next coven *dragoma,* or for Ian's future daughter. Celeste believed they would be one and the same. I memorized many of the summoning charms in that grimoire, but I am nae speaker to spirits. The charms were brilliant successes for her, but not for me. Would you consider trying one?"

Janine nodded and looked down at her hands. "Of course, I'll try one. But will you tell me something first, Gwen? Did Ian's mother give you that book because she hoped," Janine hesitated. "This may be none of my business, but I'd like to know. Did she give you her book because she believed you would be the mother of Ian's daughter?"

Well, Kiki thought, *now here it comes.* She wondered when Janine would ask more about Gwen and Ian. Janine had seen how well they got on. They could not hide their deep bond, anyone could see it. Gwen gave Kiki a brief look before turning to Janine.

"Of course it's your business, lass," Gwen told her. "You know, the Triquetra encompass many meanings, Janine. In marriage, it means to love, honor, and protect. In our coven, it also symbolizes the perfect union of spheres, when head, heart, and passions are linked in a person, or linked each from you to your mate. It's a rare thing indeed, to find the lad whose Trio of Wells are linked each to your own. From the look of things, I'd say you found it with our Ian. That didn't happen for me. Dinna worry yourself about me, lassie, that's the way it is." Gwen nodded. "Even my beloved teacher knew it was never meant to be. My dalliance with Ian was just foolish child's play."

So then, that was how Gwen wanted to tell it. Janine looked to Kiki, for her take, and Kiki nodded in agreement, it was true enough.

"Is that what you have with Detective Anderson?" she asked Kiki.

"I'm not sure yet," Kiki confessed.

"So," Janine asked, "how did I get so confused with Rick? I feel so stupid, because to be honest, I fell completely head over heels in love with him. Sometimes, I can still feel it, and it scares me."

"No one taught you to be wary of a demon, Janine," Kiki told her. "I told you, he was a true devil. I could see it easily because I'm not ruled by my passions, my base, like most. I can see his aura and that he lacks essential parts to his aura, like his core. There isn't a core for the aether to latch onto in that one, and his soul is empty, vacant. Most people can't see these things."

"It's her curse, being a savant and all." Gwen grinned.

"It's my strength," Kiki countered. "It allows me to see and hear spirits. It allows me to see people clearly too. The colors of one's aura never lie, or the lack of part of an aura. It's the interpretation that can be tricky. I wanted to tell you, your aura has brightened considerably in recent days. Darkness isn't a true part of a person's essence. That muddied light is a response to something crushing it. It's very scary, that darkness, because it's not nice to see someone's soul being crushed."

"For most, it can be difficult to recognize a demon or a devil," Gwen told her. "Demons are drawn to certain women of the realm. They sense their strong core and seek to devour it, to fill their own empty void. It feels like love, because that's what they're taking. They use their intellect, charm, and good looks to weasel their way in. Most do this through the passion zone, because it's the easiest to penetrate and the easiest to confuse. Use care regarding people who seek you out, Janine, dinna allow your passions to drive your decisions. There's a huge difference between a Max Colliers and a Richard Wilkens, though they use similar manners. Max is only an ordinary rogue, one who resists developing his core, while Richard is a true devil, a person without a soul. If Miranda Daily was also a girl possessing strong spiritual energy, then that's the reason he latched onto her. She was tricked by the demon as well. The Comba charm points to her being from a witching family, and the nature runs deep, even if she dinna practice the arts herself."

Gwen signaled for Janine to light the candle, then Gwen and Kiki each took one of Janine's hands. Their free hand lay palm up, in offer for a fourth witch to enter the circle. Gwen explained that sisters in a circle could transfer their talents to each other, if they joined hands. So maybe, Kiki could transfer her sight to them and Janine could transfer her voice. But that takes practice too, so she shouldn't worry about sharing her talent right away.

They closed their eyes to take cleansing breaths. Gwen told her that the cleansing breaths were really a moment to pause in prayer and open their cores. Gwen would recite the summoning poem aloud and repeat it, over and over. Janine should join in when she felt ready. Kiki could also join, if she wished, but as Janine learned the words, both of them would go silent. They would let the *dragoma* call to the spirit alone, so the message would be clear.

"I'm a little nervous," Gwen admitted. "Putting the control to a novice, but you've participated with Kiki many times before, so we'll do it." Gwen instructed Janine, "When you recite the words to the spirit, remember to speak as if you're calling to someone you love. Reach into that core you found and speak from there. You cannot expect this spirit to respond if you are nae open hearted to her. Also, remember not to break our circle. Keep hold of our hands." Gwen began reciting the charm in a steady voice.

"Sister come, complete our ring, tis assist and ease we bring. Meet us now and reap your meed, a sister's oath we do concede, accept our vow to set ye free. So commanded, so mote it be."

Kiki remembered the words right away and joined in. They repeated it slowly for Janine.

"Sister come, complete our ring, tis assist and ease we bring. Meet us now and reap your meed, a sister's oath we do concede, accept our vow to set ye free. So commanded, so mote it be."

After Janine joined once, the air suddenly cooled, and Kiki's eyes flew open and met Gwen's wide blue gaze. The chilled air did not come with a breeze attached, and Kiki's pulse quickened. Spirits that brought the cold were usually unhappy ones. The candle flickered in a soft dance, and Kiki and Gwen both went silent as Janine repeated the words alone. Janine's voice took on a much surer tone than the one she used on their *Spectral Analysis* quests and sounded very American to Kiki's ears, not like Gwen's voice or that of her late Auntie Celeste.

"Sister come, complete our ring," Janine said loudly. *"It's assist and ease we bring. Meet us now, and reap your meed. A sister's oath we do concede. Accept our vow to set you free. So I command. So mote it be."* She repeated it confidently.

The night descended into blackness as the candle fluttered out. Only the stars above cast their meager light upon them. Kiki felt a sliver of burning cold move tangent to her empty hand. *Was it a cold finger touching her?* Kiki tried to turn her head, but couldn't. Her neck felt like a solid stiff pillar. She could not move at all, but she could sense another presence there, right next to her. She tried to remain calm by inhaling and exhaling slowly, but her body had become a frozen paralyzed prison with only her eyes as small windows. *Oh no, they should not have let a novice call on this one.* She felt more cold fingers moving. They were slowly adjusting and perfecting their grip, encircling her hand to grasp it. The cold seeped through her skin and crept deep into the tissue.

Across from her, Gwen's eyes were round circles in the dark, rimmed with her white sclera, her blue irises strained to the empty spot in the circle and her skin reddened. Kiki forced her own eyes to strain in that direction as well. She could just make out a shadowed form in the darkness, sitting quietly, hunched over. A slender woman, motionless, limp limbs, yet vibrating with intensity.

Straight hair hung past the specter's waist, skirting the ground. The dark night caused her hair to appear very black, and a few strands flowed in a breeze that wasn't there. Her icy hand gripped Kiki's, sealing them together like the cold metal of a vise. Cold continued to seep into Kiki's hand and inched toward her wrist. Her appendage felt like it was lodged in a frozen block of ice.

Kiki had never been in such a situation before, immobile and at the mercy of an angry spirit. She could not make a sound and tried to calm herself with gentle breaths, *never let a spirit feel your fear.* She was frightened and could feel her heart beating faster and faster, running out of her control. She could neither move, nor speak, to break the spell, and that unnerved her. On her other side, Janine's warm grip was a comfort and she hoped Janine would not let go. Janine's hand felt like life, while the other hand felt like death.

"Who are you?" Janine asked the question in a strong voice.

A soft raspy voice answered. "A sister."

The cold continued to creep up her arm, and Kiki was happy for the sachets Gwen insisted on making for their séance. Placed over her chest, the sachet would surely keep her heart warm and beating. The old sisters told tales such as this and they always came out okay. Janine asked another question.

"Did Richard Wilkens kill you?"

There was no answer, but Kiki watched from the corner of her eye, straining to see. The woman gave a slow meticulous nod of her head. Her head drooped all the way down, chin to chest, then snapped back up rapidly. *Yikes!* The woman repositioned her head slightly toward Kiki. Did she hear Kiki's silent outburst?

Kiki noticed dark patches of abyss for eyes. She remembered Randy saying they were like kaleidoscopes of shadows in his dreams and Kiki could see what he meant. She reminded herself that this spirit wanted their help, she wasn't there to terrorize them. The cold grip tightened. *In response to her thoughts?* They tightened again. *Yes.*

"What is it we can do for you?" Janine's voice still came strong and steady.

"Find me." Her voice trickled out, then increased in volume. "Find me. FIND ME!" The voice increased in pitch, almost to a screeching, but also slowed down like a warped record. "Help me go where I belong. There is an empty place to be filled. Fill it!"

"Are you here? In this spot? Will we find you right here?" Janine asked quickly.

Kiki could detect a frightened pitch in Janine's voice, and her warm hand loosened. Kiki could feel her own panic. *No! Don't let go*, Kiki thought, but she had no voice to speak.

"Where are you?" Janine sounded desperate.

No, no, Janine, calm down. You must speak from the core here. This ghost will only answer if you speak from your core. Kiki wanted to advise her, but her lips were sealed.

"An empty place needs to be filled." Rasped into the air. "Fill it!"

"Tell us what happened to you," Janine demanded. "Where to find you."

Kiki felt the cold grip tighten again as a cackling laugh swirled in the air. She happened to glimpse Gwen and saw the blue rolling behind red lashed lids. If she passed out now, the ghost would leave as well, but Kiki had no voice or ability to move, no way to tell Janine to tighten her grip and pour her warmth into them, they needed her. Kiki felt completely helpless. The raspy voice whispered in such a way that it seemed like the words meandered about, passing into and out of her ears. Janine suddenly tightened her hold, and

Kiki's own eyes rolled up into her head, where she entered the vision of death again.

She crept down a hall in her bare feet, careful not to make a sound. She left him in the bedroom sound asleep, breathing deeply, and his faint snoring followed down the hallway. She felt afraid to sneak away, even though she desperately wanted to leave. Old habits die hard. Where did he hide her shoes? He was always hiding her shoes. She worked her way to the front door, silently clutching the key that she took from his pocket. The key to the deadbolt. He hadn't used that key in ages before suddenly bringing it out again.

The house was a prison, locked down to keep her in her place. The thick double paned windows were sealed shut, unable to open. The deadbolts all required a key on each side of the door, and there were deadbolts on every door, even the inside doors, so he could controlled who entered and exited the house.

He revealed himself again, and she could no longer deny it. She'd hoped he might change, that she could change him, but not anymore. He didn't lift a hand during their disagreement, didn't say a harsh word when she confronted him. He just quietly locked her inside the house with a familiar steely expression in his grey eyes. That was all it took to silence her, and she felt the violence hovering just below the surface of his skin. What she once took for undying, dedicated, passionate love was always something else. Something just as intense. Something malevolent. An incubi, a demon. Something that followed her and enslaved her. Now she was terrified, and upset for being complicit and blind. Guilty. Weak. She would no longer be the his woman, she would no longer be his victim. She wondered what they had created together.

She tiptoed toward the door wearing sweat pants and a university sweatshirt. The key slipped easily into the deadbolt, and she turned the knob silently. Relief flooded her chest. She felt tears form behind her eyes. She would be free again, and maybe she could set everything right. She would run down Thatcher Street, and then down Chicago Avenue to the all night diner. She would call Mary at the University to fetch her. As she pulled the front door open, it made a sucking sound that echoed in her ears. Then, she felt the air stir. Someone was watching. She turned to look up the stairs.

He stood silently in the shadows, casually regarding her. In the next moment, he bound down the stairs vaulting over three steps at a time. She flung the door wildly, stubbing her toe in the process. But there was no time to acknowledge that shooting pain. Tears flooded her eyes, blurring her vision. She sprung into the night. She could feel his silent pursuit.

She sprinted onto the deserted street and turned to follow her planned route. But that plan was no good, she realized. He would tail her all the way to the diner and then he would drag her back before anyone was the wiser. If she ducked onto a porch, he would surely grab her before she could knock on a door or get anyone's attention. She needed to run somewhere she could hide, somewhere people didn't think he was so charming. She bee-lined across the street into Thatcher Woods. The trees would give her cover and she could dart around quickly, losing him in the brush. She could give him the slip with a little help from the trees.

The ground became rough with twigs and uneven little rocks as she zig zagged through the oaks. She moved toward the softer grass of the glen, toward the pond. The snapping branches from behind helped her ignore the piercing pokes of the weeds. She didn't bother to turn around to see if the gap between them was closing, that was always a surefire way to lose a race. She bent forward and sprinted faster, away from the sounds of him following. She could never pretend she didn't understand him now. Pretend she didn't realize she had been a prisoner all this time. His reaction to her fear would not be nice. She cracked the shell open on the polite world they created, and she gave away all her cards by running out that door. He knew she would never go back into the house again, not willingly.

Her feet naturally avoided the rough ground and sought out the soft grasses of the pond glen. The cushioned earth drew her bare feet further and further from the oaks, and she knew it was a mistake. As the tall grasses and cattails reached her shoulders, she hunched into the flapping blades hoping to hide. She should not have let her feet decide the direction. Every now and again, she felt a little slice as the thick grass cut her. Suddenly, the edge of the pond appeared and she stopped.

She tilted her head to listen. Nothing, just the buzz of insects and the croak of a frog. Did she lose him? She took slow deep breaths and carefully walked the edge of the water. She spied a few large logs on one end of the pond. A place to hide and wait for dawn. She strained to listen for his movements but felt plugged up with the sound of pulsing blood thumping in her head. She crept toward the logs and sunk between their protective cover. Her eyes darted in every direction until they were finally drawn to the glass surface of the pond.

The flat water reflected a perfect sky. Clouds shrouded most of the full moon, and the stars played peek-a-boo through the haze of the strato-layers. It was a breathtaking sight. Calm. Beautiful. Quiet. She did it, didn't she? She lost him. She would lay low for a few minutes to be sure. Perhaps she should wait until daylight to move. Early morning joggers and dog walkers loved Thatcher Woods. Another soul would make it safer. A movement in the water startled her. It was only a turtle swimming in the moonlight. She loved turtles, once had a stuffed turtle to cuddle in her sleep. She let out a very long, slow breath. Her breathing came quieter and softer. The drum of her pulse ebbed off and her vision widened. The beautiful night easily distracted her from her predicament. Was she really running from the man she loved and their spawn?

As if on cue, she suddenly felt his eyes on the back of her head.

"Did you think you got away?" he whispered. "The breeze carried your scent."

She twisted around and glimpsed his displeased grimace. The devil her grandmamma always warned her about.

How had he moved so quietly? His hand shot out and grabbed her by the neck, shockingly swift, choking her, but not completely. Under his strong fingers, her rare, silver, Saint Comba pendant necklace cut into her. His free hand reached out and tore the chain from her, rubbing her skin raw in a painful line. He flung the precious keepsake into the distant grass, a treasured item she never removed, not even to bathe. That pendant had always irked him. Would she ever be able to find it in those weeds? Forget everything else, she would never forgive him for throwing her charm away.

"Devil!" she gasped and glared at him. She began to fight.

He answered with a tightened squeeze on her windpipe, shutting off any further protest. He slapped her hands down easily with the muscular arms she once found so attractive. She realized his plan. She could see it in his eyes. He planned to leave that necklace in the tall grass, forgotten forever.

And her as well…

"Tell us where you are!" Janine's voice broke the spell of the vision. "Tell me now!"

The ghost cackled. Her voice became a soft lullaby.

"The turtle turns. The turtle turns and gently crawls into these arms."

The voice faded as she cackled into the night. Kiki felt the cold grip on her hand disintegrate. The spirit was departing, she could feel it. Her chest released a tight contraction and open up in relief. Kiki watched Gwen go limp.

"Wait," Janine called out. "Wait! I want to thank you. Thank you for saving me."

And in just the softest whisper of an echo, "Thank you for saving me."

And just like that, the paralysis was broken. Kiki's body slumped down. She felt exhausted, as if she had held the plank position in yoga for a very long time and sweat dripped down her brow. She swung her head around and saw nothing in the empty spot. She could have imagined it all. But that vivid death vision was too terrifying to be imagined. Across from her, Gwen also had slumped over, eyes closed. Had she seen it too? Janine had tears on her cheeks. They both scooted across the grass to check on Gwen. Gwen's ginger eyelashes fluttered and then she slowly straightened up flexing her hand. Kiki glance at her own hand and flipped on her electric torch. The ghost had bruised them both.

"Why didn't either of you say anything?" Janine asked, still panicked and upset, wiping the tears from her cheeks. "Didn't you see her? Hear her? Feel her? For crying out loud, you were each holding her hand!"

Kiki couldn't help smiling a bit. How ironic was this?

"I was a bit frozen," Kiki told her. "Completely paralyzed. I couldn't speak, but I heard it all and saw her from the corner of my eye. Did you see the death vision? It was very vivid and more complete than the one at the statue. Not as confusing. She was strangled."

"Aye." Gwen took in several deep breaths. "I could nae move a muscle as well. It was a brilliant summoning. Amazing and terrifying. I dinna see a vision of death, but something very different. Perhaps a future. A collection of women gathered hand in hand, joining in a circle one after the other. You did very well, Janine. That one was definitely the spirit of a witch. I'm just happy you held onto my hand. I felt the cold might have gone to my heart."

Janine admitted, "I almost let go. Your hands were so limp and very hot, but I didn't see a death, or a circle of women, I only saw the ghost. You both saw a vision? Something more than the ghost?"

Kiki and Gwen both nodded. They would go over it together, but somewhere else. Kiki was quite certain it had been Richard Wilkens in her vision, though he did appear different in the darkness. The moonlight cast harsh shadows across his face, warping it slightly and deepening his faults.

Their altar sat on the very spot of the spirit's death. How did Janine manage that trick?

"'Twas exactly like the tales the old ladies tell." Gwen stared over to Kiki. "Unbelievable. Now you know what it's like when she really tries." Gwen gazed proudly at Janine.

"I thought it was me, all this time. Gaining a talent," Kiki said.

"We still don't know where she's buried." Janine's brow furrowed. "Where her bones are. The detective said the cadaver dogs sniffed all around this park and found nothing. I don't know how we're supposed to find her. Do you think she's right here, in this spot?" Janine moved the rock alter. "What if we dig right here?"

"She told you where she is." Gwen shifted and sat up straighter. "She said the turtle turns and turns, then crawls into her arms. That's where she is."

They each looked at one another, then slowly stood and searched around, but only blackness and the sound of frogs could be detected. Kiki steadied herself and noticed Janine was a little wobbly as well. Then, Janine snatched up a torch and snapped it on. She pointed it in every direction, illuminating the vegetation around them. All they saw were trees, trees, and more trees and a small meadow. Janine stared into the distance.

"These trails all have names. I can't remember if one is named after a turtle? Didn't Randy find the medallion in that direction, somewhere. Maybe that's where she is. The trails wind around, they turn. Maybe that's what it means," Janine said. "Kiki, do you think you would feel her presence if we got closer? We can follow that map to where he found the charm and feel out the area."

Gwen added her light to their sphere, but she pointed it in the opposite direction. "Before we go hiking into the brush, take a gander at this."

Their eyes followed the beam of Gwen's torch over the black flat surface of the lake. A multitude of stars reflected off the water as wavering points of light, because the surface wasn't serene. Something made gentle ripples. Janine added her own light to increase the luminosity along the surface of the water and Kiki suddenly saw it, something sticking it's head up in the center of the pond. It turned. It turned again. Then, it disappeared below the surface. *Diving down to crawl into somebody's arms, perhaps?*

They stumbled into a pub to search out a stiff drink and meet with Detective Anderson. For the early hours, a fair number of burly men hunched against the bar watching late night television. As usual, Gwen and her flaming hair attracted attention. She volunteered to fetch the drinks and sauntered over to flirt with the barkeep. Kiki wonder if Janine realized what Gwen was up to, feeling out a little male attention to replenish her energy. When Gwen returned to the table, they each shared their visions.

Detective Anderson appeared sometime later, tired, but happy to see them. He waved away the offered whisky and asked the bartender to send unsweetened black coffee instead. He gave Kiki a nice smile and she felt very pleased to see his large brown eyes. Janine told the detective where she believed someone might find Miranda Daily. He didn't balk at all that they summoned a spirit to reveal the location. He only nodded and smiled as his pink aura sent out a blanket of understanding. He could probably have the pond searched without too much difficulty. He had a buddy who liked to dive in murky water. Kiki didn't know if he said that to make Janine feel better, or to show support for their mystic endeavors, but she didn't care. She was just happy to see him.

"Bob," Kiki interrupted the conversation. "Would you consider attending a pagan ceremony with me, over the solstice, in Scotland. Perhaps, you could take a vacation. I'd enjoy showing you around the island."

He face opened in surprise for the first time. "That sounds interesting," he beamed.

"Be careful of my invitation," Kiki warned. "I might ask you to participate in a ceremony, or ritual, of sorts. Nothing illegal, but you would need to keep an open mind."

"Let's make a deal," Detective Anderson said. "No matter what, I will definitely attend any festival you have in mind, and, if my diver finds Miranda Daily on the bottom of that pond, it'd make a firm believer out of me, and I'll participate in any ritual or ceremony you want." He smiled, "No questions asked."

Well, Kiki thought, *perhaps she would now embark on the next chapter of her trilogy, from maiden to mother, she certainly waited long enough*. That last summoning put a fright into her and she needed to get on with it. She had no doubts that they would find someone in that pond, and that she was a strangulation victim. If it wasn't Miranda Daily, she would be very surprised. After chatting a while longer, they bid farewell to the detective, Janine was due to the airport for her flight back to California.

True to his word, the detective asked a friend to explore the bottom of Thatcher Pond and scour for debris. The bones were easily found, still pretty much intact. Eight kettlebell weights marked the location and were used keep the body from floating. The divers noted that the turtles were using the bones for their nightly rest, almost as if they were lying in the arms of the skeleton to sleep. They couldn't positively identify the skeleton, that would take a few weeks, but a rough examination of the neck area showed the hyoid bone had been snapped, a sign of strangulation. It was enough to delay the parole board's decision.

Epilogue

Janine

Soon after Janine returned to Davis, Kiki messaged that she met with Miranda's family and returned the charm necklace. Kiki hoped to buy the charm, but they refused to part with it. It originally belonged to Miranda's grandmother and had been passed down for generations. No current witches, Kiki said, but she could feel a wee bit of the ancient blood in the air. The family planned to send someone to Turkey, to return the charm to Miranda and personally check on her. They were not willing to accept that the skeleton in the pond was their girl.

On a personal note, Detective Anderson attended the solstice festival. Kiki felt hope that he might even agree to participate in her upcoming awakening under the Harvest Moon, but she was still apprehensive about fully describing it to him.

Then came a text from Carlos, full of photos of his twins playing soccer and an obviously pregnant Maria. They waited to announce it. Carlos already started at a local news station as one of the weather men. He finally got his suit and tie. And, did she know, all weather-men were expected to be funny and crack random jokes? So, it was his dream job.

Ian never messaged her, he always called, but she let every call go to voicemail and listened to them late at night. She was afraid she would break down, or beg him to come to her, that she would hinder him from getting on with his life. He was always sweet, missed her, and looked forward to when they would be in the same place again. He hoped that she was sleeping well. She always sent a text back to him, well thought out, upbeat, and noncommittal.

Then, Kiki sent a startling message in August. She was moving back to Scotland. The show shifted with a serious turn, focusing on the science and gadgets more, and they planned to film from a research laboratory point of view. Ian finagled the changes after the audio tape debacle involving Max Colliers, and Max agreed to everything. Kiki would not be needed until the culmination feature, when they went ghost hunting for the season finale.

Perhaps the most frequent messenger was Gwen. She sent short, one sentence messages that Janine suspected was the beginning of her education into the coven. A salt lamp could help tamp down her passion urges. August first was the Lugnasad, a good day to make an oath of change, and embarrassing visualization exercises that would help her quickly find her core, or base, or head.

At the end of the summer session, she found herself with two weeks to spare before the start of the fall term. She debated a visit to her sister, to work through their issues. If she flew all the way to Texas, perhaps she could also visit Ian, but she wasn't sure where he was, or if she should interfere with his life. His messages indicated that they were going to film and work out of a research lab somewhere, but where? Perhaps, they were expanding the workshop in that Texas building. After the fallout with Max Colliers, she didn't think they'd want to work that closely anymore. But men were different than women. They let go of their hard feelings much more easily. She decided to ruminate the pros and cons of going to Texas on her morning run, but when she opened the door, she found a surprise waiting on her door step.

Ian McNally stood just outside, looking unsure if he was going to knock on her door or not. Luggage rested at his feet, and he gave her a sheepish smile. Janine jumped out and hugged him on the doorstep, then invited him in, because he felt stiff with her public display of affection.

"Are you here for a visit?" she gushed. "I was just thinking of visiting you."

Something felt wrong because he was blinking, a sure sign that he was uncomfortable. He glanced around her small living room.

"I'm not here to visit," he said.

"Oh, are you passing through?" She glanced at his bags. Where was he going? "Is everything all right?"

"Everything is fine," he said stiffly, his demeanor scared her. Did he stop by to tell her in person something she might find hard to bear? Something he could have done on the phone if she would have answered his phone calls? He must have seen her worried expression, because his blinking slowed down and he gave her a reassuring smile. "I'm not visiting, I'm moving here. I'm going to teach two classes at your university as a guest lecturer this fall, and, we are going to be filming out of a lab on the Berkeley campus, so I'll commute back and forth."

She pulled his crossed arms apart and slipped into them and hugged him firmly. He still felt hesitant and stiff? Was he unsure about dropping in without notice, that she'd feel her privacy was invaded?

"It's okay with me," she assured him, "if you're thinking of staying here for when you need to be in Davis. I've been aloof, I'm sorry. Maybe you're afraid you're overstepping your bounds? Don't think that, Ian. I want to be with you. I would love it. It's exactly what I want. Don't you think it's perfect?"

"Aye, lass, I do." He finally smiled at her. "I do believe it's perfect. Here we are, in the same place, right?" But his eyes were still blinking and speeding up slightly. "We should come to an agreement first, don't you think? I want to have an agreement." That sounded very familiar. He had asked for an agreement once before. *To move slow in their relationship and take things rationally.* "You allow me stay here on the days I need to be in Davis, and I can… I can… Perhaps, I can get you a discount on your tuition, if you agree to be…"

She started giggling. What was he talking about? "Ian, I want you to stay with me, and you know I don't need a discount on my tuition. How would you even manage that anyway? Do you want me to be a research assistant? I'm too busy, and how would that look? Living with your research assistant? But, we can go as slow as you like. It's what you asked for at the beginning, and you were right, as usual. I have an extra room that I use as an office. It won't be any trouble to set it up properly and make it a private bedroom for you."

"That's not what I meant." He pulled something out of his pocket. Was it a ring box? What was he doing? What was this? She suddenly felt out of breath, weak in the knees. Ian helped her sit on the sofa and settled next to her. He held her hand in his. His blinking stopped and he stared into her eyes with that steady melting gaze of his, bright eyed and sure of what he meant to say. He was definitely holding a ring in his hand. It had a central diamond linking two Celtic Triquetra knots.

"Ian, what are you doing?" she whispered.

"There's no moving slow with you, lass, so I'm asking you for an oath." Ian took her hands. "And soon. Maybe on the equinox, that's a good day for joining two halves, right? Will you marry me? I want no misunderstanding about what we are to each other. I know that I want you, and I want you to wear my ring. I've been thinking on this for a very long time. We belong together, don't you think? A perfect fit. You advised me to do what I needed to be happy, and said you'd support whatever I needed to do. This is it." He used the smoky blue eyes that always melted her into a wobbly mess, and in his voice, there was just a touch of a dare. "So then lass, what will it be?"

What will it be indeed?

The End?

Eager to learn happens next, or discover the back story to Janine and Ian's romance? **Turn the page for information on the missing pieces of the *Spectral Analysis* puzzle…**

Reviews Help Authors

Thank you for reading. If you enjoyed this story, consider leaving a review on Goodreads, Amazon, B&N or your favorite bookstore

Spectral Analysis
Seeking Lost Souls

A fractured past, entwined with a new inflamed desire, is the perfect combination to aid skeptical Janine into believing the paranormal…but will her enlightenment occur in time to subvert a tragedy?

Don't believe in ghosts? Well, neither does Janine Stinger, even though she operates some of the tech equipment on a ghost hunting TV show. Apparently, her new and passionate romance with Ian McNally has triggered some unsettling flashback emotions and… she thinks she feels something, and hears something, and eventually sees something that might be a ghost. She doesn't want to believe in ghosts, but if she doesn't believe, that means she's screwed-up in the head, and her violent past still haunts her. But then again, if she does believe, that means the ghost is coming after someone precious to her. What will she lose? Her fragile psyche, or a precious child?

Spectral Redemption

An ancient curse, reeking of passion, betrayal and murder, force Janine and Kiki to question the men they love, all while ominous events send them spiraling towards a deadly conclusion.

Spectral Analysis enters a research and develop stage to create all new devices to record paranormal energy. This gives Kiki time to reconnect with her pagan coven, where it's revealed that the charm's curse is bigger than anyone imagined and that Janine Stinger may be a key player in resolving that ancient mandate. As dark forces bend their actions toward a pattern of love, betrayal and death, Kiki wonders who will succumb next? Kiki? Janine? Or will the curse take them both? The story concludes when *Spectral Analysis* heads to Scotland to investigate paranormal energy on the island of Skye and the ghostly messages become clear as the final dark act is at hand. Love, betrayal and death mean that someone must kill and someone must die. Someone will be the last one to fulfill the dictum, but who will it be?

About the Author

Joanne Alain Cook is a mother, wife, sister, teacher, artist, officer, and writer. She retired from the USAF after serving both in the active duty and reserves as a C-130 navigator, executive officer, and maintenance officer. Joanne is of Korean/American heritage and has lived in Texas, Japan, Georgia, and California. Her adventures have taken her to every hemisphere on Earth, and she has spent many hours flying in the air and scuba-diving under the sea and lounging on her sofa while reading. Joanne currently teaches science in Northern California. She lives in Sacramento with her handsome husband of twenty-plus years, beautiful brainy daughters, goofy Labrador, angry bearded dragon, frightened chickens, and clueless fish.

Drawing by Alaina Grace Batten